# DRAGON'S
# JUSTICE 5

## BRUCE SENTAR

D1528334

Cover by Yanaidraws

# CONTENTS

# THE STORY THUS FAR

Z ach hadn't realized just how much his life in Philly would change when he had helped a beautiful woman after her small biking accident. He'd dismissed her gold eyes as a moment of confusion, but that moment with Scarlett was the start of his introduction into a new world.

Bumbling about in a world he barely understood, Zach made a misstep with an elf, landing himself in a duel. Without the famed warrior Morgana Silverwing, he probably would have lost. But the drow vampiress took him under her protection and helped him develop his paranormal skills.

Slowly, they pieced together Zach's supernatural nature, from fire breathing to supernatural strength. While he hadn't achieved a full shift, they began to believe he was one of most important paranormal species for their ability to produce mana: a dragon.

Working side by side with Morgana as a mercenary brought him deeper into the paranormal world. While investigating a new drug, Zach found himself up against a pack of werewolves being led into violence. Zach had no choice but to take down the alpha, Chad, and temporarily hold the connection to the broader pack. And in the process, he began a friendship with Jadelyn, a beautiful siren who had an arranged engagement with Chad.

But after taking down Chad, one mystery remained. Who was the skinwalker that had escaped the drug warehouse?

Most of the semester passed, and Zach built a relationship with Scarlett. The adorable kitsune blew his mind, and he fell hard. She would always be his first, but it didn't take long before she started to realize that his nature would lead to sharing him with others, even before she knew he was a dragon. But for a time, he was only hers.

When the Order of the Magi came into town at the same time as the swamp troll migration, Zach and Morgana were enlisted to keep the swamp trolls migrating from the Great Lakes to Florida without stopping in Philly where the dumb yet powerful creatures would create a mess in the city.

The usual work of diverting hungry trolls at night and running security during the day turned more problematic as the troll occurrences seemed more calculated.

Zach makes a new friend in Sabrina the succubus, and we learn more of Morgana's past in the war with the Church from the 17th century.

The Magi and Paranormals were already in a tense situation, and the trolls weren't making it any easier.

All the while, Zach was still struggling with the death of the wolf alpha and his new status among them. Some wanted him to be their alpha, while others wouldn't accept a non-wolf. Their head bitch, Kelly, was pushing for Zach to step up and join them as alpha.

Zach's friendship with Jadelyn began turning into something deeper, and blessed by Scarlett, they began a relationship. During a date with Jadelyn—a needed respite from the chaos—there was an attack from the trolls.

In the moment of danger, Zach shifted for the first time into a gold dragon and protectively marked Jadelyn as his mate.

The attack was revealed to once again be the work of a skinwalker, and Jadelyn was at the center of both, giving Zach an urgency to solve this and protect his newest mate.

Zach went to find Kelly to get her help, but what he finds is a pack in chaos. The pack needs an alpha. They want it to be him, but he thinks it should be Kelly. Using his power, he pushed the pack link to her, making Kelly the first female alpha in history.

When another attack occurred against the Order of the Magi, Zach teamed up with a succubus-wizard in training, Sabrina, to help him thwart the catastrophic attack. Yet things needed to be solved soon or the Order and the Paranormal of Philly might come to blows.

Zach gets the support of the paranormal council, and the hunt is on for the old god Nat'alet who is responsible for the skinwalkers and the attacks on the Order of Magi.

Jadelyn accepts Zach fully and brings him to her siren's wedding much to hers and Scarlett's father's disagreement. Though, the two fathers' primary disagreement with him is that their daughters and wives won't tell them just what Zach is.

When they find the forgotten god Nat'alet, they corner him in an abandoned mall, and Zach faces off against the god with the support of the Winter Queen.

Unfortunately, Nat'alet has something that the queen wants, and trades it for her to leave the fight.

Left alone, Zach and Morgana fight Nat'alet as our favorite dragon continues to master his shifting and discovers he can become a silver dragon as well.

But things aren't looking good. Morgana reveals her secret: she's been empowered from drinking archangel blood, but it comes at a cost.

Zach taps into a strange power in his anger and defeats Nat'alet only to nurse Morgana back to health at the cost of his own consciousness.

When he wakes, Morgana is gone.

Like that's going to stop him. Zach enlists the help of Morgana's friend T, the crazy elf alchemist, and rushes off to Switzerland and the secret paranormal city of Sentarshaden with Jadelyn, Scarlett, and Kelly.

There he sees his first dragon as the second princess of the Highaen family, Yev, is revealed to be a dragon during their winter ceremony honoring the giant tree that looms over and protects the city.

Pushing that aside, Zach hunts down T's daughter and an injured Morgana.

Then we learn of Morgana's full history, that her tree was behind enemy lines and that her trip into heaven had left lingering wounds that she only kept at bay by drinking the blood of minor angels.

Determined to help her, the two of them go on a mission to Austria, tracking down Morgana's tree in a templar base and finding it is being used to sustain a portal between the celestial plane and earth.

Morgana performs a ritual while Zach fights off angels and eats a dragon bone, causing him to grow and gain flight. With Morgana recovered, they are off.

They have a harrowing escape from the templars only to learn that the Highaen princesses are being targeted by the group.

In an attempt to meet a dragon and protect the city, Zach gets himself and Morgana hired to protect them.

After a failed attempt on Yev's life, her sister Tyrande is kidnapped by the nephilim Helena. They had pulled out all the stops, and a great silver dragon enslaved by the celestials fought in Sentarshaden. If they do the same to Tyrande, then the tree of Sentarshaden would be theirs to control.

The dragon recognizes Zach as his king and he fights his enchanted enslavement to his death, asking in his last moments for Zach to take his power by consuming him.

Zach does so with a wrinkled nose only to discover that he's growing as he does so and becoming more powerful.

With the Highaen at risk of a leak, he denies Yev's pleas for help with her sister, yet Zach and his team go in alone to save her.

Zach and the girls work together. Morgana steals her tree back and takes their portal to the celestial plane, but not before an archangel appears.

With the portal gone, Helena is freed from her own shackles and turns on the archangel. With her help, Zach defeats the archangel and returns Tyrande to the Highaen family.

Zach's secret is out, and on returning home, Rupert, Jadelyn's father, turns a new leaf and welcomes his son-in-law with open arms as the whole world knows what Zach is.

Even the Bronze King, king of dragons, opens his arms to Zach and calls a conclave of dragons. The message is delivered by two of the Bronze King's wives and their daughters who are pushed upon him.

Zach heads to the conclave of dragons as things begin to grow more complex. The fae and the paranormal council want his involvement given his new status. But he doesn't have time before the conclave begins.

On their way to the conclave, even the three letter government agencies know who he is, though, not what he is.

The conclave starts with a disaster—a dragon was wounded on the way.

That doesn't stop them, but they seal the island in preparation for the week-long event that is a reunion among the dragons and negotiations amid the flights.

Dragons have a long history, including two reincarnating beings known as Tiamat and Bahamut. Zach fears he might be their son, but that would forebode a great disaster.

Thankfully, there are many lovely dragons eager to meet Zach and distract him from those problems. His first mate Scarlett is screening ladies and coming under her own strains.

Amid all of this, a murder occurs on the sealed island, and who better than Zach and Morgana to figure it out.

When they get too close, they realize a dragon that is supposed to be dead is at the conclave. Zach and Morgana spring into action only for Ikta, the spider queen, to reveal herself. She'd long been thought dead by the dragons.

Sealed by Tiamat and Bahamut, she's back to reclaim her power from the dragon conclave.

After she reclaimed the first half of her power, Zach is in a race to find her second half with the unlikely help of

Tiamat's memory stored in a crystal. Tia asks Zach to call her mom before she's willing to help.

They race to Tiamat's hidden hoard on the island, only for Ikta to block Zach's exit and demand a duel, in the custom of dragons. But what she wants as her prize is him.

Zach slips away into Tiamat's hoard along with his ladies as they explore mounds of gold, get into a little sticky fun, and find the second half of Ikta's power.

Consuming the second half of her power, Zach boosts his magic, only for it to be used against him in the duel with Ikta.

She tries to use her magic inside of him to control him, and almost succeeds, but our favorite dragon comes through in the end to banish her from the island and conflict with the dragons.

Zach wraps up the conclave, courting Tyrande after already having her sister. The leaders of the dragons push him to take an honor guard home made up of six dragons from the remaining flights.

He returns to Philly with even more women.

Maddie and Frank have had enough and demand answers for all of the strangeness lately and that he suddenly has eight women hanging on his arms with another six following him around.

Zach doesn't give them a satisfactory answer, and their friendships are beginning to fray.

# CHAPTER 1

T he clinking of gold was music to my ears as I swam through the mounds of my hoard with a satisfied grumble rumbling from my chest.

"Zach! We've been looking everywhere for you. You are going to be late to the council meeting." Jadelyn crossed her arms at the edge of my hoard, staring me down. "Stop playing with your gold."

Ducking back below the mounds of gold, I sank to the bottom of my hoard and pushed myself through the coins.

It was fun. I wasn't sure exactly how to describe it, but as a dragon, it was like a kid's joy and a lover's embrace at the same time. Fuck, gold was wonderful, and my gold was damn near perfect.

I popped my big draconic head out at the edge of the pile where Jadelyn stood.

My platinum blonde mate was unamused as she arched an eyebrow at me. "Zach." There was a warning in her tone. "We don't have time."

I let out a low rumble, and she softened a touch, running her hand along my snout.

"If I'd known you were going to be like this with your hoard, I would have made you leave it all at the conclave."

She brushed a few coins off of me and kissed my snout. "Now come on, my big dragon mate." She stood, waiting.

I grabbed the ledge and shifted back into my human form, pulling myself up to her stark naked. Jadelyn bit her lip, looking me up and down once before shaking her own head.

"We have to go," she said, more to herself than to me. "Get some clothes on before I jump you. You still haven't put a baby in any of us."

Pausing halfway to getting clothes out of my bracer, I raised a brow. "What was that?"

"Nothing." Jadelyn pushed my back and shooed me up the ladder that led out of the enchanted space under my mattress.

"Pregnancy is not nothing," I shot back. I already knew that Yev and Morgana had stopped any preventative measures, and Yev had been showing up in my bedroom most nights.

It had only been a few weeks since the dragon conclave had concluded, but it felt like everything had changed.

I'd left most of my classes at the university, and with a little help from the Scalewright family, I had been enrolled in an independent study. That would give me time to learn magic from Sabrina and the honor guard of dragons.

So far, none of them had wriggled their way into my bed, but they weren't subtle about their hope that one day I would invite them in.

It was partially expected of me. I had the ability to revive dragon flights that had gone extinct. But I also had time, and I didn't want to rush into creating a bunch of dragon babies just yet. I wanted to focus on my growing family of mates.

Until then, my dragon guard would just help me be a better dragon. My ability to wield my magic was still limited, and since I'd stolen half the power of Ikta the spider queen, I needed to get it under control.

"Council meeting," I said, finishing getting dressed. "Why was this one so important?"

"It isn't, but my father says the whole council is uneasy if you aren't there. Philly has almost a dozen dragons living in it now; their voice needs to be present. And it doesn't help that Maeve refuses to vote, saying that if you aren't there, the decisions don't matter." Jadelyn rolled her eyes. "She wants to be in your bed, too."

"I've gotten that sense," I teased Jadelyn as my hands wandered down to her hips and pulled her closer. "But I'm having a hard time thinking about anybody but the beautiful woman in front of me. The council doesn't need me just yet."

Jadelyn put her hands over mine to stop them and playfully nipped at me. "No. You are the Dragon King, and that comes with responsibilities."

I let out a low groan as I pulled her closer still.

"I love you too." Jadelyn tilted her head back and closed her eyes.

Taking the offered kiss, I let it linger as she wiggled her hips into mine.

Scenting her, I felt instantly relaxed with my mate close, but a lingering sense wanted me to gather the rest of my mates and stuff them in my hoard for safe keeping.

I was so lost in Jadelyn that I didn't hear the door.

"Oh, my king, are you ready to nest? Is Lady Scalewright pregnant?" Amira came in asking. Her bright green eyes were wide in anticipation.

"I'm not pregnant," Jadelyn countered with a sigh. "Maybe after school."

Amira bowed, her short, black bob knifing down with the motion. "I'm sorry. The king just looks like he's being overprotective."

Frowning, I had to reconsider. Ever since I'd come back from the conclave, my dragon had been much closer to the surface. It was influencing my actions to a far greater degree than before.

I'd always liked being close to my mates, but I was feeling far more possessive.

"No, I think I'm just going through a phase." Grumbling, I tried to push the nagging dragon instincts away. I let go of Jadelyn with a kiss on her head and straightened up. "Let's go."

Almost to prove to myself that I could stay focused, I headed out.

On my way out, I waved at Tia and Bart in the crystal that had its own little shelf pointing to the doorway. Tia bounded off the little bench and waved excitedly at me, her wild, red hair bouncing behind her.

They weren't technically my parents, but my parents were their reincarnation. For whatever reason, my parents hadn't gone to the conclave and deposited their most recent reincarnation's memories into the crystal like the past ones had.

As a result, Tia had no memory of having me, but I was the child she had always wanted but could never have.

Closing the door behind me, I walked into the Atrium, and my honor guard of dragonettes fell into line behind me. They had apparently been waiting for me to come to the council meeting.

"Afternoon, my king." Polydora bowed with a smirk on her face. "I expected it to take longer after Lady Scalewright joined you in your room." She turned to Jadelyn. "Is the king quick in bed?"

Jadelyn just laughed like musical chimes. As a siren, her voice was always pleasant to my ears, even more so after she'd sung her song for me at our siren wedding.

Remembering her song, I had another instinct to grab her and drag her back into bed. I staggered in my step for a moment as I regained control of myself.

My instincts were getting more intense.

I wondered if all the talk of making baby dragons was doing something to me. Because while I certainly enjoyed my women, I'd never had such intense urges to bed them immediately before.

"My mate is anything but quick. I couldn't risk him getting started, or we'd miss another council meeting," Jadelyn felt the need to clarify.

Polydora shrugged it off. "Why should they not wait for my king? A dragon comes and goes as he pleases. That goes double for the Dragon King."

I held up a hand to stop the chatter as we entered the council chambers.

All six of the dragonettes filed in behind me. Polydora was the oldest and had become the de facto leader of the group. It helped that she intimidated plenty of people as a born warrior of Amazonian height. And she carried an intense aura of dominance, as did all the dragon females, even the more shy Sarisha.

As we mounted the circular arena, heads turned.

The Paranormal Council met in a chamber that sat over a circular pit. Those being questioned would stand in the pit, and I'd also learned from personal experience that it was where duels occurred. Sometimes I saw the scratches and scuffs on the floor below and thought I remembered the moment they were made.

"Zach, my boy, right on time. We were just about to start." Rupert slapped his chair. The man looked like a bust of Poseidon come to life. We hadn't gotten along from the start, but ever since he'd found out that I was a dragon, he'd been far friendlier to me.

"Dad, you've been waiting for him." Jadelyn rolled her eyes and sat between her father and me.

"Only a little. After all, you can't rush a dragon," Rupert laughed while the rest of the council watched.

The Paranormal Council had three leading factions, or at least, they had before. Now they had four with the dragons among them. There were the sirens, led by Rupert Scalewright. The elves, who hated Morgana and my very existence. And then there were the fae, who were hot and cold. But Maeve, the Lady of Fall, was the one representing them at the moment. And she was very much on my side.

Maeve had been trying to make up for her mother's misstep when I'd been left to what the queen had believed was a losing battle for me before she knew that I was a dragon. She'd been wrong.

Beyond the three leading factions, lesser groups were also present among the council. Kelly had replaced her father on the council; she was working to reinforce her standing as alpha of the college pack. The uniqueness of her pack was drawing attention and wolves from all over the country. Calling its growth rapid would be the under-statement of the year.

For the first time, non-alpha males could have kids. And that was having a noticeable effect on recruitment.

"Now that we are all here, we need to talk about the mongrels that are flooding Philly," Sebastian spoke for the elves.

Rupert snorted and waved their concern away. "It's mostly college-age kids coming to join packs. They are harmless."

"Harmless is not two civilian attacks in the last week. They are rampant and disorderly. The bigger packs in our city were killed last year, and though Kelly is an alpha, she is young and inexperienced." Sebastian's voice was like a whip crack.

Kelly, my mate, gripped her chair with white knuckles. If she lashed out at Sebastian, she'd only be reinforcing his opinion of her being inexperienced. But I could tell that her instinct was to rip into his throat.

This was the new world of politics that we were all getting used to.

It took a moment, but she was able to finally settle before speaking. "Sebastian. Philly is changing. We have a dozen dragons, and the Dragon King himself living in our city. Not only are werewolves flocking to the city, but almost all the paranormal presence has increased as well. The city is going through growing pains, which is why we need to work together."

It was everything I could do to not smile as the elves glanced my way. I wanted to give Kelly a big thumbs up from across the chamber, but a glance at each other would have to suffice.

"She's right. Philly has become a hot spot for young paranormals. We would be better suited to welcoming them and integrating them. Tyrande tells me the elves have been welcomed by the two communities here easily enough," I added, giving Sebastian a healthy dose of side eye.

"Of course. As they should be. They are peaceful, law-abiding citizens of the city. They haven't been the cause of several crimes. And it's worth noting that the council still hasn't heard if Silverwing Mercenaries will take on the tasks we've put before it."

Elves were supernaturally good at sharp, accusing glares. I decided it was just extra emphasized by the sharpness of their faces.

I studied his face for a moment, following the random train of thought for a moment while I let him stew before I spoke again. Unfortunately, Morgana was nowhere to be seen. The only blue women were the Fall Lady and her assistant.

I wasn't surprised Morgana wasn't present; she hated administrative meetings like the one we were in. She'd only attended them in the past because I was a subject matter, and she liked to flex just how scary she could be.

"Morgana has it under control. Unless there's one specific task that you would like to bring up here at the council?" I prodded him.

Maeve cleared her throat. "I think we all agree that those newcomers are mostly welcome, but a few troublemakers are appearing. There have been reports of several vampire attacks that have even caught the police department's attention." She glanced behind Rupert at Detective Fox.

"She's correct, and we've been doing what we can to suppress it." Detective Fox winced a glance at me. "But I think we need Morgana's help in crossing that gap."

Maeve's assistant cleared her throat. Despite only wearing a whisper of silk that left nothing to the imagination, she held her head imperiously. "The fae have killed a number of vampires sniffing around our park."

Jadelyn leaned close and whispered, "Fae blood is like a drug to vampires. Not quite the level of dragon blood, but something they'd strive for."

I nodded, thanking her for the assistance. "Then I'll speak with her after the council meeting to see what we can do."

A gnome stood on their seat to get everyone's attention. "Some of us were wondering if more dragons were moving into the city? There are already enough of them that it is concerning some races with... tense relationships."

"For now, I think the migrations after the conclave are nearly settled," I answered quickly. Most of the dragons had no intention of moving around their roosts and hoards, but my honor guard had come along with Herm, Tim, and their mother.

And of course, their harems. Which meant there were nearly a dozen dragons in a city that had previously had one that didn't know he was a dragon.

Gnomes and dwarves had a long-standing feud with dragons, so I understood their concern.

"I'd also like to say that I wasn't raised with the long-standing history between your race and mine. As the king of dragons, I can say that there is no bad blood between us," I tried to put it eloquently, without losing my ground.

"So you'll pay a recompense, then?" the gnome asked excitedly. "That would go a long way to smoothing things over. After all, it was the dragons that raided our homes for centuries to steal our gems and gold."

The very thought of giving up part of my hoard to the gnome had the armrest of my seat cracking before Jadelyn put a hand over mine. The beast butt its head against my chest, demanding I reduce the gnome to ash for even thinking of my hoard.

"Our king owes you no gold. Be satisfied that he even wishes to dismiss the feud," Polydora spoke out of turn.

I had to turn and scowl at her, though I appreciated her words. The beast did even more, purring as it watched her closely. She had broken decorum masterfully and bowed her head to me as she stepped back as if I'd chastised her.

"Are her words your own?" The gnome's voice hitched up as he spoke.

"As I said, I have no part of this history. To me, there is no debt to pay in either gold or blood. As of now, the only thing that would cause me to act would be any further action by your people." I leaned back, fighting to keep the smile off my face and pumping my fist.

I sounded like a veritable badass.

Mother fucking king of dragons.

# CHAPTER 2

"Ah, there you are. My favorite son-in-law." Rupert slapped his hand on my shoulder as he caught up to me after the council meeting.

I raised an eyebrow. I was pretty sure I was his only son-in-law unless he had another hidden daughter somewhere.

"I have something I'd like to talk to you about." Rupert cut through my silence. "I was thinking about hosting a welcome party for the dragons that just moved into the city. I'd invite the rest of the council with the hope that it might help ease the tensions a little."

"Sounds good. Just let me know when." I waved to my father-in-law and wrapped an arm around Jadelyn's waist as we headed out of the room.

As soon as we were out of eyesight, she buried her face in her hands. "He's going to go over the top. He always does. Expect something ridiculous."

"Like what?" I asked, suddenly more apprehensive about the party.

"Last time he did something like this, he had a two-story ice cream sculpture made. The time before that it was an actual cake house." Jadelyn just sighed.

While it certainly wasn't the point she was trying to make, I was most interested in how a house could be structurally made out of cake. But Maeve walked up, disrupting my cake house thoughts.

"It must have been magic," I concluded, turning to Maeve.

"Of course. Most things are magic." Maeve smiled. She was trying to seem warm, but her cool blue skin and frosty silver eyes made that difficult.

She was right. The simple answer was magic. "Probably. What can I do for you, Maeve?"

The Fall Lady was clearly trying to make amends for her mother. And if I was honest, it was working. So far, she'd proven herself honest and helpful.

"The queens and I would like to invite you and the other dragons to a small celebration," Maeve stated as her attendant stepped forward and handed me a formal envelope. It felt thick, like an expensive wedding invitation.

I didn't fail to notice how the attendant brushed her hand along mine, lingering just a little extra.

"Inside the fae realm?" Jadelyn asked while I was distracted.

I stared at her attendant, feeling myself drawn to her. Despite being covered in a sheer outfit, there was a mystery to her. I opened my mouth to speak, but Maeve's voice shook me out of my daze.

"No. Of course not. We will close off a section of Wissahickon park for everyone to use." Maeve glared at her attendant. "Do not attempt to glamor him. If you offend him, I will not protect you."

The sudden swell of desire I had popped like a soap bubble.

"My apologies. He's absolutely teeming with desire; it was in my instincts." The attendant quickly stepped back and bowed her head with a flutter of her lashes at me.

I wasn't entirely sure if it was an accident.

"She's a nymph," Maeve explained. "Please do not hold it against her."

I blinked away the moment of brief confusion. "It's fine."

But even as I said it, I felt a bit of anger boiling up inside of me. I didn't like being manipulated. It was yet another reason I wanted to learn more magic. And it had me more concerned about being in a room with the fae.

"Zach?" Kelly had come around the side and prodded me. "Don't tell me the little nymph got you."

I snorted. "No. The little fae just surprised me. My dragon is quite the little horndog after all." Focusing back on Maeve, I answered her previous questions, "No, I won't hold it against her this time, and thank you for the invitation. I will do my best to attend, though I would ask the fae be warned ahead that I dislike magic being used to manipulate me."

"Of course. The rules of hospitality will be kept. Though, it is a fae event. You should still be careful." Her eyes wandered over to Jadelyn.

"We'll make sure the Dragon King knows the rules. The last thing we need is for him to be roped into breeding little fae nymphos for the rest of his life," Kelly spoke up instead of Jadelyn.

Maeve winced the slightest bit at the lack of tact, but I just smiled.

"Wonderful." Maeve bowed slightly and excused herself, pulling her nymph assistant away with a tight grip.

Jadelyn let out a soft sigh. "She must care about that nymph."

"What makes you say that?" I asked, surprised at Jadelyn's revelation.

"She barely reprimanded her. She even protected her. Maeve's had that same assistant for... as long as I can remember. Winter and Summer have a new assistant nearly every season," Jadelyn replied.

I wasn't sure what to make of it, but I had to admit that Maeve actually having loyalty to someone was a plus towards us being able to work together. "So she might have some redeeming traits?"

"Maybe. But regardless of her, you're going to be attending a fae event. There are rules and cautions you need to take." Jadelyn squinted at Maeve's back.

Polydora snorted. "The Dragon King doesn't need to worry about fae glamors and promises."

Despite her confidence in me, I'd learned from Ikta that I could be swayed. And the glamor incident with Maeve's assistant only reinforced that.

"Let's add it to my independent study. Thank you for helping me navigate that invitation." I kissed Jadelyn on the cheek, ignoring the wave of jealousy from the dragonettes.

"Your teachers for independent study deserve some credit as well." Jadelyn chuckled, no doubt feeling some of their auras.

I grunted. We hadn't gotten very far in our lessons. At the moment, we were still in the basics of magical theory. Sabrina, a succubus studying under a world-renowned wizard, had been the one to help most in magical theory.

She'd seemed happy to be able to teach me what she knew. She loved experimenting with magic.

"Come on. We need to go find Morgana. Apparently, we've been getting jobs that need taking care of."

With my new schedule, it had been harder to find time to spend with Morgana. She ran a nightclub, helped out new vampires coming into town, and ran her mercenary business. Finding time when she was free and I wasn't needed for something required us to be deliberate.

But I loved our time when we were together, so it was easy to prioritize.

Reaching out, I was able to sense the direction of the mark I'd placed on her when my dragon had made her a mate.

I walked through the Atrium, the space Morgana had made to connect various paranormal locations in the city. Stepping out into her club, it was too early for the club to be raging. At the moment, vampires, goblins, and some other less welcome paranormals busied themselves working.

I could still sense Morgana, but she wasn't nearby.

"Where is Blueberry?" Kelly asked, trailing after me.

I had a pretty long tail of women at the moment between Kelly, Scarlett, Jadelyn, and the dragonettes. I was only missing the Highaen sisters and Morgana. "You can grab a seat at the bar; I think she's deeper in the place."

When I had first stepped into Bumps in the Night, I had been shocked to find out that it was bigger on the inside than it could possibly be. Magic, or more specifically, Morgana's spatial magic, made it that way. When someone got vamped, their magic changed; Morgana was unique in her spatial magic outside the celestial plane.

But her magic likely had something to do with the fact that she still had a connection to her elven root tree, which happened to be supporting a portal to the celestial plane. She hadn't figured out a way to solve it beyond locking the tree up in a space rigged to collapse if the angels tried to use the portal, thus locking them out of earth.

As I walked down the steps to the next section of the club, it sprawled out before me. Non-paranormals likely thought the club just extended underground as they walked further and further into the club. The area, usually filled with dancing patrons, was currently well lit and being prepped.

I continued on, taking a left turn on the third floor, noticing the burlesque dancers practicing on stage. I gave them a wave as I ducked into an employee only entrance, feeling space warp around me.

The bar was a fucking spatial maze, but I just focused on the mark I'd given Morgana and followed it through. After another half dozen rooms, a training dojo, a kitchen, and even what looked like the first floor of a housing complex, I finally entered the garage.

Dozens of sports cars lined the stalls, and all of them were Morgana's. Another vampire was currently waxing one of the sleeker models, but my attention moved quickly off that vampire and onto the beautiful drow working at a table in front of a wall of empty foam shapes. Normally, it held a small arsenal of weapons.

"Cleaning your own guns?" I asked as I strolled over to her.

"I feel more confident in them that way. Nothing ruins a mission better than an idiot mixing up a firing pin." She glared in the direction of the young vampire who was waxing the cars, and he suddenly went into double time on each stroke as he avoided eye contact.

Trying not to laugh at his discomfort, I picked up a Glock and got to work helping her clean her weapons. "That makes perfect sense."

I wasn't really a gun guy, but I'd gotten used to the handguns out of necessity from working with Morgana. Claws and fire were much better weapons if I needed to kill someone.

"So, what brought you down here?" She glanced behind me, her interest growing. "No entourage?"

"I haven't been that distant, have I?" I frowned at the gun in my hand before looking back up at Morgana.

"You've been busy enough that you had to miss several missions." Morgana's red eyes bored into me.

I wanted to refute her, but I knew she was right. I put the gun down on the table and moved closer to her. "You're right. I need to rein the other distractions. Getting Herm and the dragonettes settled took a lot of time, but that's done. I do have some new social responsibilities popping up, though. Rupert and Maeve want to throw a party."

"Together?" Morgana nearly dropped her gun.

"No. Oh god, no. That would be... a disaster. Separate parties." Just the idea of Rupert trying to share the spotlight as host with the Fae Queens and Ladies made me chuckle.

I wasn't sure who would win out, the Fae Queens or Rupert's wife, Claire.

"That could have waited for tonight. Something else?" Morgana waited.

"Yeah. Council stuff though. I'm far more interested in getting you to come with me on two dates." Giving her my best grin, I tried to not make my visit entirely about business.

Morgana leaned over and kissed my cheek before nuzzling my neck and letting her fangs scrape at my skin. Her narcotic venom made my skin tingle, and it was entirely my own reaction as I felt myself hold my breath in anticipation of the bite.

She waited for a moment before sitting back, simply leaving a lingering kiss on my neck.

"Tease."

"We have company." Her eyes shifted to the vampire that was waxing her cars. "Later, I want to ride my dragon." The bedroom eyes she gave me made me want to ignore the lingering vampire in the room.

"What was the council business?" she asked, dumping a cool bucket of water on my libido.

"Vampires. With all the paranormal flocking to Philly, a few vampires have apparently been harassing the fae."

Morgana winced. "Fucking idiots. Sounds like some fresh blood getting a tasty whiff. They can never control themselves around fae and dragons. But if they're that fresh, that also means someone is turning vampires in the city."

She wrinkled her nose, and her hands blurred as she put the gun back together in record time. Once it was assembled, she lovingly slid it into its spot on the wall with a satisfied, fang-filled smile.

"I'm guessing there are rules around turning vampires?" I prodded.

"You don't make fresh vampires and walk away. They are the maker's responsibility until the new vamp can get things under control."

"Like when you tell a human about the paranormal?" I tried to connect it to something I knew.

"Exactly like when you tell a human about the paranormal. Though they become vampires, as far as the council and everyone else is concerned, they are governed the same until they get their legs underneath them," Morgana explained.

I nodded. That made sense. When I'd first been inducted into the paranormal culture, I'd wanted to tell my roommate. But apparently, then he would have become my responsibility forever. It was too vital that the paranormal remain secret with all the weapons non-paranormals had now developed.

If he had betrayed the paranormal community, it would have fallen on me. Usually, telling a non-paranormal was accompanied with marriage.

"So, whoever is turning them, if that's what's happening, would be held responsible for them attacking the fae."

"Yep, they'd be in epically deep shit," Morgana clarified. "The queens would have the right to kill the vampire that created the attacking vamps. Trick is, vampires don't exactly register their new fledgling vamps, so it can be hard to prove who was their maker."

"So how do we find who made the vampires?" I needed a way forward on this case. I had given my word to the council.

Morgana grinned. "You need a live vamp and a wizard. I'm going to go out on a limb and guess that the ones that attacked the fae aren't alive anymore."

Given what I knew about the fae, that seemed like a solid guess.

A race who spent their entire lives either preparing for, or in, an eternal war weren't exactly merciful. The Winter and Summer courts were constantly at war, balancing out the other and keeping the seasons regulated.

"Also, the council made it sound like I'd been slacking on a few jobs?" Morgana had implied something similar, and it said something that I'd been so busy I wasn't even aware I'd missed any.

Morgana shrugged. "The elves gave me a battery of tasks. Most of them are bullshit. One stuck out though." She pulled her phone out of the spatial pocket she kept in her bra. "Sex demon attack. I only thought to bring this one up because of your friend. If she got sloppy, she needs a reminder to clean up after herself. Or if it's not her, we have another fun sex demon running around the city."

Morgana gave me her phone. On it was the corpse equivalent to a dried-out prune that had been left in the sun far too long.

"Shit. This is a sex demon kill?" I couldn't even make out the gender of the corpse. "Kind of disgusting."

"They inflame lust and use it to drink the person's mana. It does about the same thing to a man that it does to a woman." Morgana made an intense slurping noise. "They don't look like that until a few hours after."

"This person literally orgasmed all of their fluids out?" I stared at the picture in disbelief.

"No," Morgana laughed. "The sex demons drink people's lust. Though, I'm sure this person might have literally cum a bucket's worth before they died. They stop retaining moisture for some reason after. You could ask your friend for more. I don't know it all. Demons aren't exactly forthcoming on the specifics. But different demons feed on different emotions."

"Then how do you know this is a sex demon?" I asked, still staring at the photo, unable to pry my eyes away.

"Because it happened in a crappy motel, and they weren't beaten black and blue. The investigators also found the body with clothes scattered around the room and an unopened wine bottle." Morgana said it dismissively, as if it were a foregone conclusion. "All adds up to sex demon."

It certainly did sound like the person had been having a good night before they were turned into a shriveled-up prune.

"Keep me updated please. I know I've been busy, but after dinner tonight, I'm coming with you on whatever mission you have," I insisted.

Morgana nodded. "But the van won't seat a dozen."

"There aren't a dozen of them, and I'll only bring one." I knew that would make her happy. I'd figure out how I was going to convince the dragonettes I only needed one bodyguard later. The trickier part would be not having a bunch of hurt dragonettes at whom I chose to come with me.

"Fine," she replied, grabbing the next gun to clean. "But take a nap first. We'll go hit up some of the vampire haunts and see what we can find. That means we can't even start before ten, so get some sleep while you can."

Something about Morgana's lip caught my attention, and I leaned forward, kissing them and pulling her closer. The guns and tools on the table rattled as they were displaced. Very little got in my way when I wanted to have one of my mates.

Morgana took a deep breath and shouted, "Rick, get the hell out of here."

He didn't need to be told twice; he darted out of the room with vampiric speed as I lifted Morgana up. Her fangs danced along my neck once more, teasing me.

I growled, and I could hear her satisfied smirk. I smacked Morgana down onto the table, bending it slightly with my force.

She ground herself into me.

"Don't be gentle," she cooed in my ear as her nails scraped down my back.

# CHAPTER 3

Maddie squinted at me across the table as I passed the salad to Scarlett. I could tell Maddie was trying to catch my attention.

Wanting to find more time for my human friends, but not having much extra time at all, I had decided on a family meal night. I'd brought my mates, the dragonettes, and Sabrina over to the apartment I shared with Frank. Frank's girlfriend, Maddie, was one of my best friends, but without understanding I was a dragon, it was hard to explain the large number of women currently congregating around me.

I stared intently at the salad on my plate instead of looking up.

Maddie gave it another moment, but then she couldn't help herself, whispering, "Another one?"

Maddie had been growing increasingly uncomfortable as each woman joined my harem. I'd been changing quickly, and she still thought of me as the guy she knew before I'd found out I was a dragon.

But she was one of my closest friends. We'd known each other for so long, and I didn't want to lose her friendship. I was hoping that if I just overloaded her with everybody, she'd start to relax.

"Another what?" Sabrina looked up from filling her plate with salad.

"Sabrina is helping me with my independent study," I filled in, not for the first time.

"Uh huh." Maddie stared at me as she stabbed her food harder than she needed to.

She didn't believe me. And I didn't blame her. She didn't have all the facts to understand the situation, so it was feeling pretty absurd.

"Zach's actually a pretty outstanding student. We are working through basic theory quickly." Sabrina smiled across the table.

I wilted.

Basic theory was killing me. I wanted to blast things or build giant magical towers, not discuss the basic languages of magic or the various approaches to channel mana. Apparently, after that, I had to learn the languages. Then I'd finally get to practice some magic.

While I was certainly getting a good foundational understanding with Sabrina, I'd been excited when my dragonettes taught me to use some draconic language. Although, so far, I'd only been able to do the magical equivalent of a fire hose, to which they informed me that the foundations would be necessary to fine tune any of it. So, I was stuck with Sabrina's methods.

"Oh. So you are some chemistry wizard? You barely look like you could drink," Maddie shot back at Sabrina.

Frank, my roommate, began nudging his girlfriend to cut it out.

"Oh. We were invited to some parties today," I cut through the awkwardness and announced to the rest of the group.

"Parties?" Tyrande perked up. Her pointed ears were tucked into her hair, and her eyes, which normally swirled with rich magical colors, were hidden by an amulet similar to Morgana's.

Jadelyn sighed. "My father is hosting one. Maeve is hosting another."

She opened her mouth to ask a question, but then stopped, eyeing Frank and Maddie. Guessing at her question, I tried to answer it for her.

"Don't worry, Maeve's party isn't at her place," I said quickly. "Though I accepted both."

"Maeve, as in hotty hot Maeve from statistics?" Frank was all smiles. He had been crushing on the Fall Lady hard. Though, I didn't entirely blame him.

I'd been trying to get Maeve to stop encouraging Frank, or at least have another fae glamor him so she was less appealing. At first, she had let him think she might be interested in hopes of getting closer to me. But she had frozen him out since I had asked her to.

Maddie's fork landed dangerously close to Frank's hand. "Who's Maeve?"

Frank stiffened before leaning back and scratching the back of his head with a laugh. "Some girl in class that totally has the hots for Zach. She's drop dead gorgeous, and he's being dense." He paused. "Though not as pretty as you."

Maddie snorted and went back to her meal while Frank silently pleaded with me. For what, I wasn't sure. Either he wanted to come along, or he needed help with Maddie.

"So, these people are okay with you parading around with... all of them at these parties." Maddie waved her utensils at my mates.

"Not that it's a problem," Frank tried to soften her words.

"I understand. You two think my life choices are a little awkward. Which... is why I think next year I'm going to get my own place, Frank." I'd been trying to decide how to tell them, but if our friendship was going to survive, I needed my own place. I couldn't handle the constant judgment from them.

Frank opened and closed his mouth several times before hanging his head. "I get it. You probably need a little more space and some privacy." He chose to take it another way and grinned at me.

"Yeah," I agreed. "More space."

***

The rest of dinner was awkward, but Scarlett did try to perk it up with some of her incredible muffins.

As we were clearing the table, my mind was swirling with thoughts. In a way, the meal had begun to feel like a little of a goodbye to the two of them. We only had a few more weeks in the semester, and they'd both head home for the summer while I stayed in Philly.

Next year was my senior year, and I didn't even know what that meant as I shifted to independent studies. But I still wanted to graduate. I could probably wrap up my studies in another semester if I pushed myself, or I could take a light load both semesters and work on magic on the side.

Shaking my head, I pushed the thoughts away. I'd make those decisions another time.

"Come, that dinner wasn't satisfying for me," Morgana whispered in my ear, her hands roving under my shirt.

"Stop that. There are others."

"They aren't looking. Just a taste. It'll look like a play bite." She nibbled at my neck, and I tilted my head aside, exposing my neck to her with a sigh of relief as I felt her fangs and her venom.

She had only taken a sip before I removed her from my neck and pulled her around to my front. "If I didn't know better, you were getting a little hungrier for me."

We didn't get to flirt for long before Maddie cleared her throat.

Morgana rolled her eyes and sauntered away with grace that made me wonder how, even with her magical guise, anyone mistook her for a human.

Prying my eyes off her tight, leather clad rear, I met Maddie's eyes.

"Look. You know that I don't like this." She waved vaguely at the ladies cleaning up. "But I don't want you to just cut Frank and me out because of it."

I held up my hands and leaned against the counter. "Who said anything about cutting you two out?"

"Come on. I'm not an idiot. I don't approve—something seems wrong. But you are all adults, and no one seems unhappy with the situation." Her eyes focused on my neck, a crease forming in her brow. "You're bleeding."

I wiped at my neck. "Shit, sorry..." I struggled to come up with an excuse. "Must have scratched at this bug bite."

"Let me." Maddie grabbed a paper towel and wiped it away. "Huh. I don't see a bug bite."

I was distracted with being caught potentially in a lie and just diverted the conversation. "Don't change the subject. I do believe you were in the middle of apologizing."

She playfully slapped my chest. "Oh, shut up. You know you're stuck with me, but Frank is a whole other level. You know he'll track you down and make you share your pheromones or whatever has all these women around you."

I laughed. "Sorry about that."

Maddie snorted, but then her face became more serious. "If Maeve was a problem, would you tell me?"

"Absolutely. And she's not. I had a talk with her," I promised Maddie.

"Good. I like Frank, but he still sort of wants to skirt chase." She rolled her eyes. "Maybe he'll settle down."

I wasn't so sure about that, but I hoped for Maddie's sake that he did. I didn't know what Frank would do without Maddie.

"Look. I know this seems strange to you, and there are things I can't tell you, but we are happy," I promised my friend.

"You all look happy, which is what is so confusing. I mean, how can this work?" She held up a hand to stop me from responding. "Nope. I don't want to know the intimate details." She smiled at me. "Thanks for dinner, Zach. I think we're going to head out for a bit, but I'm glad I got a chance to see you."

Maddie ducked away, grabbing Frank's hand and urgently leaving the apartment.

As soon as the door closed, Polydora raised her hand. "Did we do something wrong? They fled."

"No. I think our harem is just too much for her to comprehend. Let's finish cleaning up and then I'm taking a nap before I go out with Morgana to visit some vampires."

Tyrande walked over and kissed me on the cheek. "We'll turn in for the night. We have to get up early for some calls back home."

She let her magical facade drop and showed me her beautiful high elf form for a moment before heading into my bedroom. The bedroom had a portal back to Jadelyn's manor where she and Yev were staying.

Yev came and gave me a kiss before following her older sister. The scent of my dragon mate lingered, and I savored it.

"Do you have transportation arranged for us to follow you on your trip tonight?" Polydora asked.

I groaned in my head. I had been dreading this conversation. "Actually, I'm just going to take Trina with me."

Trina perked up. "Really?"

"Really. We are heading into some vampire dens. I thought your death magic and healing might be useful," I added.

Amira perked up.

Technically, the black dragon and the copper had the same type of magic, but Trina just came to mind first since I'd spent more time with her. I was comfortable with her.

"Why her?" Amira asked. "I have the same magic. Is it because she's metallic?"

I should have seen that coming.

There were several other stares at me in the room, most pointedly, from Chloe and Larisa. They were blue and white dragons, respectively.

"No. I have no problem with chromatics; Yev is a green," I pointed out. "Trina went through the challenge at the conclave with me."

"Trina, you will call us if things go poorly?" Polydora asked the other dragon.

"Hey," I protested.

The dragon girls all shrugged.

"Male dragons aren't exactly known for asking for help," Polydora added. "Plus, it is her job to ensure your security, which means calling for backup if needed."

Trina gave Polydora a sharp nod.

Letting my thoughts roam, I realized Sabrina might also be useful on the mission. She could help in figuring out the difference between a vampire or demon kill.

"Sabrina, do you have time? There's a sex demon causing problems in the city too."

She stood up straight, a touch of hurt in her eyes. "I didn't do it."

I blinked. "Never thought you did. I just wanted to ask some questions."

"Oh, sure. I can help answer them, but I can't be out too late tonight. I need to rest for an exam tomorrow. Normal class work on top of tutoring you is taking a lot out of me," Sabrina replied a little sheepishly.

Several of the dragons stared at her like something was wrong. I had to work to not laugh at the fact that they couldn't understand why she would turn down the chance for more time with me. They all were singularly focused at the moment.

"Okay then. Ladies, as much as I'd love your company, I need to get some sleep if I'm going to be out with Morgana all night. Trina, Sabrina, meet me at the bar at ten." I led Sabrina over to my bedroom and walked through the closet.

If I didn't leave, there was a pretty good chance I'd end up in bed with at least one woman, and then I'd never get any sleep.

"Where are we going?" Sabrina asked, but she didn't seem concerned as she followed me.

"My place in the Atrium. Had to get away from the dragons."

"They are oozing the desire for sex," Sabrina said flatly. "Not surprised you feel it."

Halfway to opening the door, I looked at her. "You can sense that?"

"And your own desire is through the roof. I am a succubus." She sighed. "I think some of the dragons are putting off pheromones. It got really bad when they were close."

I grumbled to myself. It was the last thing I needed, but it made me feel better about being a horndog lately. If my honor guard of dragonettes were the problem, that somehow made it better.

I'd been a little worried that it was some sort of Dragon King result. Like my body was going through some sort of new pubescence. Horror hit me as I wondered if that was really a thing.

Distracted in my thoughts, we reached my room in no time.

Sabrina looked around before sitting down in a chair with dragons carved into the wooden arms. I grabbed a spot near her.

"So, what can you tell me about demons? Morgana thinks there was a sex demon killing in town."

Sabrina bit her lip. "You don't suspect me, do you?"

"Not really. You don't exactly seem the type. Though... uh... if it isn't insensitive, how exactly do you... feed?" I stumbled over my words.

It felt like a very personal question. That, and I was pretty sure it involved sex.

"Well, let's talk about the basic theory of magic and mana. We know all paranormal abilities run off of mana as does magic."

I tried not to groan as she went straight into teacher mode, her legs crossed as she pushed her glasses up firmly onto her face. I did not want more magical theory, but I needed information for the case.

"Right. Mana is a physical particle, but only something with a soul can store or manipulate it." I had learned at least that much.

Sabrina nodded along with me. "Correct. And emotions are outpourings of the soul. That's why people under high emotional stress have trouble controlling their magic. Demons manipulate emotions and the soul. We heighten an emotion to the point that their souls pour out mana, and then we collect a specific flavor of emotionally tinted mana."

I opened and closed my mouth a few times. "So, you make men really horny and then..." I made a slurping noise. "You suck up all the lusty mana?"

She frowned at me. "Crude, but yes. I also don't have to be the one to make them lusty, nor do they have to be men." She raised an eyebrow, and I suddenly understood what she was trying to say.

"Shit. I didn't mean to assume. Are you—" I decided to shut up before I made it worse.

Sabrina laughed. "I'm bi, or maybe omni." A husky chuckle rolled out of her. "Sex is in my very nature. I'm not picky."

I didn't know what to say to that. Previously, she hadn't given off much in the way of sexuality.

"Oh. OH. We were giving you a buffet tonight?" I realized that, if I was understanding how she fed correctly, we must have been giving her a feast.

Sabrina sighed. "A table of horny dragons was a lot, I..." She blushed. "I should tell you that I fed off of you. It was too tempting." Red tinged her cheeks, and she was avoiding looking me in the eye, going as far as to cover her face.

"Sabrina, that doesn't bother me. You have to eat too, and it's only fair when you're surrounded by all that lust." I tried to be gentle. I could tell it was something she was self-conscious about. But I had to ask one question. "It won't hurt me or the women?"

Sabrina went from covering her face to waving her hands wildly. "No, nothing like that. You'll be fine. As a dragon, I take no more than would normally leave your body."

"As in, you've been doing this for a while?" I asked, surprised.

Sabrina shot up from the chair, her face beet red. The sudden motion knocked her glasses off her face, and she quickly fumbled to grab them.

Her human guise was gone. Instead, she had pale pink skin, goat horns that curled out of her head and plump lips that made my jaw ache and my mouth salivate.

I wanted to taste them. No, I needed to taste them.

"I'm so sorry." Her words brought me up to her eyes, which were filled with raw, lusty hunger. I became hard in an instant.

Fumbling some more, she got her glasses back on, and her succubus nature was hidden away once more. A more bashful girl with glasses and a sweater that was a few sizes too big stood once more in my room.

"I keep it under wraps. My nature causes more trouble than it's worth," she grumbled.

The compulsion to push her up against the wall and use her to slam through it was gone, but my body was still quite flush, and my pants were tented. I was avoiding the urge to adjust myself and draw more attention to it.

"Oh, it's fine. Thank you for the information on demons. But I really should get some sleep. Are you good to meet at Bumps around ten?" I rushed her out.

"Yeah, I can do that. How do I get out of here?"

"Go out that door. Two doors down, you'll come out at Bumps." I hurried Sabrina out of Morgana's wing and closed the stone door behind her.

"Fuck," I said to myself as I marched back into my apartment. Flipping the dragon-claw styled shower knob to cold, I stepped under it and dunked my head.

I would not be getting any sleep until I relieved myself of the current need in my body.

# CHAPTER 4

"**B**uckle up," I advised the others as I clicked my seatbelt into place.

We'd hopped into Morgana's armored minivan, which, despite the normal look, had been outfitted to match a tank's intensity.

"You are a dragon. A car crash is barely going to hurt." Trina crossed her arms.

"Just wait until you see Morgana's driving. This is so you don't fly out early." I patted my trusty seatbelt.

Sabrina seemed to take my advice more to heart, quickly buckling her seatbelt and chanting a few words under her breath to enchant it.

Morgana frowned at me, speaking in her Swiss accent. "What you see as careless driving is just highly skilled."

Trina paused, and while still trying to appear nonchalant, I saw her quickly buckle her seatbelt.

"I still don't understand why we couldn't take the red one." Trina had seen the other sexy luxury cars Morgana owned and was not at all impressed with the minivan.

"That one barely seats two," I said. "Besides, this thing is actually pretty decked out. Morgana's goblin friends in Sentarshaden gave it enchanted siding and an engine that requires Morgana to buy enchanted drive belts. Otherwise, she'd strip them instantly."

I had grown an appreciation for the ugly vehicle after watching bullets bounce off of it on numerous occasions.

Morgana started the engine with a roar and immediately slammed her foot down, gunning it out of the stall. She managed to nearly hit three of her beautiful sports cars as the van swerved its way through the garage.

Trina was hanging onto the oh-shit handle for dear life. "Warn me first."

"I did," I replied, trying to hide my smugness but failing. "Happy to be wearing that seatbelt now?" I managed to contain the laugh bubbling up my throat, but only barely.

"Watch it. I'm the one who's supposed to patch you up if something goes wrong. You want to stay on my good side." Trina smirked right back at me, twirling her hair. It fell over her shoulder in a messy braid. She looked cute as she played with it, swirling the light brown hair just over her tan shoulder blades.

She'd gone casual but cute for the night. She'd paired jeans with a white top and a plaid shirt, but she'd tied the plaid shirt just under her chest. My eyes were drawn to where it pulled tightly across her breasts.

I found my dragon perking to attention as I became more self-conscious, remembering that we had a succubus in the car. Looking up, I met Sabrina's eyes, wondering if she was feeding off me.

She could see where my mind was going, and her face became slightly frantic. "I wasn't!"

I looked to reassure her just as Morgana spun the wheel and took a sharp turn, my body flinging against the side of the car. I grumbled over at my beautiful mate, who seemed quite pleased with herself.

Looking back at Sabrina, I went back to trying to make her feel more comfortable. "We talked about it, Sabrina. It's all good."

"What are you two talking about?" Trina frowned, looking between Sabrina and me.

Morgana looked into the rearview mirror, taking in the blushing succubus and pieced it together. "Putting on a show for the succubus, love?"

"I told her it is okay. Everybody has to eat," I replied.

"Wait." Trina's mouth gaped. "She's feeding off of you? I didn't think she was part of your harem yet." The copper dragon looked more than a little jealous.

Sabrina's face got even redder still. "I'm not part of his harem. He just puts off a lot of lust, and... I just take little sips."

Trina calmed and turned to the succubus with a big grin. "Poor girl. I understand your pain. His lust has to be delicious. After all, he's the Dragon King. I'd love a taste of him myself." She winked at me.

Sabrina's blush spread to the tips of her ears and down her collar.

"Cut it out. Don't tease her," I growled at Trina, my chest rumbling louder than my size made it seem possible.

"Apologies, my king." Trina was quick to get serious and bow as low as she could, strapped into the seat. "You've brought her along, so I simply assumed you must be adding her as one of your mates." The small quirk of her lips told me that she was still intentionally messing with Sabrina.

"Eep," Sabrina squeaked and sank down in her seat, apparently trying to make herself smaller.

I rolled my eyes at Trina, but continuing the conversation seemed like it was just going to make Sabrina pull more into herself.

"Buck up, buttercup. She's just messing with you. Don't give her the satisfaction." Morgana turned around in her seat to comfort the succubus, keeping one hand on the wheel. The van was roaring at a solid eighty miles an hour through the streets.

"WATCH THE ROAD!" Trina screamed and pulled her legs up while clinging to the oh-shit handle.

"Oh, relax. There's barely anyone out at this time. Besides, didn't you say a car crash would barely hurt a dragon?" Morgana huffed a sigh as she turned back to focus on the road, the car lurching as she hit a curb on her next turn.

I heard Sabrina muttering a few more enchantments under her breath, holding on to the seat belt as she rode out the current blush spread across her face.

Letting silence settle across the group, I relaxed into the seat as best I could with Morgana's driving, letting my mind wander. It didn't feel like much time passed before we were pulling up to a well-lit club bouncing with music and a bright neon sign, 'The Bloody Mary', complete with a little blood drop.

"I thought they'd be... I don't know, a little less obvious." Now that I was a part of the paranormal world, I just couldn't understand how it wasn't obvious to everybody else.

"Surely you've noticed by now that the best way to stay hidden is to be right under their noses." Morgana got out of the car. "Besides, I know the owner. He's a little flamboyant."

Sabrina perked up, curiosity shining in her eyes. "I thought you weren't friendly with the vampires."

Two steroid chugging goons stepped away from the door and flashed their fangs at our group.

"I never said I was friendly with them, just that I knew them," Morgana replied over her shoulder as she sashayed up to the club's bouncers like she owned the place.

"Morgana Silverwing. What the fuck are you doing here?" Goon number one stepped forward. But it was goon number two that made the fatal mistake of touching my mate.

As his hand descended towards her arm, I moved towards him faster than he could dodge away without giving away his nature in public. He was face to face with the pavement a moment later.

"My. Mate." My chest rumbled deep enough to make the window panes buzz.

It was everything I could do to leave him and the current limb in my arm intact. Every part of my dragon instincts wanted to crush him. My beast butted its head inside my chest, thrashing around.

"Hey, man. Wait... fuck." The first goon held up his hands, his eyes going wide. "You're the..." He paused, realizing there were onlookers. "King."

"Yep! And my mate," Morgana clarified helpfully, looking smug as shit.

"Okay. We can fix this. Jack, if he lets you go, you're done for the night. I need you to get out of his sight as quickly as possible. Got it?" The man in my grasp nodded ever so slightly, and the man still standing turned to speak to me.

"We apologize for the slight. It's in our culture to rough house given our extreme healing. He did not mean to insult you." As he finished, I had to admit that the respect was helping my dragon calm down slightly.

I felt Morgana step up to me, pressing her body into me. "It would probably be more trouble than it is worth to make a mess here, Zach. And I'm sure he's very sorry." She smirked down at the vampire on the ground, who nodded at her statement.

"Fine." I shoved off of him and straightened my shirt. "Let's go."

Jack was on his feet and rushing away at normal speed.

Goon number one gave me a friendly smile that showed off his fangs. "Come on in." He parted the velvet rope, and we cut the line.

"I need to talk to Ricardo." Morgana got down to business as soon as we were walking through the doors, the doorman walking in behind us and making sure the vampires checking IDs didn't make the same mistake.

"Ricardo isn't in charge anymore," he replied.

Morgana paused in her steps. "Is he dead?"

A suave looking man with a few too many shirt buttons undone swooped in. "Not dead, but at times, you have to know when to throw in the towel to survive. Isn't that right, my dear Morgana?"

The new man tried to grab her hand to pull her close, but she drew it away before he could snatch it.

"Ricardo, you can't be that friendly. My mate might misunderstand and not realize that you are just from another time, with different greetings." Morgana stepped back, making the vampire bring his attention to me. I caught his attention quickly.

"Rumors are true?" His nostrils flared as he took a deep breath. "Yes, that's the smell of a powerful dragon. It is an honor to meet you." He tucked one hand to his chest, the other behind his back, and bowed. "Forgive me, the old Italian ways are still alive and well with me."

"Boss, he nearly killed Jack for putting a hand on Morgana," Goon one coughed into his hand. It was a not-so-subtle whisper; I heard it easily.

Ricardo chuckled and patted his back. "Well, we'll just have to entertain our guests properly, then. Morgana, we have a show about to start. Come, join and watch. Then you can talk business with our new leader."

"Fine. But we'll need a booth." She was already making her way towards where she wanted to sit.

Our host graciously bowed. "Of course, after you."

But she was already strutting away, making him hurry after her. I followed after my beautiful mate, taking my time to scope for any threats in the area as I walked beside Ricardo.

"So, if you stepped down, who's in charge now?" I asked Ricardo.

"Deniz. He came over from Turkey. He has the support of some of the bloodlords, and enough power that it was easier to give way to him." Ricardo made it sound far simpler than it actually was.

But the fact that this vampire was from Turkey certainly got my attention. That was the same area that had shot down one of my dragons, and the dragon in me stirred forcefully. I could only assume Deniz was related to the group that had attacked.

My dragon wanted blood, but I was a king now. I needed to understand more of the facts before I acted.

"So, what kind of show are you putting on?" I made small talk as I continued to scan around.

The patrons of the club seemed heavily clothed in leather and latex. A guy walked past me with a ball gag in his mouth and a pair of leather pants that were far too tight for him.

"It is a little more risqué here than my shows," Morgana admitted.

"Your tame little dances? What's the fun if there isn't blood and semen spread across them by the end?" Ricardo laughed as Morgana slipped into a nearby booth.

Across the way, there were two women fawning over a man, but I could tell he wasn't the predator of the group. His eyes were glazed over as the women showered him with kisses and licks before sinking their fangs into his neck.

"Lovely place," I commented dryly.

"When you live as long as some of us do, vanilla gets boring and you start to branch out." Morgana shrugged before looking to the other two for support.

Trina held up her hands. "Don't look at me."

Sabrina just ducked her head, the blush on her face seeming to become permanent.

A woman walked up to our booth in a latex bunny outfit and leggings with a few tears in them. "What can I get for you guys?"

"Do you have anything sanguine and from the 80's?" Morgana asked.

"We do, a Roma Gerindalt. Will that do?"

"Perfect."

The bunny waited, turning to me. "And you?"

"I'll take a Moscow mule," I ordered, hoping I wasn't about to get Russian animal blood in a vampire club.

"Cosmo," Sabrina spoke up.

Trina just ordered a beer.

"Cosmo. Huh, never would have guessed," Trina commented.

Sabrina just scratched the back of her head. "It was the first thing I could think of. I didn't want to make her wait for me to come up with something else, and I hate beer."

Sabrina was such a puzzle to me. Her nature should make her an extreme extrovert, but her personality definitely leaned the other way.

A drum roll sounded as I scooted closer to Morgana in the booth.

Spotlights flared and shrank in onto what I had thought was an empty table with a tablecloth as we'd walked in. But as it became lit, I realized it was a circular bed placed on a pedestal.

A young, tatted-up man walked into the lights, holding a chain. And on the other end of the chain was a woman crawling on her hands and knees as he led her up to the bed.

"Morgana, uh. She's human, and he's very not human." I looked at the scene with my dragon eyes.

"Yeah, she's probably going to get fed on," Morgana said offhandedly before twisting to look at me, a bit of sadness in her eyes. "This is a good chance for you to see exactly what vampires think of humans."

"Not much," Trina snorted.

The bunny server girl came back with our drinks and passed them around. She was human, and I wondered how long she'd last.

I welcomed the distraction as the man on stage began wrapping the woman in the chains. She moaned and groaned with ecstasy, and I noticed Sabrina wiggling a little in her seat. The room was probably full of sexual energy.

The man on stage pulled the chains tight, causing her breasts to jut forward and shake before he bent her over the bed and sank his teeth into her thighs.

"He's drinking from her?" Trina asked Morgana.

"Yes, the thigh is a quality spot. It's easier to hide the bite marks than the neck." Morgana stared at my neck.

"Down. You've had enough. Maddie saw the blood after you nibbled on me at dinner," I grumbled over the screams of the entertainment.

I was ready for it to be over. While the other patrons seemed to enjoy the display of bondage, it felt forced to me. There wasn't any chemistry between them.

Trina looked on with interest until she noticed I wasn't watching. Sabrina's eyes were focused on absolutely anything except the stage.

"It is strange that after everything I've been through that this isn't very interesting?" I commented.

"It makes perfect sense. When you can have me, or any of a half a dozen gorgeous ladies, I'm not surprised that a plain girl doesn't interest you." Morgana tossed her hair with a smirk.

I laughed, pulling her tightly against my side. "You're right. That must be it." I leaned down to kiss the top of her head while my eyes continued to scan the room. I wanted to locate the Turkish vampire.

"Calm down." Trina put a hand on mine. "Your eyes are shifting."

I nodded, appreciating her intervention. Taking a deep breath, I tried to change the conversation. "So, is anyone here tasty, Sabrina? There's got to be a lot of lust going around."

She wrinkled her nose. "Nothing compelling. Mostly the vampires are hungry, and the horny humans are like trying to subsist on air."

"Compared to my king, they would all be like eating dirt," Trina agreed. "So, you should work with me to woo the king into our bed. That way, we can both enjoy him."

"Cut it out." I rolled my eyes at Trina. Out of the corner of my eye, I saw the woman slump down on the bed, looking very pale.

Looking over, I watched as several men came and picked her up, carrying her off deeper into the club. Nobody seemed concerned, and I hoped that meant she would recover just fine.

Before I could ask Morgana, I saw the man that had been part of the show have an attendant whisper in his ear and look our way. He took a deep sip of a drink before slightly turning in the direction she indicated, taking us in.

Taking another long sip, he put the drink back on the table and stood.

"Ah shit." I connected the dots. "I have a feeling we're about to meet Deniz."

# CHAPTER 5

As the vampire walked over to me, I knew that my intuition was right. This was the man who owned the club. The bare-chested vampire strolled up to our booth, and one worker scrambled to get a chair in place for him.

He turned it backwards, straddling it and leaning forward casually as he scanned our table, his eyes landing on my mate.

"Morgana," he said with a thick accent. "I heard the famed killer was here. To what do I owe the pleasure? Want to introduce your friends?"

I didn't miss how his eyes flickered over to me. He knew exactly who I was, but it didn't seem that he was going to admit it.

It was some sort of power play.

"Denis, was it?" Morgana acted bored and messed up his name. And I didn't miss that she ignored his question, replacing it with one of her own. "I've never heard of you before. Which of the bloodlords do you do grunt work for?"

The vampire barked a laugh. "My name is Deniz, actually. And those stuffy old men are busy playing with baubles in their castles. I much prefer to play with women. They're so much sweeter. But I was turned by Yusuf Wallachia."

He grinned from ear to ear when he said the name. I assumed those in the vampire circles would recognize it, but it meant nothing to me.

"Interesting. The Wallachia family hasn't tried to spread past the Balkans in a very long time. Don't you think coming here might be seen as an expansion attempt?" Morgana took a sip of her drink, looking almost bored as she let her eyes rove around the bar lazily.

"I'm just having a little fun." Deniz leaned back while holding onto the chair with a cocky grin. His ripped and tatted body was clearly on display, and he knew it. It seemed like his prized possession.

"You never introduced me," Deniz addressed Morgana once more.

"Because we both know you don't need it. This is my mate and partner, Zach. And these are Sabrina and Trina." Morgana was short.

Deniz breathed deep. "Dragons. Two delicious dragons." He eyed me before looking back at Morgana. "There was a rumor that you are now with the king of dragons, Zach Pendragon." His eyes flickered back to me. "I didn't know we were among royalty, or I would have dressed for it."

"Hard to dress up when you don't dress much at all," I replied dryly, enjoying the small snicker from Trina. He bristled, but I moved us on before he responded. "We are here on business, unfortunately."

I let just a little of my dragon aura slip free to keep others away from our booth. Deniz could feel it and narrowed his eyes at me.

"For privacy," I said simply, although flexing my power felt good. "After all, you let humans wander around here, and we have sensitive matters to discuss."

"A man has to eat." Deniz grinned wide, showing off his fangs. I could feel his nature wanting to rebel against my aura. His eyes sharpened as he looked at me. "What business do you have? This is time for pleasure."

I didn't beat around the bush. "It seems vampires aren't being so careful in Philly anymore. We came here on behalf of Philly's council. We are getting significant complaints of freshly turned vampires hunting in the open. The fae are concerned; they've had several attacks on their people. Spring is fading, and Summer is about to be at the height of her power. If it isn't solved, it is likely she will come and resolve it for herself." I tried to add some urgency into the statement, hoping it would make Deniz be more open.

While the fae hadn't outright said they would become more involved, what I'd said was factual. They were nearing the Summer's apex, and it was possible they would retaliate.

Deniz nodded. "But I'm still not clear why you would come here. I keep my vampires in line." He gestured about to the club, where several vampires were obviously feeding in public. "You have no problem from me."

"Given the change in vampire behavior and a change in leadership, you can understand why we'd be concerned." I narrowed my eyes and folded my hands on the table. "Fix this, Deniz. If you are going to claim leadership of the vampires in my city, then this is your problem."

"A dragon does not command me," he sneered back.

I didn't react, keeping my head held high as I stared him down. "While you are in Philly, the Paranormal Council does command you. Otherwise, you won't be welcome in the city. And I can assure you that removal would be the kinder option of our choices."

Deniz's club disgusted me, and I'd be more than happy to burn it down. But he was clearly well connected, and this was a matter for the council. While I had serious sway on the council, I didn't command it.

I looked over at my mate, who still had a bored look on her face. But I knew better. She was calculating and adding her own context over everything she was hearing. I was eager to be alone to get her thoughts, and maybe relieve a bit of her own hunger.

Deniz pursed his lips and shrugged with his hands out. "I suppose then that I should join this council if I'm to lead the vampires. Things are difficult being new, but I'll get a handle on my brethren. A few must be acting up."

His tune changed on a dime, and I knew he had ulterior motives.

"Come to the next council meeting. I'll make sure someone sends you a message," I played along. "There you can represent the vampires." Honestly, I looked forward to not playing messenger. And it never hurt to keep my potential enemies where I could see them.

"Yes. That would be great. Philly will come to understand that vampires are good for everyone." Deniz grinned at me like we were best friends. I smiled back, letting my dislike for him shine in my eyes.

"Well, that settles the issue, and I'm afraid I have no need to stay here longer." I pushed off the table. "Shall we?"

I stepped out of the booth, holding my hand out for Morgana. She scooted around the booth and took it, rising gracefully as her eyes met mine.

My beautiful vampire didn't even look at Deniz as she moved past him. Although Sabrina seemed a bit more anxious, side eyeing the clearly dangerous threat still sitting at our table.

Waiting until the women were past me, I turned my back on Deniz and followed them to the exit.

"That didn't go so well," Ricardo commented dryly, leaning against the wall near the exit. "Anything we should know?"

"There's a problem with new vamps running wild. If he doesn't get it fixed, the Council will respond," I replied, figuring he may also be able to help quell the problem.

Ricardo swallowed and stayed where he was against the wall.

We moved out into the street, and I was glad for some space until I spotted Helena standing on the sidewalk ahead.

"Helena, what are you doing in my city?" I moved into a naturally defensive stance in front of my mate.

Standing in front of us was the white-haired nephilim that had been a large part of the Church's attack on Sentarshaden, Ycv and Tyrande's home. While she'd helped me defeat the Archangel in the end, I still didn't trust her.

But then my eyes zeroed in on the woman next to her, and my eyebrows shot to my hairline.

Agent Till—an agent I'd only met once when they'd been trying to pin Jadelyn and her family for illegal shipments—stood right beside the archangel.

"Who knew tonight could get even more interesting?" Morgana commented from behind me.

Looking them over again, I noticed that Helena had a badge resting on her right hip.

I groaned, already sensing the mess this was about to become. "Agent Till, what brings you to Philly?"

I took a few steps to the side to get clear from the night goers entering the club.

"After I requested a new partner and a change of post, they put me on casework. I'm here about a recent problem." Till eyed me, like she was wondering if I was the problem.

"I see. Well, maybe we can help. Silverwing Mercenaries works in Philly. And I'd be happy to do anything that gets this one out of my city faster." I grinned before turning my attention to Helena. "You didn't tell me you joined the FBI."

Till stepped forward, her brow furrowing. "I have a few questions. Why did you call this your city? And what is your relation to Agent Albright?"

I shrugged off her first question. "Helena and I met on a trip to Switzerland."

"Something like that," Helena agreed. "I have heard the rumors since then. But I'm afraid that the woman next to you is a suspect in the case we are currently working."

Following her line of sight, I expected her to be picking a fight with Morgana, but it was Sabrina that she was looking at.

"No. I don't know why you are here, but she didn't do it." I growled, taking an aggressive step towards Helena. "Till, I think you made a good call in getting a new partner, but I'm afraid to tell you that you've picked up someone who's nothing but trouble."

To my surprise, Helena stepped back in response to my aggressive stance. "If he won't let us take her, then we can't."

The surprise was evident on Till's face as her eyebrows shot up into her hairline.

"You didn't come here for her anyway, did you?" They had no way of knowing she'd be at the club.

"No. We have a meeting with Deniz Wallachia," Till replied quickly. "I do not know who the lady next to you is. We are looking into a series of murders." She frowned at Helena, then at me. Clearly, she was smart enough to know there was something she didn't know.

I looked between the two ladies. "Be careful in there. If two federal agents die in my city, it'll be a problem."

"Zach." Helena stopped me. There was a frown on her face, but it didn't seem like it was directed at me. "I'm sorry for what happened before."

I eyed her. "I don't need the apology. Tyrande does. She's in the city. You and I won't be okay until my mate forgives you. If you can earn that forgiveness," I growled.

Helena might have turned tables and fought the archangel when the connection to the celestial plane was gone, but she still had endangered Tyrande. It was up to them to settle it. Until then, I'd stand by my mate.

"I'll do that. After it all, I am working with the FBI to fix problems." Her terminal resting bitch face softened just a little before she nodded and turned around.

Till joined her, and I heard the agent ask. "Mate?"

Helena grumbled something in response as they sauntered up to the bouncers, flashing their badges.

"Sabrina, are succubi that rare?" I was surprised that she'd been the target of the investigation so quickly. She had also jumped to the conclusion that I'd suspect her after learning about the death.

"We are very rare," Sabrina softly stated. "If it looks like a succubus killed someone, it is understandable that she would make me one of her suspects."

I looked over at Trina. "Think you girls could take another in your house? I don't want anyone jumping the gun on Sabrina if we can help it."

"That's okay, you don't have to do that," Sabrina protested.

"Nonsense. If you are getting roped into all of this, we can help." Trina nudged Sabrina and shot her a wink.

Whatever the copper dragon was plotting, I was sure I'd find out later. But if the dragonettes could look after Sabrina, I'd feel better. I was becoming busier by the day, and she'd be safer with them.

Something was happening in Philly, and I intended to get to the bottom of it. New vampire power dynamics, a demon feeding, and FBI agents descending on the area. I had my work cut out for me.

My phone rang and I looked down, seeing a phone call from my 'Fabulous Foxy Lover'. Scarlett enjoyed changing her contact info from time to time. I smiled, answering immediately.

"Scar, what's up?" We started making our way back to Morgana's van.

"Hello, Zach. It's Detective Fox."

"Oh my, what a deep voice you have, Scar," I joked with my father-in-law. I could hear Scarlett behind him, saying something, but I couldn't make it out.

Detective Fox cleared his throat. "Sorry, I'll give the phone back to my daughter when I'm done. I wanted to give you a heads up. The case triggered something up the chain; we have federal agents in town."

"Yeah, they're FBI. I'm one step ahead of you. We just ran into them while asking a few questions at a local vampire watering hole. And we know both of them. Helena was the nephilim from the battle at Sentarshaden, and Agent Till was present when Jadelyn's family's barge got pulled over," I explained.

Scarlett squawked in the background. "Helena! That pigeon brained bitch is in the city? Dad, give me the phone."

Detective Fox sighed. "I'll do my best to direct them away from you," he replied before the phone crackled as it was passed to my mate.

"Zach, did I hear that right? Helena, as in the very one who kidnapped Tyrande, is in this city?"

I could tell that Scarlett was getting agitated. "Yes, Scar, the same Helena. I told her to apologize to Tyrande, and I think she might actually do it. But I think we have bigger concerns. Put me on speaker."

There was a pause as Scarlett worked to let her issues with Helena go for the moment to focus on what we needed. "Okay, you're on with dad and me."

I climbed into Morgana's van and buckled in. "We went to see the vampires and got a surprise. They've gone through an abrupt leadership change. Some guy named Deniz Wallachia is now in charge."

"Wallachia?" both of the kitsunes replied in sync.

And their reaction told me more than enough. "Yeah."

Morgana cleared her throat, and I put it on speaker. "You have Sabrina, Trina, and Morgana here as well. I think Morgana is about to tell me about this new vampire."

"I don't know Deniz, but I do know his line, Wallachia. Vlad Wallachia was a vicious Romanian ruler. He was so ominous that he was nicknamed Vlad the Impaler."

My eyes went wide. "As in the inspiration for Dracula? Wait, was Dracula real?"

"Yes. The Wallachia family is one of the three big families among vampires. They have multiple bloodlords among their ranks," Morgana explained.

Detective Fox added on. "And they are bad news. Wallachia should not be expanding into America." The detective continued, "They still have a vicious reputation. Though their family extends by whom they turn now. If it is really Wallachia coming into our area, the entire council will want them gone."

I hadn't expected that strong of a reaction from the detective. But based on Morgana's expression, she agreed with him.

"Your thoughts?" I asked my mate.

"The Wallachia are brutes. They and the other two families have been isolated in the Balkans since the seventeenth century. The Church would take action if they stepped outside of that. Maybe that's why Helena is here." She thought after a moment.

"Except the Church just lost their celestial support, and Helena betrayed them." I closed my eyes, realizing the implications. "Fuck. By cutting off the celestial plane, we opened the door to vampire expansion."

Everyone was quiet enough that I knew I was at least partially right. I didn't regret our decisions, but it seemed that the global politics of the paranormal were sensitive enough that we'd caused a secondary reaction.

"Without the Church, there are others that might grow bolder as well," Sabrina commented quietly.

Her comment reminded me of the demon attacks in the city, and I followed her train of thought.

"Okay, so Philly is getting an influx of paranormals, and without the Church, some players are looking to expand. Did I get that right?"

"That means there are more problems on the horizon," Detective Fox echoed my concerns.

"Thanks for the talk, father, but we need to run. The council gave Silverwing Mercenaries a few other cases we need to work on." I hung up on him and let the phone slide off my hand and into the cup holder.

"Sabrina, is there a similar club for demons?" I asked.

But she shook her head, causing her black hair to fall in her face. "No. We are solitary most of the time if we are remaining on this plane. But if you know what kind of demon you are looking for, they tend to haunt the places where they can feed."

"Interesting. Do you have an example?" I asked.

"Like a succubus lingering outside a brothel," Morgana commented as she darted around a car that wasn't moving fast enough for her. "But there's always a number of options. Staking them out doesn't make sense until we've narrowed it down. Let's head down to the station and see if the morgue has more answers for us than Deniz."

# CHAPTER 6

We'd spent the night tracking down a few of the council's other problems, and I might have taken a little of my anger out on them.

Particularly an elven drug dealer.

But we got the council's backlog of work done before I pulled up to the dragonette's place. "Alright, this is the place," I announced to Sabrina as Morgana pulled up into the drive of a large home in a very nice neighborhood. It happened to be not that far from the Scalewrights' home.

Before the van even came to a full stop in the drive, I was hopping out of the car and opening the back car door for Trina and Sabrina.

"That was unnecessary." Trina came out first. "But thank you."

I leaned down and kissed her cheek. "Thank you for tonight. You did well. I know you didn't want to heal that elf."

Rather than reply, she held her cheek with a big grin plastered on her face. "Anytime, my king. You are even welcome to come in and avail of my help in bed."

"He certainly doesn't need any help in bed," Morgana chuckled.

"Even so, our partnership is clearly strong. Tonight was proof of that." Trina patted me on the chest and stood on her tiptoes, puckering her lips and closing her eyes. She was pushing for a little more reward.

Shaking my head, I drew the short woman up and went to plant a peck on the waiting lips. But she went from patiently waiting to actively engaging in an instant. As I pulled back, her arms wrapped around my neck, and she pulled herself against me.

Laughing into her lips, I grabbed her just a little tighter, enjoying the moment.

Her kiss became slightly more aggressive, her tongue vying for dominance over mine. My dragon instinct kicked in, and I pushed her up against the van a little extra hard.

Thankfully, it was reinforced.

It was slight, but I could feel the corners of her mouth curve up in victory. The little minx knew exactly how to get a reaction from a dragon.

Realizing we were in public, I managed to pull my beast back. Trina smiled in victory as she bounced a few more steps away from the van, letting Sabrina get out.

As Sabrina exited, Trina turned to her. "Come on, Sabrina, how was the taste?"

I felt my cheeks heat up. That Sabrina fed somehow made it feel like she was a part of the intimacy without me knowing.

"Very good. You got him riled up." Sabrina came out of the van holding her glasses to her face. "But he was already pretty riled up."

"OH MY GOD!" Chloe bounded out of the house; the other dragonettes were all peeking out of the front door. "I want a kiss like that."

Most of the dragons came in small packages, but Chloe was all curves stuffed in torn jeans and a metal band t-shirt that was perfectly small for her. She was also the youngest of the dragons.

"You have to *serve* the Dragon King well. I did that in spades tonight; you should have seen the *services* he asked for." Trina exaggerated the words suggestively, standing more proudly than I'd ever seen her as she faced the other dragon women.

Polydora was next out of the door. "You mislead. I don't smell him on you like that." The Amazonian woman scowled at Trina until she got a sniff and relaxed. "The competition is still on."

"Competition?" I asked, having a feeling what that challenge must be. But my question was ignored as the rest of the dragonettes came out and chatted with Trina, wanting to know what happened.

"Sabrina looks like she's in the line of fire for some issues around town. The king has asked us to help house her until he can resolve it," Trina cut over the crowd and pulled the succubus close to her.

"A succubus? My king, are you intending to take her into your harem?" Sarisha looked up at me through her eyelashes. The exotic brass dragon had the brightest blue eyes. Along with her dark skin, it made her enticingly exotic.

"Is there a problem with that?" I asked, genuinely wanting to know if they'd have an issue.

"No. Sex demons have long participated with dragons. Though, often not a permanent arrangement," she stated plainly before looking at Sabrina again. "She is beautiful, but young for a succubus. Very young."

I didn't know what passed for young, but given everything, it was probably better if Sabrina was young.

"Thank you. Please look after her."

"We will. She seems to have an excellent shot at your harem." Sarisha was succinct and nodded to join the rest of the dragonettes.

I used the moment to grab Morgana. "I think we should head back to your room. There's a few things left to do before we sleep."

"Sleep?" Morgana batted her eyelashes at me. "Who said anything about sleep?"

I spanked her leather clad rear and hustled her into the van while I waved goodbye to the dragons.

I'd barely grabbed the oh-shit handle as Morgana peeled out of the driveway. It wasn't far to the Scalewrights', where we'd use one of Morgana's doors to the Atrium to get to her room quickly.

While she drove, I couldn't keep my hands off of her, letting my fingers trail up her neck and caress her pointed blue ears. As my fingers ran through her silky, silver white hair, I caught the barest smell of her natural perfume. It smelled like the coppery tang of blood, but covered over by flowers.

"I love you too, my mate." Morgana smiled at me from the side.

"Mine," I growled. "Love you too. Thank you for the help tonight. I enjoyed going back out on jobs. It feels more natural than meetings."

Her hand traced unknown shapes on my thigh, and my cock was trying to stretch itself out so that it could get some of those soft touches. "You have taken on a lot. You only found out you weren't human at the beginning of the school year."

It was hard for me to believe it had only been one school year. "Are you telling me to take it slow?"

"In life, yes. In the bed? No, my mate, take me hard and fast. I heal quickly." She grinned wide enough to show off her fangs. "But maybe you should slow down on the administration piece of it. Or if you trust Jadelyn enough, you could have her manage it."

The seriousness of the conversation warred with the urgency my body was feeling as her fingers continued to run along it. "Jadelyn would be great. But everyone on the council will see her as favoring her father."

"Won't others see the same from you?" Morgana asked.

I could see her point, but it felt different. "Maybe, but then there are some things that are easier if I'm personally involved. Like the fae."

Morgana hummed to herself as her finger found my shaft and traced lazy lines up and down it. A sense of calm swept through my body even as I wanted her to pull over so that I could take her right there on the side of the road.

"The fae who wants to join your bed? Yes, I'd imagine they'd be favorable towards you," Morgana laughed. "Maeve will probably use your absence to request private audiences with you. I'm sure if Jadelyn grants even one, Maeve will play just as nice with your siren as she does with you. If anything, you'll empower your siren to lead more."

Morgana paused. "Or is this about being a dragon and a king? Do you crave to stay in charge?" Morgana purred as she pulled into the circle drive, and I could feel her nail scratch along my thigh.

I let out a low growl that made the van vibrate. "Inside."

"You'll have to catch me first." Morgana hopped out of the van and tossed the keys to a security guard before she took off with a chuckle in the wind.

My dragon roared, predator instincts instantly engaging.

My shoulders and legs crackled as my bones tried to shift. Luckily, I had more control than that now. Instead of shifting all the way, I let my legs shift to give me a boost as I gave chase.

She wasn't going full speed; she was moving just fast enough to stay out of my reach. She ducked into the side entrance to the Scalewright mansion and up the staff's staircase, trying to avoid anyone who might be there.

I had to be making a colossal amount of noise as I chased up after her and through a door that led to the Atrium, but I couldn't give a shit about it at the moment.

I bounded after her through the stone gargoyle door that led into the Atrium. But instead of taking a left into my room, she took a right into her own.

My instincts flared, knowing that she was trapped. I slowed down, taking my time as I savored my victory.

Opening the door slowly, I growled, "Trapped now."

"Oh no, whatever shall I do?" Morgana wasn't a great actor, but it didn't matter.

I pushed the door open fully, taking in my beautiful mate. She'd used her speed to change. Morgana was wearing a sheer, black slip and stockings that were most certainly not going to survive the night.

She braced herself up against the wall, one leg slightly raised up.

I prowled forward, and she couldn't keep the smile off her face as she watched me approach.

"Mine," I growled, pushing her up against the wall and rubbing myself against her through my pants.

Rather than respond directly, her nails dragged across my chest and up my throat until they came to the tip of my chin, drawing us together.

I claimed her lips roughly, dragging myself against her and feeling her soft mounds squish against my chest. My hands wandered down her hips, cupping her delicious ass and spreading her thighs to wrap around my hips.

Her tongue slipped into my mouth, tasting me and dragging my lip against her fangs.

I could feel her venom running through my system. Knots all over my body seemed to unravel and relax into the moment. With my draconic constitution, I wasn't going to turn into a glassy eyed doll, but it still felt relaxing.

As I kissed her, I could feel the heat of her sex penetrating my jeans. Her desire for me only excited my dragon all over again.

I slammed her into the wall and broke the kiss, trailing my lips down her neck to my mark. My jaws crackled, and I bit down again.

"Yes. Yours." Morgana bucked against me as I marked her once more. This time, it wasn't magical, but it still felt immensely satisfying.

Mine.

"Bed." I hoisted her up and tossed her on the mossy bed. Roots formed the bedposts and came down from the ceiling. It wasn't a typical bed, but whatever she did to cultivate the moss made it soft and springy in a way that a true bed couldn't mimic.

I shucked my shirt and jeans, letting my rock-hard member spring up into Morgana's face as she leaned forward like she was going to whisper to it.

But instead, she kissed it softly, her tongue darting out and licking it from the tip all the way down to the shaft as she looked up through her lashes at me. Her bright red eyes nearly glowed in the dim light.

"Mmmm," Morgana murmured as her hand came up to pump me. She moved her mouth down to each of my balls, kissing and lightly sucking on them as she pumped her hand up and down.

Then she looked up and sat slightly back as she pumped, letting me appreciate her body.

The drow vampire was beautiful, and she knew it with the smirk she wore. There was something about her soft, blue skin that made her breasts even more inviting.

"Like what you see?" she asked.

"Yes. You are gorgeous, Morgana."

"And yours. All yours." She proved that by leaning forward and swallowing my cock down to the back of her throat. Keeping eye contact with me, she began to bob.

Each time she went down, she nestled the head in her throat, humming around it and sloppily letting it back out of her slippery throat.

My body yearned for more, and Morgana liked it a little rough. Getting a fist full of her hair, I pushed her all the way down and pumped several times into her throat, enjoying the slick sheath.

When I let up, she dragged her fangs along my length in warning. The sensation sent a thrill through me.

She made a ring with her fingers and squeezed the base of my cock before slathering it with her tongue. Her venom had made it near euphoric. With every lick, I could feel myself peaking, but her fingers tightened, and she denied me the release as she continued to please me with her mouth.

I growled in frustration and grabbed her head again, slamming her far enough down that she was forced to remove her fingers.

There were two pricks on my skin. They were barely noticeable if I hadn't known it was coming, but the drow vampiress knew how to work my body.

The sensation of her venom was washed out as I groaned and came. It felt like buckets of cum as I pumped, sheathed wonderfully in her throat as she hummed.

I let myself finish and savor the vibrations of her throat. I let myself slowly come down from the sensitive bliss, and Morgana obliged, continuing to swirl her tongue over me.

When Morgana pulled back, she licked her lips. "So sweet. Like a little forbidden treat."

"Forbidden treat, you say?" I smiled as I pushed her down on the mossy bed.

Morgana's nails raked along my side and over my shoulders. "What a monster." She grinned as she spread her legs.

I playfully bit at my mark on her again as I worked my cock around her labia, parting her folds and feeling myself plunge into her warm and ready depths.

"Morgana," I grunted as I savored being inside of her.

"My mate," she whispered before she bit my ear and dragged her nails through my hair. "I want you to pound me into the wall from behind."

I pumped a few more times, making sure I was lubricated before I flipped her over on the bed and circled her puckering anus. "Careful what you ask for."

I was rough, shoving it into her, eliciting deep moans of happiness. Her body arched, and I took the opportunity to grab onto her breasts, kneading them in my hands as she stretched out around me.

When she was ready, I shoved her forward to the headboard of the bed and rammed myself home.

Her ass was still tight, and it felt glorious with my already sensitive member. Her venom continued working through my body as I lost myself in her, driving into her repeatedly.

She cried out and worked herself back on me while she clung to the headboard for dear life.

My thighs clapped her ass, and the sound drove me even harder. Her hands slipped off the headboard, and I drove her into the wall as I pumped into her.

"Fuck. Fuck," I groaned before I lifted her shoulders up so that I could get my hands on her chest.

The change in angle squeezed her ass around me, and I sandwiched her between the wall and my chest as I continued to drive myself wild in her ass.

Her fangs found my arm and bit me as she reached behind herself, her nails digging into my scalp and neck.

I felt the tension building in my body to near unbearable levels before I came, filling her ass and bucking her against the wall several times. "I love you. You drive me wild."

"Mmmm," Morgana said, a putty-like smile spreading across her face. Then she playfully turned and pushed on my shoulders to make me lie back on the bed. "I want to ride you now." Morgana bit her lip, smearing a little blood before she licked it away.

Smiling, I flopped myself backward, ready for the show I knew she'd provide.

Morgana moved sensually as if in a dance, her hands sliding along my thighs and up to my abs as she swung her legs over to straddle me.

Then she rose up, holding her sex just over my rod.

"My turn." Her sultry eyes met mine as she gleefully sank down on me. I shuddered with pleasure, knowing what was about to come.

# CHAPTER 7

I walked through the university, making my way to the science building where Sabrina and I would practice that day.

Sabrina was walking in from the other direction at the same time.

I gave her a friendly wave. "Morning. How were the dragonettes?"

"Uhh..." She hesitated to find the words for whatever she was thinking. "It was interesting. They very much want more information on you."

Holding open the door, I let her enter first.

The science lab we used was one of the older ones in the campus building. It came with a dozen dinged up lab benches and a score of scorch marks on the ceiling and floor. It was the perfect place to get away with a little damage if one of my spells went awry.

There might have been more fortified places for that, but this let me keep the illusion of going to classes. That was important to me.

Jadelyn's father had helped convince the school to let me and Sabrina use it for my independent study. Obviously, they didn't know I was studying magic.

"Are any of them joining us today?"

Sabrina couldn't meet my eyes. "They got in a small fight this morning after Trina tried to assert dominance over Polydora."

I struggled not to laugh as I pictured it, setting my bag down on a nearby table. "How'd that go?"

Sabrina pulled out an old-battered tome and sat on the lab bench next to me, a sigh leaving her.

"Not well. Poly wrecked Trina, but then the others joined in, and it became a whole mess. They probably won't show up until they aren't sporting enormous bruises." Sabrina shrugged it off and flipped open the tome.

I watched her. Something seemed different about her.

Looking her over, I realized her sweater was a size or two smaller than normal, still a little baggy, but much more formfitting than usual. And her skirt was shorter than usual.

My dragon nose was picking up some perfume, which my beast was upset at for masking some of her normal scent. She smelled a little like someone the day after a bonfire.

She'd put more effort into her appearance. I coughed into my hand, trying to hide my attention. "So, what's on today's agenda? Learning more theory? Maybe we'll dive into the physical properties of mana and how it functions with chemistry?"

"Actually, after seeing you last night, I thought we could learn a spell." Sabrina looked at me over the rim of her glasses. "If you had anything besides those crude blasts, you could have restrained that elf."

I snorted.

An elf had decided to run away from a predator when we had needed to question him. Really, I don't know what he could have expected. "All I did was throw a trash can."

"Yes, well, I'm pretty sure you could have launched it into space if you had a different trajectory. Trina had to spend twenty minutes healing him before he could talk," Sabrina replied, putting me in my place.

When the elf had crumpled to the ground, I'd realized I had probably overdone it. But in my defense, he ran, and that triggered my instincts.

"Do you have a problem with elves?" Sabrina asked, curiosity in her eyes.

"No. I'm married to... three? Well, two of them are more like half elves. Well, at least Morgana and Yev both look like elves, but you know..." I was rambling and trailed off.

"True. I'm glad you don't because that would make your wedding with the Highaen sisters awkward." She laughed a little.

It was the first time I'd heard her laugh. She had a soft, rolling chuckle.

"Wedding?" I was still stuck on her words.

"Oh! Um, I just assumed?" Sabrina started rambling. "They are high elves, and royalty at that." She held up her hands defensively.

I rubbed the bridge of my nose. "No one has said anything about a wedding. But you are right. The girls probably all need some sort of formal celebration. To my dragon, I've marked them. Nothing else is needed and nobody else will ever have them."

Sabrina didn't say anything, but I could see her opinion that I needed to do something more as she focused down on her materials. "I want to teach you a restraining spell. It's quite simple, actually."

"Oh?" I perked up at that. "What are the words for it?"

She licked her finger and paged through the tome. Amira's mother had provided it to her in hopes of winning some favor with me. Sabrina had been excited about getting her hands on it and seemed more than able to understand it.

She shifted into her teacher's tone. "We discussed this. Words have power, but not as much as physical representations. So rather than learn the words, we are going to enchant a stick."

"A stick?" I had hoped for something maybe a little more awe-inspiring. "Won't that break under the strain of a few uses?"

"We will make a few; you'll need the practice. This spell is stronger holding, but reliant on the stick staying intact." She put the tome down in front of me. "I looked through the tome this morning. This one feels like the right place for you to start, given your needs."

I could read the words for the spell, but I knew she wanted me to pay more attention to the enchantment listed out. It was a string of characters vaguely resembling a chain. I was glad it was relatively short and easier to memorize. "I don't suppose you already came with sticks?"

Sabrina smiled and pulled a whole handful of twigs out of her purse before reaching back in. "Here's a needle to do your etching."

I picked up the little needle. It looked like one from a sewing machine. I pulled back the twig, seeing if it would break. It seemed decently firm.

"How the heck am I supposed to etch that?" I pointed at the diagram in the tome. "Onto these little sticks." Finesse wasn't exactly a dragon's strong suit.

"Practice." Sabrina smiled smugly.

"Are all succubi sadists?" I grumbled, picking up the needle and pricking the twig as a test. It worked pretty well for scraping off the bark; the wood was harder though, and my first attempt snapped the twig in two.

"No, but it is funny watching the big bad Dragon King hunched over and struggling with a little twig." Sabrina laughed before taking my hand in hers. "Here, hold it a little further back."

"Can't I just use my claws?" I asked.

"I have claws too, but they just don't make as great of lines. Here, look." Her hand turned slightly pink, and her nail grew black and long. She scratched at the wood in a small arc, but it was rough, sort of like a sketch.

"Versus this." She held the needle, and in one clean, curved line, she drew the same shape.

I scratched my chin and took the needle from her, scratching out the enchantment in tiny detail on a twig. "What happens if I mess up?"

"Finish it as long as you don't break the twig. With a little luck, you might be able to make a few working ones today, even if they are flawed." She pushed the pile of twigs to the side. "You missed a line here."

I grunted and noted it before continuing.

\*\*\*

Sabrina patted me on the back as I swept the pile of broken twigs into the trash. "You snapped the last three before we finished, so maybe it's best if we stop for the day. I need to get to my actual classes soon, anyway."

I snorted, and a little smoke came out of my nostrils. "Yeah, I don't think I'm going to make any more progress."

The pile of errors was large, but I'd managed to make three somewhat functional twigs.

Sabrina picked up one of my successes. "Not bad. Even if you did these perfectly with the twigs, they'll probably only last two minutes. The mana flowing through the enchantment will heat up the twig. It'll probably either char your enchantment off or burst into flames."

She looked at another twig. "These might last half as long with their flaws."

I nodded. There had been no reason to use nicer materials for practice, and the utility of the spell wasn't meant to lock someone down for days. It certainly would have been handy on the elf the night before.

"What's the range of this?"

"Line of sight, essentially. If you wanted to leave someone locked down by this spell, you'd want to leave the twig in the room with them. Distance will also affect the time this lasts." Sabrina handed me back the twig, and I carefully placed them in my bracer.

There, they were nice and secure, and more importantly, couldn't be used against me. While they were not the most impressive thing, I was quite proud of the twigs. They represented progress. My first enchantment.

"You should be happy. You actually mastered that quickly," Sabrina commented. "Most wizards take weeks to get a working enchantment with that many symbols."

"Wait, was this a complex one?"

"Oh, no." Sabrina gathered up the tome and stuffed it in her bag. "This is child's play compared to what you can really do with enchantments, but it's complex enough that a wizard would have done several easier enchantments first. Maybe it's because you are a dragon."

The beast preened in my chest. The smug bastard was just a clump of instincts, but I swore he was alive.

"I'll walk you to class," I replied, getting up out of my chair and following her out the door.

"You don't have to," she replied quickly, but she didn't move to rush away.

"Nonsense, you are helping me, and I'm a little worried that Helena will do something. You two are opposites. I guess... I'm not sure how that works. Are the celestial and the demonic planes at war?"

After she was quiet for a moment, I realized I might have stuffed my foot in my mouth.

"No, not really. I actually think we are more alike than they would ever admit. The celestial plane feeds the same way as demons, only they tend to focus on different emotions. Joy, love, devotion, and things like that. An angel could turn people into husks just like demons if they pushed. There have been more than a few cults like that." Sabrina rolled her eyes.

"Cults?" I asked curiously.

We stepped out of the science building, and she led me across the campus sidewalk. She kept her voice down, making sure she wasn't heard.

"You know when you hear about closed door cults where people become obsessed and think they're in a utopia? Those are often angels pushing on people's emotions and feeding off of them. We are not that different. People just give those emotions a more positive spin, but anything to an extreme is bad."

I nodded. What she said was interesting. And it also made me think of the Church and the templars. Angels were likely feeding off of them, but at a low enough level that it wasn't killing them.

"So, what's on the schedule for tomorrow? More sticks? Or do we play with new enchantments?" Now that we had stepped into actual magic, I was like an eager child. I tried to play it cool, but the look Sabrina gave me told me she wasn't buying it.

She squinted up at me. "Don't think you just get to skip all the steps. But... we can look through some of the other small enchantments to see if they would help you."

I did a little fist pump. Magic! We were doing actual practical magic!

"This is the building. I can go by myself." She gave me a look, telling me that I wasn't supposed to follow her any further.

"That's fine. But be careful and call me if anything comes up."

She laughed. "Yes, mom." She rolled her eyes, but I could tell that she was pleased.

"You know," she continued. "Giving someone like me that sort of privilege is going to make people say things." She paused in her walk, seeming to pay close attention to what I'd say to her vague statement.

I shrugged. "It's not as if they don't already say things about me having eight mates. Let me get the door for you." She was carrying a heavy bag.

"Thanks." Sabrina ducked in, and someone was coming out the other way, so I kept it open.

But I regretted that decision as Agent Till stepped out.

"Zach Pendragon, interesting seeing you here." Till turned as I let the door close behind her.

"Is your partner lurking around here?" I asked, looking around for Helena and wondering if I should charge in after Sabrina.

"No. She likes to disappear and do things on her own. I don't like it, but she gets results." Till had a small frown on her face.

It bothered her more than she let on. But it made sense to me. Helena would have to hide her paranormal activities from her.

"It bothers you that she connects dots you can't," I guessed.

"Yes. Things used to be so simple, but recently..." She trailed off and motioned for me to follow her.

I didn't have anything pressing, and it didn't hurt to work with her more. Having friends in law enforcement would likely be useful as the king of dragons.

"Recently, things have been... strange. Everything isn't adding up," she started.

I nodded, letting the silence linger for her to figure out the right words.

"Take you, for example. You're just a student. There's nothing out of the ordinary except you are isolated because your family is dead." She paused, realizing she was being insensitive, but I just nodded for her to continue.

"Then you got involved with the Scalewrights and a small mercenary company out of the blue. And people say weird as hell titles now about you. Dragon king? What even is that supposed to say? I thought maybe you were some kind of kingpin, but there's no evidence of that either."

She tried to stare at me, as if that could somehow solve her curiosity.

"You think I'm part of some secret shadowy organization?"

"Maybe. But even then, it doesn't make sense. When people join organizations, there's training. There is a recruitment phase. You just went from ordinary to 'Dragon King' overnight. That doesn't happen. Which means, either you somehow hid it all for a long time, or there's something special about you." Till raised an eyebrow at me, asking for an answer.

I could only grin. "There is something very special about me. But I can't tell you what it is. Doing so would put myself at risk, and you wouldn't like what it meant for you."

"Meant for me?" she asked quickly, pausing in her steps.

I decided to lay it on thick. "You'd become mine. My responsibility and mine to do with as I pleased. Never again in your life would you have an option of walking away from me."

"I don't know if that sounds more like marriage or slavery," she commented dryly.

Snorting, I barely held in the laugh. "I'd like to think marriage isn't close to slavery, if you do it right."

"True. I'm married to my job, anyway. No time for relationships. There's too much travel and secrecy to keep something up. But you've managed to pull off whatever you're doing, plus many relationships. Helena said you were married to multiple women. But often I hear the term 'mate'." She showed her hand a little too much.

I was uncomfortable with how much information she had compiled on me.

Till saw it in my face. "I have to admit that I've been paying special attention to you lately. After Dubai, my partner went wild trying to look into you before I got the transfer processed."

"Is he going to be a problem?" I reined myself in, working to suppress the growl that wanted to escape my throat.

"I don't believe so. He's going to end up tanking his career soon in his obsession." She shook her head. "But even if he was a problem, what would you do about it?" She turned back towards me, seeming to hope for more data points.

"Problems don't exist if they disappear." I gave her a wicked smile. "But he's safe as long as he doesn't come after me or mine."

Till couldn't stop staring at me. "I don't get it. What caused this transformation?"

Before I could answer, Maeve was walking towards us. She waved to get my attention. "Hello, Zach. Who is this?"

"Maeve. This is Agent Till, an acquaintance of mine who works for the FBI. We were discussing some recent problems that have brought her to the city." I tried to tell her with my eyes that they were the same problems that were cropping up for us. "A new business owner is in town. Deniz Wallachia."

Maeve's smile plummeted to the depths of an icy cold frown. "Yes. It seems that news of his arrival circulated last night. Given his family's history, we should be careful. Please, if the FBI needs anything, let us know and we will assist how we can." Maeve's smile at Till was tight, but it blossomed when she faced me. "I'll see you around."

Till had a raised eyebrow as she watched Maeve leave. "That one is maybe even worse news than the Scalewrights. I don't know how you attract them like honey."

"Maeve's not so bad. Her mother is a right bitch, though. Stiffed me pretty bad once. Maeve has worked hard to distance herself from the impression her mother gave me."

The agent just stared at me like I was a freak of nature. I wondered just how much she knew about Maeve and her family.

My phone started ringing, and I fished it out of my pocket, holding up a finger to stop whatever Till was about to say.

"ZACH!" Frank's voice was panicked. "Man, I didn't know who to call. It's Maddie, she's in the hospital and… and…" He was speaking so quickly that he could barely get a word out, but he'd said enough.

"Frank. Take a deep breath. Which hospital?"

Till dangled a pair of keys in front of me, and I snatched them out of her hand.

"I'll be right there, Frank," I said to him, hanging up the call and turning to Till, waiting for her to point to the right car.

She held her hands out for the keys back and walked over to a car. "I'll drive if you answer a few questions on the trip," she stated.

This time, I did let out the lowest of growls. I didn't like being cornered. But for Maddie, I'd do it. "There are things I can't say, but I'll do my best."

## Chapter 8

"So, what do you exactly do for Silverwing Mercenaries?" Agent Till asked as she pulled smoothly out of the parking lot.

She drove a nice car, but it wasn't Morgana-level nice. If I had to guess, the BMW was used before she'd bought it, but it wasn't that old of a model. She was practical and focused on functionality, not appearances.

"Mostly settle low-level disputes. It isn't flashy. Lots of sitting in cars, trying to find people," I undersold our day-to-day work.

"Who are your clients?" Agent Till asked in reply.

"I'm afraid I can't just give out that sort of information. Mercenary-Client Privilege is of the highest importance," I joked.

The side eye glare I got from the agent told me she wasn't amused; she clearly wanted the answer to her question. "You said there are some things you can't tell me. Is that one of them?"

"Generally, it is a poor habit to share that sort of information. But there's one I believe you already know. I've done some work for the Scalewrights."

"That's how you met Jadelyn and the two of you became involved?" Till pushed further.

I chuckled. "If by involved, you mean committed for life, then yes. We'll have a formal wedding sometime in the future."

"Just like that?" she asked.

"Yep." I had a smug grin plastered on my face as I remembered my siren's wedding with Jadelyn. That had been a night to remember.

Till scoffed. "Wipe that grin off your face."

"No. She's beautiful, and I smile when I think about her." That was a good thing. My mates made me happy.

We had pulled off of campus, and I could see the hospital rising above the other buildings a few blocks over.

"But you have other women. At least, reports have you being very friendly with Morgana Silverwing, as well as a cheerleader from your school. Jadelyn has to be too proud to let that slide. What would happen—"

I cut her off. "If she found out about Morgana, Kelly, oh and her bodyguard Scarlett? She already knows. And she is okay with it. Scarlett was the one to push her towards dating me," I explained.

Till sounded like she was choking on something. "That's ridiculous."

I took the comment in stride. It would have looked ridiculous to me as well not too long ago. But now I felt differently, and I could not care less what she thought.

"It's my life, and I'm happy." I folded my arms behind my head with a smile that I just knew would piss her off.

"So, what do you call them?" Till asked, pulling up at a stoplight just a block away from the hospital.

"My harem." For the first time, the word sounded natural to me. "Mine," I added, growling a little.

She shook her head. "I don't understand."

"Who says you have to?" I turned to her with my face set. "I don't understand why you are married to your job, or why you decided to become an FBI agent. Do we really have to understand each other?"

She stared ahead through the red light as it turned green. Despite the green, there was a moment's hesitation before she put her foot on the gas. "Then just one more question. What is between you and my partner? Is she going to join your harem, too?"

This time I laughed so hard that I had to hold my stomach. "No. We were on opposite sides of a situation. She wronged one of my women, and until any bad blood is settled, I'm more likely to rip Helena's head from her shoulders."

"If you kill my partner, I'll come after you," Till warned me with a squint of her eyes, making small wrinkles form at the corners. Till was probably beautiful even a few years ago, but the years were wearing on her. The job had worn her down if I had to guess.

"Agent, if you come after me, you'll die. If your entire agency comes after me, they'll all die. Ask your partner. She knows what I can do." Till had pulled up to the curb, and I hopped out. "Good talking to you."

"Wait, you don't just—"She started to protest, but I hurried into the hospital, checking my phone for the room number that Frank had sent me.

Finding the elevator, I went up to the fifth floor and hurried down the hall. Even before I got to the door, I knew something was wrong. I could hear Maddie screaming inside.

I nearly ripped the door off its hinges as I dashed inside, finding two nurses holding Maddie down. But what caught my eyes first were the fangs she was flashing at them as she screamed.

A nearby doctor was measuring out a dose in a syringe as I stood, my brain trying to comprehend what I was seeing. Maddie's eyes moved instantly, fixating on me as she inhaled deeply. A look of hunger crossed her face as her struggling redoubled.

"Zach!" Frank leapt up from a chair and rushed me, throwing his arms around me in a crushing hug. "I didn't know who else to call. Maddie's gone crazy! She had been muttering something about figuring out what was wrong with you and getting your blood tested as she charged off. And then the next thing I know, I'm getting a call that she's been mugged. I don't know what they did to her, but it's like she's some animal!"

"Frank." I grabbed his shoulders and rooted him to the floor. "Slow down." I was still processing what he was saying, dread filling my gut. I waited for Frank to get ahold of himself before I moved over to the bed next to Maddie.

She needed to be sedated, and the two men were having no luck holding her down. I grabbed her shoulders, pinning her to the bed. "Nurses, steady her arm for the doctor."

They looked relieved for me to take over. I had a feeling her strength had taken them by surprise. Vampires were a lot stronger than they looked.

The doctor got the syringe in her arm and pushed down the plunger. It was only moments later that Maddie started slowing down. By the count of ten, she was relaxed, her eyes distant and her eyelids fluttering down.

"Thank you. But you can't be in here," the doctor told me.

I scowled at him enough to make him back up. "She's my best friend, and he's my roommate. I'm not going anywhere."

The doctor muttered something under his breath, but he headed out of the room, leaving me with a frantic Frank and a passed-out Maddie. I ran my fingers through my hair, trying to figure out what to do next.

"Maddie," Frank said weakly as he came up on her other side and put a hand on her shoulder. "Zach, I don't know what to do. They said it was drugs, but Maddie would never do drugs. Definitely never do them without me."

I sighed. I'd only gotten a glimpse of her fangs, but the sinking feeling in my gut said that Maddie had been turned. But I couldn't tell that to Frank. "It'll be okay. I think I know what is wrong. Let me text a few people."

Frank looked like he was about to cry, but he didn't ask questions. He simply nodded. For once, my secrets didn't matter, just the solutions I could give him.

I stepped away to text Morgana and Trina. Pausing one more moment, I texted Maeve. If someone had an ancient cure for vampirism, it might be the fae. But as I texted her, I groaned, realizing her party was the next night and Rupert's was the night after. This was shit timing.

Texts sent, I tucked my phone into my pocket and was about to go inspect Maddie further when the door opened.

Agent Till entered the room.

"What are you doing?" I growled with enough force that she actually stopped.

"Investigating. You seem to be at the center of some of this mess. Plus, I don't have any leads to follow at the moment until my partner gets back." Agent Till gave me a tight smile that told me I was firmly in her crosshairs.

As much as I wanted to throttle her and kick her out of the room, I held myself back and focused back on Frank. She'd only dig her heels in deeper if I made it clear there was information she could gather. So I just let her linger in the room.

"Frank, you said something about my blood?" I focused back on my roommate.

He dipped his head. "I told her it was a stupid thing to try. She said she had a little of your blood." Frank grabbed her purse and started going through it before pulling out a paper towel in a ziplock baggie.

I touched my neck, remembering when she had wiped a little of my blood off my neck at dinner the previous night. "Fuck. They said she was mugged, but that's her purse."

"Exactly." Frank held the purse up higher, as if it were the key piece of evidence. "They didn't take anything. She called me saying she'd been attacked. When I got there, her shirt was a little torn, but everything else was fine. Well... except for her. She was wild. She kept trying to bite me while I brought her to the hospital." He frowned in concern.

"Did she bite you? We should get you checked out." I tried to hide the anxiety I was feeling.

"No, she didn't bite me. She just scratched the hell out of me." He showed me his arm, which looked like a cat had gone to town across it. "I buckled her into the back seat of my car, and the nurses helped me when I got here."

My phone pinged. The three ladies confirmed they were on their way.

I shot a quick response that we had two humans here to make sure they didn't come in such that they'd give the paranormal secret away. If Maeve ripped open a portal, it would be hard as hell to explain.

Morgana was the first to arrive, wearing her amulet that made her look like a blonde Swiss model as she strutted in wearing her classic leather pants and corset.

"Oh. Agent... Tips was it?" She smirked at Till.

"Till. Morgana Silverwing, what are you doing here?" Agent Till replied gruffly.

"Zach asked for my assistance." Morgana's eyes flitted to Maddie on the bed, and she frowned. Walking over, Morgana lifted Maddie's eyelids. She checked a few other places, but I could tell she was just covering for her inspection of Maddie's mouth.

"Hi, Morgana. Can you help her?" Frank asked with a pleading face.

I turned to the agent. "Please, this is a personal matter. I'd appreciate it if you gave me some space." I paused, realizing I needed Frank out of the room as well. "Frank, why don't you go with her? I have a private doctor and another friend coming in to look at her. Let them do their work, and then, when they have something conclusive, we can figure out where to go from there."

Frank frowned. "You have a private doctor?"

"Yes, now go. Please." I was feeling the strain of not being able to tell him what was wrong with Maddie. We were best friends; I hated keeping something so important from him.

As they left, Maeve came into the room, followed shortly by Trina. The door closed, and I felt magic from Maeve wrap around the room.

"No one can hear us. Zach, what happened?" Maeve asked.

I blew out a breath. "My roommate and friend have been getting suspicious of my recent activities, including my growing harem." I held up the baggie. "It sounds like Maddie here took a paper towel with some of my blood and wanted to test it. They think I'm involved with drugs."

Morgana lifted Maddie's lips to get a look at her fangs. "Looks like she's started the transformation to a vampire. Someone fed her their blood."

Maeve shook her head. "This is why it is bad for the paranormal to be too close to the mundane. Or we should eradicate all vampires. The pests can barely contain their urges." Her eyes flicked to Morgana. "Not you, of course."

But my blue mate waved off Maeve's comment. "She hasn't finished the transformation. To do that, she'll need to drink a decent amount of blood. Her body will need the mana to finish the transformation. She's running low on her own stores and getting desperate. And if she doesn't complete the transformation, she'll die."

Trina looked at me. "What do you want to do, my king?"

"Is there a way to stop this?" I asked all three of them.

"You could kill her," Trina offered simply, confirming my worst fears.

Morgana shook her head, but Maeve pursed her lips in thought.

I realized Maeve might have an answer for me. "Maeve, what do we need?"

"We have records of a cure for early vampirism. Most of it is pretty simple. The hardest part is that you need the fangs of the vampire who turned her." Maeve tapped her lips. "It has to be the one that turned her; there's a connection between them."

Morgana snorted. "That's a myth."

But Maeve didn't give in. "I can only tell you that there are records of fae using it successfully. The bloodlords have worked to remove it from even our records. Besides, many would wish to make the transformation. Immortality is a heady draught for humans. Before you try to take it from her, you should give her a choice."

Maeve looked a little sheepish, knowing that she was critiquing me. But I appreciated the clearer perspective she brought to the situation. My head was still in scrambles.

"No, you are right. She should have a choice. I just... rushed ahead on things. Uh... how does it work as for the paranormal rules if I expose myself to her at this point?" I asked.

Trina cleared her throat. "She'll forever be a part of the paranormal community now. Even if Maeve's concoction works, she is already paranormal."

Maddie stirred in bed, groaning and rolling around.

Trina picked up her chart from the foot of the bed. "Yes, she's very paranormal. She should not even be able to move yet. Her partial vampire nature is kicking in and removing the sedative from her system. We need to make a choice here soon."

"We will need to kill the one that turned her, anyway," Morgana said, stepping up close to Maddie's head. "The one that turns a vampire has power over it. Regardless of her choice, they will need to die for your friend to be free and to prevent her from being used against you, which I won't let happen."

"Used against me?" I asked, surprised at her leap in logic.

Maeve nodded. "At this point, we must consider that the vampires are making a move on our city."

"Why Philly?" I asked.

"The fae," Trina replied quickly. "There are a limited number of places where the fae realm connects permanently to our world. Philly is the only one I know of."

"We keep them secret on purpose," Maeve replied; I could tell that she was worried. "There is much power in the fae world and in its people that could be used by others. It must be protected. But we also cannot seal ourselves off; we must remain connected or else we would have no support when something like this happens."

I cringed, hating that my conflict with the Church had led to this imbalance. But it was clear the vampires had just been waiting for their opportunity.

"We'll figure this out. We are having another council session to discuss this tonight. Vampires running around turning people is not okay." I'd send messages out through Rupert to ensure we had a council session.

"No, but she was likely targeted because she was carrying your blood. That very well might have tempted a vampire beyond their ability to control themselves," Trina pointed out.

"Either way, the city has a problem on its hands, and we need to work together," I reiterated, looking at Maeve.

Maeve bowed slightly. "You will have the fae's full support, and I know you can obtain the sirens' easily enough." She smirked a little.

I nodded, already forming a plan in my head. I turned away ever so slightly as Maddie's eyes popped open, and she lunged for me.

Morgana had her restrained and slammed her back down on the bed before I could even react. "Be a good girl and have a drink."

There was no intelligence in Maddie's gaze, but Morgana cut herself and dripped some of her own blood into Maddie's mouth.

That was all it took for Maddie's focus to switch to Morgana. Her tongue wiggling out of her mouth, trying to catch the blood as she slurped, like she was trying to suck Morgana's blood out at a distance.

It was completely animalistic.

"She's starving. The human brain nearly shuts down when a human is starving; it is the same thing. A little blood should help her regain some clarity." Morgana let her blood continue to drip.

True to her words, Maddie started visibly calming. Soon, she was licking the blood off her lips, confusion entering her eyes.

"Where am I?" Her wide eyes moved around the room until they found me. "Zach?"

# CHAPTER 9

"Hey, Maddie. You were attacked and you're in the hospital." I moved closer. She seemed to have control over herself, but her nose wiggled.

"You smell so good," she moaned, disgust filling her face. "Why the hell do I want to take a chunk out of you?" Maddie tried to hold her head, realizing in that moment that Morgana was still restraining her.

Maddie licked her lips again, tasting the blood that still lingered on them. She smiled at the taste and then frowned, moving her hand up to touch the liquid and confirm it was blood.

"Wait, did you just put your blood in my mouth?" she nearly screamed at Morgana. "That's some sick shit." She looked over at me. "Zach, I knew things were fucked up, but what the hell kind of drug cult have you gotten yourself into?"

She tried to get out of the hospital bed and come towards me, but Trina was there in an instant and decked Maddie, slamming her back down on the bed.

"Do not approach my king. We do not know if you can control yourself." Trina stood like a wall between us.

"Control myself?" Maddie's eyes were wide with a mix of panic and hysteria. "Like you all have control? You throw yourselves at Zach all dinner long."

"Maddie," I warned her, trying to keep my voice calm. She'd been through a lot. "I've told you before. There are things you don't understand."

"Yeah, I've got that. But unless you are suddenly going to enlighten me, shut the fuck up," Maddie snapped.

I paused, realizing she had a point. Deciding to go for the most direct route, I took off my shirt and handed it to Trina amid a few stares.

"Uh... what are you doing, Zach?" Maddie looked at me hesitantly. "If you're about to do some sort of weird cult orgy thing, I am so not into it."

I rolled my eyes. "I'm proving a point." My body crackled as I let my upper body start to shift.

Gold scales rippled down my form as my shoulders broadened and my arms stretched out, claws forming off my fingers. And of course, my jaw elongated as my face became draconic.

"Wha— HELP! HELP!" Maddie started screaming at the top of her lungs. "There's a monster!"

I held up my gold scaly claws. "It's me Maddie, Zach. There are a few things you need to know."

She pushed herself as far up the bed and away from me as she could, fear shining in her eyes. "What the fuck. This must be a nightmare. What kind of drugs are they giving me?" Maddie looked to Morgana for help.

"Sorry, this is neither." Morgana undid the clasp on her amulet. As it fell off, she returned to her normal blue self.

Maddie's eyes went wide as her attention went back and forth between the other two women in the room.

Maeve dropped her glamor and became the cold-looking winter fae that she was, complete with her silver eyes.

"And you?" Maddie pointed a quivering finger at Trina.

"I don't want to ruin my clothes." She crossed her arms and scowled at Maddie. "But I'm like my king." Trina pointed at me.

"Your king?" Maddie looked back at me. "Zach, what the hell is going on?"

"You're probably starting to get most of it." I shifted back to normal and took my shirt from Trina before putting it on. "The world is full of supernatural beings. I'm one of them. So is everyone here, and all of my mates are as well. My kind is rare and endangered. It's typical for us to have several mates."

Maddie looked around the room as we stood, letting her digest the information.

"This isn't the drugs? This is real?" she asked. She was calming down, but there was still a frantic edge to her.

I nodded back at her.

"Okay. Okay... this is nuts, but okay." I could see her thoughts going a million miles a minute before she seemed to settle on her next question. "Why now?"

"That's the right question," Morgana said from her side. "We are telling you now because of what happened to you. Feel inside your mouth. Were your teeth always that sharp?"

Maddie pricked herself with her fangs and winced. "No, and I never found myself liking the taste of blood." It sounded like she was about to cry as she put it together. "Am I... a vampire?"

I sighed. "Yes. You were attacked by a vampire and are in the process of turning. Maeve here thinks there might be a way to reverse the process before it completes, but that would require us to find who did this to you."

Maddie looked down at her hands and couldn't look up to meet my eyes. "Okay. So I'm some sort of newbie vampire. What are you?"

"I'm a dragon. Morgana is a drow, which is a type of elf, but she was turned into a vampire. Maeve is a winter fae, and Trina is a dragon like me."

"What about the others? Jadelyn, Scarlett, Kelly?"

"Siren, kitsune, and werewolf," I answered, ticking off my fingers.

"Are unicorns real?" Maddie asked.

I paused, realizing I had never met one. I turned to Morgana to let her answer.

"Yes, but they are pompous assholes," Morgana answered flatly. I vaguely remembered Rupert talking about an associate having a son-in-law that was a unicorn.

"What about—"

Maeve cleared her throat. "I think you can ask your questions later. We are more curious about who turned you."

Maddie nodded. "Right. Oh, uh... I don't know if I can be of much help. I decided to take a shortcut through a kinda shady area of town. One moment I was walking, and the next I was being pressed to the ground. I thought..." She shuddered.

I knew what she thought and wanted nothing to do with that train of thought. Thank god it hadn't happened.

"Can you be more specific about where you were when you were attacked?" I urged her.

"Can I see my phone?"

I didn't know where it was, but I pulled up a map on mine. "Here."

"Okay. I got off the train here and was headed to this location. I think I cut through here." She backtracked her route on my phone.

Taking note of the spot, I dropped a pin and shared it with Morgana.

"Thank you. That'll help us." I tucked my phone back into my pocket.

"What happens to me now?" Maddie suddenly was brought back to her present situation.

I hesitated to give her hope, but she needed to know all of her options. "Well, you are in the middle of your transformation to a vampire. Morgana could answer a lot of your questions. But what concerns me the most is that it sounds like whoever sired you has the ability to keep you under their control unless they die."

Maddie's eyes widened, but I continued. "Given that you were just attacked and turned, and we've had other vampire attacks in the city, my guess is the two go hand in hand. And Morgana and I already accepted the job of removing whatever is causing our vampire problem. I'm going to find them and take care of them, Maddie. I won't let somebody control you."

She sagged just the slightest bit in relief.

"But I'm going to stay a vampire?" she asked.

"We don't know yet. Maeve thinks that there's a way to help revert you, but we're not positive. And to do it, I'll need to kill the person who attacked you." I looked away when I talked about killing. Though I'd come to terms with it, I knew that Maddie wouldn't understand.

"You kill people?" she asked quietly.

I nodded. "Paranormal society is a lot more violent. I actually was forced into a duel to the death on my first day learning about it. That was back at the beginning of the school year."

"Scarlett?" Maddie asked, starting to piece everything together.

"She and Morgana helped me adjust. I was born a dragon, but... never knew I was one until I got into a fight with Chad after the bar that one night."

Maddie's eyes went wide, and she covered her mouth. "I remember that night."

"Yeah..." I trailed off. "That night I kicked Chad's ass, and he went all werewolf on me. Still kicked his ass, but that was the start of it. It has been a bit of a whirlwind."

"Yeah, having girls trailing behind you calling you 'my king' must be really hard." Maddie's snark was back in full force, and it made me smile. It meant she was doing better.

Trina cleared her throat and started in on a very serious tone. "Because he was born the king of dragons, he has a large amount of responsibility. I am part of an honor guard that helps protect him; he is very important to our kind."

Maddie blinked, shocked by her tone. "So, what is so important about him?"

"I'm a sort of dragon that is a mix of all the colors. The dragon population is important for the paranormals, and several of the colors have completely died off. Through me, I might be able to restore them."

"Wait... like kids?" She frowned. "How does that—"

Maeve cleared her throat. "I'm glad to see you are doing better, but you have decisions to make, and we all have work to do. Zach, I hope you will still have time to attend the party tomorrow night." Her eyes flickered to me again, and I realized I might have dropped some new information when I spoke of multiple colors.

"Of course. I am happy to meet the fae formally as the Dragon King. My honor guard will be there as well, and I'll bring along the other dragons in the city." I turned back to Maddie. "Morgana will stay with you and answer your questions. I need to go tell Frank that you are okay."

"Frank!" Maddie tried to get out of bed, but Morgana held her down.

"He'll come in as soon as he knows you are well. But we must talk. Either we resolve your condition, or you become a vampire," Morgana warned her before she put her amulet back on. "Do not talk of the paranormal, and resist the urge to bite him. You will kill him if you do in your present state."

Maeve returned to her human glamor and dismissed the magic around the room.

I joined her, and we stepped outside the hospital room, Trina trailing behind us.

"Zach." Frank shot up from where Till was talking to him. "Is... is she..."

"She's awake and wants to see you." I didn't even finish my sentence before he bolted past me and into the room.

Till and Maeve's assistant remained out in the hall with us. The nymph looked like a secretary about to shoot a porn video in her glamor.

"Agent Till, I would like a momentary word with you," Maeve stated, motioning for the agent to follow her.

I had my suspicions as Maeve pulled her away, but I was distracted as her assistant got close enough that her chest brushed me.

"I wanted to apologize for earlier." She was close enough that her sweet scent hit me like a potent aphrodisiac. Her hands touched my chest like the softest silk.

Fuck, she wasn't even using her magic. Just her person was that alluring.

"No need. I think I understand your nature better," I replied.

She pushed her lips into a pout that made me want to lean down and see if she tasted as sweet as she smelled.

"My mistress would not like it if I couldn't earn your forgiveness." The nymph looked slightly away, but glanced back up at me through her eyelashes. "Do you forgive me?"

"Yes. What is your name?" I realized I didn't even know that.

"Evelyn Daexisys Flutterwink." She gave me a brilliant smile that made my heart flutter, and she winked as she said her last name. "You may call on me anytime you wish. I'll serve you in *any* way you desire."

"Evelyn." Maeve's voice was like shattering ice. "Get off him. We are leaving." The fae lady watched me for a moment to see if I was upset.

"I will see you both tomorrow. Maeve, Evelyn, was just asking for my forgiveness." I tried to not make trouble for her assistant.

Maeve only narrowed her eyes and tugged Evelyn away.

Trina chuckled behind me. I'd forgotten she was there with Evelyn in front of me. "I think she was asking for a little more than that. What a hussy. Don't blame either of you, though."

Rubbing my forehead, I started to grow concerned about the party coming up. "Are they all like that?"

"We should probably give you a cultural crash course for class tomorrow," Trina replied, keeping her words generic as Agent Till returned her focus to me.

The agent looked at me and shook her head. "I have no idea how you do it. But I have other things to worry about right now. Don't think we are through." She turned sharply and left in the opposite direction of Maeve.

"Got the attention of an agent, too," Trina gasped playfully and covered her mouth. "Maybe there is hope of you single-handedly repopulating the dragons." She barely suppressed her laughter.

"Laugh all you want. When I have you pumping out eggs and laying on your brood for centuries on end, we'll see who's laughing," I returned the playful banter, but the look in her eyes told me that Trina was hungry for at least parts of the image I presented.

"You'd give me my own brood?" she asked hopefully.

I shrugged. Thuun had explained dragon reproduction to me. It had made me feel like I was back in third grade getting a talk about the birds and the bees.

Dragon women nested with their eggs as they waited for them to hatch, but my other mates would follow their own gestation process. Their draconic heritage would come through later in their lives. It was like how Yev appeared like a high elf from her mother.

Trina was still staring at me with her dark, baby-crazed eyes, waiting for an answer.

"We will both live a very long time. I'm in no rush, but I assume I will eventually give in like the conclave expects and take you all into my family." Relenting, I realized it was just a matter of time.

She stepped forward and kissed me on the cheek. "Thank you. Hearing that gives me a lot of relief. Even a few years isn't much time for me. Though if you want to relieve any of your stress, I'm more than willing to help sooner." She winked just like the nymph had, a smile breaking across her face.

Not wanting to interrupt whatever Frank and Maddie were going through, I sat down, and Trina joined me. "Then tell me a little more about yourself. Your parents were raised in ancient Rome, and your upbringing was pretty strict from the sound of it."

She snorted. "They were very much stuck in the old ways. A lot of the old dragons are rooted in the past. We go on a survival trip to teach us independence."

"Tell me about that. Would you be in wolf-filled woods where you had to fight for your life?" I imagined a movie I'd seen once.

"Nothing that dramatic, but there were elements of it. If there'd been a wolf, I would have just shifted and eaten it. Actually, I wish there had been a wolf." Trina looked wistfully at the ceiling. "No, I was sent out into the desert. It was mostly about finding an oasis and digging a den nearby so that I could hunt creatures that came to the water. I learned more about the cycle of life and balance in the world."

"How so?" I pushed her to continue.

Trina sighed. "You can very easily over hunt an oasis. As a dragon, I need a lot of food and can consume far more than I need. In order to survive, I had to learn how to nurture the oasis and the population while feeding away from it."

"Brutal. But I can see how that would be necessary. If you tainted the area around the oasis with blood and death, nothing would come."

She nodded. "I toasted a few oases before learning that lesson myself. After I came out of that, though, I knew myself better. I went back to college, then med-school. Then I became a doctor and worked my way through a number of specialties as I reinvented myself over the years."

Copper dragons like Trina had death magic, but that also meant they could stave off death and heal. It made sense that she went into medicine.

"What was your favorite specialty?" I asked.

"Surgery is fun. I like being able to actively *do* something, you know? Giving meds and doing checkups only to send them to a specialist or surgeon to get the actual treatment is boring." She shrugged.

I chuckled. "No, unfortunately I don't really know. My life has been much shorter than yours, but I can imagine that being active in a solution is far more preferable to just passing it further along the system."

As I said it, I realized I was echoing a lot of my recent feelings as I sat in council meeting after council meeting. Maddie being in the hospital spurred me on to solve the latest vampire crisis myself. There might be council meetings and parties still required of me, but I was ready to get my hands dirty.

The desire built up in me, and the beast rattled his cage in my chest, demanding he be let out to track and hunt.

"What do you say about a little trip? I'd like to go get a look at the area where Maddie was attacked before we go to the council tonight." I grinned.

Trina's own grin mirrored mine, and I realized just how savage she could be "Time to hunt?" Her eyes gleamed.

"Something like that." I got up and pulled her along with me as I shot Morgana a text, telling her that I'd see her at the council meeting. My beautiful drow vampire would not be pleased to be left out, but Maddie needed her more.

# CHAPTER 10

I got out of Trina's car and wondered what the hell Maddie had been thinking, walking through the area that surrounded us. Windows had metal bars protecting them, and a few buildings were boarded up.

She should have turned back, and I had a feeling she would have if she hadn't been so focused on trying to get my blood tested so she could help me. Maddie was the type to be laser focused on something when she wanted it.

"This is a shit hole," Trina commented as she looked around. "If I walked through this area, I'd have to get my claws dirty."

I looked back over at the dragon. She was in a tight t-shirt that she was in the process of tying up, paired with skin-tight jeans.

"What?" she asked as she looked at me.

"Why do you always tie up your shirts?" I asked.

"So you check out my voluptuous rack." She rolled her eyes at me. "Don't pretend like you don't. I've seen it. One day, I'll wear you down."

I just chuckled and continued into the alley where Maddie thought she had been attacked. Trina locked her car and then did it a second time, to be sure.

The alley had the stink of long forgotten trash and people with no reason to move it. I wrinkled my nose and recoiled a little.

"The Dragon King is afraid of a little stink?" Trina teased.

"Just sort of hit me like a hammer," I shot back and strode forward into the alley as I shifted the inside of my nose.

Thankfully, with that move, it went from an overwhelming stink to individual scents as I gained the sense of smell of a predator. But I could still taste it in its full vividness. I gagged a little but tried to hide it from Trina.

There was an area of the alley that was disturbed, looking like a recent scuffle had occurred. There were drops of blood leading back out of the alley.

"She managed to get back out to the street before Frank got here," I noted.

"She seems like a tough girl. We'll help her get through this," Trina reassured me, stepping over to where there was the most blood and a few scraps of torn cloth.

We both took deep breaths as we tried to scent the area.

My shifted nose picked out distinct scents, and I pushed aside the smells of the garbage and area. Then I highlighted the remaining smells and tried to follow them.

"This way." I went back through the alley, almost to the end, but then I lost it.

Turning back, I found the scent again. But each time, I lost it in the same spot.

"Look up." Trina pointed at an open window.

"It couldn't be that easy, could it?" I replied.

"If it was some fresh vamp that smelled your blood, this might make sense. She passed his window, and he went wild." Trina threw out a plausible explanation.

I eyeballed the window relative to the building. "Third floor, a few past the corner."

"We'll see what it looks like inside. The windows on the front were boarded." Trina went back around to the front door, which was indeed locked, with a board behind it.

I grunted as I twisted the door handle, and it snapped off without much effort. No one was watching us, and I pushed in, prying the board away from our passage and entering.

The building was half finished. It was all concrete and studs on the inside. Dry wall had only been put up in a few parts, and it was all water damaged.

"Looks like someone's failed project," Trina commented.

I wiped some dust off a nearby wall stud. "It has residents, though. You don't get dust without people."

My alarm bells were going off. If there was one vampire here jumping out to feed and turn, that meant there were probably others besides Maddie that had fallen to the same tactic.

With most of the place boarded up, I shifted my eyes to see better in the dark. We walked cautiously through the first floor, expecting something to come out of the shadows, but it never happened.

Instead, we made our way over to the stairwell, which seemed the most finished out of anything in the structure. As we neared it, I heard the first signs of life. The sound of quiet chattering made its way down the stairs to us.

I put a finger to my lips and crept up the stairs, heading directly for the third floor.

My heart was pounding in my chest, but I was loving the adrenaline rush. I wasn't sure what we would come up against, but I wanted to catch whoever had turned Maddie. I was not giving up this chance.

As we got to the third floor, I crouched and peeked around the door frame. Multiple forms huddled on the floor, and they talked in hushed voices. I didn't bother listening.

I shifted, letting my clothes rip off my frame as I grew several feet and wrapped myself in armor like gold scales. Powerfully built and armored, I thought of this as my dragon knight form.

Even as I rounded the corner, the group was already scattering at the sound of my clothes ripping.

"Get him," a raspy voice screamed, and their sudden surprise turned into a feeding frenzy.

They were fast.

A hag of a woman with torn clothes and gray stretched skin came at me with her mouth wide. I smacked her aside, or at least, I tried to.

She grabbed onto my arm and clung on with the desperation of a drowning rat. Her fangs slammed into my arm, but she couldn't penetrate my scales.

Trina was there in a heartbeat, her fist crushing the vampire's skull and sending her flying.

"My king." She took a deep breath, but I stopped her.

"Don't. We need their fangs." I wasn't sure if her death breath would ruin those too.

Trina was shifted to match my dragon knight form, yet she scowled at me. "Fine."

"Contego," I shouted as a shield popped up in front of me, blocking the next vampire. Then I grabbed the vampire by the back of the throat as my shield faded.

Even the one with the crushed skull would heal enough. We needed to inflict as much damage as possible and force their healing to its limits. Or we could remove their heads. Morgana had always taught me that was a solid backup.

My other clawed hand grabbed the vampire's chest, and I tore the head off. There was surprisingly little blood from the vampire.

Trina's back bumped against mine, and we fought with our claws as a dozen vampires surged towards us.

They had the advantage in numbers, but their strength was pitiful. A few times, one was fast enough to try to get in between us, but with our strength, we crushed them.

My claws tore through vampires, and before I knew it, everything had stopped except mine and Trina's heavy breathing.

"I think they're done," Trina said. "So, how do we know which one turned, Maddie?"

Blinking, I stared at the carnage. "Uh... I'm not even sure which head goes to which body."

We both said the answer at the same time. "Magic."

So I shifted back to being human and pulled my phone out of my enchanted bracer. Sabrina picked up on the first ring.

"Zach? How can I help?"

"Who said I needed any help?"

Sabrina just sighed. "It always seems like you are in some sort of trouble."

"Well... now that you mentioned it, I could use some magical assistance. I need to see if any of the dead vampires currently surrounding me was the one that turned Maddie."

"What?" Sabrina squawked before lowering her voice. "Maddie was turned? Where are you?"

I puffed up my chest a bit, happy that she was concerned about Maddie, and not so concerned about dead vampires. I quickly gave her the address and promised to tell her everything when she arrived.

"The succubus is coming again?" Trina prodded one of the bodies with her foot and stepped over near the stairs. "We should probably make sure the rest of the building is clear as well. Although, I would have expected the noise to bring any of the others to us."

She had a point.

"Let's go sweep the rest of the building. The last thing I need is more surprises." I grunted and shifted back into my dragon knight form as we headed down to the second level.

It turned out to be clear, and we made our way up through all eight floors.

We found two more vampires, but they weren't much of a fight compared to the dozen that had been on the third floor. They could barely move, like they had little blood. There was also a pile of dried out corpses on the top floor.

By the time we had finished, a taxi was pulling up out front and Sabrina was getting out and staring at the neighborhood cautiously.

"Up here." I waved from one of the few windows not boarded up.

The cabbie exchanged a few words with Sabrina, and I could see she was trying to reassure him that she'd be all right. I appreciated the taxi driver not just dropping her and flying off. He saw the risk the area posed.

But finally Sabrina seemed to appease the cabby, and the car drove off as she made her way into the building.

"What is this about Maddie being turned?" she asked from the stairwell, pausing only briefly when she stepped out onto the third floor.

"Long story. The short version is that Frank called me to the hospital after I dropped you off at that class. Maddie was bit and turned in the alleyway down there. Maeve thinks she can help her if we get the fangs of the one who did it to her." I then gestured at the bodies. "We could use a little help figuring out the right one."

Sabrina nodded and walked in a circle around them. "I need you to move their heads into a pile. Then we need a piece of Maddie after she's been turned."

"A piece?"

"Hair would do," Sabrina clarified. "Vampire lines will trigger the same magic that determines paternity, so we can just do a paternity test."

"You are not the baby daddy," I joked.

Neither of them got it, so I sighed and dialed Morgana.

***

"You killed all of them?" Maddie asked, staring at all the surrounding bodies.

She'd been discharged from the hospital and tagged along with Morgana to the scene. Morgana was trying to keep her close in case she needed help in curbing her hunger.

Apparently, her lack of straight answers had led her into a fight with Frank, who had stormed off.

"Trina helped." I put some of the blame on her.

"Come over here." Sabrina motioned for Maddie. "I need some of your hair."

"Sure." Maddie yanked a few strands out. "Whatever you need."

Sabrina took the strands and wound them around the diagram she'd drawn on the ground. It was far more intense than the ones I could do.

"If the one that turned me is here, does that mean I go back to being human?" Maddie asked.

"Only if you want to, and only if the fae's process works," I told her, not looking away from Sabrina's work. "The urges you have can be controlled."

Maddie was quiet, but nodded. "Morgana told me that Maeve's solution might not even work. I just... it would mean so much change."

I was certainly sympathetic. When I'd found out I was a dragon, it had indeed changed every aspect of my life. But I wouldn't wish for a normal life again.

And I could see the temptation in her eyes. The paranormal world was more intense, but it also was magical, literally.

So many human problems disappeared the moment you became a vampire: aging, disease, physical prowess. Morgana didn't even have to watch what she ate. She could pack as much blood as she wanted.

"If you want to finish the transition, I'll support you." I pulled her into a hug.

"Thanks. It's a lot to take in. You briefly described your transition. Has it made life better or worse?" she asked.

I noticed Morgana's ears twitch, and Trina did a very poor job of trying to look elsewhere.

But I didn't care if they listened. "Better. Things are more dangerous, but I'm surrounded by such strong ladies. We've been through things that have made me feel more alive, and my life is certainly richer." I paused. "Would you tell Frank?"

She licked her lips. "I... I don't know. If we figure this all out, I feel like I either need to leave him or tell him. It isn't fair to keep him in the dark. He'll sense enough that he'll push me away, anyway."

I nodded. Frank adored Maddie, even if he was obsessed with the idea of a harem. I wasn't sure what he'd do without her. "We'll see. There is still time."

Sabrina's work glowed brightly, and a searching red light wavered over the vampires present before disappearing in a puff.

"What does that mean?" Maddie asked in a hurry.

"That whoever turned you isn't here." Sabrina clicked her tongue. "I'm not quite sure where to go from here. This seemed like it would be the place to find them."

Morgana had been inspecting the vampires and moved to do so a little more aggressively. "Can you redo that with one of their hairs?"

"Why?"

"I want to know if they were all turned by the same vampire."

Sabrina nodded and started to use her chalk to change the diagram.

"What are you thinking, Morgana?" I asked, not sure where my mate was going.

She opened one of their mouths. "The vampire fangs are pristine, especially when compared to the rest of their dental care... or lack thereof."

"Meaning the fangs are new?" I thought I was following her train of thought. Vampire fangs were still teeth, and they should all show similar wear and stains if they were old.

Morgana pursed her lips. "Given how they acted and how fresh their fangs look... I'd guess these guys are less than a few days old, maybe even less than a day old. A few of them are only partially transitioned."

I nodded. "You think a single person or a group came and turned all of these people? It might even be the same person who turned Maddie. But why?"

"War tactics," Morgana said. "It was done in the seventeenth century too. To slow down the Church, vampires would go in and turn an entire small town, then command them to stay indoors until someone came. They would transition and then grow ravenous. When the Church rolled through, they would trigger an ambush."

"That's awful." Maddie covered her mouth.

"War is awful," Morgana said, wrinkling her nose. "Such tactics would get the entire paranormal community against the vampires in these times."

"Then let's bring this to the council tonight," I growled and scratched my feet on the floor.

Trina coughed. "You can't prove it was Deniz."

She'd figured out what I was thinking. After their killing of a dragon on her way to the conclave, I had a bone to pick with the Turkish vampires. Deniz would make a marvelous example.

"Sabrina, can you do another one of these spells at the council meeting tonight? If he shows up, I want to nail him to a wall." My eyes were shifting, and the beast was pitching a fit in my chest. "He does not get to come into my fucking city and make a mess."

"I could, but if we do this and it doesn't lead to Deniz, then what? He's old and can play politics in the vampire courts. It won't be him. He could have had somebody turn them for him. Hell, he may have even targeted Maddie, smelling you on her, to piss you off. To make you make a political misstep," Morgana warned me.

My beast really didn't like the idea of being manipulated. But she was right. If Deniz was behind this, then I was playing a game with someone who was likely ten times my age and experience.

I needed to be more careful.

My beast begrudgingly relaxed, seeming to agree, even as visions of ripping off Deniz's head and solving the problem easily wafted through my mind.

# CHAPTER 11

I sat in the council meeting, leaning my chair back as I waited for the meeting to start. For once, I was early. And I'd brought quite the crowd with me, but they were all staying in the back for the moment.

"Hello, Zach." Rupert noticed me as he walked in. "Seems you are getting busy again, but you'll still make time for my party?"

"Wouldn't miss it," I told him and wondered what extravagance he was going to pull for the dragons.

"Great." He slapped my arm as Jadelyn came up and sat in her seat at his side.

Part of me wanted to claw her back to my side, but I knew she could help me better by being a different voice on the council.

She caught my look and gave me a soft smile. "If you don't have other things after this, how about we retire together?"

The beast in my chest couldn't have been happier; it practically took over to tell her yes.

Instead, I just gave off a satisfied rumble that earned me a brilliant blossoming smile from my siren.

"That's a yes. Are we taking any of the others into bed with us yet?"

Rupert choked next to her, and she just rolled her eyes.

"No one new. But I imagine Tyrande might pop in tonight," I said quickly. The schedule around my bed was becoming more complex than I'd like.

Jadelyn tapped her lips. "Two little princesses all for yourself. Such a greedy dragon."

Damn right. Mine.

But that reminded me. "When will we have a formal wedding? At one point we had discussed it, but it never really came back up, and now I'm hearing whispers that Tyrande and Yev will want one."

Rupert jumped in, seeming more interested in the current topic. "Claire would very much appreciate it if there was a formal wedding. Though, I understand by dragon customs that you are already mated."

I smiled. I could sense how important it was to him, likely because it was so important to his wife. Claire was my favorite mother-in-law, so I had no issue giving into her wishes.

Detective Fox came up behind Rupert and his fox ears twitched. "Ruby would also like to have a formal wedding. They could be joint." His eyes wandered to Jadelyn and Scarlett to see if one of them was going to have a problem with it.

"If we keep it paranormal, then doing it jointly won't be a problem. Everyone would understand. But then there is the struggle of what to do for future wives." Jadelyn looked over her shoulder at Scarlett. "You are the first mate. I think you should have the say in how we organize all of this."

There was some surprise on both of the fathers' faces as Jadelyn deferred a wedding decision to Scarlett.

I tried to hide my own surprise. Jadelyn was the type to dive into wedding planning if given the chance.

"I have to decide?" Scarlett pointed to herself, unable to hide her shock.

"Yes." Jadelyn nodded. "Our mate has made it abundantly clear that you have the role of first mate. All of us, myself and the Highaen sisters included, will have to settle with what you decide."

Scarlett looked to me for help.

I raised my hands in the air. "She's right. But you can take some time and discuss it with the others if you want." Please don't let a wedding be what causes my harem to implode.

She gave me a sharp nod and looked down at the ground in thought. "I'll have to think about it."

The rest of the normal crowd at the council were filling in their seats, and a few that didn't normally show up were wandering in and standing near those that they considered friends.

The city knew that something was happening.

"It seems the majority of the council has joined us. There are a few matters to attend to today, but first and foremost, we have a nephilim in the city seeking admittance in accordance with an FBI case she is working on," Rupert read off a sheet.

The doors down below opened up and Helena stepped forward, shielding her face from the bright lights behind us.

I knew from my own experience that it was difficult to see past the bright lights to the faces above.

"Hello. I'm Helena. I am on a case with the FBI in search of the person responsible for a series of demon killings up the east coast. We've tracked these killings along the way. They've moved to Philly and have three confirmed kills so far. That is outside their pattern, giving us reason to believe they have settled into Philly," she quickly and succinctly stated her purpose. "I wish for the council's cooperation in the investigation and hiding our people's nature."

Detective Fox cleared his throat. "I understand you've been working on behalf of the paranormals through the agency recently. Though, this is the first I'm hearing of a third kill."

Helena turned to him, and based on her movements, I'd bet that the lights weren't hindering her vision at all. "That is correct. I do this to be useful to the paranormal community after the closure of the celestial plane. I wish to find my place. And the reason you haven't heard about the third murder is because it is sensitive in nature. Federal agents were made aware of it prior to local PD. I can share the details with you in private."

I wondered what that meant. The most likely scenario I could play out was somebody important must have been the victim.

There was a slight pause among the council as they also tried to pick apart what she'd said.

"I'm here to progress the investigation quickly, without disrupting the paranormal," she reiterated her goal, and it had the effect she wanted. The council moved off her previous statements and began chatting.

Maeve lounged in her chair and waved her hand nonchalantly to get everyone's attention. "While I'm sure you have come with good intentions, my understanding is that Zach Pendragon has prior experience with you. I'd love to hear his thoughts on the matter before making my decision."

Clearing my throat, I bought myself a moment to think before I spoke. A million thoughts raced through my head as I tried to piece them together into something more eloquent.

"Helena and her partner, Agent Till, are both known to me. While I would consider neither an ally, they have not shown themselves to be enemies at this time. They are interested in solving their case, and I do not believe either of them would pose a disruption to the city. However, I am interested in moving this along quickly. Cooperating with Detective Fox and the local PD would be in everyone's best interests."

Mentioning the local PD, I turned to Detective Fox for his opinion. "The local departments will be involved in this. That won't tangle everything up in red tape, will it?"

He shook his head. "No. I'll make sure it goes smoothly."

Turning back to Helena, I noticed that she was staring straight at me. The lights were not throwing her in the slightest. "Then you have my vote in admittance to the city."

"Mine as well," Maeve quickly echoed me. Enough others followed our lead that there was no reason to call it to a vote. The majority had already voiced their opinion.

"Thank you." Helena bowed, spilling out her white wings for a moment before she stood and turned to leave.

Morgana rubbed my shoulders for a moment. "Better than I would have done."

"Slowing her down does nothing but keep Agent Till in the city and a demon or angel on the loose killing and drawing more attention to us." I sighed and rubbed my brow. "In this room, I need to look out for paranormals, not just myself."

Rupert spoke to the room as I was whispering to Morgana. "Next up. There is a junction on—"

A door swung open, and murmurs began immediately. Deniz trooped into the council meeting with a slew of vampires trailing behind him.

"Ah. I see this is where the magic happens, as you say. Which seat is mine?" He looked around the circle, but there were no empty seats.

The vampires had never had a seat among the council, tending to stay inconspicuous. They got little love from the other paranormals. Some even would go far enough to call them a disease or a necessary evil.

I raised my hand. "Rupert, I propose we put aside the junction and use this time to discuss Deniz Wallachia moving into Philly, as well as the recent rise of vampire incidents in the city." Rather than grandstand and risk being outplayed by Deniz, I kept it more civil. Although, I purposefully tied the two topics together.

But if he was behind Maddie's attack, and especially if it had been intentional, keeping my calm was going to take serious self-control. Looking over my shoulder at Sabrina and Maddie standing at the wall behind me, I nodded.

Sabrina nodded back and pulled out a hoop shaped object. Then she held her hand out for a hair from Maddie.

With that started, I focused instead on Deniz.

He was doing a flourishing bow to the council. "Zach Pendragon, king of dragons, has introduced me, but allow me to introduce myself."

He stood back up, tall. "Deniz Wallachia, member of Vlad Wallachia's sixth court. I've come over to America to help bolster the representation of my people. My people are marginalized because we are seen as a danger. I hope to correct that misconception and reintegrate the vampires of Philly into your community." He grinned wide, showing off his fangs.

It was a decent speech, but I wasn't buying it. And based on the faces around the table, many of the other leaders were trying to figure out his true intentions as well.

Maeve tapped her fingers on the table as she watched Deniz. "Unfortunately, your arrival and hope of integrating vampires is coming at the same time as we are seeing an increase in vampire attacks. And some against my people." Maeve's eyes flashed a little in warning.

He gave her a roguish grin. "The Fall Lady herself. I'm honored to be in your presence. You, of all people, must know that when leadership changes, there are often rogue elements that break out and must be corralled. I'm afraid that is the cause of your current problems."

"Oh, let's be clear about one thing. They are not my problem." Maeve's eyebrows rose as the room cooled ever so slightly. I saw the paranormals near her shiver slightly. "The rogue vampires are most certainly your problem."

"Agreed," I added. "Even Summer and Winter take joint responsibility for their people as a whole. If they can do that while at war, surely you can take responsibility for the vampires in the city."

Deniz's lips twitched, but he nodded as he looked around the council table. "I see. Things are done differently where I am from, but I will do my best to adapt. Now, where should I sit? If you expect me to rule over the vampires of Philly, certainly I should have a seat at this council."

"That is fair." Sebastian steepled his fingers. "Would others disagree?"

"His seat is contingent on him resolving the issue among his people and proving himself as a leader," Maeve stated, and I saw Deniz's movements halt just ever so slightly at her statement. I got the feeling he wasn't used to being managed.

But enough other voices agreed that it settled the matter.

Rupert began to speak just as Sabrina's work went off. A red puff of magic floated into the air, sifting about.

And the council room turned into a battleground. It was like the red mist had declared war, as everybody tensed and drew on their power, ready to defend themselves at a moment's notice.

The clump of mist searched for a moment before dispersing.

"Explain yourself," Sebastian roared at me.

I held up my hands for him to settle down. "It was a simple spell to seek the vampire who turned one of the recent victims. I wanted to be sure they were not present with us here in the room to settle all our fears and confirm the story we heard here today."

I worked to hide my disappointment that I hadn't been able to point the kills towards Deniz, but I had a feeling he would be too clever for that.

"That is no reason—"Sebastian was cut off by Maeve.

"As purely a member of this council, his actions would likely be considered an attack. But in his role as the investigator of the vampire problem, they are appropriate. He needed to confirm that the source of the problem was not here and privy to our discussions, and if he had given warning, it could have skewed the results. I support his decision." The winter fae eyed me across the chamber, and I tried to convey through my eyes that I appreciated her backing me.

"I apologize for the sudden surprise and concern that it brought you, but what Maeve says is true, and I stand by my decision." I paused and looked around, waiting to see if anybody would object.

"You do not trust me? What reason have I given you for this?" Deniz shifted straight into playing the victim.

"Trust is earned. When you step up and bring this problem under control, then you will be on your way towards earning that trust from me. Until then, I will continue to do what is in the best interest of the paranormal of this city. It's not personal."

"So you say." He eyed me for a moment before stepping up to the table. His lips twitched, and he looked around the council, but no one vacated their seat for him. So instead, he settled on standing over a space between the elves and Kelly.

"Well, then," Rupert jumped in, moving the conversation on. "Deniz will represent the vampires, contingent on the removal of the rogue element in the city. I will remind everybody here that the primary purpose of the council is to keep all of us safe and hidden from humans. These rogue vampires put that at risk." He gave Deniz a pointed look before settling into the next topic.

The meeting continued with a few new arrivals into the city, making themselves known and various committees and groups providing their latest updates.

We worked through the topics, and it became my turn to provide an update on the vampire attacks.

I cleared my throat. "The investigation into the recent uptick in paranormal deaths has revealed well over several dozen vampire killings. In working to track these killings back to a source, we found an abandoned apartment building with fifteen freshly turned vampires. My partner indicates that it had parallels to a war tactic previously used by vampires. Vampires were turned and starved with a compulsion to remain hidden. They stay that way until somebody walks into their trap."

Deniz's eyes were wide with outrage, and he slammed his hands on the table. "You would insinuate that we are at war?"

"That was not what I stated. I was merely conveying the information my partner provided me as we work to investigate these deaths. But if you have additional information, that would be helpful. Can you confirm if during the seventeenth century war with the Church that the vampires used the tactic I described?" I ignored his anger.

"Yes. But there is no war."

"Of course." My tone was placid, waiting for his anger. "I never mentioned a current war. I believe you brought that up."

Deniz fumed, but he managed to keep his wits. "Do not twist my words, young Dragon King."

"I am concerned about this development," Maeve jumped in. "Deniz, you must act swiftly before a greater problem arises. If it is indeed this rogue element, it seems they are preparing for a larger scale uprising. It would be in everyone's best interests if you solve this immediately."

The final word came out so harshly that I had to hold myself from wincing and continuing onto the next part. "Agreed. If it continues to escalate, it may force us to remove all vampires from the city before an infestation grows to the point that it can't be contained. Finding over a dozen unattended, freshly turned vampires is a large problem."

"Agreed." Maeve shot me a smile. "And if needed, at the height of Summer's power, the fae could take a brief concession from our war to bring Summer's strength for such a task."

Deniz must have had whiplash from how quickly he was looking back and forth between the two of us. He was breathing so hard from his nostrils that I could hear the air rushing even from where I sat.

Morgana leaned over my chair. "Harsh, but maybe necessary."

It was about as close to a praise from her as I was likely to get.

"My people are not pests. If you should try to purge us from your city, you will find yourself on a war front," Deniz threatened me.

"Interesting that you bring up war so soon after denying that it exists. And I did not say purge, I simply said remove. The method of removal is still up for debate." I remained amicable in my tone, watching him seethe.

"But I do suggest that you solve your rogue element problem before Summer comes, because the fae are far more experienced at war than any of us can imagine. I would think that it wouldn't be much of a war, more of a slaughter if it comes to that." I was very glad at that moment to have Maeve on my side. But it didn't mean the vampires wouldn't cause a colossal mess in the process, potentially exposing paranormals to humans.

I still needed to stop an all-out war if I could.

"Let's take a step back," Rupert tried to play peace-keeper. "War is off the table. But, Deniz, your people are threatening all of our safety with their aggressive actions in the city. We, the council, will need to do what we think is best to prevent that."

Deniz snorted and turned, storming out the door.

Sebastian raised his hand. "I think we all should confer with our people given new information."

"Agreed," I replied, echoed by many of the others at the table.

The meeting adjourned, and everybody began to disperse. I stood to head over to Maddie and Sabrina as a heavy hand caught my shoulder.

Detective Fox was standing next to me. "You are playing a dangerous game."

"I don't have the luxury of time on this one. The apartment was a trap, one that I tripped. And one of my best friends was attacked and may now live her life as a vampire. This is escalating. So I'm simply escalating in return," I growled, having trouble keeping my frustration out of my voice.

"I see, but it's not your problem anymore. Deniz is now in charge of solving the problem," Detective Fox reminded me.

I snorted. "Fine. He can work on the rogue vampires, but I'm still investigating who attacked my friend. It would be interesting if the two were related, no? And we also have the case around the demon or angel attack that has now attracted the feds. So it's worth keeping tabs on all the happenings in the city in case any of them become related."

He hummed in agreement. "Yes. I would like your help in that case. You seem already involved with both of the agents?"

"We've met a few times. Agent Till is human and highly suspicious," I understated her curiosity.

"Got it. Why don't you come down to the station tomorrow morning and help me debrief with them? Help us fill in any details," Detective Fox offered.

I didn't think I had much to add, but if he wanted me there, I'd be there. "Not a problem. I'll adjust my class tomorrow as needed."

We were supposed to be going through fae customs in our next class; Sabrina had promised that my honor guard would lead me through it.

"Detective," Jadelyn interjected herself. "If you are done with my mate, there was something we had planned after this."

My father-in-law blushed slightly and cleared his throat, moving away a little faster than was polite.

I rose from my seat and took Jadelyn's arm in mine as the dragonettes and Scarlett hesitated.

"Jade, I have some first mate duties I need to see to. You are in excellent hands." She looked almost a little guilty. But I was proud of her stepping away from the role under Jadelyn and becoming my first mate.

"Of course. Being his first mate can take priority over being my bodyguard." Jadelyn put a hand on my arm, telling me to be quiet. "Is it alright if I take him tonight?"

"Yes. Though, I think Tyrande is waiting in his room. Work it out with her."

Jadelyn's eyes sparkled as she focused back on me. "What a lucky dragon."

# CHAPTER 12

As promised, Tyrande was lounging on my bed when Jadelyn and I walked into my room. But unexpectedly, she was lounging with gold coins scattered all around her, wearing a shiny gold dress that was pouring over her onto bed. It looked like it was meant to be ripped off.

I let out a low growl as I took in the view. My dragon instincts were raging inside of me, and I didn't really want to hold them back.

"Oh, that's brilliant. I'm totally going to steal that," Jadelyn said, her arm still looped in mine. It was the only thing preventing me from lurching forward and taking Tyrande right then and there.

"I have a dragon coaching me," Tyrande joked good-naturedly. "But if you don't let go of him, I'm afraid you are about to lose your arm. You're welcome to join me though!"

She lounged back on the bed, the coins jingling as she raised her arms above her head and exposed herself to me.

Jadelyn's arm slipped out of mine, and I was on Tyrande in a heartbeat. I pushed her down to the bed and huffed her scent mixed with gold.

"Not my gold," I grunted, pleased.

"No, I came with a little offering to your hoard. If I put a little gold in there, can I use your gold in the future?"

Nuzzling her head to the side and working my way down to my mark. I nibbled at it. "Nope. Mine. You belong in my hoard. If you take coins out, they must stay in this room."

I'd know too. Somehow, my dragon had cataloged every coin's specific shape and smell. There were different scratches and dents in the soft metal that made them all unique like snowflakes.

Tyrande tried to calm me by kissing down my neck. "Of course, my mate. I just wanted to cover myself in your gold. I wanted to smell like it, let you feel it on our bed as you take what is yours."

The beast in me preened at her words.

Jadelyn came up behind me, pressing her soft chest to my back. "I should start taking notes from the dragons. You have him extremely worked up." Her lips came up close to my ear and the wet noise of her lips parting sent tingles through my body.

I waited until she began singing a lovely note made just for me into my ear. It was like the softest silk coursing through my ears and wrapping my brain in bliss. The beast basked in my mate's song even as my body warmed and the front of my pants became taut.

"We have to have our tricks if we are to compete with that." Tyrande pushed her chest up and parted her lips, giving me a wonderful come-fuck-me look.

"How about we work together?" Jadelyn pushed on my back.

After Tyrande scooted out of the way, I let the ladies roll me onto my back while the two beautiful blondes hovered on either side of me.

"Two princesses. Such a lucky dragon," Tyrande teased.

Jadelyn had said the same, but I didn't voice that as someone's hand brushed my pants. I couldn't see which it was, though; both women were leaning over my chest expectantly.

"You two are asking for trouble," I grunted, my body aching to be with both of them.

Tyrande leaned down and kissed me. Her soft lips parted to let our tongues wrestle. Instinctively, I reached up to grab her hips, but I ended up with a handful of two different rears. Jadelyn's was soft and a smidge smaller, but Tyrande's was firm, nearly elastic as it rebounded from my fingers.

Tyrande pulled herself off with a satisfied smile and dipped down away from view. Then Jadelyn leaned over and started kissing me, moving my hands to her soft, inviting breasts.

My zipper sounded beneath her, and I felt the cool air on my cock just a moment before it was swallowed in Tyrande's warm mouth.

I grunted and thrust up into her, but both of them held me down. Jadelyn kissed me and bit my lip, making it clear she wanted me to play rougher with her chest.

Tyrande was working wonders on me, and I wondered if there wasn't magic at work as she sucked me, her tongue running up and down the bottom of my shaft, driving me wild.

Jadelyn pulled back for just long enough for the lovely siren to wiggle out of her pants and slide down her thong.

My attention was split between watching Jadelyn's pert butt free itself of her tight pants and Tyrande holding back her hair as she bobbed on me, taking me all the way into her throat.

"Lean back," Jadelyn warned me as she mounted me again and put her sex in my face, then she slowly lowered it onto me as she faced Tyrande.

I got a nose full of her scent, and it did nothing but make me harder before I started lapping at her folds, letting my tongue quest for her clit.

At that point, Tyrande stopped and exposed me to the cool air once more before I felt her move around on the bed. The way that Jadelyn pressed down on me further told me she was helping Tyrande before I felt her warm skin touch me again.

Slowly, I felt her sink back down on my cock, and I could imagine her holding Jadelyn's hands for balance as she rode me several times, testing herself.

My two mates were facing each other, one riding my face while the other rode my cock.

"You stopped licking, my mate," Jadelyn said, wiggling herself firmly on top of me as sensations that weren't natural flooded my cock. Tyrande was most certainly using her magic.

I licked Jadelyn from top to bottom and made her shudder as I found her clit and licked it long and slow like a favorite ice cream.

She must have encouraged Tyrande as a result because the high elf started bouncing furiously on me, bringing me higher and higher until I grunted into Jadelyn's folds and erupted into Tyrande.

It was a satisfying start to the night as they popped off me and I pushed Jadelyn into the bed, ready to take what was mine. My two mates, surrounded by my gold coins, was a high point of the day.

I took them in turns, loving my two mates.

***

I could tell that Jadelyn and Tyrande's legs were nearly jelly as we wiped ourselves off from our extra fun shower.

"That was amazing," Jadelyn sighed.

"I always thought shower sex was supposed to be terrible." Tyrande tousled her hair and sat down on the bed next to her shredded gold dress.

"Siren." I laid down on the bed, already dry. "She's made for sex in the water, and I was covered in her."

Tyrande made a face of surprised understanding. "Got it. Then I won't try that again on my own."

"Maybe we should get some sleep?" I grabbed the covers as both of them settled in on either side of me. They were wiped and I needed to get at least a little sleep if I was to go after the case tomorrow. There was still the urge to take them again, but it was dull enough that I pushed it aside. My mates had well and truly satisfied me.

"Tyrande, we should talk about having a wedding, or weddings," Jadelyn said from her position on my right.

"Uh oh. Do we want to include the big, broody one in that conversation?" Tyrande teased me.

I grunted. "I'm right here, and I'm not broody. Jade, I thought you handed over that decision to Scar?"

"Oh, I'm not going to make a decision," she quickly corrected me. "But weddings are fun to talk about."

"Scarlett is deciding?" Tyrande tensed up against me. "Not that she shouldn't have a healthy say in it. But it's all up to her?"

"She'll talk to you," Jadelyn reassured Tyrande. "But she'll decide if we do separate weddings or a joint one."

Tyrande let out a gargantuan sigh. "Well, I hope she picks separate ones. I've always dreamed of my wedding in green and under a big, beautiful tree before taking him back to Sentarshaden and him joining the family."

"Don't you have enough green? Weddings are all about white." Jadelyn leaned over my chest, and suddenly, I realized they weren't about to sleep.

"Maybe your weddings. But traditional elven weddings always have green. Green is very important; it's the color of life and healthy growth." Tyrande's voice got heated and her shoulders were moving as she did something with her hands that I couldn't see in the dark.

I thought I'd settle the argument. "Gold. Everything is going to be in gold. Gold everywhere, because it is my wedding, you are all mine."

There was a momentary pause, and I thought I saw sympathy on Jadelyn's face in the dark.

"Green is really better." Tyrande picked it back up and patted me reassuringly on the chest. "Trust me."

"White," Jadelyn shot back.

I realized this would not stop anytime soon.

Tyrande snorted. "You are anything but pure now. White is purity, and green is growth. Green makes so much more sense. We want our family to grow with little ones, don't we?"

"Excuse me?" Jadelyn scoffed. "I'm not pure? What do you think, husband?"

I held my hands up and scooted out of the bed. "That I should go sleep in my hoard tonight. We'll plan it out over a family dinner and be good to go."

It got oddly quiet after that, and I moved to the corner of the mattress and lifted it up.

Light shone through the room, giving me a glimpse of their faces. Both of them were staring at me as if I'd just told them the Easter Bunny wasn't real.

"There's no way we can settle this over just one dinner," Jadelyn assured me.

"Yeah. Weddings take months and months. There are hundreds, if not thousands, of decisions to make," Tyrande agreed with her, and I rapidly understood that I was in for a lot of wedding talk. Each woman in my harem wouldn't add linearly to the conversation, but become multiplicatively more complicated.

I nodded in understanding. In this one thing, the Dragon King would admit defeat and retreat. "Lots of nights in the hoard, got it. See ya tomorrow."

I dove into the spatial pocket under my mattress even as they picked up their argument again on the best color schemes. But their chatter held notes of excitement behind the arguments for or against their particular preference.

As the mattress fell back in place, blissful silence descended on me again. I was too tired for that shit. Maybe I could convince Scarlett to just make the decisions quickly for everyone.

Standing in my hoard, seeing my gold, made me perk up. All of my lovely gold. It was amazing to see how the light

from the enchanted bulbs glittered off my gold. Turning
to the familiar vials of panned gold, I froze.

Both were there, and my father's vial was as I'd left it.
But my vial had tipped over, and the contents were gone.

I raced over and froze before picking it up, my sleepiness
suddenly gone. The glass of the vial was clean. There were
no smudge marks. Picking it up, it only smelled of my gold;
there wasn't anyone else's scent on it.

My beast was roaring in my chest. Somebody had done
this. Someone had touched my hoard and they would pay.

The only people who knew about those flakes were
my mates and the dragonettes. Polydora had mentioned
that gold gathered with a dragon's own claws had magical
properties. I tried to decide if one of the dragonettes could
have done this to me.

But they should have left a scent. And my hoard was behind several protections that clearly hadn't been breached.

I was suspicious and stared at my hoard, shifting into
my dragon form and wading into the gold. Letting it clink
against my scales, I swam through my gold, checking each
and every coin or article of jewelry. My big dragon brain
worked in full overdrive as I did a swift inventory, hoping
to find something else to help me track the thief.

A moment later, I heard a tinkle of gold coins further
away from me.

My body went rigid. I stopped in my movements, my
ears focusing hard on locating the next ping. Sure enough,
a few more light tinkling sounds of my gold reached my
ear. I crouched low, staring just over the surface of my gold.

I caught a piece moving about thirty yards away, my
eyes homing in on the spot as I prepared to attack. I could

feel every ounce of my body focused as I became a full-on predator.

Springing out of the gold, I roared with a fury that could only be a dragon whose hoard had been disturbed.

There was a scattering of gold coins, but it almost seemed like a TV show on silent as my roar drowned everything else out. I snapped my jaws down on the section of gold that had movement, but there was no squish or crunch.

More gold clinked in my mouth, and I stood there, confused.

Something pushed against my gums and a gold, slug-like slime pushed its way out of my teeth. For a moment, the creature that looked like liquid gold paused on my snout before diving back into my hoard. The thing couldn't have been much bigger than a rat.

My jaw dropped and gold coins clinked out of my jaws and onto my hoard. Just what was that thing?

I clawed at my gold, pushing the area around, trying to spot it again, but it kept darting between the gold pieces. No matter how I dug around, I couldn't catch it.

Growling, I dove back into my gold and scoured my hoard. I had to find this creature living in my gold. But the creature had felt unique. It was like gold having come to life.

Back and forth I swam through my hoard, pushing aside all the treasure, searching for the creature. I searched and searched, but no tinkling of gold reached me. Whatever it was, it had gone into hiding among my gold and I couldn't find it.

Frustrated, I went and sealed the space so only me or my mates could come and go. Nothing would leave my hoard, and I would find this creature again.

When it didn't show, I stopped and waited with just my eyes resting above my gold.

Hours passed, and my eyelids became heavy. At some point, I drifted off into sweet dreams of resting among gold laden fields and the occasional game animal skirting past me only to find themselves a new home resting in my belly.

Sweet dragon dreams filled with gold-covered mates.

## Chapter 13

"Sleepy dragon, it's time to get up." Scarlett was bouncing on my snout.

I grumbled and lifted my head, surprising the Kitsune. She faltered for the briefest moment before regaining her footing.

Then she rode out the rising of my head as if it was a walk in the park. "Zach, my dad sent me to get you. And the two beautiful women in your bed said you all stayed up quite late."

I grunted. "No. They stayed up late talking about wedding details."

An exhausted sigh slipped out, and it transformed into a yawn. Scarlett had to go low, clinging to my snout to stay on.

"You need to settle this whole wedding thing ASAP."

"Weddings take months to plan, dear," Scarlett admonished me.

I had been waiting to try a new trick, and that moment seemed like the perfect time. Making my eyes big and pitiful, I gave her dragon puppy dog eyes. "Please."

Scarlett held her stomach as she burst into uncontrolled laughter. "Don't do that. The eyes— and the dragon— it makes no sense."

While she belly laughed, I frowned. That did not have the desired effect. Grumbling, I sank back down into the gold.

"Nope, sorry, dragon boy. You have to go see my dad. He's waiting for you." Scarlett stomped on my nose as it sank under the gold. "I'll handle the wedding talk. It won't go away, but I'll manage it."

"Really?" I poked my head back up. "Can everything be gold too?"

Scarlett sighed. "No, but I can help you pitch for gold accents."

Laughing, I rose from the gold and shifted back. This bracer that the girls had gotten me was really something. I often forgot it was there, carrying all my items within it. With that thought, I grabbed out a fresh set of clothes and got dressed under Scarlett's watchful gaze.

"Sometimes I really want to just kick the others out and claim my spot as first mate," she commented.

"I'm not against it." I bobbed my eyebrows before putting my shirt on.

Scarlett blew out a breath. "Being the gateway to the Dragon King is almost giving me a high. Do you even realize how many times a day I'm asked if a woman or someone's daughter can get a meeting with you?"

"Aren't you busy with Jadelyn's security?" I grew more concerned.

She snorted. "Less so now. People don't exactly want to mess with her now that you stand behind her. It's been quiet, and the dragonettes are pitching in to protect your mates more."

"Do we need to get you an assistant?" I asked aloud, quickly glancing over at my gold and wondering if I'd have to spend some of it.

"That... might not be a bad idea. Or we can get you one, and the two of us could share her?"

"Share?" I couldn't help but grin at a meaning that she hadn't intended.

Scarlett knocked me upside the head. "You know what I meant! Get your head out of the gutter. You need to see my father."

I stuck my tongue out. "Will do. Oh, and we have the fae dinner tonight. Don't be late." I was bringing all of my mates.

It was hard finding the time for them all, and I suddenly had the urge to go track down Kelly. It would just be a short trip through the Atrium, though it would make me late to Detective Fox. I pushed the urge aside, but I made a mental note to make some time for my werewolf.

Heading out of my hoard, I passed two sleeping beauties before walking out into the Atrium with Scarlett. She wandered down the hall. I had no idea where a number of the doors went. Many were enchanted like Morgana's.

"This one goes to a coffee shop across the street from the station." Scarlett stopped at a door.

"Why?" A coffeeshop didn't seem like the type of thing to need passage into the Atrium.

"For emergencies," was all Scarlett replied before shooing me through the door.

I stepped out of an employee only door into a coffee shop. I looked around, taking in the vibe. The glasses, flannel, and trendy haircuts told me all I needed to know.

But the workers were subtly not human. I couldn't put my finger on what exactly they were, but it wasn't human, that was for sure. One of the workers waved at me excitedly, and I nodded.

"You're here for... for my coffee?" he said excitedly. There was a little sprig of a leaf that popped out of his hair.

"Can I have something quick? I have a meeting at the station." It seemed the least I could do to order something when I was using their door.

The man turned and got to work quickly before coming back with a steaming hot cup and putting a lid on it for me.

"The Dragon King special!" He winked as more than a few of the surrounding hipsters took note of the drink's name.

I could tell they were anxious to try the new off-menu specialty.

I took a sip of it. It didn't burn me. After breathing fire, a little hot coffee was nothing. It was very, very warm, almost magically so, as it settled in my stomach. A relaxing energy spread through my limbs. "That's great. I'll have to come by more often."

The man couldn't stop grinning as he went back to work, not even asking for money.

Fishing a twenty out of my bracer, I stuffed it in the tip jar and went on my way. The police station wasn't far.

Walking up to it, I noted that the police station was hustling and bustling. Having the federal agents in town must have kicked everybody into gear.

"You're late," a woman wearing a blue uniform stated, waving me down and indicating to follow her.

"Hello?" I said, cautiously following her. "I'm here to see Detective Fox."

"I know. I'm here to bring you in." She smiled at the receptionist who was sitting behind bulletproof glass and used a badge to unlock the door. "No idea why Fox needs a kid like you, but he's just down that hall, only room on the right."

As she left me on my own, I glanced around. The bullpen was a hub of activity, people coming and going, and not all of them were doing so of their own free will.

Heading down the hall, I opened the door to find a small conference room. Detective Fox perked up as I stepped in. Helena simply frowned, but Agent Till looked like she was about to have a cow.

"We were waiting for him?" Till flung a hand at me.

"He might have some helpful information. And it is best to keep him apprised of your investigation." Detective Fox didn't really want to answer her question. "Your partner asked for information that we had, and I agreed if we could have a consultant informed."

Till looked at me like she wanted to pick me apart. "Who the fuck are you, really?"

"No one." I sat down. "You okay with this, Helena?"

She shrugged and put a hand on Till. "Leave it."

"How are you both okay with this?" Till kept shaking her head in disbelief. "Fine. Whatever. Let's get this show on the road."

I sipped from my coffee and settled into a chair as Detective Fox pulled out a stack of files and laid them on the table. He kept them close, not yet offering them to the agents.

"We have the investigations on the two victims we processed, but you mentioned a third." He kept his hand on the files.

Helena pulled out her phone and put it on the table with a picture of a dead man in a suit. My father-in-law snatched it up and expanded the photo. The victim's skin was wrinkled beyond belief, but Detective Fox recognized him.

"That's Representative Halmer." He blew out a heavy breath. "We have a dead congressman?"'

I cursed. I didn't pay much attention to politics, but if that was him, then the hornet's nest had well and truly been kicked.

"Yes. As you can understand, the situation has become very sensitive as a result. We cannot let the news break before we have a rock-solid suspect," Till explained.

I had a sinking feeling in my gut. Her suspect was paranormal; given the state of the body, it was a demon or angel. We certainly didn't want that scrutiny into the murders.

Till continued. "Do you have any understanding of why or how the criminal is desiccating these corpses? When I ran it past the lab, they thought either these bodies had been put in a vacuum or someone had used a tub full of industrial grade desiccant. Both are fairly impractical, but they were stumped."

Detective Fox leaned back and eyed me for a moment to see if I had a better way to explain it.

"It is more likely a drug that is causing their bodies to stop retaining water." I made something up on the spot. I wanted to make the process less time or money intensive.

Needing an industrial grade machine would create a lead that would take us away from the actual investigation.

The agent looked at me incredulously.

"That would explain some of what I've learned too," Helena, to my surprise, supported my claim.

"Then we need to add it to the bureau's database, because I've never heard of anything like this," Till snorted and stared at all three of us with a slight squint. She wasn't stupid. She could sense that there was something she wasn't being told.

But at the moment, she had no way to connect the three of us together cleanly.

"I don't have a definitive sample, only a rumor," Helena said smoothly. "If we can get a sample back to the lab, then we can talk about that. Or would you like to have that conversation with the director?"

Till wrinkled her nose in distaste. "Fine, so, some secret drug. Given to a congressman, an accountant and..." She took one of the folders, and Detective Fox let her. "... a soccer coach. What do they have in common?"

"Money is always the most common," Detective Fox said, opening the folder for the accountant. "We need to understand what money was floating around the congressman."

"Can't. Not unless we open a formal investigation and believe his death is related to his political activities. Until then, his bank details are sealed." Agent Till pursed her lips. "And we can't let this go public until we have a name to give the press."

That seemed convoluted and murky. "Aren't donations public record?"

"Well…" Agent Till waffled her head. "That's tricky. Money often funnels through multiple organizations, and the final donation is public record. But who funds the action committees is almost impossible to get unless you go into them with a warrant."

"Then he's useless." I looked at the photo of the congressman. "We need to identify what both an accountant and soccer coach have in common."

Detective Fox was on it though. "Given the nature of these two incidents, we have been working on identifying any connections they may have." He flipped in the folders to what looked like notes. "The only connection we found is that they frequent the same dive bar. And it's certainly not the kind of place you'd find a congressman."

Helena snorted. "You'd be surprised where you find congressmen. Can we get the place's name? We might be able to get a specific request like this pushed through to check his credit cards to see if he went there often."

Fox underlined the name and turned the folder to her. Both agents took notes on their phones.

"Thanks," Till said and shifted her focus to me. "Since you seem to have all the answers, what's your leading theory."

"Well…" I fudged the truth. "This is a brutal way to kill someone, maybe they did it to cover their tracks? But there's emotion in it. They could have just thrown them in a river, but this feels like there's more emotion or intent behind it."

I continued on. "In terms of the connection, I could see a way the three of them play into the hands of somebody else. There's the congressman for connections, and the accountant who's good with shuffling money. But both of them are either too smart or too scared to get physically involved. The coach? He's probably desperate and willing to put himself in a risky situation to make some solid cash. Whatever they were into was planned by the killer."

I almost believed it myself, rather than making up something for a demon killing. "Given that they moved up the coast before killing here in the city is odd, though."

Those were feedings I guessed. But the killings in Philly seemed like an odd pattern. I wanted to know if there was more to the killings than just feeding.

Till grudgingly nodded. "Okay, any theories on what they were into?"

"Drugs, people, or weapons are really the only things that offer enough money to do something this stupid," Helena tossed in. "We should check out the bar."

Till nodded and glared at me. "So help me god if you show up at the bar. I don't know why everyone in this city seems to look to you for answers." She turned to Fox. "Is he an informant or something?"

"No. He's my son-in-law," Detective Fox deadpanned.

She threw her hands up in the air and marched out of the police station.

"Thank you. I'll update you on the progress of the investigation." Helena paused. "I don't want to presume to order you around, Zach. But it might be best if you steer clear of my partner."

I only nodded, and she took that as leave as she hurried after her partner who was storming through the station.

"That went well." Detective Fox smiled and collected the folders.

"Why didn't you just give them the bar in the first place?" I frowned.

He stopped what he was doing and smiled. "It's just how it is done. Information isn't free. If I didn't make it a little painful, they wouldn't have given me the congressman's name. This is a mess, though."

"Which part?" I asked, cringing a little.

Though he was right, this whole situation stank. We had a dead congressman and a nosy FBI agent circling the drain around a paranormal problem.

Fox shrugged. "We have to get there before them and kill the demon. If they show up to the dead corpse, I'm sure Helena can find enough to pin it on them. But we absolutely cannot allow for a demon to go to trial or Till to confront one."

"Because the demon won't stay hidden." I realized it would break our secret if it had to survive.

"No, it'll go poof. She can't catch one, even if she does with Helena's help. The demon will disappear the second she takes her eye off of it."

The detective eyed me for a moment with a more fatherly look, and something told me some guidance was about to be given whether I wanted it or not. "And you need to be more careful. Stop riling up the agent, or she will dig into your life more than any of us want."

He waited until I gave him a nod.

"What do you think about Helena?" I asked.

"Do you really need more, boy? If you neglect my daughter—" His build up to a threat was cut off when I lifted a hand.

"Never in a million years. I meant, can we trust her? My past with her is... contentious, and I wanted a second opinion. Can we trust her on this case?" I clarified before I had a huffing and puffing father-in-law.

He scratched at the orange scruff he called a beard. "Probably. I looked into her. She's been squeaky clean since Sentarshaden. She had a case in Montana a few months ago, and I have a friend on the force up there whom I gave a call. They said she was nothing but helpful. If anything, she was trying to ingratiate herself."

A bit of sympathy filled his face. "Kid, she just got cut off from the authority she believed in, just after she started to realize she was on the wrong side. She's now alone, trying to protect herself and find ways to give back to the paranormal community. If anything, I'd say she's trying to repent."

I let his words soak in, not quite sure how I felt. Either way, I doubted Tyrande would forgive her. So for now, she remained under watch.

# CHAPTER 14

After finishing up at the station, I swung by the coffee shop again. I thought I'd order another 'Dragon King special'. But to my surprise, I wasn't the only one. I heard a couple a few places in front of me ordering it as well.

"What's the Dragon King special?" a girl with a knit hat in front of me asked the couple that made the order.

Someone on the other side of the rope divider heard her. "You don't know the Dragon King special? It's this place's hottest off the menu item. It is amaze-balls."

Apparently, it was the new 'thing'. If I was getting hip coffee drinks named after me, I'd hit a new level of stardom.

The line moved forward, and a good half of them were ordering this new special drink. Honestly, I thought it was pretty tasty myself, so I didn't blame them.

When I got to the front of the line, the para winked at me. "Don't worry, I'll get you the extra special."

The barista sold coffee like a pro, but when I watched him make my coffee, he pulled a little bean out of his coat. I let my eyes start to shift only for a second to see the magic in that coffee bean he added to mine. Then my eyes shifted back before anyone noticed.

Taking my Dragon King special, I stood to the side, and he never again pulled out a magic bean for the coffee. At least satisfied that he wasn't giving college kids magic coffee to keep them coming back, I headed into the Atrium.

Slipping down the hall, I ducked into my room to find it empty. I was disappointed, but it was probably best for my time management.

Grabbing my bag, I went back through the door to my apartment and came out of my closet. The liquid gold creature was in my hoard, but there was little I could do about it until I knew more. That and it wasn't getting out of there.

Already, I could hear shouting in the apartment I shared with Frank. There was a huge temptation to just turn back and find another way to class, but I took a deep breath and stepped out.

"—just tell me," Frank ended some plea he was making to Maddie.

Maddie shifted her focus to me, as if she just found a life preserver in the middle of the Atlantic.

Frank noticed and turned. "When did you get in last night?"

"Late," I lied. "You two need to stop fighting. Maddie almost died and you are picking fights with her?" I frowned at Frank.

"She's not telling me something. She won't even kiss me." Frank looked like he was in near tears.

Maddie couldn't look at him. "I told you. I just need to process things."

"You freaked out and ran across the apartment when I tried to kiss you," Frank lamented.

I knew what was really happening. Maddie was being extra vigilant of her new saliva and its potential effects on Frank.

"Probably some of the drugs she was on." I went to my usual multipurpose excuse. "Some of them can cause paranoia. Just give her some time?"

Frank didn't like that answer, and his eyes shifted back and forth between the two of us. "Were these the drugs you were involved in, Zach? Is that why they talked to you alone at the hospital? There must be a reason the FBI agent wanted to talk to you. What do you know?"

"He's not into drugs." Maddie stomped her foot, and it sounded like she nearly cracked her bones with it.

"This!" Frank gestured at her. "This too! You suddenly do a one-eighty on Zach? What the fuck happened in that hospital room?!"

"Nothing," Maddie insisted, putting her hands on her hips in a classic 'don't test me' pose.

Frank closed his mouth, but he looked like a volcano ready to erupt, and Frank rarely lost his cool. After a few loud grunts, he took a deep breath and looked at Maddie. "I love you, Maddie."

He grabbed his bag and stormed out.

My best friend wilted and braced against the wall as she slid down to a sitting position and grabbed her legs with tears pooling. "Fuck. How did you manage this? Keep everything a secret?"

"Well, I haven't had a close relationship with someone who didn't know." I sat down next to her. "But you saw how it strained our friendship."

"Not helping," she informed me.

As I sat next to her, I noticed her snotty nose begin wiggling. She took a sniff of my scent. "Your blood smells fantastic."

"I'll break your nose if you try to bite me," I replied.

"Maybe the pain would be nice?" Her voice broke over a sob she was trying to hold in. She was hurting, and she wanted to feel it.

I sighed. "Maddie, don't do that. We'll work through this."

"No. I either need to tell him or break up with him. But the way Morgana explained it, if I tell him, he's my responsibility." Maddie sighed. "I won't be able to survive just feeding off of him, and there's a pretty large risk that I would kill him if I try before I get this under control."

"You could always get a harem to feed on," I teased.

She glowered at me. "Ha," she said with zero amusement. "Harems aren't the answer to everything."

I bumped into her with my shoulder. "Okay, so if you could find a way around this, would you tell Frank?"

Maddie bit her lip and nodded. "Yeah. I think I would. I love him, Zach."

"I know." I paused before bringing up the elephant in the room. "You seem to talk like you will forever be a vampire. You're not thinking about returning to being human?"

She opened her mouth to protest, but then snapped it shut. "No, I'm not. Morgana said I only had a few days, and I'm coming to terms with what I am becoming."

"We'll still find whoever turned you, regardless of what you decide. I won't let anybody have control over you," I explained.

"Morgana explained that to me too," she whispered. "Thank you."

If they could make it work, then I was willing to help. "Make sure Frank is okay with it. You can explain the consequences, even if you can't tell him why. I'll see what we can do about helping him survive your bites."

"Really? You think there's something?" She lit up with excitement.

I chuckled. "Yes, Maddie. There's now magic in our lives. You'd be surprised what we can accomplish."

"But what would something like that cost?" Maddie's hope started to dim. She didn't have a lot of money.

"How about you let the Dragon King figure that out?" I jokingly puffed up my chest, and she rolled her eyes, but I got a laugh out of her.

Relaxing back into the wall, I returned to being serious. "The fae would happily do me some favors, and if it involves actual payment, I have that covered."

She peered over at me. "Are you suddenly rich?"

"Like I said... Dragon King." I grinned. "Fuck yeah, I'm rich. I work for payment in gold, and I had a rather large... inheritance." That sounded better than saying I'd stolen all of my dragon parents' gold.

Mine. My dragon instincts reared up.

"Next you are going to tell me that dragons have hoards." She laughed at her own joke.

But I didn't laugh. I sat there, a little awkwardly, until she noticed.

"Oh. Oh shit, you have a hoard? Can I see it?" Maddie gave me big puppy dog eyes.

"Not now, but sometime later. Maybe we can take Frank too." I didn't like letting others into my hoard, but

I'd put up with it if it made Maddie happy. The thought of visiting my hoard seemed to be distracting her from her negative thoughts.

"Is it big?" she asked.

"Huge. My real mother, Tiamat, had a vast cave of treasure. She's kind of an airhead."

Maddie's jaw dropped open. "You met your freaking mother, and you didn't fucking tell me?! What the hell, Zach!"

I scratched the back of my head. "Well, it isn't my mother, really. She's likely dead at this point. It was an image of her memories she and my father were storing in a magic crystal. So... I couldn't really tell you without you being in the paranormal know."

"You just had to keep this all bottled up?"

"My mates helped me," I said quickly. I owed them a lot.

She grunted. "Right. Okay, so now that I know, what's with all the girls?"

"It's a dragon thing. It started when I wore Scarlett out to the point that she pushed me onto Jadelyn. And then Kelly and Morgana just kind of happened. And while we were saving Morgana, I built up a bond with the Highaen sisters that went deeper—"

Maddie held up a hand. "Wait, I've heard of the Highaen now. They are like the rulers of elves?"

"No, they are the rulers of Sentarshaden, which has an enormous population of elves."

She let out a low whistle. "So you have quite the impressive bevy of beauties. You must be quite the catch. What's with the six new girls?"

"I'm the king of dragons. Do you remember when I went away for a week last spring?"

Maddie nodded, listening intently.

"I went and held a conclave of dragons, where I led a group of dragon leaders. It was a little intimidating, honestly. Many of the dragons were thousands of years old." I paused, letting that sink in for her. The age of the paranormal community was hard to wrap your brain around after being human for so long.

"Okay." She nodded. "And you did kingly stuff? Wait, did you have a throne?"

I laughed. "No, no throne, but I do lead us. I needed to help us decide if we were going to go to war with another organization. That and I had to arbitrate over dozens of minor disputes among their groups." A sigh ripped itself out of me, and my chest rumbled with a depth far larger than my human frame.

"Got it. Dragon kings have to do a bunch of not-so-exciting work. So the new girls? They are all dragons like Trina?"

I nodded. "They are an 'honor guard' sent by the other leaders. Really, they all hope that I mate them and have more dragon babies."

"Because the world needs more dragon babies?" she hazarded.

"Pretty much. So, when you feed, you are really feeding on mana. All paranormals rely on mana, and dragons are one of the few species that produce it naturally. If dragons were to decline or die off, so would the entire rest of the paranormal world." I felt like that was almost comically too much, but it was the truth.

Maddie nodded. "Harem and sex to save the world. Got it. You lucky dragon boy."

I gave her a joking grumble. "Dragon man." I emphasized the second word.

She laughed, leaning over and nudging my shoulder as we sat against the wall. It felt so good to be back to us. I hadn't realized how much I'd missed Maddie.

I waited, knowing more rapid-fire questions would be coming my way.

It didn't take long. "Okay, so that explains a little. You are an incredibly hot commodity and sex with you could save the world. But how are they okay with it?"

"Scarlett wasn't at first," I told her honestly. "We dated a good three months before she got used to it. After that, they sort of had to be okay with it to start because I wasn't going to ditch Scar. The dragons don't mind at all. It's just part of dragon nature."

It was very much a shift in identity. One that I was still adjusting to. I wasn't human. I was a dragon, and with that came a difference in what was expected of me. And it also came with a whole bundle of instincts that I still thought of as a separate entity in my chest.

"Well, when you put it that way… I guess it makes sense. But this is an example of the type of thing that might break me and Frank apart. I'm scared, Zach."

"I'll back you one hundred percent if you get him to agree to the stipulations of telling him," I said again. "Deal?" I raised my pinky.

"Deal." Maddie pinky promised and sighed before pushing herself up off the floor. "I guess I have some work to do, then. See you later."

She rushed out the door. I wasn't sure if she was trying to get away or just needed some space to think through her next steps. Either way, I was late for my class on fae customs.

Grabbing my bag, I left the apartment and headed across campus.

I let my mind wander as I walked. Talking with Maddie had made me realize just how much my life had changed. But then my thoughts drifted to showing them my hoard. Frank's face would be so priceless. I grinned to myself.

He'd be far more impressed than Jadelyn. My dragon hadn't loved her reaction. It was like I'd shown her some mundane gold pile. Kelly's had been better, though. Her wolf and my dragon had played in the gold.

As I thought about her wolf, I decided to find time to drop by and see her. I played through my schedule for the day, and I had some time after class. I'd go visit my beautiful werewolf.

I got to the chemistry lab and opened the door to find Amira waiting patiently inside.

"Are you teaching me today?" I asked.

"Yep. Most of them would rather start getting ready for dinner tonight," Amira replied, as if it was normal for dragon ladies to prep for nearly half the day.

But if I was honest, I had no idea what that entailed.

"So, fae," I started simply, coming up to the lab bench and sitting down next to her. "What do I need to know?"

The black dragon watched me for a moment. She was a petite thing with short black hair cut at a sharp angle.

Amira was pale, looking more like her mother rather than her father, Herm. But she had the brightest green eyes. They seemed extra bright against the neutral colors she normally wore. And she was doing so again today, wearing a white blouse tucked into a black pencil skirt. She looked professional, but her body wasn't hiding.

"Well, first off, you need to understand the fae," she started getting right down to business.

I tried to be an excellent student and jump right in with what I knew. "They fight wars constantly, rotating power between the queens, with the ladies leading the vanguard of each effort."

Amira shook her head. "I meant more about their culture. They tend to be much more emotional than humans. You see it a lot in their art and their children. They are a very vibrant people, but given the nature of war and the schemes in the courts, the fae learn at a young age to create facades and rein in their passion so that others cannot manipulate them as easily."

"That seems... sucky," I commented.

She shrugged. "It is who they are. But when there is a party and rules of hospitality are in play, they can let loose." Amira stared at me over the bridge of her nose, waiting for me to jump in.

"So, this isn't just going to be a party. This is going to be a rager."

"Yes," Amira said with little emotion. "They will be fairly unrestrained. There will probably be an orgy before the night is over, if not several. Sex is fairly casual for them. Only once they bear a child with someone is it considered a coupling. Children are rare, but like most paranormal species, they can have kids with other races, especially those more virile than their men."

"Fae dudes don't have great swimmers?" I asked, surprised at the revelation.

"It is a mix of factors. With the typical restraint they show, men are rarely willing to give women that sort of trust. After all, during sex, the fae are quite vulnerable. Also, the fae are a matriarchy if you haven't picked up on that yet."

I nodded. I'd heard of queens and ladies, but no kings. "Do the queens have husbands?"

"Probably not permanent ones. Those fae men would likely be targeted during court schemes and would take a bullet for their queen. Again, they wouldn't be coupled until they had a kid. So they may have a number of men cycling through their bed until that happens," Amira tried to explain it.

I understood the concepts but didn't get how it could happen.

But I was becoming used to the strange new cultures that existed in the paranormal, so I just accepted it for the moment to move on. "So sex is freely given and taken. And then at some point, sex leads to a child and those two people are then a couple? How do they know who the baby daddy is?" As soon as I said it, I knew the answer. "Magic."

"Very much so. The fae realm is much richer in mana than in this plane. They are experts in magic, and mana literally has seeped into their very being. Mana is an element of logic and laws; thus, they have some rules forced on their very beings," Amira continued. "They cannot lie, but they can be misleading or obscure. You have to be careful and specific with your questions. Also, if they say something three times, it is binding."

"Like an apology," I remembered Maeve being surprised that she had apologized to me three times over her mother's betrayal. That meant she apologized in such a way that it was binding and she owed me. I wondered what that had effected between the two of us.

"Yes. And these things go both ways. Saying something three times creates a spell-like structure for them. So apologizing three times would put them in your debt and you could force them to do something. While that is in place, they also wouldn't be able to harm you such that it could prevent them from fulfilling their debt."

She paused and stared at me closely. "But it works the other way, too. Say that tonight you should thank someone three times. They could create the same sort of structure back to you and be able to force you into a favor. I suspect that more than a few will try to get a favor out of you."

"That's not so bad," I replied.

"What if the favor is to impregnate them? Dragons are known for being quite virile." She paused and let that sink in as she switched her legs for which one was on top. I found myself following the movement.

Then I realized she was waiting for me to reply. "That would further create a connection between us, and we'd become a couple." I realized how far the simple apology could be stretched. "Got it. Be careful of who I thank. Does this carry over between conversations?"

"If the conversations are close, I wouldn't say something thrice to someone tonight, but over the matter of a few days or a week, nothing would happen," Amira explained.

I nodded, glad I wouldn't be tracking statements I'd made to each fae for the rest of my life. I would have definitely slipped up. But knowing this new information did make me rethink Maeve's behavior, including that she'd apologized three times. I wasn't sure what that truly

meant. From what Amira had said, it did seem meaning-
ful.

It could just be a way to show her sincerity, but I had a
feeling there was more to it.

"Good. Now, we need to talk about the risks with their
food and wine. Then we'll run through some misleading
verbiage they use with some exercises to get you used to it."
Amira smiled, and I could tell I was about to process a lot
of new information.

# CHAPTER 15

"We are out of time, and I need to go join the others getting ready for tonight," Amira ended our little class.

I stretched while I processed what she'd just said, looking for the trick. She'd been testing me all class, and now I was dissecting every single word.

But there was no trick. "Alright, I look forward to seeing you ladies tonight."

Getting up, I headed out, but she followed me out and lingered by my side. I started heading towards Kelly by sensing my mark on her, but Amira stayed by my side instead of running off to get ready.

She was quiet as she walked, but she still stood tall. Amira was like a soldier walking into battle most of the time. At the moment, she gave a more pensive feeling, but you could tell she was ferocious deep down.

"Why haven't you taken any of us... dragonettes to bed yet? We are clearly interested in joining your harem. Many other dragons would have conquered us and added us to their numbers."

I made sure no one was listening before I answered, "It isn't about conquering you girls. Besides, I know next to nothing about you."

"You know both of my parents," she stated bluntly. "That should put me ahead of the others."

Rubbing my forehead, I could tell that she needed answers. And if she was being direct, I could do the same. "I need to get to know you. There needs to be feelings shared between us before I'll make a move on any of the dragonettes. If you are keeping score, Trina is in the lead."

Amira's eyes went wide. "Trina is going to win?"

"There isn't winning or losing. But I know her better than any other dragonette, and I like her. Even then, it's only been two weeks. I didn't mate with Jadelyn until I'd known her for almost a semester. Scarlett and I had been dating for almost half a year before I marked her." I sighed when Amira's face was expressionless. "The point is, I need to know you. I won't take somebody to be a mate and then forget them. If we're going to spend our long lives together, I need to make sure that's the right thing to do for myself, the other person, and my other wives. That takes time."

She nodded along. "By this explanation, it would put the succubus and the Lady of Fall ahead of the dragons."

"Yeah, maybe," I said carelessly.

"What about me? Where am I?" she asked.

I winced. We really hadn't spent much time together. We'd had a few classes together, but that was the extent of our bond so far. "It is probably best I don't start making this a literal race and giving everyone positions."

Amira sighed. "So I'm last."

"No, not at all." Although if I told her the truth, she wasn't near the front.

"My mother will be so disappointed. After you appointed her to speak for the black dragons, she wanted to offer me to you, yet you keep ignoring me."

"So is this a dragon thing? I help her and she offers up her daughter to me?" I asked.

Amira nodded. "Yes, but it is also a little selfish on her part. You are the Dragon King, and connections to you are beneficial to her. But regardless of your status, this is commonplace, like trading a daughter to another king in return for some favor."

That seemed highly archaic. My silence proved to get my disapproval across.

"You disapprove. But it is the way of things." She shrugged.

"But what do you want?" I tried to pick through her views to the heart of it.

Amira bobbed a little with her steps. "It would be an honor to mate with the Dragon King."

Nothing about her own feelings, and nothing specific to me. "So, if I were to thank your parents for your service as an honor guard and send you back with the promise of a favor for your parents, what would you do?"

She frowned at me. "I would return to them. You would have dismissed me, and they would earn a favor out of it." Then she looked down at the ground. "Is that what you are going to do? Have I upset you in some way?"

"Then you don't want me to send you away?" I tried to push her towards a decision.

"It would be the right thing for me to accept such an offer. But I do not want to," she stated firmly.

"Why?"

"Because I want to mate with the Dragon King." This time, she said it a little more forcefully, causing a few passersby to look at the two of us strangely.

I gave her a small scowl and kept us moving before we drew too much attention. "Thank you for saying it, but maybe we keep more vague for the sake of the ears around us. But you should know that, to mate with me, it cannot be out of a sense of duty. You should feel something towards me."

"I feel lucky to be a potential mate to the Dragon King," she said as a frown shifted into a smile.

"No. To Zach Pendragon. Not just the Dragon King, but to me. Listen, think about it and talk to some of the girls. We can talk later tonight at the party. I have to go visit one of my mates."

"But you need your honor guard," she protested.

A quick glare from me shut her up.

"No, I don't. Besides, I'm going to be in the middle of a wolf pack with my mate, the alpha. It will make no difference if I have my honor guard. Besides, didn't you need to get ready?"

She wrinkled her nose but nodded. "Please call us if there is any trouble."

I nodded. With the pack, there was always some sort of trouble, but it was typically something more rambunctious that Kelly would step in to stop. Nothing concerning.

Amira eventually faded off, and I continued my trek up to the stadium. Football season was over, so they were currently in spring training and would soon get into summer training.

I picked up my pace, eager to get to Kelly. We hadn't spent much time together recently. I'd been busy with the Dragon King business, and the popularity of the pack and their expansion had kept Kelly incredibly busy as well.

By the time I got to the stadium, practice was going on as usual, but this time, the first few rows of the stadium were loosely filled with werewolves cheering on those on the field.

The pack had more than doubled in size, maybe even tripled, but it was hard to tell at a glance.

Kelly was talking with some girls, many of whom were showing baby bumps. It had been a little more than four months since the beta wolves had access to H's concoction, which allowed them the ability to impregnate their partners.

As I walked through, a few of the wolves on the field and stands noticed me. Howls broke out, one after another, like they were competing for who could be the loudest.

Kelly whirled around with a scowl, looking like she was about to shout at them, but it transformed into a brilliant smile when she saw me. "Alpha!"

The howls cut off and many of them were shouting 'Alpha' as it built into nearly a chant.

Kelly was beautiful as she stood up. Where some of my mates held a beauty marked by extravagance, she had an effortless girl-next-door feeling to her with her heart-shaped face and tight cheerleader body.

She raced across the stadium, wrapping her arms around me and hugging me tightly for a moment before jumping down and spinning at the wolves with a howl that cut through their cheering. "Shut up. I'm your alpha. He's my alpha and only my alpha."

"Alpha-alpha!" someone shouted, only to get hit upside the head by someone next to him.

"Get back to practice," Kelly growled, and I could feel her pull on her alpha magic and push them all to get back to it. Then she grabbed my hand and pulled me over to the bleachers.

"Thank you," one pregnant wolf squealed as I joined the bleachers. The others followed the lead, thanking me.

"Uh. No problem." I scratched the back of my head and looked at Kelly for an explanation.

She rolled her eyes. "They are very happy with the current arrangement."

"Yes. Please, sit. If there's anything you need, just let us know. I get to have a little cub with my Ben! He's so happy, and I just can't stop smiling." A pregnant wolf patted my leg.

"Please. I should be the one getting up and helping you all with anything you need. You all look so lovely." I scratched the back of my head.

More than a few of them lovingly rubbed their bellies.

"Like those bellies? Want me to have one just like that?" Kelly teased me with a roguish grin and ran her hand above her stomach, pretending to rub a full belly.

The beast in my chest rose and demanded I try to do just that. Attraction and lust ran through me as I took in my beautiful werewolf, and I had a feeling that, if Sabrina was around, she might have passed out from the sudden spike.

"Oh, he likes that, alpha." One sniffed in my direction. "Maybe you should leave the rest of practice to us and go spend a little time with your alpha."

"You sure you'll be okay?" Kelly asked the girls, but she was already moving towards me and the exit. I tried not to laugh.

A red head snorted. "They eat out of the palms of our hands now. The bitches rule this pack."

"That's just because we control the potion," another joked.

They all laughed, but it was a happy laugh. The few that didn't have baby bumps started eyeing the men on the field.

"This is really working?" I asked no one in particular.

"Yes it is, Dragon King. The pack has tripled in size and never before have they been so happy. I swear, some of these betas worship you," a wolf answered.

"And they ALL know it is only possible because Kelly is who she is and that you are her mate," another clarified the statement. "Even if Kelly wasn't so kick ass, she has all of our support. The betas won't touch her."

"You should have heard what happened to this new guy. He came in and tried to rally support to challenge Kelly. The way Tay described it, the betas basically turned on him as one and nearly tore him limb from limb before tossing him out onto the street. They ran him out of the state for even thinking about challenging Kelly." The girl held her pregnant stomach as she laughed.

It was clear that the wolves were more than just happy with their situation, but willing to defend it to the extreme.

"Okay, then. Mind if I take my mate away for a little?" I asked the bitches.

"Shoo. We'll keep them on task for practice. Get us some more 'special ingredient' so that we can keep the betas happy," another hooted.

"Get some!"

"Ride that dragon!"

The girls started to cheer us loudly, making both of us blush as we hurried away.

"Those girls." Kelly rolled her eyes.

"I think it's cute. Unlike the other alphas I've seen, you are loved. Most of them are just feared." I bumped my hip to hers.

She nodded, a slightly somber tone entering her voice. "It was the way my father led. If you make the effort to help them get what they need, it goes a long way."

I couldn't stand to see my alpha wolf down, so I wrapped her in a huge hug. "He'd be proud to see what you've done with the pack. Heck, I'm amazed at their reaction to you."

Kelly just leaned against me as the shouts from her bitches faded into the background. "So, are you up for a little resupply for H?"

I moved from hugging her to hoisting her up into my arms. "Can't I get a little time to talk with my favorite alpha?"

"I'm your bitch. There's a difference." She kissed me all the same. "Also, you should know that I'm off everything. You are at risk of putting a pup in me now."

A heavy breath ripped itself out of me, making Kelly giggle. "Sure you just wanted to talk?"

"Oh, we'll do more than talk in time."

"Locker room." She pointed to the one with the 'girls' sign. "The girls will give us some space. Pretty sure Taylor will wait outside."

"The new head bitch?" I asked. Kelly had stopped holding both positions when a new girl came in and was tough enough to knock some heads around when problems happened among the girls.

"She's a tough nut and single." Kelly raised an eyebrow, waiting for me to respond.

"I don't think I need any more girls, Kelly. The dragonettes are lining up and already getting antsy that I haven't touched any of them. Besides, after the wedding drama, I think I could slow down."

"Wedding drama?" Kelly perked up.

"Scar will talk to you about it if you don't know. Jadelyn and Tyrande got into a fight over the color scheme that lasted long enough. I went into my hoard to get some sleep." And ran into that strange little gold creature, but I didn't go into all of that. Kelly might want to go find it, and I wanted to spend time with her. I'd figure out that creature later.

Kelly let out a peel of laughter. "You ran away?"

"They wouldn't stop fighting, and I wanted to sleep. It was a tactical retreat," I grumped.

"The big bad Dragon King running away from wedding talk. Although, that was an intense first two to discuss it with. They will want to go all out. What's the plan?"

I deadpanned. "Showing up once it is all settled. Scar will talk to you."

Kelly grinned. "I'll stop talking about the wedding if you give me something to keep my mouth busy with?" She wiggled her eyebrows as she trailed a finger down my chest.

"Oh, is that how this works?" I kissed her lips and pulled her close, feeling her tight body rubbing up against mine.

"It is. Besides, we are about to go to a fae nympho party. We should probably try to tire you out a little." She winked and kissed me again, grinding her pelvis into my lap.

I snorted. "You think you can tire me out? Is that a challenge?" I growled and pinned her to my lap as my hand slipped into her tight, hot pants, finding no underwear.

"Oh, I might have had a heads up that you were coming." She grinned. "We girls keep in touch, even if you haven't managed to pull us all into the same place yet."

Nuzzling her head to the side, I growled. "Stick you all in my hoard and pump you full of little pups."

Kelly pressed herself to me with need. "Careful what you promise, big boy."

"Oh. I always fulfill my promises." Launching myself off the bench, I pressed Kelly to the lockers. She groaned and hooked her legs behind me, hips tugging me closer to her.

"Don't pussyfoot around it, alpha." She leaned in and whispered in my ear, "I want you. Now."

# CHAPTER 16

"That should hold us over for a while." Kelly put the stopper on a large glass flask we used to capture the ingredient for H.

I pulled Kelly into me, feeling more connected to her after getting some time to play and talk. But now it was growing dark, with stadium lights streaming in through the locker room windows.

We'd ended our time getting cleaned up in the shower, and I was working to dry off so that I wouldn't be late to the fae party.

"Alpha?" a voice called in. "There are some people here to see you two."

I frowned, unsure who knew where we were.

Kelly seemed unperturbed as she pulled a slinky black dress out of a locker and slipped it on. "Tell them they can come in with his suit. I have a flask for you, too."

Moments later, a tall girl with a messy ponytail of red ringlets walked in, trailed closely behind by two of the dragonettes.

Kelly held out the flask to the other wolf. We hadn't done the best job of getting it in cleanly, but that didn't seem to bother Taylor as she took it with eyes that flashed the orange of a wolf's.

"Get that to H. Do not think about taking any extra," Kelly instructed.

"Of course, alpha." Taylor nodded eagerly. "And if you ever need any help to get some of this, I'm your girl. Okay?"

Kelly snorted. "If he ever needs additional help, I'm sure he has plenty of offerings."

Taylor didn't give up, turning to give me a lusty look before sauntering away, swinging her hips.

But she only made it two steps before Larisa and Polydora throttled all of us with their fear auras. Despite both of them being done up and in sparkly floor-length dresses, they reminded everyone here that they were dangerous.

The auras washed off me instantly, and I grabbed Kelly to prevent it from affecting her.

Taylor stumbled two steps before catching herself and throwing a pissy glare at the two dragons. "Watch yourselves. The pack doesn't bow to anyone but our alpha."

"Ooh. I like you. You're a tough one." Polydora grinned right back. "Want to fight?"

"Not now. I have an important task." Taylor held onto the flask with care.

Polydora's eyes went to it, studying it for a moment before she realized what was inside. "What is that for?" the bronze dragon demanded.

"Polydora, stand down," I growled. "Kelly's pack uses it for a potion for fertility among the betas. Given the difficulties of an alpha female in werewolf pack structure, it is important to them."

The Amazonian woman snapped back to me. "But, my king—"

"Enough," I cut her off.

She bowed her head, and she looked particularly submissive, with her hair curled and tied up in a bun with little tendrils hanging down to frame her face. She and Larisa were wearing dresses to match their dragon colors.

Polydora's dress was particularly interesting. It looked like it was tightly woven chain mail. I wondered if they literally made it of bronze. The weight wouldn't bother her nearly as much as a human.

Turning my attention to Larisa, I took in her blindingly bright white dress. It hugged her body like a second skin, except where there was a large cutout showing off her toned back.

"Your suit, my king." Larisa held a garment bag out while Kelly jerked the towel out of my hands.

"Thank you. We need to get him dressed quickly. The others are waiting."

Others? But I was swept up by the girls and didn't have time to give it much thought.

Moving quickly, the three girls helped me get into a suit so black it almost felt like it was absorbing the nearby light. Gold buttons glittered off my chest and my cuffs, standing out even more against the dark material.

After I was dressed, Larisa held out a black velvet case with a gold watch, and Polydora pulled out a gold tie for me. It even had little dragons embroidered on it.

"For you, my king." The tall bronze dragon offered to tie it.

I let her help, not wanting to admit that it would be difficult for me without a mirror. She slipped it around and effortlessly tied it around my neck.

"Do this often?" I asked, surprised she knew how to do it so well.

"I've been practicing all day," she replied, not meeting my eyes.

Larisa giggled. "Be thankful you didn't end up like the mannequin." She made a hanging noose gesture.

"Frustration is part of life." Polydora glared at her companion. "Come on. The rest of the girls are waiting."

We headed out, making our way through the stadium as Kelly and I got a series of catcalls from the large audience of wolves that seemed to have stayed around far past the normal practice time.

Blushing, I put Kelly's arm through mine properly as we walked, opening the door of a stretch limo that pulled up for her. As I swung the door open, I was met by a cabin filled with my mates and the dragonettes.

"So, this is how people go to a fae party?" I asked, feeling out of my element.

"A party where the entire park is shut down with security surrounding it and magic to block satellites? Yes, we roll in with limos and make it look like some sort of extravagantly wealthy party. But it's extravagant anyway, so it's not hard." Jadelyn rolled her eyes.

"Extra extravagant," Yev agreed. "Picture a movie with a billionaire and then triple it."

"It's all made with magic, though," Polydora clarified. "Both queens will be in attendance, which is incredibly rare. And they will be drawing power from the Faerie directly. It will almost be an extension of the Faerie itself."

I started getting both anxious and excited. I hadn't felt this way since I'd first entered the paranormal community. There was so much I didn't know, and so many possibilities.

"Sounds like a blast. And I've got my instructions. Don't say things thrice and don't let a nymph get in my pants." I smiled, knowing I'd get a reaction.

Sure enough, all of them gave me glares.

"Yes, that would be good," Scarlett drawled, drawing my attention to the Kitsune. She was wearing a particularly lovely blue dress that made her orange curls distractingly vibrant. "I have accepted that you have a harem. There is no need to cheat on all of us with some nymph floosie."

The rest of the girls were clearly in agreement.

I gave her a warm smile, letting her see me appreciate her body. "Did you say something? I'm a little distracted."

I let hunger fill my eyes, quickly reciprocated in hers. She moved towards me, but Jadelyn grabbed her arm, giggling. "Easy, girl. There's no room in here for him to go all dragon, mate."

"You will be protected. There will be a dragon with you at all times," Polydora declared. "Rules of hospitality do not allow us to act against a fae for simple glamor, but we can drag you away or break the glamor ourselves. We will also be on the watch for tricks."

"Thank you." Jadelyn reached over Scarlett and patted Polydora's leg. "I feel better knowing that you all are watching over him."

My siren was wearing a pretty teal number that hugged her hips and ended at her shins with a flare.

All of them were dressed to perfection. I noticed that the metallic dragons all went with the same style of dress as Polydora, only made out of their own metals.

The chromatic dragons were a little more varied, but they all wore full length dresses of their color. Although, Chloe's was more sheer cutouts than fabric.

All of them accented themselves with gold jewelry to match me subtly.

Morgana was wearing a red velvet dress, complete with a corset. She reached into it at that moment and pulled out a flask. "Anyone need something to take the edge off?" She took a sip from the flask.

"Gimme that, you damned Blueberry." Kelly held out her hands eagerly.

"This might be too strong for you, Furball." Morgana held it out halfway.

"Shut it." Kelly snagged it and took a shot from the flask. As soon as the liquid touched her tongue, her eyeballs popped wide and held it out as she coughed. "What the fuck is that?"

Larisa grabbed the flask and took a sniff before sipping it. "Shit. That's strong. Shojo whiskey?"

Morgana nodded. "It takes some magically infused alcohol to affect most of us."

I held out my hand, but Polydora pushed it down. "My king, you will be toasted and cheered by many of the fae with fae wine. I would suggest you abstain from drinking until then."

Frowning at her, I paused for a moment before holding off. Last thing I needed was to be smashed before we arrived.

The girls passed the flask around, and I noticed that those without enhanced healing turned it down. I'd just have to get a sip another time. But I enjoyed the effects of it across the group. The girls loosened up, giggling and dancing around as we rolled through town.

We chatted idly until the limo came to a rolling stop. Only then did I look out the tinted windows at the party in a valley of the park.

My jaw dropped and nearly hit the floor.

The only words that fit it were magically extravagant. The entire park was lit up by floating lights that seemed alive as they moved and danced around. They swirled around floating crystal chandeliers, splashing the light down among the patrons.

All party goers were dressed up, dripping with jewels and perfectly tailored clothing.

"Those are will-o-wisps. Minor fae that don't do much more than float around people and take sips of people's alcohol." Scarlett pointed to one that came down and drank from a cup that had been left unattended at a table before wobbling back up to dance among the chandeliers.

As I followed her flight, I realized that one chandelier was different. At one end of the party was an absolutely enormous chandelier that wound over part of the celebration like a giant serpent.

"I'm going to guess that's where the important people are," I said.

"Most likely," Morgana agreed.

"By the way, how the hell are we hiding this from the normals?" I continued to be awed by the display.

"You were eyeing all the girls instead of the road," Scarlett snickered. "There was a police blockade just outside the park, and I'm sure there are wards in the woods to keep any adventurous kids out."

I nodded, glad that I could enjoy myself and not worry about paranormals being outed.

A line of servants stood nearby, and two of them peeled off the group to approach our limo. One opened the door, and the other waved their hands. With their motion, a rug rolled out of their sleeve and made a path between the car and the party below.

"Name?" the servant asked, holding the door.

"Zach Pendragon," I spoke up from further up the limo.

The servant did a double take and looked into the limo to see me. "Of course."

He did a quick about face and snapped twice at the line of servants. His jaw moved, but I couldn't make out what he said. Whatever he said had the entire line of servants peeling off, leaving the limo behind us waiting.

Fae magic swirled, and the plain red carpet turned to gold, expanding and filling in with flying dragon motifs around the edges. Lights stretched out overhead, illuminating the area like it was broad daylight, and a brief splash of fireworks in the shape of a gold dragon went off above us.

The line of servants pulled out nearly a full orchestra and cut right into a dramatic, upbeat fanfare.

"Uh... what the fuck?" I commented, watching the completely overdone welcome.

"Welcome to fae extravagance." Jadelyn patted my knee, preparing herself to exit the limo.

Each lady was helped out of the limo by a waiting servant amid the music that was turning heads as the party nearly stopped to watch them parade out and down the gold carpet into the party. Not that I blamed them. My ladies were stunning as they walked the carpet down to the party.

When it was my turn, I was surprised to see Maeve waiting for me with her elbow out.

"Surprise," she said with a winning smile.

The Fall Lady was wearing what looked like an odd cross between a military uniform and a dress, complete with a big, blue silk bow tied around her waist that caught the will-o-wisp light that was dancing amid the party.

"Very surprised. You must have won Scarlett over if she let you walk in with me," I replied, getting out last and taking her arm amid the servants that backed away from her, watching with wide eyes.

After stepping out of the car, I noticed that the fae working together were split. They either had a natural, yet tan skin tone and vibrant hair, or they had varying degrees of blue tone to their skin and subdued pastels for their hair, which came in a multitude of colors.

"Are you uncomfortable?" Maeve asked. Her arm was a little chilly to the touch, but I tapped into my silver dragon abilities, and I didn't notice it again.

"Not at all. I'm quite resistant to the cold. I am a little surprised at you taking me into the party and all the opulence." Knowing we may not have another moment alone during the party, I added. "By the way, in my fae crash course, I learned the significance of you apologizing thrice."

"Mmm," Maeve hummed, giving some time for us to pass the last of the servants and making our way down the winding carpet down to the party. It gave us a moment of privacy. "You didn't react initially. I suspected you might be unaccustomed to our ways."

"Now that I know, it seems you owe me a favor." I smiled.

She nodded. "Though, until you call on that favor, I must do my best to protect you. Because of that, I'd ask you not to call in the favor."

"Why? Does it require this compulsion to be on my side?" I asked, wondering again how much of her recent behavior had been a result of the compulsion that would follow the thrice apology.

It was Maeve's turn to be surprised. "You'd... trust me that much?" She frowned, as if thinking through it for some trick.

"So far, your support amid the council and with Maddie's vampirism, none of those were part of that compulsion, were they?" I pushed further to understand her.

"No. Only to protect your person," she replied quickly.

Which meant all the times she'd helped me had been of her own volition. I was happy that it wasn't part of a compulsion from apologizing three times.

"Then I would say you've earned my trust, if not my friendship," I stated plainly. Even if she had some ulterior motive, she had gone out of her way to help me. Until she proved otherwise, I would trust her.

"Interesting." She seemed to have trouble processing my statement. "Then I am a friend of the Dragon King?"

"Are you trying to get me to say it thrice?" I raised an eyebrow and thought through the implications of such a thing. It wasn't binding, such as a promise, instead cementing a relationship. One that would certainly benefit both of us.

Realizing there was no harm in it, I pushed forward. "Maeve, Lady of the Fall, is my friend, and as both Zach Pendragon and the Dragon King, I accept your friendship."

There was a small tingle as something passed between us.

Maeve's eyes went wide. "You should not give things like that away so easily."

"It wasn't easily. We have been helping each other in the council for some time, and you have helped me personally on several occasions. We have built this over a period of time," I explained my rationale.

"Yes, well, if you don't mind, I'll keep an eye on you tonight. Should any fae attempt to ambush you, they will fail as they find my dagger in their back." She paused. "My friend." She struggled to say it, and I suddenly wondered just how many friends she had.

"So what sort of surprises are in store for me, besides the welcoming fanfare?" I asked, hoping for some spoilers.

Maeve pointed to the long, winding chandelier. "You will be given that as a gift when you head out. My mother made it as an apology, but she doesn't understand you beyond that you are a dragon, so she is trying to make up by giving you something of high value. If you understand it is an apology, you can try to get two verbal ones from her, and when you accept it, name it for what it is. Another apology."

I raised my brow. "That would indebt her to me. Also, I imagine she'll be furious."

"Oh, she most certainly will smash many things upon her return. But she will calm down. And by the time you see her again, she will respect your guile," Maeve coached me. "Plus, it will protect you both by having her aid, and it being publicly known."

"Your advice is a grand gift. I'm glad we had this moment," I said, somewhat dreading the bottom of the carpet as dozens of expectant fae looked up at me.

Maeve smirked. "Yes. As I have gained your friendship, it is the least a friend could do. Now, get ready. You are about to be the center of attention," she warned, a cheerful facade falling over her face as she glanced out emotionlessly across the crowd.

# CHAPTER 17

M aeve led me across the carpet to the edge of the winding chandelier. The beast in my chest wanted to stare at the glittering lights, creating a beautiful array of shimmering gold that danced along the party.

I wanted to put it in my hoard and watch the light flicker across all my piles of coins and trinkets. I pictured it for a moment before a flicker of the creature I'd found in my hoard popped into my head. I wondered if Maeve knew anything about it, but at that moment, we lost all privacy as several fae pressed in upon us.

"Ah. The Dragon King. Here, have a drink" An excited fae lady pushed a drink into my hand. She was, like the rest of the fae, beautiful.

Polydora appeared at my side, taking the drink from my hands and sipping it before handing it back to me. She then stationed herself behind me and loomed over the fae. "It is suitable. Please do not hand my king drinks like that again."

The fae lady forced a smile on her face as her eyes roamed my face. "Forgive me. I was just so excited to meet the Dragon King. Ah! Where are my manners? I'm Lady Dresdeth, of the summer court." Her eyes twinkled for a moment at the mention of summer.

I'd already guessed which court she belonged to based on her tanned skin and vibrant pink hair. It seemed that the title of 'Lady' must be more common among the royal fae of each court. But she clearly held some sway, because the others mobbing us parted and gave her a bit of extra space.

"Well met, Lady Dresdeth. Why don't you help me meet some of these others?"

She immediately hooked her arm on mine, and I noticed Polydora looking at it like she was trying to decide if she should bite it off or not.

But Lady Dresdeth didn't seem to mind one bit. "It would be my absolute pleasure."

The fae lady paraded me around the ball, winding around under the utterly massive chandelier. I noticed the others were very polite as she walked, moving out of her way gracefully as she sauntered through. My honor guard rotated out twice as she introduced me to nearly everyone.

I knew enough of my habits to be careful. The more time I spent with her, the more likely I'd accidentally give her three 'thank yous' just out of habit.

My ladies were being led through by Maeve behind me. It seemed that the important people flowed this direction while the less impressive people who had come early slowly made way for them and shifted down further away from the end. Based on the social hierarchy, I assumed the fae queens would be at the end of the winding procession.

I found it was an intricate dance, thinly veiled behind glittering dresses and gold goblets of wine. While I gained an appreciation for fae beauty through the party, I also became wary of just how well-connected Lady Dresdeth was as she seemed to hold influence over nearly everybody.

"Thank you," Lady Dresdeth laughed, but her eyes shone with meaning as she patted one of the fae.

The person who had received her thanks beamed like they'd gotten the best thing in the world.

"You know, Lady Dresdeth, I haven't quite gotten an idea of what you do amid the summer court," I said.

"This and that. Really, a little of everything. Honestly, I probably have my hands in a few too many pies, but one has to do that to have a firm hand on a fae court." She wrinkled her nose. "But now isn't the time to talk about court or duty. Tonight is a night for celebration."

"Of course. What is it you do for your own enjoyment?" I asked her as the fae bowed off the moment the lady failed to continue the conversation.

"In my off season, I have a wonderful chateau at the edge of some mountains. It is beautiful, and I spend a lot of time gardening." She sighed wistfully.

"Sounds peaceful," I commented, not knowing much at all about gardening.

She only grinned from ear to ear as she leaned in conspiratorially. "I cheat." She wiggled her fingers and magic sparkles darted off. "It is still very relaxing, and I enjoy doing much by hand."

The party opened up as we reached the end. In the center of the new area stood a platform only a foot off the ground, but it was as if the platform was sacred. Many fae avoided touching it. On the platform were two large thrones and several tables laden with food.

I realized I had noticed little food as we'd walked. Most of it had been on the edges of the party, and the sight of the spread in front of us made my mouth water enough to distract me for just a moment.

But it didn't take long before I noticed the throne that was currently occupied.

The winter queen sat on the other side of the table. Her cold, silver eyes glared my way, and I shivered for a moment before realizing they were landing on Lady Dresdeth.

The Winter Queen's ire only made Lady Dresdeth smile more. "Come, my Dragon King and entourage. You are all welcome up here."

Several of the tables had occupants. Some fae were standing up on the platform, but more notably were members of the council, Herm, and his wife, Amara.

I nodded at them as I caught their eye before continuing to scan. The Summer Queen was nowhere to be found, her throne left empty.

Lady Dresdeth noticed it had drawn my attention. "I wanted to meet you in a less formal setting. Do forgive me." Then she strutted across the platform and up to the throne.

As she spun to plant herself, her gown extended to flow off her legs and down the steps of the throne, pooling out onto the platform. As she sat, her eyes turned the gold that I had come to expect from her, and her hair turned a vibrant green of new growth. She was instantly recognizable, and I cursed in my head.

"Did you know?" I asked Larisa, who was currently acting as my guard.

"No. I didn't even sense the glamor. The Summer Queen is nearing the height of her power; there are few things that could match her. But if you had a handle on your magic, you could be one of them." She squinted at me as if accusing me of not working hard enough on my magic.

The surrounding fae clapped excitedly for the Summer Queen as she took her spot.

The Summer Queen waved her fingers at me and cleared her throat while staring at me. "I welcome the dragons to our lovely party, and more importantly, to Philly. It seems partnerships with the dragons are already blooming, and for that, I am thankful. We celebrate change and growth. And we look to solidify our friendships. As such, I'd like to ask the Dragon King for the third time if he would accept my hospitality in the fae realm."

I respected how she called out that the question would be my third response, but I despised that she'd put me on the spot in front of everybody. I played through my response, trying to make sure I didn't corner myself.

The party grew quiet as the fae waited to hear my response.

I looked around the party, taking in the opulence and glittering gold around us. An idea sparked in my mind of how the queen could repay me.

"Do you host weddings?" I asked.

The crowd was quiet.

"Weddings?" The Summer Queen repeated my question in a neutral tone before a beautiful smile blossomed on her face. "I would love to host the Dragon King's wedding."

I turned back to my wives to see what they thought of it while the merriment kicked back up into full swing.

My wives looked surprised, but none of them seemed put off by the suggestion. I had a feeling they were enjoying the gowns and setting as well. A few even seemed pleased.

I had a sudden moment of inspiration. "My mates seem to like the idea. I'll let you work out the details with them."

I figured it couldn't help to have some reinforcements to sort out the various wants of my wives. And a little magic wouldn't hurt either to keep me from losing much from my hoard to pay for it.

The Summer Queen gave me a knowing chuckle. "That I can do. Though we'll have to work through missives after the party."

Her statement prompted Scarlett to step forward and start discussing in low tones with the Summer Queen.

Not to be left out, several of my mates quickly stepped forward, turning the space in front of the Summer Queen into a mass of conspiratorial whispers.

I glanced from the group to the Winter Queen. Her face was icy as usual, but there was a flicker of interest from her as I looked her way. Thinking back to Maeve's suggestion, I ignored her for the moment.

My honor guard rotated again, and Amira was at my side looking towards her parents. I waited before we headed over to them.

"So, have you thought about my offer? Your parents are right there. If it's what you want, I will walk over right now and thank them for sending you to my honor guard. You could go back with them." I wanted to make sure she didn't stay with me out of obligation. If we were going to build anything, I wanted it to be real, not some trade for her parents.

Amira swallowed loudly. "No. I'd like to stay with you. But I would enjoy speaking to them while I stand by your side."

"Ah, of course. They'd love to see you presented next to the Dragon King. But you are long lived. You could just wait for the next one." My tone was a little harsh, but I was also frustrated by the situation. I didn't know where her loyalties landed. The thought of a transactional relationship made me annoyed.

I had absolutely no interest in a mate that there was no love between. Six were enough wives that loved me; I didn't need to marry to see if love would develop.

"You are Zach Pendragon. You are the Dragon King of my generation who was born a human but somehow managed to take on an old god within a year of your first shift. Then you fought the Church near single handedly and sealed the celestial plane because two of your mates were threatened."

She turned to face me straight on. "You fought the Spider Queen, one of the world's most feared powers, and protected all of us. You are strong and powerful. I would be proud to be your mate. Your position is of less worth to me." Amira stopped and stared into my eyes.

I paused. Wanting my strength wasn't exactly what I had in mind, but it was better than her just wanting to be with the Dragon King because her parents demanded it of her.

Processing my feelings, I held out my elbow for her, deciding to give us a shot. "Come, let's talk to your parents. Lean on me and laugh when I tell a joke."

Amira put her arm around mine and leaned ever so slightly on me. I tried not to snort. It looked more awkward than anything else, but she was trying. Amira was far from a blushing bride.

"Like this?" she asked, her body rigidly leaning.

"Relax," I replied, taking a step towards her parents.

She let out a staccato of little chuckles and once again I was trying to keep my cool. It was almost cute how unnatural giggles were for her.

But the sound caught the attention of her parents, both of whom looked like they were staring into some alternate reality as they noticed their daughter laughing.

My instructions for her were clearly not going to work.

"Act natural. That wasn't a joke," I sighed.

Her chortle cut off instantly, replaced by her normal stoic expression. "Better?"

"Yeah. That's probably better." At least her parents wouldn't think I'd replaced her entire personality. I stepped up to the table with Herm and Amara. "Hello, I'm glad you both could make it."

Amara beamed at her daughter, pointedly looking several times at where Amira held my arm. "It's a fantastic surprise." Amara caught herself. "The party I mean. Fae parties are things of legend, even for paranormals."

"They sure know how to put on a show," I agreed with her before turning to her mate. "How are you, Herm?"

Despite the camaraderie we had built fighting together during the conclave, Herm was glaring at me like he wanted to tear my head off. But I understood why as he glanced towards his daughter with a loving expression.

I had a feeling that no matter how many years you prepare, a man was rarely ready to give away his baby girl.

Amara bumped Herm to prod him into speaking. His eyes moved from his daughter back to me, the love in them fading away before he spoke. "Good. We moved into Philly just fine. And Tim and his harem are just down the street. But I have to admit that being in such a crowded city makes me feel a little constrained. I need to stretch my wings every now and then."

"We love it here," Amara butted in, clearly not feeling that her mate was showing enough enthusiasm. "You should come by our place for dinner this weekend. We brought along Amira's hoard with us, and I'm sure she'd love to show it off to you."

"Mother." The stoic dragon stomped her foot as her cheeks flushed bright red. "My hoard is my business."

Amara only grinned at her daughter's reaction, waving it away. "Right, right. I just thought that since you left it at home, you must not be too concerned about it. I almost took it for myself."

Her daughter's eyes flashed dangerously, but Amira's parents just laughed.

"We won't touch your hoard. At least, not until you find a mate. Then we'll happily let them safeguard your hoard," Herm promised her.

Amira snorted, causing both her parents to grin. The moment lingered as the conversation lulled, and my mind wandered back to that little creature back in my hoard.

"So... how has Amira been performing?" Amara asked suggestively, causing Herm to nearly choke and my attention to snap back into the moment.

The former Greek general had a weak poker face when it came to his daughter.

"Admirably. We were talking about some sort of bonus, but she couldn't make up her mind on what she wanted," I fibbed and pulled Amira closer.

This time, she leaned on me slightly less stiffly.

"Yes. My bonus. We haven't decided yet." She kept her responses short, sounding a little bewildered.

"Well. You will have to think hard and take advantage of a bonus from the Dragon King." Amara glared at her daughter, trying to drive something home.

Wanting to shift the conversation, I decided to see what either of the dragons might know about the creature I'd found. "Is it typical for creatures to live in hoards? There's a little slug-like creature living in mine. I keep my hoard in a spatial pocket that Morgana made me, so nothing should have been able to get in or out."

All I knew was that it was a magical creature, and given its draw to treasure, I assumed it might be attracted to hoards. Any hope I'd had that they would know about the creature faded quickly as they looked at each other in confusion.

"Something is living in your hoard? Sometimes dragons let pigs or chickens live there as a snack, but even then the dragon brings them in," Herm hedged.

Amira frowned at me. "Why have you not told your honor guard about this before?"

"It's recent, and it didn't seem to pose a threat. I tried to catch it the other night. It was annoying, and it escaped me, but it didn't attack in any way. It's definitely magical." I was a proud Dragon King, and I didn't need anyone's help to manage my hoard. Besides, it was sealed.

Herm rubbed his chin. "What does it look like?"

"It's about the size of a football... I think. It changes shape. Really, it is almost like fluid, and it is gold. It also smells just like my gold." I held my hands out to show the shape, but then mashed them together. "I waited, and when it came to the top of my gold, I attacked. But when I tried to bite it, the little bugger slipped between my teeth."

Herm frowned. "Is any of your gold missing? Maybe it came in with something you added to your hoard?"

I shook my head, but then slowed. "There was this gold I've had for a long time. I dug it out of the ground myself."

Amara's eyes went wide. "You, the Dragon King, dug up your own gold?!" She got progressively louder as she said it, and then hushed herself down. "Given your powerful heritage, that gold would be unbelievably potent." Her eyes flicked to Herm.

"You think he made an elemental from it?" Her mate picked up from where she had been going.

Amira's face became the definition of shock. "But the mana requirements to make an elemental are so astronomical that they aren't naturally formed anymore."

Both of her parents nodded. "Yes, that is true. But long ago, when mana was richer in the world, they formed naturally. The only ones still around are those that are ancient. Once in a while, a human magus manages to make one artificially, but it can take decades and are incredibly weak."

"I've had this gold for a while. Almost a decade." I thought back to when my father had taken me into the hills to pan the little flecks of gold. "What do I do about it?"

Amira took over the conversation. "If it is made from your mana, it should be attuned to you. Your mana will feel familiar, so it won't harm you and should adapt to help you."

I raised an eyebrow for more information.

"It will grow rapidly for as long as you continue to feed it mana. Given that it is living in your hoard, it is also likely soaking up some of the mana from your gems and gold," Herm explained. "They are extremely loyal creatures. That is one reason they are a prized creation by many wizards who manage to make one. The fact that yours is made of gold is brilliant... maybe I should make one."

Amara smacked him. "I will not have you disappear for years to make one. We all don't have the mana capacity of our king."

I stepped in before they began fighting like a married couple. "So, if I let it live in my hoard, it might grow into a powerful follower?" I asked.

"Yes. It will grow quickly now that it has formed, and it will grow in intelligence sharply as well. Try feeding it some of your mana directly and talking to it. In no time, I'm sure we'll see it standing next to you." Amira had a funny face.

But before we could talk about the budding elemental in my hoard more, there was a disturbance at the party.

I turned quickly, scanning for my mates in case there was danger. Determining that they were safe, I scanned the area for what was causing the disturbance.

There seemed to be two groups attracting attention.

One was a swath of people wearing leather and flashing their fangs, the other was a group of spider women carrying a gauze-covered structure. The wind swept the gauze aside, and Ikta beamed at me for the brief moment before the cloth fell back down into place.

I almost had to wonder if it was on purpose.

"Oh great. Here come two batches of trouble," I grumbled.

# CHAPTER 18

"Ooh. This should be entertaining," Amara commented as we watched Ikta come parading in.

"More like bad news," I grumbled. Thankfully, the vampires and wild fae seemed to be separate. The horrors that would come of them working together boggled my mind.

"Do we have a stake in this, my king?" Amira asked me.

I frowned, trying to work through the same question. "We support the fae if needed. Vampires are a problem for everyone. As for Ikta, we avoid conflict. She can't do anything to us in her present state."

The vampires pushed to the stage first.

"Queens." Deniz threw his arms out. "I apologize for our tardiness. It seems that our invitation got lost. Luckily, I heard that there was a party to welcome new paranormals to the city, and I couldn't be left out as a new arrival." He grinned like they were best friends.

Unfortunately, I realized from the way he phrased it that he had found a way to be invited.

"Welcome." Summer's face had lost its warmth. "Though, no other group brought so many people."

Behind him were two dozen vampires, many of whom were looking around hungrily at the fae, who were stepping away in response.

"We wanted to experience the fae's famed hospitality. And I hear the beverages are delicious." He licked his lips as he looked around. "Although, I doubt my entourage competes with a Dragon King's harem. He has what? A hundred wives?"

"Six," I snorted.

But my words were drowned out by the rage of Winter. The temperature dropped several dozen degrees. The warm day turned to a chilly fall day in an instant.

"You will not drink a single fae while you and your people are here. Our hospitality may be famed, but we have limits."

"I thought you would treat us equally. Did you not bring food for the others?" Deniz gestured vaguely to the food. "Do the rules of hospitality not declare that all guests receive food and drink untainted by the fae. That includes vampires, no?"

"The rules of hospitality state that no one shall be harmed. Drinking the blood of my people would be harmful," Summer declared. Her power welled up and banished the cold, instead making it a little toasty.

My skin was getting a little temperature whiplash, but I shrugged off the heat with a slight tap into my gold dragon abilities.

Seeming to ignore the current conversation, the driders came up to the platform and lowered the pallet to make it even with the stage. Two purple nymphs with faces of pure beauty and lust stepped out, wearing sheer sparkling strips of cloth as clothing. They then stepped to the side, parting the curtains for Ikta to step out in her full glory.

"Ah. It seems like nothing has changed," the Spider Queen stated as she glided out. "The two queens still bicker endlessly. It seems we have all sorts of guests, and there's a conflict in the rules of hospitality. Whatever shall we do?"

Ikta tapped her fingers along her cheek, giving us her most sincere forlorn look, which still wasn't very sincere. A smile crept along her face as she spoke again. "Perhaps a third party could settle this? I'd be happy to assist. I'm very knowledgeable in fae laws."

Ikta's eyes glittered with malice towards the two queens as she tilted her head, waiting for their response.

I cleared my throat to get her attention. She glanced my way, and seemed even more pleased by my attention, but as I glared, she seemed to shrink ever so slightly. She shifted a little uncomfortably before straightening up and turning to the queens, waiting for their answer.

"A third party with the knowledge of your people. That would be perfect to settle this. We are hungry after all. It would be rude to keep us waiting when the rest of the party is feasting." Deniz was watching the queens intently.

The queens shared a look before nodding. "Declaring yourself a third party means you have no relation to the fae. We agree you can settle this."

Ikta laughed. "No relation to the current leaders of the fae, that is certain. However, I and my people are fae." She pursed her lips.

The queens didn't acknowledge her statement, but they also didn't revoke her ability to be a third-party decider for the moment.

Ikta stood for a moment, her eyes flicking between the queens, Deniz, and myself as she tried to decide on the best course of action.

"Very well. The vampires need blood," Ikta started, and I could see the queens' eyes lighting up with fury before Ikta spoke again. "But... to drink from the party guests is not ideal."

Ikta walked over to the spider women who had carried her in, whispering in their ears before snapping a finger and a dark portal opening beside her.

The spider women marched into the portal, and everyone waited. The party was eerily silent for those moments until they came back with a goat under each arm.

"Goats!" Ikta shouted before cracking up in laughter. "Everyone likes goats."

"Insulting," Deniz spat.

"But they have blood, and who doesn't like goats?" Ikta frowned at the vampire as if he was the odd one. "It is food, and it harms none. Well, the goats won't love it, but they were going to be food, anyway."

Deniz bared his fangs. "How about I drink your blood to settle this?"

One of his entourage took that as the signal and rushed forward. The blur that was the vampire disappeared into a portal that popped into existence in front of Ikta, followed by a loud shout from above.

Ikta twirled her wrist, causing the first portal to turn to face upwards. The vampire came screaming down and right back into the first portal, only for his voice to reappear higher up in the air.

He came down faster this time, then faster still the next.

"I demand you stop this at once!" Deniz yelled, and it was the least composed I'd ever seen him.

"Sure." Ikta dismissed the portal near the ground, but the screaming vampire was still hurtling down towards us all.

The vampire hit the stage in a red, messy splatter, killed on impact.

"You twisted bitch," Deniz screamed. "Hospitality is nothing to you? Fine. Based on your example, we shall feed."

His entire group launched themselves forward towards the nearest fae.

However, when they each touched their target, they froze. Magic slammed down around them from everywhere. But it wasn't a single person casting the spell. It felt as if the spell was woven from every other participant, myself included.

It made my little twig enchantment look particularly pathetic.

Ikta clapped excitedly in Deniz's face. "You broke the rules of hospitality."

The vampire's face was twisted in confusion and anger as he stood frozen. At that moment, the vampire who had been sent falling to his death appeared through a portal, and everyone was bewildered.

I looked back towards the splattered vampire, finding shaggy white fur and a pair of goat horns amid the mess.

Ikta continued to clap excitedly while swirling around the frozen Deniz. "You broke the rules, even if I played you for the fools."

Herm laughed. "Serves you right for party crashing."

The Summer Queen stood and gave Ikta a bewildered look, likely trying to decide if she was friend or foe.

Too bad she was just crazy.

"Given that you were tricked, you will only be expelled. However, your inability to control yourself poses a risk for future parties. You are not welcome among the fae or our celebrations for the next century." The Summer Queen snapped her fingers, and the vampires disappeared.

Having seen what happened when the rules of hospitality were broken made me suddenly far more comfortable amid the party, although I was deeply aware of the trick Ikta had done. She knew how to play the game, and the other fae did as well. I needed to keep a sharp eye out for traps.

With the vampires gone, the party went back into full swing. Within moments, you'd never know an attack had just occurred.

I snagged a drink from a passing server as I waited for my adrenaline to slow. "Well, that was fun," I commented to Amira.

"My king, you have someone's attention," Amira said as Ikta and two of her nymphs walked over.

"Hello, Dragon King. I do hope that my choice pleased you. Though I cannot act against you, maybe one day you will let me bear thousands of dragons for you." Ikta licked her lips and bowed low, purposefully making her chest sway.

I struggled with what to say in return. She always was so blunt that it threw me off. Gathering my thoughts after a moment, I responded, "I'm pleased you got rid of the bloodsuckers. They are causing a lot of trouble in the city."

Ikta hummed to herself. "Are they now? I'd be more worried about the demon. Nasty little pests."

Raising my eyebrow, I waited to see if she'd say more. But she seemed to be distracted by the two queens. They had moved from their thrones and were walking the party, and Ikta skipped off to antagonize them.

I wanted to know what she was talking about with her demon comment, but with Ikta, nothing was ever straightforward. And whatever it was would emerge with time.

"My favorite son-in-law." Rupert wrapped a muscled arm around my shoulder and turned me to face several people of various races. "Meet Grim Darkshank and Tilly Flatbottom."

The dwarf and gnome watched me expectantly.

"Pleasure to meet both of you." I did a slight bow of my head in greetings.

"The famed Dragon King." Grim bowed. "You had said that you would hold none of our people's former grudges. I would like to know if you truly meant that." The man eyed Amira.

Amıra took the empty glass from my hand and replaced it with a full one. It was her own way of being affectionate. "Our king's words are the draconic laws. He has told the rest of us in the city not to exercise any grudge."

"Truly?" Tilly asked, his voice deeper than I expected for his small frame. I realized I'd expected him to sound like a child.

"There is no reason for me to hold those grudges. They are the past, and we can all move on together," I said calmly.

They both nodded.

"Well then, it has been a great pleasure to meet you."
Tilly held out his tiny hand nervously.

"It has been nice to meet you as well." His hand fit into
mine like a child's, and I pumped it gently. He tensed but
relaxed and let his hand rise and fall with mine.

I got the feeling that the handshake had been some sort
of test. I wondered if the dragons and gnomes were at such
odds that at one point a handshake could lead to attack.

"Are any bribes needed?" Grim asked.

I hadn't considered it. And a part of me wanted to say
yes and demand a mountain of gold, but given the tension,
I thought it better we start off on the right foot. "No."

My beast threw a fit in my chest, and I covered it up with
a smile.

"Huh." Grim traded a glance with Tilly and nodded.
"We believe you. Let bygones be bygones. That's what
humans say, right?"

It wasn't a modern phase, but I went with it. "Yep.
What's happened is in the past, and we will forge a new
future. I have no past history or grudges to carry from the
issues in the past, but I know there is still anger in my
people. And I'm sure in yours as well. Let's do our best to
not spark conflict."

Both of them nodded gravely, and I was left to wonder
again just how much damage our two groups had done
to each other. But the last thing I needed was another
enemy to deal with. Between vampire bloodlords, celestial
angels, Ikta, and a church that wanted to kill all of us, I had
enough problems.

I nodded to the group before Rupert released me. I noticed Ikta antagonizing the Winter Queen and headed that

way. Amira trailed along behind me, clearly my dragon guard for the moment.

"—according to the treaty your great great great grandmother laid out—"Ikta rambled on as I stepped up, only pausing to give me a slight glance out of the corner of her eye.

One of her nymphs gave me bedroom eyes that felt like she was about to suck out my soul.

"Cut that out," Winter snapped, breaking the glamor. "I'll not have you antagonizing Zach in my presence." She had a slight smile forming on her cold lips at having 'saved' me. I made sure not to thank her.

The Winter Queen eyed me. "How are you, Dragon King? It has been a while since we last met."

I couldn't resist. "You mean the time when you promised to help in the fight with Nat'alet only to back out at the last second after I was trapped inside?"

To her credit, she didn't so much as flinch.

"It was critical to the balance to restore part of my strength. These years with additional pressure from the world, Summer's strength threatens to overwhelm mine. To preserve the balance, I would go far." She paused and dipped her head. "But to you, I do owe you an apology. Please accept it."

"Apology accepted. Maeve has been working on your behalf to smooth things over." I wondered if I could twist that into another apology from her.

"Has she now?" Winter's gaze was downright chilling, but I was unsure if that was just natural.

"Winter, you didn't tell me you offended the Dragon King." Ikta laughed. "Zach, would you consider owing me a favor for solving her transgression?"

I wasn't sure what exactly 'solving her transgression' would entail, but I wasn't about to sic Ikta on Winter. "No, that's quite all right. I'll be the one to exact any of my own vengeance."

Ikta rubbed her hands together at the word vengeance. "Perfect."

"What of you two? Plotting world domination?" I asked the two queens.

"No such thing. This ancient relic was demanding that accords struck by my predecessors be acknowledged." Winter scowled at the Spider Queen who only batted her eyelashes in response.

"I'm not that old." Ikta tugged at her cheek, and it failed to produce any wrinkles as if that was proof.

If I understood one thing about the fae, they loved their beauty.

"You certainly don't look old. Though, maybe you are weaker. Half of your power was quite tasty," I teased Ikta. But if she was bothered by the loss of power, she didn't show it.

Instead, she just shrugged. "There are other parts of me that are tasty, or some say that my nymphs are the tastiest. The wild fae were famed for their fertility, unlike the other two." Her eyes flashed back to the Winter Queen. "I wonder if your populations are declining at all? Without the wild fae, how are you two keeping up your populations? Don't tell me you are using men of other races?"

My ears perked up. I'd been wondering about the myth that fae used human men for children. I wondered if there was any truth to it from what Ikta had just said.

"We have adapted," Winter was short with Ikta and turned back to me. "You have grown fond of my daughter?"

"Yes, though she's made a few missteps in the beginning, her genuine effort in working through that has made her an ally," I replied.

Both of the queens noted my words. Even the Summer Queen a few dozen feet away looked in my direction briefly. The queens all wanted my support. While it was nice to be wanted, the weight of each little decision I made weighed on me. I could imply the turning tide of wars based on the smallest comments.

"I sincerely hope that we can push past a slight mistake in the past and forge forward. At the time, I did not know what you would become," Winter replied, seeming to think that was a good reason for betraying my trust.

But I wasn't bothered. Instead, I was simply ready to use it to my advantage.

I scowled and pretended to be offended. "That you did not know I would shortly become the Dragon King has no bearing on what you did. You still abandoned me in a time of need."

Amira spoke up. "Even now you underestimate my king. He has the entire dragon race in lockstep with him. When you offend him, you offend all of us." She of course referred to my heritage.

Summer had seemed to notice after my return from the conclave, but I doubted Winter knew yet. I certainly wasn't advertising it.

"Amira," I scolded her, but she gave me a fiercely defiant glare.

"I will not stand for a smudge against your honor," she held her ground.

"You are relieved. Rotate with another of the honor guard," I demanded.

I needed to make a show of scolding her, even if it helped towards my cause.

Amira bowed out while Ikta giggled.

"Winter, you really don't know the fire you are playing with in upsetting the dragons. Maybe when you have your strength back, you'll understand," the Spider Queen teased.

"It seems I find myself making matters worse. I apologize for any slight I may have caused. Perhaps it is better to leave it at that." She dismissed me, no doubt hoping to avoid apologizing a third time.

But internally, I was pumping my fist high in the air. She had now apologized twice, and I just needed to twist the meaning of their parting gift.

Score one for the Dragon King. It was a minor victory, but I was far outmatched in trickery. Every victory counted.

Sarisha, in her brass chain dress, joined me as I continued through the party. She was far quieter than the other dragonettes, it was easy to forget about her.

The night had moved into full swing, and the fae were celebrating. An orgy developed off the side of the stage. Nymphs drew men of every race to them and rutted in a twisting pile of flesh amid a gully. I was glad that I'd been prepared that it would happen, or I would have been thrown off.

But I noticed that Ikta's nymphs and Maeve's assistant stayed out of the orgy, as did the queens and ladies of the fae.

After all, if they got with child, they'd find themselves married. While many of the fae would love just that, those with responsibility seemed to be more discerning.

# CHAPTER 19

The night and party had continued on without further incident, and attendance had thinned out while the now three orgies around the party blossomed. I could feel the party nearing its natural wrap up, and I was eager to see if I couldn't get my third apology from the Winter Queen.

"So, did you get two from my mother?" Maeve asked as her assistant made eyes at me from behind her.

"Maybe." I grinned. "Can I ask why you or your assistant aren't taking part in the orgies?" Not that I wanted her to, but I wanted to know.

"I have no desire to potentially marry any of those taking part," Maeve said simply. "Many of them are hoping to become pregnant and tie down a spouse. My mother has a husband, and though Summer's husband has passed, she has remained loyal to her deceased husband."

"What about your assistant?" The blue nymph made no attempt to hide naked desire as Maeve turned.

"She has other men in mind who are not currently participating. Plus, she is mine." Maeve narrowed her eyes on her assistant.

The nymph grinned. "What she means to say is that she saved my life by taking me in. I've willingly sworn myself to her, and in return, I get to satiate her desires if she is feeling them. Recently, she has needed my services more and more." The nymph wiggled her eyebrows at me.

Maeve's cheeks flushed before her eyes flashed with anger.

"Does that mean you're a package deal?" I asked, stepping in.

The nymph's cheeks blushed purple. "Yes, as I'm bound to serve Maeve. I would happily serve her future husband as well." Her glamor came up in full force as she batted her eyelashes at me.

"Do not glamor him," Maeve scolded her, though her tone was light.

"He practically asked me to," Evelyn complained. "I would share."

Sarisha coughed into her hand next to me. "Please do share with the dragons, too."

"Of course," Evelyn beamed. "I'm a nymph. Sharing isn't a problem."

Maeve glared at her for her words. This time, the look was harsher. "A Dragon King does not share. Do be careful with how he would interpret those words."

Evelyn's eyes went wide. "My apologies, mistress. I only meant that I would be more than happy to be amid a harem's writhing on the bed. Do you think my skin tone would look good amid your other mates?" The question was directed at me, and the little nymph was purposefully directing the conversation back towards sex.

Thankfully, something else drew us out of the cycle.

Just then, the Summer Queen clapped her hands, and little fireworks shot up into the air, growing in intensity until they lit up the night. I noted the effective way to get everybody's attention. The orgies slowed down and stopped to look up at the stage.

Summer and Winter stood from their thrones and stood before the audience.

"We thank all of you for joining us tonight. Our brief recess comes to a close shortly, and we have one last thing to do," Summer spoke first.

Winter picked up where she left off. "To celebrate all the dragons who have joined our party, we offer a gift and our thanks." She lifted her hand to the chandelier above, and it floated down towards me.

I watched it come down, wondering if I had enough room in my bracer to fit it. Because getting it put on the back of a large truck bed seemed excessive and dangerous.

"Morgana, would you be a dear and make this a little more carriable?" I had to raise my voice to reach my mate.

Morgana had no problem stepping forward and using her spatial magic to reduce the space that the chandelier took up. It created a strange paradox. Looking at it was almost uncomfortable, but I could grab hold of it and not smack everyone in the party.

There were murmurs around the group.

Morgana rarely showed off her spatial magic, but she had become more frivolous with it now that she had my blood. Its potency and availability allowed her to be free of guilt when using it. And in return, I feasted at her bar. The steak was to die for.

It was a win-win.

"I appreciate the gift to the dragon kind and the apology to me it represents." I took the chandelier in hand and drew it into my bracer as an enormous wave of magic crashed over the Winter Queen and myself.

She gasped as a connection was forged between us. Her silver eyes went nearly white with fury, and the surrounding crowd went completely silent.

"You," she hissed, but the effect was somewhat muted as Ikta started howling with laughter amid the silence.

Despite Ikta's outburst, the Winter Queen didn't lift her gaze from me.

Summer cleared her throat. "Well, what a way to end the party. And I am happy to see us cement the relationship between the fae and dragons." She tried to play it off as if the third thanks was on purpose.

It had the desired effect. The crowd collectively let out a breath and then cheered while the Winter Queen attempted to relax and not show her anger. But she never took her eyes off of me.

Maeve gave me a little finger wave across the party, but she didn't dare come over at that moment while her mother watched closely. And I couldn't blame her. I could only imagine how enraged her mother would be if she realized Maeve had helped coach me.

The dragonettes and my mates gathered around me protectively as the party came to a close, and we headed out.

"So, did you girls come to an agreement with Summer about the wedding?" I asked as we trooped back up the slope to the limo.

Many of them looked between each other, finally settling on Scarlett to give me the news.

"It will be complex, but with Summer's help in the Faerie realm, there should be no problem giving each of us the wedding we desire," Scarlett replied.

I swallowed around a lump in my throat. "Each of you is getting a wedding?"

Jadelyn laughed. "Look at him fret."

"Not exactly." Kelly clung to my arm and gave me puppy dog eyes. "But we want it to be perfect and have our own moment with you. We can say our vows thrice, and in Faerie realm, they will be compelling, so be prepared to make a bunch of vows. Otherwise, you just need to show up."

Nodding along, I accepted it as I filed into the waiting limo. "Not a problem. That is the least I could do for each of you."

Yev pulled my head to the side and kissed me as she got in. "Thank you, mate. I promise it won't be too hard, but it will be memorable for all of us."

While she was peppering me with kisses, someone else's hand was wandering up my thigh. Surrounded by my mates while also having the dragon ladies pumping out pheromones in the tight limo, I quickly came to attention.

Jadelyn knocked on the divider between us and the driver. The window slid open.

"Yes, Miss Scalewright?"

"Please drive around for a while. There's no rush getting back. Also, discretion would be preferred."

He nodded professionally and slid the window back up, keeping his face forward toward the road.

Then Jadelyn crawled across the floor towards me. "I always wanted to do it in the back of a limo."

My eyes flickered over to the line of dragonettes, who were holding their breath as Jadelyn continued crawling on the floor, coming up in front of me and nuzzling her face along my thigh into my lap.

A single note rang out of her throat as she looked up, filling my head with soft, silky pleasure. I was at hardened attention immediately.

"Jade, I love you." I cupped her face and ran my fingers through her soft hair.

"What about me?" Scarlett leaned over Jadelyn, trailing a kiss along my neck.

I knew Scarlett needed a little extra attention in the harem, so I pulled my Kitsune in close, crushing her to me as my hands wandered down to her hips and sought for the bottom of her dress.

My cock came out of my pants, and I felt Jadelyn go down on me as my hand went up Scarlett's dress and found no underwear.

She smiled into the kiss and captured my lip, holding me there as my fingers went to work.

There was moaning to my left as Yev pinned Kelly to the seat and asserted her dominance over the alpha wolf. I wondered who would be dominant among those two. I dominated both of them, but I wasn't sure who would shake out on top.

I craned my neck for a moment, only to have my face pulled back by Scarlett. She smiled at me as she captured my lips as she bounced on my fingers.

I let out a moan as Jadelyn trailed her tongue along me, leaning over and taking me deeper into her mouth. I found myself lost in the moment until a phone ringing startled me out of it.

Polydora picked the phone up off the seat and answered it in hushed tones.

Scarlett and Jadelyn ignored the call, continuing to kiss and suck on me.

I heard Polydora's voice hitch each time that Scarlett moaned and thrust herself down on me. I couldn't help but smile into my kiss with Scarlett.

"My king, it is the Agent Till," Polydora stated, clearly not pleased with having to interrupt me.

"Is it an emergency?" I pulled myself away from Scarlett for a moment.

"She sounds frantic," Polydora reported sheepishly.

I growled low enough to make the windows of the limo vibrate. "Get the details from her and direct the driver. I'm not to be disturbed until we are close."

A little of my frustration at being interrupted came through as I grabbed Jadelyn's head and thrust it down on me, hurrying her up. I came out of the moment enough that I noticed all the dragonette's staring at me with wide eyes.

I paused, feeling self-conscious for a moment. But after the orgies we had all just witnessed, I decided to let go of that awkwardness. Instead, I enjoyed their eyes, letting myself feel powerful.

I smiled at them as Jadelyn worked with my member. Maybe one day I'd line my honor guard up and fill them up one by one to brood.

The beast roared in my chest, demanding that I make 'one day' into 'today', but I pushed it aside. The current moment was for my mates.

Looking over, I noticed that Morgana had pushed Tyrande up under her dress and was sighing blissfully as the high elf lapped at her. Noticing my attention, she pulled down the top of her dress and began fondling her breasts, leaning back and moaning a little extra for me.

I could feel myself about to explode into Jadelyn as I watched.

Firm hands found my face, and I was once again looking deep into my Kitsune's eyes as she came on top of my fingers. Sinking down on top of me, she collapsed to the side, nuzzling and kissing my neck as Jadelyn worked to finish me off.

***

We pulled up to the location around twenty minutes later. It wasn't as long as I would have liked with my mates, but it had at least been enough to take the edge off.

Later, I'd grab my mates and take them back to my hoard.

Stepping out of the limo in front of a dark warehouse, I straightened my tie and shook out the sleeves of my suit.

"My king, she appears to have been attacked, along with her partner. For the moment, she has sequestered herself inside this building." Polydora stepped out of the limo alongside me.

My mates were laying lazily in the limo, seeming to have no interest in anything but enjoying their post orgasm bliss.

"Polydora, with me. The rest of you protect my mates."

The agent's BMW was parked up against the chain-link fence, right by a hole in the fence that looked as if it had been there for some time.

Frustrated at being disturbed, I went with the most direct route. I used a quick wash of my ice breath and froze the fence in front of me. Then I backhanded the brittle metal, breaking off a section large enough for me to duck through.

"What else do we know?" I asked Polydora.

"Not much. Agent Till said they had an encounter with very fast people. Vampires, I expect." Polydora ducked through the fence with me. "My king, what do you intend to do?"

"Kill anything that moves and pull the agent out of wherever she is hiding. Then I'll take my mates back to my hoard and enjoy the night as I had intended."

I tried to tell myself it was just a minor diversion, as I tried not to get upset at the agent for needing my assistance. It was necessary that I pull her out of this though. A dead FBI agent would be a colossal mess for the council.

The warehouse was closed up, but a lock wasn't going to stop me. I stepped up to one of the bay doors and shifted my fingers to golden claws. They sank easily through the sheet metal of the door, and I jerked the bottom.

I had expected to break the lock, but I ripped the bottom frame out of the lock with the screeching sound of tearing metal.

"You have alerted everything here to your presence," Polydora stated the obvious, and I rolled my eyes.

"Thanks, whatever would I do without you?" The sarcasm was dripping from my voice as I heard a rapid pitter patter of bare feet on the stone floor.

A haggard vampire came around the corner.

I didn't hesitate, pulling one of the twigs from my bracer and activating it. The vampire froze before it could move, and I stepped up to it to get a better look.

"Fresh," I said and reached over, opening its jaw before tearing out its two fangs. After learning the signs from Morgana, it was the first thing I checked.

Then I was curious about how the enchantment would do. I waited, seeing if the enchantment would hold, and it did. Smiling, I gave myself a mental pat on the back for good work before I tore the vampire's head from its shoulders.

I paused, acknowledging that some of that might have been left over with frustration at the interruption, but it was highly therapeutic.

"Kill all the vampires and keep their fangs intact if you can. It's possible one of them was the one that turned Maddie." I kept my focus on what was important.

"Yes, my king." Polydora stepped up to a forklift that looked like it had been left in mid-operation and ripped off one of the forks before crushing part of it in her grip to make a more manageable handle.

The bronze dragon now had a sword. Or maybe it was more like a metal bat. It didn't need to be that sharp with how hard she could swing it.

I was a little impressed with her quick thinking. "Come on." There was more noise amid the warehouse, and it seemed focused in one of the far corners.

"This place appears to have been in operation before this attack." Polydora noted. It felt like fork trucks and pallets of material were suspended in the middle of a workday rather than being put away.

"No," I disagreed. "This was in operation before it was set up as a death trap for Agent Till."

The whole situation reminded me of the abandoned apartment building.

"The war tactic that Morgana mentioned?" Polydora asked before assessing the situation. "I suspect it would be highly effective if someone else hadn't already sprung the trap."

I was more concerned that whoever was behind the attacks had turned everyone in an active warehouse. It was far less subtle than an abandoned apartment, and it was much more likely to draw human attention.

The urge to just wipe out all the vampires on my own was growing as we walked through the large metal rack. Moving towards the corner, we approached a partition in the warehouse. From what I could see, there were over a dozen vampires scrabbling over and around what looked like a freezer door.

Many of them were wearing reflective vests and hard-hats, only confirming my theory that the location had been recently turned and left as a trap.

Polydora held out her 'sword' for me to hold.

I took it, and she took off her dress, handing it to me as she started to shift. I tried not to look, but it was hard not to as the beautiful woman shimmied out of her dress.

Polydora gained little height, but she filled out and packed on muscle underneath a new scaly armor.

Then she held out her hand for her sword back. "I will be only a moment, my king. Please keep my dress safe. I like this one."

I nodded dumbly as she stalked forward like a big cat, ready to pounce. Although, the large forklift sword she was carrying made her look far more deadly.

The first vampire to turn and lunge for her was torn in half by the blunt sword, and it was messy. The vampire's entire midsection went missing with a casual swing of Polydora's weapon.

I wasn't sure if it had been on purpose, but the blunt blade caused maximum carnage. I knew at a single glance that the vampire's healing would be strained with wounds caused by the heavy blow.

The rest of the vampires present turned instantly, aware of the danger now among them. They moved to attack Polydora as one.

The Amazonian dragon stepped around casually, almost as if she were practicing a dance in the privacy of her home. But as she moved, her weapon swung out, catching vampires with each swing and tearing them apart.

Not a single one got close to touching her.

It was almost beautiful in a gory way to watch her fight. The dragon in me smiled in satisfaction to see how effortlessly she tore apart the dozen vampires.

I was still watching with a slack jaw as she finished and whipped her weapon to the side to splash a little blood off of it and away from her.

"What would you have me do now, my king?" Polydora put her hand on her hip and cocked it to the side with a raised eyebrow.

It took me a moment before I was able to speak. "Pop the door open. I don't think we need to hide ourselves anymore. It sounds like our friend Agent Till just got a crash course in the paranormal."

# CHAPTER 20

Polydora smirked and stepped up to the freezer door, stabbing her weapon into the frame and using it as a pry bar. In one fluid movement, she peeled back the metal door.

I paused at the loud noise, bracing for any vampires that might come out of hiding, but nothing stirred.

Polydora ripped the door off and stood to the side.

I called in before I stepped into the doorway. "Agent Till? We got a call for a Silverwing Mercenary pickup?"

"Fuck. Is that you, Zach?" The agent held her gun out and crept forward, shivering from the cold.

I put myself in the doorway so that she could see me. "Please put down the gun. I'd rather you not accidentally shoot me." Just in case, I covered the parts of my body under my suit in gold scales.

"You wouldn't believe wh—"Her eyes went wide as she caught sight of Polydora in her dragon knight form. "Behind you!" She raised her gun and fired off three times at my guard as Polydora was picking the teeth from the fallen vampires.

Thankfully, dragons weren't bothered by a 9mm round. All three bounced off of Polydora. Polydora glared at Agent Till.

"Cease your fire before you harm my king." Polydora slammed a wave of her fear aura into the agent, and I groaned. It felt a little excessive. Agent Till was clearly already about to pee herself.

Till stuttered and dropped her gun. "Wha-what?"

I motioned for Polydora to stand down before I walked over and picked up the gun. Removing the magazine and round in the chamber, I handed it back to Agent Till.

"Please don't shoot my guard. Poly does good work, and she'd be damn hard to replace."

The dragonette in question snapped to look at me, tilting her head. She'd noticed that I had shortened her name. And based on her face, she wasn't sure what to make of it.

"Guard?" Till came out of the freezer, and I lifted a hand to create a small magical light.

There was blood splattered over her face and chest, and I quickly did a scan of her body. She didn't look harmed. "What the hell happened to you?"

Agent Till looked around, taking in all the dead bodies around her that were somewhat mashed, then refocusing on the glowing ball of magic.

Her eyes grew wider as she went into shock. Her expression became almost glazed as she looked up at me and focused back on my question. "These people moved so fast. One got in the freezer with me. I shot her in the head at point blank range." She wiped at her face. "It got messy."

"Don't touch it." I was suddenly worried that vampire blood had gotten into her mouth.

"She'll be fine. It takes a significant reduction in blood before vampire blood can be effective," Polydora informed me, guessing where my mind was going.

"Vampire blood?" Till commented, her eyes once again finding the dead bodies scattered around, looking at Poly, and then she just sat down on the ground. "What is all this?"

Poly held up her forklift sword. "I made a mess, too. They were vampires."

Agent Till was quiet for a long moment.

"Okay, let's suppose I believe vampires are real." She looked up at the bronze dragon. "Then what are you?"

"I'm a dragon. This is my hybrid form; my kind are capable of shape shifting."

Looking around, I saw no additional danger. "Why don't we get you back to normal and get out of here? I need to call for a cleanup crew."

Polydora stabbed her weapon into the ground and shifted back into a naked woman with thick black hair, cut right at her shoulders. "My dress, please?"

I handed it to her, and she slipped the bronze chain dress back on.

Having held it, I could confirm it was indeed made completely of the metal, which now made me appreciate just how well it was tailored to her.

Till watched with wide eyes. "Dragon." Then she looked at me. "Dragon king?" Pieces were falling into place for her. Even if she was bombarded with the sudden situation, she was an investigator to her core.

I only smiled. "Come on. You weren't supposed to know any of this. Whoever made this trap for you broke a lot of rules tonight. Where is your partner?"

"They took her," Till said.

I stopped in my tracks. "They took her? I don't believe it."

"Why no— oh, she's something too, isn't she? That's how you two know each other." Till started seeming to come back together, her mind working through the pieces and making sense of everything.

At least it calmed her down having a puzzle to solve.

"What is Helena?" she asked calmly. She seemed to take all of it much better than Maddie. But she'd seen many types of humanity through her work; she'd likely already come to terms with the monstrosity that humans could become. Now she just had actual monsters.

"An angel, or nephilim, if you wish to differentiate between the two. She was born of a union with a human, which makes her an angel, but she is tied to earth rather than the celestial plane." I tried to keep my explanation simple as we walked back through the warehouse. Then I pulled out my phone to text Detective Fox, hoping he wasn't too drunk on fae wine to assist.

I had a feeling this was going to become an enormous case for the police department. What a headache.

"They still took her. There were some that weren't crazy like the rest," Agent Till replied, seeming to be back to her old self.

"Did you get a good look at them?" I got excited. If she'd seen who had set the trap, it could speed along our investigation. "Also, what were you both doing in this warehouse?"

Till scowled at me. "I'm the one who should ask the questions, and this is an active case." She hesitated. "But since we just killed a dozen people in there, and you are calling a cleanup crew, we are completely off the reservation, I suppose."

Till scowled again. "We were tracking our case, and for whatever reason, the congressman had visited this warehouse several times. He also had a major stake in the business. We came to investigate."

I frowned. Politicians were often businessmen before they took office. "What's so odd about him owning a food warehouse?"

"It wasn't in his declaration. And when we tried to call them, no one answered. So we drove out here, noticing that it looked recently abandoned," Till explained.

"Then you went in and bam, vampire ambush," I simplified, not needing to hold back as a growl rumbled in my throat like a jet engine starting up.

The agent watched me closely. "That was far too loud to be you."

"Oh. I get a hell of a lot bigger when I'm pissed off." I couldn't help the smile that broke out across my face. "You won't like me when I'm angry."

"Did you just—"

I held up a hand to cut off the agent. "So, the vampires attacked. What happened to Helena?"

"Well, we were walking through, and suddenly, the wild ones came out of the metal racks. And then two men and one woman just appeared. You said they're vampires? Does that mean super speed? They were just a blur, and then they were there."

"Supernatural speed. We aren't in a superhero movie. But yes, they do. And the ones you call wild were recently turned and likely were starved to set that warehouse up as a trap."

We stepped out into the light, out of the warehouse as I prompted Agent Till to continue. "So you had three, and they managed to get Helena on their own? An angel is very strong, especially one tuned to earth like Helena."

"You sound like you know from experience," Till stated with a raised eyebrow.

I scratched the back of my head. "We may have gotten into a few tussles over a situation in Switzerland. She's pretty freaking tough; I threw her through a lot of walls."

Till just blinked several times, seeming to not know what to say. "Okay. But they still held her and bound her before hauling her off. I don't know how they did it. Magic maybe?"

I grunted, deciding not to show off my lack of magical knowledge. "We'll figure this out. If I get you in front of one of Detective Fox's sketch artists, can you get me a sketch?"

"Definitely," she replied, her detective voice back in full force. But then she noticed the limo for the first time. "So, did I interrupt a party?"

"Sort of." I grinned, and Polydora stepped ahead to open the door.

My mates were lazing about inside, restoring their energy for when I got back. The limo clearly smelled of sex, and more than a few of them had their dresses askew.

"Ah," Till commented dryly.

"The Dragon King has a responsibility to sire many children," Polydora stated proudly, as if that explained everything.

"Agent Till?" Scarlett sat up quickly, her tails disappearing.

"It's okay, Scar, some vampires let that cat out of the bag."

Scarlett nodded as her ears and tails popped back into existence. "Shit. What happened?"

"We can get into that later." I crawled into the limo, snatching Tyrande off her seat to put her on my lap before turning back to Scarlett. "Text your dad to have a sketch artist ready tomorrow morning. Tonight, I'm taking my mates back to my hoard for some much-deserved fun."

Polydora scooted Agent Till to join the rest of the dragonettes in the limo while I pulled my mates around me.

\*\*\*

We were sitting in the Scalewright's main parlor. Breakfast was well underway, and I was on steak number five, after a few plates of waffles, of course.

"Rounder face and a little sharper nose," the agent directed the sketch artist. She glanced over at me with a strange look.

Till had been doing that all morning after Poly essentially held her under house arrest in Morgana's room.

I was unsure if it was the amount of food I ate or my weary mates, but something had made an impression on her.

The sketch artist made the changes and showed it to her again. "Yes, that's her face. And then she had hair down to about here." She pointed at the paper.

Till returned to watching me.

Scarlett shifted uncomfortably in her chair, and that took my attention away from the agent.

"Everything okay, Scar?"

"Yeah." She scratched at the base of her tails. "Just so itchy. I haven't been this itchy since I grew my second tail."

"When do you normally get your third?"

"When I'm thirty, so a while. Maybe I need to go see a doctor." She grunted and scratched at the base of her tails again.

I looked over at Trina, who was standing in a line with the other dragonettes as they surveyed the area. Jadelyn's security team always made them try to act a little more official.

But before I could call her over, Detective Fox walked into the room and smiled at me. "The emergency council meeting will begin in half an hour."

"What do I do about her?" I pointed to Till.

"The council will decide her fate," he said low enough that the agent didn't hear.

I nodded and raised my voice. "Is the sketch done?"

"Yes, sir." The sketch artist was a siren, and he raised the clipboard to show us a woman.

I gasped. "I know her. She was the woman at Deniz's club that he fed on for his little sex show. Get the other two sketched out. Maybe we can nail Deniz." My excitement built.

"Let me see." Trina came off her position by the wall and grabbed the clipboard. "That's the woman. So, she's been turned since the show."

Detective Fox rubbed at his stubble. "That changes things. We'll present this to the council. Though Deniz will probably show up and contest this."

"I can't wait to see how he tries to weasel out of this." His head would look nice on a platter, maybe one made of gold.

"You cannot go killing people unless they are guilty, my mate." Scarlett rubbed my back, trying to calm me down.

Grumbling, I leaned back in my chair. "We watched him feed on this woman. The vampires completely shifted their behaviors when he came to town."

"It's not enough," Agent Till spoke up. "That's barely even circumstantial. You need much more than that to be sure he's guilty."

"I didn't ask you," I growled at the agent, annoyed at her logic.

She tossed her hands up and rolled her eyes. "Well, excuse me for being practical. I thought you were some kingly big shot around here. But you must just want to surround yourself with beautiful little fuck dolls and yes men."

The next thing I knew, Till was rocketing across the room and crashing into the wall.

"I threw you softly," Amira said, straightening her clothes and walking over to a groaning Till. "Don't act like a baby."

"Amira." I narrowed my eyes at the black dragon.

"She is welcome to say what she wants, but to insult you is not something I'll tolerate. She'll just have to find another way to criticize you." The black dragon shrugged off my glare.

Till rolled over on her side. "Fuck. Okay, I take back the fuck dolls."

Amira hoisted the agent off the ground with one hand as if she weighed nothing. "I wish to be the king's fuck doll. Do not take that one away."

Till only looked at me with a bewildered expression. "Help?"

I tried not to laugh.

"Lay on the couch." Amira hustled the agent back on the couch and then her hands glowed a dangerous looking purple as she pushed magic into the agent.

"Oooh. That's worse than being thrown." Till let out a sharp cry.

"Healing is often worse than getting injured," Amira agreed. "I like to think it makes the lessons more pronounced."

Satisfied that the agent would be okay, I replayed what she'd said, trying to figure out if it was true. Was I really surrounded by so many people eager to please me that I wasn't getting valuable information anymore?

There was a moment of uncertainty before I felt confident that she was wrong. My mates were more than willing to spare my feelings and tell me the truth. What Agent Till saw was their more submissive side in public.

"Agent. I guarantee that my mates and the dragonettes are quite capable of bringing me back to reality, though they do so in private. Among my people, I am king, and among the paranormal community, my people are respected. As you can see, my honor guard is more than happy to defend me, so please choose your words more wisely."

Till rubbed her head as Amira stepped back. "I'll take that under advisement. Are you going to go all murder-dragon on Mr. Wallachia?"

"My course of action is still to be determined. But Deniz is a vampire, and he comes from an area that recently angered dragonkind," I gave her the shortened background.

"So, it's personal. That means there's even more reason to be absolutely sure before going after him," Agent Till said. "Can vampires kill a dragon?"

I grew a little angry even thinking about it. "They can with an enchanted fighter jet when the dragon was traveling a long distance to an important gathering."

Till just made a round 'O' with her mouth. "Right. Magically enhanced fighter jets are the level of munitions required to take a dragon out."

"The king would require far more," Polydora interjected. "Thalia, though older, was less than half the size of our king."

Till's curiosity was passing the professional line. "How big exactly is your king?"

Some of the girls giggled, and Detective Fox decided it was time to leave.

"I'll come get you when the council is gathering," he muttered over his shoulder.

"Thank you, father-in-law," I quickly shot back before he left. "Now, Agent Till, despite your amusing curiosity, there are two more sketches you need to finish before our council meeting. We can discuss everything else later if there is time."

My mates were still snickering as I went back to my food and the agent worked with the sketch artist again.

"So, Zach, there is a little rumor going around from the dragonettes that you have an elemental living in your hoard. I did not see it last night," Tyrande started up a conversation.

I nodded. "The gold I collected with my adoptive father might have something to do with that. It disappeared, and Herm believes that it might have collected enough mana to become an elemental of gold. It would match the description of what I saw."

That caught more than a few girls' attention.

"A gold elemental?" Yev asked, her eyes glittering. "I want to see it!"

"We can go search for it later; the council meeting will start soon," I replied, my dragon desperately wanting to hunt with its mate through the gold.

"And we all know that if we let him go play in his hoard, we'll have to drag him out to get to the council meeting. The meeting he called." Jadelyn gave me a knowing look, her lips pursed in amusement.

I shrugged. "I like my gold as much as my mates."

Kelly frowned at me. "I'm unsure if I'm supposed to be offended that he likes gold as much as me, or honored that a dragon likes me as much as gold."

"Honored," Trina piped up. "There's nothing a dragon loves as much as gold. That you are on the same level means that he really loves you all." She managed to keep any bitterness out of her tone.

# CHAPTER 21

I was holding copies of the other sketches that had been made from Agent Till's description of the vampires with a frown plastered on my face.

They weren't who I'd hoped to see. If anything, they gave more credence to Deniz's claim that there was a problem among the vampires, but it wasn't related to him at all.

In my hand was a sketch of a man that Morgana informed me was Ricardo's number two and Ricardo himself. That, along with the woman that Deniz had turned, made for a rather unfortunate picture of someone working behind Deniz's back.

The well-connected Turkish vampire certainly had created enough motive for Ricardo. When I explained the situation to Agent Till, she had said that was enough motive to make him a suspect over Deniz.

I still wasn't sure how her case of the sex demon attack had brought her to a warehouse full of vampires, but it showed that the two were somehow connected.

As I studied the photos, the rest of the council were being handed the same images.

Sebastian sat down at his seat, taking the copies and scowling over at me. "Let's get this going. I have important things to do today. It seems we have two major issues to deal with; why don't we deal with the most important one first."

I was nodding along with him, but then paused when he didn't give me the floor.

"A human has become informed of the paranormal. Those who broke the laws that have kept us all safe for hundreds of years were swiftly killed, but now an FBI agent has been brought here with knowledge of who and what we are." He waved his hands, and one guard brought Agent Till into the circular ring below us.

She paused and stared around the circle at the shadows arrayed before her. "I am here investigating a case, and I would like to request your help—"

"Silence," Sebastian snapped. "You do not speak. You have no master, nor are you paranormal. You have no voice among those of us here."

I winced. She had started as we had coached her, but the situation had flipped on its head because the elves were too stuck in their ways.

Till did not look amused at his statement.

Sebastian continued. "She should be executed to preserve our secrecy."

"No. In this, you are wrong, Sebastian," I barked, causing a silence to fall over the council. "She's a federal agent looking into the death of a federal legislator. If you kill her, it will only bring an army of investigators into our city looking into what is already a paranormal crime."

The elf grimaced. "So, you have failed. Detective Fox has failed to keep the paranormal out of the focus of this investigation."

"You are going to pretend as if you have no duty among this council to preserve the paranormal? Another building was filled with freshly turned vampires. That was the reason for Agent Till's knowledge of paranormals. And also has now led to Helena's kidnapping, an angel who came to this council for support and was given such," I reminded him.

I didn't think Sebastian was working with the vampires, but his bigotry might just end up killing Agent Till and bringing a bigger headache to my city.

The elf turned his nose up at me. "I don't see you taking custody of this human."

"You didn't give me much of a chance. You hurried straight towards eliminating the threat. Interesting for an elf to be more bloodthirsty than a dragon." Even as I said it, I knew some of my anger was from the grudge I held. The elves' choice to duel me to the death on my first day in the paranormal world wasn't exactly a warm welcome.

"Then, by all means." Sebastian gestured down to the agent.

I cleared my throat. "Agent Till. Per our customs, a human can only be a part of our paranormal society if one of us takes them in. Any mistake you make would be on me. Among paranormal customs, you would be mine."

Her eyes widened. "As in a servant?"

I paused before answering. "This clause was customarily used for servants and wives."

She scowled at me, but I wasn't the one who set history. The best I could do was move forward and try to help protect her.

"So, would you consent to becoming my servant in the eyes of the paranormal community?" I certainly would not ask her to become my wife.

"Well, if that's the only way to stay alive, then I suppose I'll say yes. I'd hardly call this consent in the legal form, though," she remarked dryly.

Sebastian hissed. "She already shows disrespect for our laws. I hope that this doesn't come back to harm you, Dragon King."

"Now that she is under my care, let's hear what she has to say. Please, Agent Till, continue," I urged her.

She shot me an eye roll before continuing. "My partner, Helena, and I were attacked last night when entering a warehouse for the case. I'm told my partner is an angel. I watched as she was captured by the vampires in the sketches that have been distributed. I was forced to lock myself in a freezer to survive, and then I called Zach to see if he could get me out."

I picked up the conversation. "Two of the three vampires are likely known to many of you. Ricardo and his right hand. The woman was last seen as a human being fed on by Deniz. Ricardo may have turned her after that feeding, or she could have been turned by someone else. We don't have that information right now.

With no objections, I continued. "Agent Till will work with Detective Fox and me as we try to locate Ricardo and his associates."

"Am I late?" Deniz trooped up into the council meeting. He ripped the sketches from the gnome leader, Tilly's hands. "What is this?"

"Ricardo was seen at a warehouse full of freshly turned vampires last night." I decided to provide as few details as possible. "He is currently the subject of this meeting."

"I have not seen him for a few days. I figured he was licking his wounded pride at losing his role in the city."

Deniz shrugged. "Is he the one responsible for the current mess?"

Kelly snorted. "You tell me. Aren't you the one working on investigating it yourself?" She was rightfully pissed and glaring at the vampire.

The rest of the council was waiting for his response.

"We have only just started." Deniz shrugged. "I was not aware it was this bad. But as the investigator on the case, I would have thought I would have been pulled in as soon as such a finding occurred, and not at the council meeting."

Rupert cleared his throat and spoke calmly, trying to keep the peace. "It would seem that Ricardo's actions have attracted the attention of the FBI. To prevent further investigation, we need to solve this with the agent below. She is now the servant of Zach Pendragon. Using his connections, we can hopefully prevent a larger investigation."

Deniz looked between the agent and me, frowning. "I see. I will have my people look for Ricardo."

Kelly scoffed again. "I would like to suggest that the entire council put in their efforts on actively tracking down all vampires in the city. We need to act swiftly. Cordon all vampires off to safe spaces and purge the rest of the city of vampires. We cannot be sure there aren't more of these buildings stuffed with starving vampires."

"What?!" Deniz spun back on her.

"Keep your people in your club and nothing bad will happen to them." Kelly said without an ounce of remorse. "Anything outside your club becomes fair game. This needs to be solved quickly, and an investigation risks more trouble. The werewolves would be willing to participate in a clean sweep of the city."

I cleared my throat. "That may be extreme, but we can plan that for the near future, Kelly. Allow me at least another day to investigate this and solve it with a little less force. But everyone should be on the lookout for Ricardo."

My werewolf mate was blood thirsty today.

"If it is not solved by the end of tomorrow, I vote we sweep the city," Rupert offered.

Several others among the council agreed to the motion. Deniz stepped over, bickering with Kelly as Rupert motioned me over.

"We'll delay my party because of this mess. We shall have it in three days. My wife would not be pleased to have it overshadowed." He grimaced.

I nodded. "Probably for the best. Either way, we'll hopefully have an answer by then. Either we sweep the city, or we find the source."

The old siren pressed his lips together. "Yes, let's hope we don't have to sweep the city. It can be dangerous for everyone involved. But we must preserve our secrecy."

This situation was definitely reinforcing with me the need to keep abilities and magic under wraps. Little by little, our secret was unraveling.

I looked over and noticed Trina was walking up the steps with Agent Till in tow.

The agent was not pleased as she crossed her arms and glared at me. "So, do I call you 'Master' while batting my eyelashes now?"

"It wouldn't hurt, but you don't have to." I couldn't help myself, enjoying the fire that sparked in her eyes.

Chuckling, I focused back on the issue. We needed to hurry. "Agent, I'm as invested in solving this as you are. We need to track down these vampires and your partner. I'm concerned about why they would want her. Do you have any theories?"

Till stopped being so prickly about the new status the paranormal council had thrust on her and focused back on the case. "Well, we have this representative, who I now assume was killed by paranormal means?"

"Demon or angel," I informed her. "They feed off of someone through their emotions."

"Like Helena?" Till blinked.

"Yes, though she's bound to earth, not another plane. I was under the impression she didn't need to feed to recover her mana as a result. But she might be capable of it." I hadn't thought about that before.

In Sentarshaden, I'd learned she was the daughter of the archangel of love. So I had to assume she had such abilities.

"Are they common?" Till asked.

"Not at all. Sabrina is the only registered demon in the city, but there very well could be another. The angels were either sealed off or went to ground this winter," I explained, once again a bit stuck without many threads to pull on.

"Why did they go to ground?" Till asked, her investigative nature once again coming into the discussion.

"Because they became my enemy. I destroyed one of their large strongholds and sealed the celestial plane. With Morgana's help," I added. "What about this business? Were there other owners?"

Till nodded and pulled out her phone to swipe through it. "There were, but none of them flagged when we looked into them."

"What about our accountant and soccer coach? Did they have any relation to this business?" I pushed her.

"What was the soccer coach's last name?" she asked, looking at her phone.

"Garrison," I remembered from the folders.

She typed for a moment and then held up the screen for me to see. There was an email with the list of major shareholders and the congressman was highlighted. "Think he has any relationship with Susan Garrison? She's another large shareholder of the warehousing company."

"The accountant. Any shares?" I realized this could be the connection.

But Till shook her head. "But he could be doing their books. Actually, I'd bet on him being their bookkeeper."

The circumstances certainly were lining up. This company was missing from the representative's declaration, and the soccer coach's wife had a large stake in. "What do you think this business was for?"

"Who knows? Drugs, money laundering, smuggling, or even human trafficking are all open with a warehouse," Till rambled off a list.

"Helpful," I said dryly. "Let's head on down to the station and see what we can figure out about Mrs. Garrison before we pay her a visit."

Looking around, I collected Sabrina, and Larisa fell into line behind me.

"What kind of dragon is the pipsqueak?" Agent Till asked. The white dragon was barely breaking five feet tall, but she was the second oldest of the dragonettes.

Larisa glared daggers at her. "You'd barely fill the gaps between my teeth. Remember that before you call me small. I'm a white, and I have no problem turning you into a popsicle for me to munch on."

"Wouldn't be very tasty," I commented. Dragons loved the taste of mana, and Till was the epitome of human.

My guard snorted. "Be thankful that my king wants you around for now."

Till raised an eyebrow at me for her attitude. "And the demon?"

"She's great with magic," I said honestly. Even though we had a few dragons around, none of them really seemed to have Sabrina's academic expertise.

"Thank you." Sabrina blushed a deep scarlet and looked down at her feet as she followed along. "Not many people think of that first," she mumbled under her breath.

I frowned, trying to understand what she meant.

Reaching out my arm, I pulled her a little further ahead of Till and Larisa as we left the council chambers and moved down the Atrium towards the coffee shop.

Waving a hand behind me, I gave Larisa the signal that I wanted a moment of privacy with Sabrina.

"What did you mean, people don't think of that first?" I asked the blushing succubus. "You are amazing at magic. It's no wonder that Sir Benifolt took an interest in teaching you."

The British wizard was supposedly one of the most brilliant minds among human magi. He took in the succubus as an apprentice before I met her.

"Yeah. There you go again. You are talking about my brain, my skills and not— not my nature." She couldn't meet my eyes as she stumbled over the words.

"That you're a succubus?" I pushed to the heart of the issue. "What does that have to do with anything?"

Sabrina stared up at me through her glasses, which she used to suppress her sex demon nature. "Because my succubus nature is all anyone ever sees."

She frowned when I didn't seem to get it. "They see my chest, my body and what it can do, but they never see me as someone with a brain. Zach, a low-level succubus like me in hell is not treated much better than a fuck doll, a prostitute at best." She met my eyes, searching them for something. "Even when I became a wizard, when people found out about it, once again I was viewed as sexual and nothing more."

"Oh. Well, I don't see you that way. And we are certainly not in hell," I offered. "And I'll bet you managed to leave hell with your brain, not your charms."

I had noticed that her baggy clothes had been getting slightly tighter the last few days and her skirt was now above her knee. While she didn't want to be seen purely sexually, she was getting more comfortable showing her body.

Sabrina smiled beautifully. "I did. A horny teenager summoned me into his dreams, and I led him to make a summoning circle amid an area rich with mana. I structured it so it should last a very long time. Then I came out and made it as permanent as I could."

I raised an eyebrow. "Summoning circle. Does that mean that there's someone out there with power over you?"

"No." She shook her head vehemently. "He died." Her eyes became saucers as she realized how it sounded. "But not by me! It was gang related violence. And he had no control over me, anyway. After I was summoned, I wanted to stay here. I'd been working on more and more complex magic. It's just so fun to take a magical puzzle and work through it. Every time a piece fits perfectly into place, there is this rush. I— I just can't explain how great it feels."

The nerdy succubus couldn't stop grinning as she thought about practicing magic.

It was infectious, and I smiled back at her. "Then I'm glad you are the one teaching me. One day, I bet you'll be the best wizard out there." I made sure to emphasize that she was a wizard and not a succubus.

Sabrina paused and put a hand on her glasses, lifting them slightly off her face. Horns appeared above her brow and her skin was dusted with a slight pink tone.

I was sucker punched by a desire to pin her up against the wall and rut her through it, making her moan and scream my name endlessly. But I reined that in and clenched my jaw, forcing myself to meet her pink eyes as they drew me in like two pools of overflowing lust.

"I am a succubus, though, Zach," she reminded me.

Grunting, I kept myself in check. "Well aware. But I might suggest not doing that if you don't want a bite mark on your neck. It seems I'm a little susceptible to you." My body was rigid as I tried to stay in control.

"You are overflowing with lust." Sabrina studied me as she put a hand on my chest. Her breath was a faint pink fog that seemed to push everything else out of focus and make her beauty crystal clear. Her curves magnified to the point that I couldn't help myself. I wanted to touch them.

She smiled as I pushed my lips to hers. Sabrina was so sweet it made my body ache. I wanted more. Pushing her up against the wall, I began running my fingers over every inch of her as I rubbed myself against her.

Her mouth pried mine open, and I felt a whoosh of relief and ecstasy rip itself from every inch of my body.

The rigidness faded, and I relaxed, still completely enamored with the succubus in front of me. But this time, I wanted to savor her for decades rather than crush her with my desire.

She pulled away, a thin gold stream coming from my mouth to hers.

"Feel better?" she asked.

"Much." I blinked several times. Now, even when she was still a succubus, I was able to resist and control myself. "What was that?"

Her eyes had little gold flecks in them now, and she blushed a deeper pink. "I wanted to taste you directly. W-was that too much? Oh no, I fucked this up." She pulled at her hair, clearly in distress.

"It was fine. A wonderful kiss." I used my hand to push her glasses back up on her face. "But maybe I'd like to kiss this Sabrina." Then I kissed the nerdy succubus again. She still sucked on my lust, but there wasn't the overwhelming need to rut her into the wall.

She looked stupefied. "You don't like me as a succubus?"

"Oh, don't misunderstand this. I like both forms, and definitely am turned on by your succubus form. But if you do that again, prepare to be marked by me. This Sabrina is brilliant on the streets. But if you ever want to let loose in the sheets... you have my permission," I teased her as she blushed even deeper pink and gave me a small nod with a smile lingering on her face.

"I'll hold you to that," she breathed.

Till cleared her throat, reminding me of their presence, only to be smacked by Larisa.

"Do not fucking ruin it. That was hot as hell, and I, for one, want the succubus to make my king fuck her until she's pregnant."

Till looked flabbergasted, and I jumped into the conversation.

"The moment is over. Let's keep going."

# CHAPTER 22

I led the group into the coffee shop and got in line for another Dragon King special.

"They named a drink after me here," I proudly told my group, wanting a little caffeine in my system as we dug into our research.

Till snorted. "Wait, are they... something too?" She caught herself.

"Silvani," Sabrina whispered. "They protect and tend small areas of wilderness. Absolutely magical farmers."

"And have the tastiest coffee," I added as we moved up in line.

We were being quiet. The hipsters seemed to have a penchant for eavesdropping, but even then, we were being subtle enough that I doubted they'd make any connections.

The line moved forward, and I ordered the Dragon King special. It was still trendy apparently. The rest of the group ordered one as well, and we continued over to the station.

"Wow." Sabrina took her first sip and her eyes briefly glowed.

The barista had given our entire group special beans.

"It can't be that good," Till took a sip and stumbled. She would have collapsed if I didn't catch her. "Holy shit.

I feel like someone just blasted my brain with caffeine." She shook from head to toe. "Someone else will need to finish it for me. One sip is all I need."

Larisa snatched it away and took a deep drink. "Fantastic. Really shakes off the icicles."

Till stared at the small dragon as Larisa pounded down the coffee. "Are you going to be okay with two of those?"

"Yep." Larisa drank from her other cup with a big grin. "Normal coffee does nothing to me. This stuff, though, it packs a lovely punch."

"Are dragons resistant to drugs?" Till asked while we crossed the street.

"Think of it more like we are ten-ton lizards stuffed in a human body. A bit of caffeine is like a drop in the ocean. It just isn't a big enough dose," Larisa explained.

"How does—" Till started.

I cut her off. "Magic. It's the simple answer to most of your questions."

Agent Till grumbled as she marched into the police station, waving her badge at the front desk. The door buzzed and clattered open as she jerked it and marched through the bullpen while the three of us kept up. She turned down a hallway to an office with Detective Fox's name on the door.

"He said I was welcome to it."

"I'm sure he really meant it." I rolled my eyes.

Ignoring my comment, she sat down and clicked around on the home screen until the badge in the background changed to one matching the one on her waist. Till continued to log in to the portal.

When her desktop background came up, I bent over in laughter.

"What?" She scowled at me. "What's wrong?"

"Your background is just a flat blue color. No photos?" I laughed. "Not even like your badge or your gun? You have to have something."

Till scoffed. "No. This is for work. I don't need to have anything on my computer. I need to focus." Her statement sounded more like an excuse than a reason.

"Oh. We could put one of the plushies as her background." Larisa pulled out her phone and started tapping on it.

"Plushies?" I asked at the same time as Till.

Larisa and Sabrina looked back and forth at each other until Sabrina sighed.

"Jadelyn has been getting all of your harem hopefuls little gold dragon plushies as a sort of welcome gift." She held her hands up as if I needed a reference for its size.

"Fuck no," Till growled, still watching her monitor. "Don't you even dare give me one of those, or make it my background."

The way Larisa giggled had me thinking the agent was now almost certainly going to get one.

"Let's get down to business." Agent Till clicked on the screen. "Look at this. Susan Garrison. She's our girl, and damn is she loaded." Agent Till scrolled down through several articles on the woman.

Many of the articles included photos of Susan wearing fancy dresses on the arms of the soccer coach, who was wearing a tux. It definitely rang of wealth.

"She seems pretty well off. If her husband was into something criminal, it doesn't look like it's for the money," I replied. "Unless, of course, her money is from her husband's illegal activities, but then why is he a soccer coach?" I asked no one in particular.

One article directly mentioned her wealth at sixty million and most of it was inherited. I let out a soft whistle.

"If that impresses you, what do you think of your mates' money?" Till asked. "I thought you'd scoff at this amount."

"Hey, I was a kid working and using my meager inheritance to put myself through school recently. Also, I have no actual figure to put on Jadelyn's wealth."

Larisa rolled her eyes. "A lot, my king. Then you have Maeve, the Highaen sisters, and Morgana."

I shrugged. "Not my gold. I only care about my gold." Doing my best to redirect us back to the case, I thought aloud. "So, we have a wealthy business woman married to one victim. Regardless of how that affects motive, I want to talk to her."

"Here's her number." Till scrolled to the top of the page again.

Dialing it, I listened as it rang several times, and then the answering machine was full. "Didn't pick up and couldn't leave a message. Let's go to her place and take a look around."

"We can't just—"

I stopped her with a glare. "Welcome to not being exactly law enforcement. That and paranormals normalize killing. If things get messy, don't hold back."

Till checked the gun at her hip. "Okay. This is just your jurisdiction, so we'll do it your way."

If that was how she wanted to justify it, then that worked out well for me. As long as she wasn't going to have a crisis of conscience part way through this, we'd be okay.

"I'll drive. My car is still here at the station." Agent Till sighed, pulling a pair of keys from her pocket and tossing them in the air.

***

I took in the quaint suburban area as Agent Till drove. It was idyllic. Kids were playing in sprinklers, people were out walking their dogs. We only passed a few cars as we made our way along the large homes.

All the lawns were a vibrant green and mowed in a criss-cross pattern that was for old men with too much time on their hands, framing in pristine houses. Not a shutter was out of place and the cars had absolutely no damage, not even some dirt.

It was almost uncomfortably perfect compared to the city.

"Just down here." Till pulled into a lane that changed the landscape. Rather than houses one after another, there was more space between them, and the houses were set back further from the street.

Agent Till pulled up into one driveway. It was a large home with peach-colored bricks and a complex roof line. "So, what do you do if someone's home?"

I turned to Sabrina in the back. "Can you check it?"

The succubus smiled at me. "I was already working on something. Let me see if this works."

She had a wooden hoop. It looked like a hoop somebody would use for needlepoint. She held it up, the etching she'd made into the hoop glowing as it activated. An image formed inside of it.

"How long will that last?" I asked, curious and thinking about my twigs.

"Twenty minutes, give or take," Sabrina replied, twisting it around and giving us a view inside the home.

Larisa bent around the succubus to get a look at the enchantment itself. "That's impressive. Very detailed."

"Thanks." Sabrina's eyes pinched together as she continued to sweep the first floor of the home and into the garage. "We have a car, but I don't see anyone home."

"Three-car garage. Looks like it might be a spare or a kid's car," Till commented.

That was enough for me. "Keep looking around with that. I'm going in." I needed to find something to open up this case.

We had time pressing in on us before everyone came out in force and cleared the city of any threatening vampires. While the vampires weren't my favorite of the paranormal, I knew it would only lead to more trouble.

I had a feeling it was all tied together. If I could solve this case, I could likely find the vampire that turned Maddie and rescue Helena.

Anxious to move, I darted out of the car and up to the door to the garage.

Twisting the handle, I applied enough pressure that it snapped. A feeling of satisfaction ran through me as it gave under my strength, swinging open easily.

"My king." Larisa was running behind me. "Don't rush without your guard."

The other two were getting out of the car, but as the air in the garage reached my nose, it wrinkled.

Something stank. It smelled like a rodent had died in the corner.

Larisa smelled it as she followed me into the garage, and her hands sprouted large, scaly white claws. "My king, there's been something dead here."

"It doesn't smell that bad. Maybe a squirrel came in and got trapped." But even as I said it, I realized that would mean that the home had been unoccupied for a while.

I got to the door to the home, and it was unlocked, but the second I opened it, I stumbled back and covered my nose. "Fuck. That's not a dead squirrel." I tried not to gag.

Till and Sabrina came in. With their less sensitive noses, they didn't pick up the smell until they took a few steps closer.

"Oh, that's awful." Till covered her nose and mouth.

Meanwhile, Sabrina shrugged it off. "I've smelled worse."

We all looked at Sabrina.

"Plague demons," was all she said and refused to elaborate, turning off her little magical mirror. "Pretty sure no one is home."

"Yeah... someone's dead in there," I said, shifting my nose. The dragon's sense of smell was better, but it also was easier to deal with the stench because it was almost analytical of the scents rather than reactionary.

Till's voice was high pitched and nasally from pinching her nose. "Multiple dead people. A single body doesn't stink this much."

That was intriguing.

I pushed in through the home, not bothering to take off my shoes. Everything seemed pristine on the main level, nothing askew or broken. In fact, it looked like it was right out of a magazine.

The only thing out of place was the stack of unpaid and overdue bills on the counter. That was certainly a reason for them to get involved in illegal activities. Things weren't so perfect in suburbia.

"Nothing here," I called back and went to check the rooms.

"The smell is coming from downstairs," Larisa called from down the hall and disappeared into a doorway.

I grumbled and hurried to follow her down the stairs.

She was right. The smell grew even more pungent as we moved down the steps. And as we reached the bottom, it was easy to see why. Blood was everywhere, splattered and sprayed over the walls. Nearby, a pile of dried out corpses was stacked in the corner.

"Looks like someone had a party," I commented, trying to lighten the morose atmosphere with a little humor. The scene really hit home.

If we didn't solve this case soon, this would be what Philly would become. The sight before me was disgusting, and it felt like a warning.

Till came down the stairs after me with a stoic mask on her face. These weren't her first dead bodies. "Okay. So, this woman is a suspect."

"Understatement of the year," Larisa snorted. "There's at least a dozen dead." She stepped up and got a closer look at their clothes. "They were wearing basically rags."

"Human trafficking then." I looked to Till for her confirmation.

She nodded in agreement. "Seems likely, given the state of them. But why ship them in just to feed them to vampires? Are there some sort of feeding rules that make them need to import fresh people?"

I scratched my chin. "No, not really. They basically have free rein unless they get local law enforcement's attention. Detective Fox would clean it up, and then the council would resolve it, and not in a fun way."

"Then why?" Till pushed again.

Looking over the bodies, I scratched at my chin. "They were recruiting? Bring in people, give them a choice? Maybe then the ones who are okay turning are given the others to feed on? This just doesn't feel like a mature vampire to make such a mess. Most of the ones I've met take pride in being neat."

I tried to think about why they would kill them here, though. That just seemed even sloppier. No, this was a one-time thing. Susan Garrison didn't seem like the type to get her hands dirty and her home ruined every time.

"It does feel very sloppy," Larisa agreed. "So, they recruit from out of the city because they don't want to make waves."

"If they are recruiting out of the city for vampires, why not demons too?" I added. "The demon could be brought in as additional security. Take out anybody moving against them."

Larisa raised an eyebrow at me, and I realized what they might need a demon to take down.

I pointed at myself. "Me? I mean, they are as tough as angels, right? Those weren't too bad."

"Those were angels under the archangel of justice. My king, I have the greatest respect for you, but dragons have their vices, and you seem... susceptible." Larisa was quiet on the last word.

I still frowned. "Doesn't make sense to me. Even if they tied me down, the city has the fae queens here. You'd need someone of... shit." They'd need someone strong who could take a beating to stand up to the fae.

And we knew one. One that just went missing.

"What is it?" Till asked.

"Helena. She was tough enough to take a beating from me in Sentarshaden. I might be stronger now, but I bet she could at least stall a fae queen." Turning to Sabrina, I raised an eyebrow. "Can they force her to fight for them?"

"No... maybe? It depends on what exactly is in town. Helena is going to have some natural defenses against any demons or angels, but I can't be sure." Sabrina thought through it out loud. "We can't rule it out."

I thought as much. "So then, the target is the next question. The fae make the most sense, but it could also be the dragons. Both of us make for tempting targets. And we'd both get in their way of ruling over this city freely."

Till raised her hand to get my attention. "If I gauge this right, the dragons seem like far more isolated targets than the fae. They'd be strategically easier."

"The portal between earth and the Faerie realm functions as a bottleneck," Larisa added. "If the vampires could hold it, they could wage a war against them, but they'd need someone to stop the queens."

"Couldn't these people do something like take his women and force him to help them?" Till pointed a thumb at me.

I let out a low growl that made the windows vibrate. "Mine."

Larisa was already pulling out her phone and texting the other dragonettes.

"If they dare go after them," I stated, my dragon instincts taking over at the mere thought of my mates being held hostage.

"Calm down. We have a guard on the vulnerable ones around the clock," Larisa chided me as she continued to type. I noticed that her fingers moved faster.

"Vulnerable ones?" I asked.

"We aren't wasting a guard on Morgana or Kelly," Larisa clarified, chortling.

I nodded. But even thinking about somebody touching my mates was making me see red. "Get them to my hoard now."

I pulled my phone out of my pocket and dialed Deniz's club. We were about to have words.

# CHAPTER 23

"Hello! This is the Bloody Drop," a hostess sang happily on the other end of the line.

"Give me Deniz," I growled into the phone.

"Who?" the hostess asked, suddenly far less cheery.

And unfortunately for her, I didn't have patience at the moment. "Your boss. Give him the phone." My voice deepened, and my body crackled as I fought to contain the shift starting to ripple through me.

"Look, prick, I don't know who you think you are—" the woman started.

"I'm Zach Pendragon. And before you speak another word, I'd recommend running that name past your superior." I waited.

There was a muffled noise on the other end, followed by silence.

But it was only a moment later that a voice came on the line. "One moment, Mr. Pendragon. We are getting Deniz for you. Is there anything I can do in the meantime?"

I took a deep breath, working to keep my head level. "I am this close to coming over and burning your entire club down. My mates are not to be touched." Anger just at the thought of my mates being in harm's way had me ready to torch every vampire in the city.

I didn't have any proof that Deniz was to blame, but he came to the city at the same time everything blew up. And being calm and collected wasn't much of an option for me at the moment.

Sabrina put a hand on my arm, trying to calm me down. "Breathe. Your mates are not in danger. Agent Till is very sorry she said that." Sabrina glared over at Till.

I knew my eyes had shifted, because when I raised my eyes to look at Sabrina, I could see her succubus form. "Don't care. This stops now."

"What is it now, oh king of dragons?" Deniz's voice came over the phone. "It seems you just can't get enough of me. I come to this city, and you seem to want to talk to me every day. I thought you'd be busier with your harem. Maybe you should take them to bed and let me do my job. You seem to struggle to do much, anyway."

Deniz needed to thank whatever higher power he believed in, because if he'd said those words to my face, he wouldn't have a head anymore.

"My mates," I growled as the phone began to be crushed in my hand. I had to force myself to open my grip a little, relieving the pressure.

"What is wrong with your mates? I have done nothing, and you constantly threaten me." Deniz sounded exhausted. "Dragons. Always so smart, but so stupid."

"What do you mean?" I replied.

"I've come here to help you. I am Wallachia. We remember what happens to tyrants, those who push the world too far. We know about the dragon killed on the way to the conclave. It wasn't us. The Gregorians are making moves." Deniz sounded like he was spitting at the phone at the mention of the other vampire faction.

Frowning at the new information, I took a moment to consider his words. "So you are telling me you came to make peace?"

The ladies in the room with me were only hearing one side of the conversation and watching me closely.

"No, we came to keep the peace. An offshoot of the Gregorians were the ones to lead the local vampires here. They were making too much noise," he replied.

"Tell me everything you know," I demanded, realizing he'd been leaving me in the dark. "I am out of patience. I'm currently standing in a home filled with humans that have been bled dry. And there are signs that whoever is behind this has been quietly amassing numbers. Helena, the nephilim, has been taken, and they appear to be working with either an angel or a demon in the city. I need to know what they are targeting."

There was silence on the other end of the phone for a long while.

"Say you are sorry for the threats," Deniz said quietly. He had what I wanted and was going to use it.

"I'm a dragon and naturally threatening. I cannot help that. But I'm sorry for my temper." I held back a smirk.

"Best I'm going to get from a stubborn dragon," Deniz scoffed. "We knew the Gregorians were bringing in more and more fresh blood. We have been keeping a close eye on blood donations and where that blood goes. The Wallachia monitor many things. We also know that Beelzebub has been called from hell."

I turned to Sabrina. "Beelzebub?"

She understood my question. "Gluttony. He takes over bodies and burns them out while satisfying his gluttony.

Very powerful demon prince." Sabrina's eyes were wide with fear. "Is he here?"

I processed her words. He takes over bodies.

I ran back through the previous murders with that information. Helena and Agent Till had tracked him, likely as he worked his way through bodies towards Philly. And the demon likely knew the supernatural killings would draw Helena's attention and bring her to the city.

He might be the lure, or he might be something even more dangerous. I wasn't sure yet.

"We have a belief that Beelzebub might be in the city. Maybe even used to lure Helena here. What are they after?"

"If they are affected by gluttony, they will want the fae," Deniz said slowly. "Or the Dragon King. The Gregorians will try to feed on and turn the fae. That's the only way they can start a war on this level and come out the other end alive. But I don't understand why they would align themselves against you."

Deniz truly sounded tired. I'd called to rip him a new one and found myself feeling sorry for him.

From what I'd learned, vampires used the mana in blood to fuel their magic and their speed. All the blood they drained was compressed within their body to aid healing, and some of the older vampires had been saving up blood in them for millennia, to the point they could do unspeakable things.

At a certain point, people stopped calling them vampires and started calling them bloodlords. Powerful vampires who had a near limitless ability to absorb blood to power themselves.

They were a problem.

"Thank you. Sorry again for all the scorched earth poli-cy." I had let my anger for vampires get ahead of everything else. Although, Deniz was also a bit of a dick.

Deniz grunted and hung up the phone.

His words made sense, and he'd help solve the issue of who might be behind the FBI case deaths. I hadn't really given him a chance since I'd met him the first time.

"Okay. Get everyone important to me and stuff them in my hoard. If the vampires are going to flip Philly upside down by going after the dragons or the fae, I want my mates to be safe." I put the phone away, knowing Larisa was already on it.

"I've texted all the mates and potential mates. They should be heading to your room in the Atrium now and will stay there until your honor guard gives the all clear." Larisa looked up from her phone.

I raised an eyebrow. "Just like that?" I was skeptical they'd obey so readily.

"Scarlett made the protocols and makes us run drills when we aren't on duty. Your first mate is well chosen. None of us really has bodyguard experience. And any of your mates that don't follow protocol will have to deal with her. Even Morgana has determined it's not worth pissing off Scarlett and does the drills, though she usually grumbles through them." Larisa shrugged and stuffed her phone into her pocket. "So, since I'm with the party, can we go blow something up?"

I smiled. "Wanna blow this building up?" I asked her. The stench bothered me, and I didn't think there was much left to see. It seemed like it might be therapeutic and take care of the evidence at the same time.

"I thought you tried to keep a low profile. Blowing up a building is about as high profile as you can get. Besides, some nosey neighbor has to have noticed us by now." Till pushed on my back and directed me out of the home.

Letting her push me, we went back out of the garage and into her car with the other two trailing behind us.

"What now? The trail has gone cold," I asked, frustrated at the situation.

Till leveled a look at me. "A lead will come. You need to be patient. You have your whole paranormal community out looking for these vampires, and Fox has put out an APB on their cars. They'll turn up soon. Why don't we get you back to your hoard and let you see that all of your mates are okay?" Till took on a warm mothering tone.

I must have been in a bad state if Till was trying to calm me down.

"Let's go." I buckled my seatbelt.

Till pulled out of the drive. "So, why are you such a target?"

"Because I'm a very special dragon," I scoffed. "I can mate to restore all the flights."

Till looked into the mirror at Larisa in the back seat. "What does that mean?"

"He's a combination of all the dragon colors. So, he's much more powerful. His parents are sort of the dragon gods," the white dragon tried to explain simply.

"Wait, his parents are Tiamat and Bahamut?" Sabrina squeaked. "Oh wow. He's not just the gold king."

I winced. "Sorry, didn't mean to hide that from you. But also trying to keep it under wraps."

"It's fine. That explains why your mana is so rich." Sabrina nodded from the backseat, confirming something she had suspected.

"Yeah, that is part of it. But I also ate half the power of a fae queen," I added sheepishly. It seemed primitive to gain power through eating, but it was the perfect task for a dragon.

Till kept her eyes on the road; her driving was far smoother than Morgana's. "Which of the two queens?"

"A third, one that has been absent for a while. So maybe it isn't that big of a deal." I sighed. "My birth is auspicious. My parents were never supposed to have a child together. Apparently, as a result, my life is supposed to disrupt the world."

Till continued on out of the neighborhood and gave me a little side eye. "That doesn't sound like a healthy amount of pressure."

I laughed. She had no idea. "I'm the Dragon King. An entire race of people, my people, look to me for guidance and to restore us to our former power. It sure as shit isn't a healthy amount of pressure. But it is what it is," I shot back.

Till nodded, reaching over to pat my leg. But as she slowed her patting, she realized what she was doing and briskly put both hands back on the wheel.

"Okay. I'm understanding this all a little more." Till tilted her head back to address the girls in the backseat. "You girls have your work cut out for you. If he keeps up this level of pressure, he's going to snap. I've seen it happen to agents before."

Rather than give her an angry retort, which would do nothing other than confirm her words, I crossed my arms and stared out the window.

Till kept driving for a while in silence before she broke it. "I've seen plenty of people pushed past their stress limits and snap, doing something that they wouldn't have otherwise done."

I snorted. "There isn't much of an option for me. The dragons recognize me as king because of what I am."

"Then get help." Till's tone wasn't polite anymore. "And if you can't figure out how to use these women who orbit around you to help, then I'm calling bullshit on the Dragon King title."

Glancing back at Larisa, I laughed as I saw clear agreement. "You have a terrible poker face."

The white dragon blew out a breath. "When shit hits the fan, you really don't use any of us," she admitted.

"Mine." I snapped my teeth playfully. "Besides, I'm supposed to be some big bad Dragon King."

Before we could get into it further, Till's phone started ringing and 'Detective Fox' flashed on her screen.

I picked it up. "Father-in-law. What's new?" My voice pitched just a little, hoping for good news.

"The car for Susan Garrison was just spotted northbound on I476," Detective Fox said as I looked up to double check the road sign we were passing.

Grabbing the wheel, I jerked it to the right, ignoring the cursing Till.

"We are taking this exit." I told Till, pulling the car onto I476.

"What the fuck!" Till cursed as I crossed us into the exit lane a little late.

"Garrison's car was spotted northbound on I476," I relayed Fox's message. I smiled, excited about the chase. I had a lead, and the predator in me was ready to hunt.

The agent floored the car as soon as she got onto the huge highway. It had two split five-lane sections.

"Where were they spotted?" I asked the detective, putting him on speaker.

"Near exit thirty-seven about a minute ago. Calling you was the first thing I did."

I looked for a mile marker, spotting thirty-two. They had a five miles and one minute lead. So around six miles total.

"I have a helicopter getting in the air in a minute. It will be out there in five," Detective Fox commented.

Squinting over at the speedometer, I watched as it rose over one hundred and kept climbing.

"Don't you have lights on this?" Larisa sounded excited.

"Do you want to tell the vampires that we are coming for them? And besides, this also isn't official business. We can't use them."

The kid in me was annoyed. I'd always wanted to blast the sirens and cruise through traffic.

But Agent Till just smiled. "But this was my favorite part of Quantico."

Her old BMW maxed out just under one hundred and ten miles an hour as she roared through the traffic, changing lanes like a madwoman. I kept track of the time as we moved. Given their lead, we'd need about eight minutes before we were likely to see them.

Till wove between the cars amid angry honks, cutting people off and causing more than a few cars to swerve as she raced up beside them.

"What do we do when we catch up with them?" Till asked. "Does your succubus have something for that?"

"Nope! I've got this one." Larisa grinned. "Just get me close enough to see them."

Sabrina nodded, a small blush dusting her cheeks at being called my succubus. Digging in her bag, she pulled out a needle and etched an enchantment on Till's car.

"What are you doing to my car?" Agent Till glanced up into the rear-view mirror, only to immediately have to look down to dart between a few cars.

"Let her do whatever it is she's doing, and watch the road," I grumbled, wondering how I ended up with such dangerously driving women. She was safer than Morgana, but dodging traffic at a hundred and ten miles per hour had my blood pumping.

We almost reached where I assumed the car would be when a helicopter came into view just ahead of us. And it was following something.

"That helicopter is going fast," I commented, realizing that the vampires might have picked up the pace as they noticed the helicopter. "Either of you have something to give us a little more juice?"

"Working on it." Sabrina had just finished the enchantment. "It would work a lot better if I had time to enchant her tires or engine directly, but I can reduce the weight of the car and reduce your resistance. Keep a good grip on the steering wheel!"

She finished and pressed her hand to the enchantment to activate it. The magic glowed red in the backseat, and Till's car pushed over one ten up into the high one twenties.

We got closer, and the car was just up ahead.

"My turn!" Larisa cracked her fingers. "Envokus." She flicked her wrist, and a spike of ice shot up from the highway, clipping their car and tottering it to one side before it stabilized.

But the car behind them ran headfirst into the spike of ice, crashing and turning the car sideways as a huge pileup started behind us.

"Whoops." Larisa looked over her shoulder for a second as we drove into a large open space with traffic stopped behind us. "Missed a little, but I'll get it this time." She shot again, and this time it worked.

The spike of ice shot up through the hood of the car, and the sudden pressure caused the hood to dip and the back to rise. A moment later, the car flipped end over end down the highway, like someone had just kicked a very large soda can.

"Fuck." Till looked back at Larisa as she slammed the brakes, skidding several dozen feet past the car even as the vampires were pulling themselves out of the wreckage.

"Oh, no you don't." I unclicked my seatbelt and burst out of the car before it came to a full stop. "Contego."

I threw up a one eighty barrier around their car, forcing them to get past me. As I moved towards them, I recognized Susan Garrison. She had black hair and looked years younger, but now, seeing her face to face, I wouldn't mistake Susan Garrison.

Jackpot.

I pulled another one of the twigs out of my braccr and activated the enchantment, locking her down as two more vampires came for me. They were fast, and they both tried to slip past me.

But a gun went off three times and one jerked back as they all hit center mass.

I didn't hesitate, stepping forward and ripping its head off. The other vampire got past me and caught Agent Till, holding her hostage with its claws on her throat.

"Leave us. Don't even dare speak to cast a spell; she'll die before you finish," the vampire threatened.

"Larisa, get the one I bound." I handed off the twig to her as I made eye contact with Sabrina in the car and then shifted my focus to the vampire holding Till by the throat.

She was an ugly fucker. Her face was a warped mask of rage, and her torn clothes made her seem desperate and dangerous.

The vampire was taking steps back as she held onto the agent, who had become dead weight in an attempt to slow the vampire. I almost laughed. She was really trying to help, but she did not know just how strong the vampire was. I doubted she was really slowing her down at all.

"Okay, we got what we wanted. You guys can have the agent." I shrugged, trying to play it cool.

Agent Till looked at me as if I had betrayed her.

"Oh? Well then, I guess there's no more need for her." The vampire chucked Agent Till over the divider into oncoming traffic and bolted.

# CHAPTER 24

I t felt like time slowed as Agent Till's body was lobbed towards oncoming traffic. But it was only the briefest moment before we all reacted.

Sabrina launched a red ring of magic that chased down the vampire before she could get far. As the red ring reached her, it sliced right through both of her legs.

She didn't hesitate after she sent the spell, immediately moving out from behind a car to chase the vampire down.

Knowing she could handle her, I leapt over the divider as a car swerved, attempting to miss the agent. I felt a rush of relief as she came out unscathed, but the big Mack truck barreling down the road wouldn't have the same nimbleness.

"Go low!" I yelled as I landed and punched my foot into the asphalt. Then I expanded my foot into a dragon's claw and tore into the cement, holding on as I put my hand out towards the oncoming truck.

My hand hit the front fender, tearing right through it as my hand entered inside of it and I could feel the heat of the engine block as I got a good grip on the frame.

The Mack truck's back end picked up, but thankfully, it was full of cargo that was weighing it down. All it did was a small hop before the whole thing came to a messy and loud stop as I shoved the engine a good three feet back under the driver's seat.

"You all right?" I asked Agent Till, turning away from the truck.

"Holy shit," she whispered, still crouched down on the pavement. "You—you just stopped a truck going sixty miles per hour with your bare hands."

"We need to go." My left shoe and the bottom of my pants were shredded as I shifted my foot back to normal, and my right sleeve was torn to hell from the truck. I looked like a mess, and I needed to leave as quickly as possible.

Cars were already stopping, and people were getting out to see if they could help.

I went over to the truck driver, who was pushing down his airbag.

I breathed a sigh of relief that he was moving. But he'd have a nasty headache and a bruise from the seatbelt. The police helicopter was touching down amid the mess, and people were pulling out their phones.

I grabbed a piece of the truck amid the wreck and used it to shield my face as I hopped back over the barrier.

Four uniforms hopped out of the helicopter at the same time and started shouting at people to stop recording and get back in their cars. Another two rushed to the two downed vampires.

"Are you Zach?" One that had been yelling at people to get in their cars turned back to me.

"Yup." I raised an eyebrow, readying myself for whatever came next.

"I work directly with Detective Fox, and these guys are all good." The man emphasized the word 'good'. "What's the situation here?"

I smiled, glad that they knew about paranormals. "Two vamps, one directly involved in the kidnapping of an FBI agent." I pointed to the vampire that Larisa was currently pressing to the ground. "Susan Garrison is the prime suspect in multiple murders."

"Gag and bag," the cop said to the others, pointing at Susan. "We'll bring them wherever you want."

"You know Bumps in the Night?" I asked with a smile.

"Of course." The cop nodded and made some motions for the others to hurry up.

"What's that?" Till asked about the club.

I grinned. "Morgana's club. I'm going in the helicopter with them. I'm not letting them out of my sight."

"You don't just take someone... never mind. We'll meet you there." Agent Till went back to her car with Sabrina and Larisa while the vampires were put in multiple sets of zip ties and tied to the seats of the helicopter.

"Coming with us?" the cop asked, getting in and strapping himself to a seat.

"I'm staying with them. Let's get out of here." I pulled a headset on so that we could communicate if we needed to in flight.

Despite the cops' best efforts, there were still some people trying to get pictures of the accident. I started texting Rupert and Detective Fox, hoping they could get ahead and spin the story.

The paranormal secret was far too close to being exposed. While I knew they'd been covering it all up for years, I worried that we were reaching a tipping point.

The helicopter lifted off, and I hung onto a handle, no longer fearing flying nearly as much as I once did. Having wings helped with that.

The two vampires were wiggling against their restraints, but they stopped once I stared at them. Susan glared at me. I wondered if she knew who I was.

The other vampire had her pants recently turned into shorts, and her legs below the cutoff looked pale and atrophied. Apparently, she was barely healing them back.

They were both relatively recent vampires.

Neither of them had a headset on, and the helicopter was loud. They wouldn't be able to hear me if I asked if they'd turned Maddie, but I was ready to rip out their fangs if they were.

I pulled out my phone while holding onto the helicopter with one hand and texted Maddie. If she met us at Bumps, we could quickly use Sabrina's spell to confirm if they'd turned her.

I started wrapping up my next text and saw Bumps in the Night in the distance. The chopper had made quick work of the distance.

The cops dragged the vampires out onto the roof while several of Morgana's staff exited, curious about what had brought the chopper down.

"Valorie." I recognized one of them. Morgana had taken the vampire under her wing after she'd been used by werewolves to manufacture a drug from her saliva. "These two need to be held. Morgana wants them."

"Poor souls." The vampire came forward and roughly handled Susan while a guy came forward and did the same to the other. "Morgana breezed through a bit ago. I'm not sure where she is at the moment."

"I know where she is. I'm going to go get her. Bring them to the gym?"

Valorie made a face and nodded.

"We should get back. Let the detective know if you need anything else." The cop that was in charge gave me a respectful salute, followed by a nod, and they quickly rose back into the air.

I followed the staff back down into the club and moved through the spatial maze until I reached the Atrium and my room within it.

Lifting my mattress, I poked my head into my hoard to see an array of my mates. The dragonettes save Larisa, and one surprise.

Maeve and her assistant had been pulled down, and they were waving their hands over my gold.

"Hands off my gold," I growled at the two fae.

"We heard there was an elemental and were curious," Maeve replied, standing up.

I glared at her and then shifted my gaze to Jadelyn. "Does she have a plushie?" Now knowing that was the sign for a 'harem hopeful'.

Jadelyn blushed. "Maybe?" She avoided meeting my eyes.

"Fine." That confirmed my suspicion. Maeve had not only started working her way into my heart, she'd been also working through my harem. "Come on out, girls. We found one of the vampires at the center of this whole mess; I need some help to get answers out of them."

"The coast is clear?" Polydora asked.

"No, they are still at large, but I feel pretty comfortable with you guys in Bumps. Between all of you, I don't think there is anyone who is going to touch you. Sabrina,

Larisa, and Agent Till are on their way. I'm going to go fetch Maddie." I laid out my immediate plans for them and pulled my head out from under the mattress, moving quickly through the Atrium to the portal that led to my apartment and stepping out into my room.

Maddie and Frank were talking outside at the table when I opened my door.

"Oh, Zach. Good timing. I... uh... Frank agreed."

"He knows?" Frank asked, frowning at me. "You have this big secret that I have to marry you to know, and he already knows? Wait, did you two get married? That is not the type of harem I was talking about, Maddie."

My roommate was freaking out, even if he'd agreed to it.

"Frank. I'd never do that to you," I replied, trying to calm him down. "It's complex, but it sounds like you are on board? This is a big decision. You are bound to Maddie forever, no take backs."

"Yeah, man. I love Maddie. I've been with enough girls to know when one works. She's my ride or die. Wait, do I get a harem with this secret?" He looked at me with a face full of hope...

...before Maddie dashed them. "Absolutely not."

Cutting through the awkward tension, I jumped in. "Okay, so if he's going to find out anyway, you might as well bring him with us. We need to check two... vampires we have in custody to see if they turned you, Maddie." I hesitated to say the word around Frank, but it was time he knew, too.

Frank did a double take between the two of us. "Vampires?"

"Come on." Maddie grabbed his hand. "Let's see what you think of vampires." She dipped her head, letting her hair cover her face. "Because things like vampires and werewolves are real."

Frank was stunned, but Maddie grabbed his hand, pulling him along. I led the two of them back into my room and through my closet, back into the Atrium.

"Wha-what?" Frank stammered as he looked around at the Atrium, but allowed himself to be pulled along. "What just happened?" He was barely forming coherent sentences as his head kept spinning.

"We are going to see my harem of supernatural creatures, Frank. Don't worry, they won't hurt you now that Maddie has taken you in. Though, should you tell anyone our secret, it will be Maddie's head on the chopping block right next to you. And I don't mean that as a metaphor," I explained, wanting to make sure he knew the implications.

"Harem?" Frank perked up, clearly listening to the wrong part of my warning. "Wait, this is your secret to creating a harem!" His eyes shined with joy. "What are you, Zach?"

I huffed. He had gotten over that shock quickly enough. "A dragon. Come on, through here."

The door led out of the quiet Atrium and into Morgana's club. It was midafternoon, so it was still relatively quiet, no loud blasting music and no patrons.

"It's Bumps in the Night," Maddie informed him. "Morgana's club."

We went down several floors and through the twisting maze of Morgana's club to find my ladies all circled around two vampires in the padded gym we used for sparring.

Both vampires were still heavily zip tied and sitting in chairs. It looked like I hadn't missed the fun.

"We just got here." Agent Till waved at me. "Ready to get started with questioning?"

Frank was staring from woman to woman. "Elf, were-wolf, fox girl, blue elf, or wait, is that significant? Wait, what's Jadelyn?"

"Hi, Frank." Scarlett waved at him while her twin foxy tails swished behind her. "Morgana's a drow, underground elf. Jadelyn is a siren."

My roommate just turned to me stupefied before making a 'nice' hand signal and winking.

"Sabrina, could you use Maddie's hair for the spell?" I urged the succubus to get started.

Maddie didn't hesitate for a second, pulling out a hair and handing it off.

"What's she?"

"One of the best wizards around," I said without hesitation, but I didn't miss how she blushed all the way to the tips of ears with a smile as she got to work. "As much as I love you both here, this might be a little messy for you two. I really just needed Maddie's hair."

Maddie glanced at me. "Will they die?"

"If one of them is the one that turned you, then absolutely. They will die." There was a cold edge to my tone. "Do you want to go back?"

Frank didn't miss my words, though. "Turned? Maddie..." His words trailed off.

Maddie grabbed his hand. "Come on down this way. I... I have something to tell you." Her voice broke a little, and I could tell she was anxious. But Frank loved her. I had a feeling they'd work it out.

My friend and recently turned vampire gave me a small shake of her head. She wasn't going back to being human again.

Frank took her hand with a glance over his shoulder at me. I just gave him a wink of encouragement and a little shooing motion. The two of them had a lot to talk about as they moved off to a connecting room.

Once they were out of sight, I motioned for Polydora to watch over them. The last thing I needed was a dead roommate because Maddie lost control.

"This will take a minute," Sabrina commented, still etching a chalk circle on the ground. "But I don't even need them to be alive for this to work."

The female vampire struggled when she said that, but Morgana was there in an instant, stabbing one of her wicked, curved swords through her spine.

"Don't even try. Where is Ricardo?" Morgana hissed.

She mumbled around the gag in his mouth.

"You have to ungag them first, Blueberry." Kelly threw up her hands. "I swear, you always jump ahead."

Morgana laughed. "Why don't you get the gag out then furball? Seems appropriate." Morgana pricked the woman again, as if she was just going to keep stabbing and asking questions, even if she couldn't answer.

Kelly rolled her eyes as her hand became clawed. With a single swipe, the cloth wrapped around the vampire's mouth broke and fell down around her shoulders.

"You fucking bitches, I—" Morgana's blade went through her lungs and stopped her short.

"Okay, maybe you were right, Blueberry, just keep stabbing. Eventually, she has to give in, right?"

Sometimes, I forgot how brutal my beautiful mates could be. They had grown up among the paranormal, where violence was far more common. Even my two princesses stood around with hard grimaces on their faces. They didn't like it, but they weren't about to stop it.

It was the dragons' reaction that bothered me the most. They looked... hungry for more.

"Zach. You don't get effective information from torture," Till whispered in my ear.

I kept my voice low. "They don't want information from her. Morgana wants to show Susan what she's in for unless she talks."

The agent was uncomfortable, and it made me smile that she was the least comfortable with the violence.

"Got it. I'm going to take a walk." She headed off to the restrooms as Blueberry and Furball continued their byplay of injuring the vampire before she could even talk, as if it were a game to them.

I realized that I wasn't as horrified as I used to be at the violence.

My mind wandered back to Sentarshaden when the Silver Slave had asked me to eat him to increase my power. It was about that time that the violence made sense.

There was a cycle of life and power that required violence and death. I had become part of it. More than that, I had embraced it when I had eaten the Silver Slave and used his power to rescue Tyrande.

Maybe when this was done, I needed to go talk to Tia and Bart. I wanted to understand how they held so much power and didn't let it change them. The idea that power corrupted absolutely wasn't so farfetched to me anymore.

Staring down at my hand, I couldn't help but imagine it coated in the blood of what I'd already done. And as Dragon King, it would no doubt grow worse.

"Zach?" Sabrina got my attention. "The spell is done."

"Do it," I told her, coming out of my musings. There would be time for that later.

She pushed her mana into the enchantment to get it started, and once again, a red mist floated up above the spell, questing about like a dog sniffing.

It didn't take long before zeroing in on the woman and lingering there as it grew brighter.

"What's that?" she screamed, trying to wiggle away, but Kelly put a foot on his chair and kept it from moving.

We all knew what that meant. She was the vampire that had turned Maddie.

My body crackled and people moved away from me as my jaw shifted, growing larger. My torso ripped open my shirt as it grew to support my head. I let myself shift to about the size of the kitchen table.

There was no hesitation. My jaws slammed close around the vampire, chair and all as I chewed and swallowed before shifting back. I had a ruined shirt, but it was worth it.

Maddie had already decided to become a vampire and we'd brought Frank in on this. I didn't need the vampire's fangs anymore.

Till was on the other side of the room with her hand covering her mouth. Apparently, she hadn't gone far. But this was what I was. I was tired of hiding my nature.

"Susan Garrison. Talk now or die." I tore off her gag.

# CHAPTER 25

S usan Garrison was watching me with a calculating expression before she turned to Maeve. "If she swears to protect me three times, I'll tell you whatever you want."

I scoffed. So Susan was only willing to talk if she was given protection. Which in itself was information. It told me that she was in over her head; whatever she'd signed up for wasn't going quite how she expected.

"Beelzebub not going so well?" I took a stab at the truth.

She stiffened. "You know? H-how?"

I rubbed my forehead. "How long have you been a vampire?"

"Five months." Susan watched me as I grabbed another chair and placed it opposite of her before sitting down.

"So, you probably aren't too used to how things are done. If I had to guess, you weren't really brought into the paranormal." I leaned back in the chair, considering the woman before me. "Let me try to work through this.

"You were a rich and well-connected woman, already..." I paused, thinking back to some of the photos with her husband. She'd already built up wealth, but perhaps that wasn't through legal means. One explanation made the most sense. "You were part of human trafficking even before this, weren't you?"

She snorted and looked away. It was all the confirmation I needed.

"Got it. You were a human trafficker, giving you enough wealth to get to know other rich and wealthy people. You don't seem like the type to get your hands dirty. So my guess is you just funded the operation and made connections with enough rich and powerful people to protect it." The story was coming together for me.

"My guess is that it included your husband, Representative Halmer, and an accountant. This thing had deep roots, but someone came to you with an amazing offer. They wanted to become your single source buyer."

There was a hum of understanding from Till. "It made things easier. That way you'd be business to business, cutting out the risk of vetting individuals or them backing out. And less work for you overall."

"When did you start working with the vampires?" I asked.

"A year ago," she said in a bitter tone. Her eyes flickering to Maeve but letting her previous idea to get three promises out of her go.

A feeling of relief surged through me. I'd known I was a dragon for less than a year. This entire operation had happened before that. Somehow, that took a tremendous weight off my shoulders. It wasn't my fault or the fault of my birth.

"So, you were supplying them with fresh blood, and at some point, you realized what they were," I replied.

"No," she spat. "We tried to back out as things grew weird, and we were turned to keep it going."

I turned to Morgana, curious. "How long does the compulsion last if you give an order to a vampire that you turned?"

"A few days to a week, but it depends on the strength difference between the two," she replied.

"Then you met with Ricardo often." I turned back to Susan. "What was he planning?"

"Things sped up the bloodlord's plans. Then that thing came in and went through what was supposed to be months of reserves." Susan wrinkled her nose. "Beelzebub, a demon, they called it... it took my husband. He became wild, and ate through months of blood bags we'd been collecting and then all the people we'd recently brought."

"Wait. You were draining their blood?" Suddenly, the scale of the operation exploded in my mind. If they were bringing in people and feeding off them directly, it could sustain a fair number of young vampires. But if they were using those people as constant blood sources and storing it, we could be looking at an army.

She nodded. "Beelzebub went through our supplies, and then they couldn't keep them all on a leash, so they stopped trying."

"The increased attacks." I nodded. The time line she was describing made sense.

Susan scoffed. "You don't know the half of it. Entire homeless communities have been wiped out. What you saw at the warehouse has echoed throughout the city and beyond. They are trying to be quiet, but they are all waiting for the bloodlord to ring the dinner bell for the fae."

"Bloodlord? Who's that?" My attention snapped to her. One of those was a very large problem.

She shrugged, caring less as this conversation went on. "Ricardo forces me to bow and stare at my feet whenever he's around. He has this horrid accent, though."

I frowned. "Do the names Wallachia and Gregorian mean anything to you?"

"Gregorian sounds right. I think that's the guy's last name." Susan seemed hopeful that maybe that was a useful piece of information.

At least it confirmed what Deniz had told us. Grudgingly, I had to admit that maybe he was helping us.

"Wallachia?" I asked again.

"Never heard of it. But they don't tell me much." She sounded resigned, but her eyes held a small plea.

I looked up at the ceiling as I thought through what she'd said. She'd filled in a lot of the background for us, and we now had confirmed the fae were targets. I also had a new target, the Gregorian family.

But one gap remained. "What about Helena? What do you know about her kidnapping?"

"That was Beelzebub's idea... but he's been hopping around bodies. His current one might be close to burning out like the others." She couldn't meet my eyes.

"Like your husband and your business partners. Were you next on the list?"

She really couldn't meet my eyes, but that only confirmed my suspicion. Susan Garrison was all about saving her life and staying in the clear herself. Everyone else could be damned.

"So, this Beelzebub is going to take Helena's body?" Till asked the crowd.

Sabrina pursed her lips. "It's possible. He's a demonic prince. If he had Helena for a prolonged period of time, he could work through her defenses."

"Then we have to get to her ASAP." Till sounded frantic. "Before she becomes shriveled like all these other victims." Finally, she turned to Susan. "Where is Beelzebub?"

"I don't know for sure. But it seemed like most of their activity was at the big brewery in Callowhill. At least, that's where they had us deliver all the crates," she hedged.

I stepped back. "Till, think you can trace her human trafficking and do that part by the books to satiate the FBI?"

That caught Susan's attention, and she got a bit of energy back. "Hey, I helped you."

"Yeah, and you'll keep helping us," I snapped. "Till, we'll keep her safe so that you can take her down publicly for the human trafficking. That should help explain all the deaths. And you can get credit for the find.

"Scar, get her out of here and have your father send someone to pick Susan up. Keep her gagged so we don't have anyone getting bit at the station."

My Kitsune was more than happy to stuff the wad of cloth back in the woman's mouth and tie it behind her head.

"I got this. Get going, and take care of this Beelzebub." She dragged Susan away by the chair as she pulled out her phone.

I glanced around the room, thinking about who I needed to take. "Morgana, Sabrina, and Maeve, with me. Poly, Trina, and Amira get in Morgana's van. The rest of you stay here and stay safe."

"Like hell I'm leaving my partner out there alone," Till complained, but a glare from me silenced her.

"Work on the case. Getting the case wrapped up and the FBI out of my hair is more important. Besides, we are talking demonic princes and bloodlords. No offense, Till, but that gun might as well be a toy."

Yev stepped forward, ready to argue with me, and I got a whiff of my first dragon mate. I felt my dragon stir in interest and pleasure.

I leaned forward, taking another deep whiff, a moment of panic that she'd been possessed. But once again, my dragon seemed pleased and not concerned.

"Something's wrong," I replied, trying to understand what had changed her smell.

Trina stepped forward and sniffed Yev before a big grin blossomed on her face. "There is no way you are going."

"Why not?" Yev demanded, her eyes shifting.

Trina leaned in and whispered something into Yev's ear, but my hearing picked out one word like someone had dropped a bomb on me.

'Pregnant'.

My hands were on Yev in an instant. I pushed her against the wall, sniffing her and biting her, marking her again.

"Zach, cut it out. You can rail my sister another time." Tyrande put a hand on my shoulder to pull me away, but there was no use.

I was fully entranced by the thought of my mate being pregnant.

Trina laughed and told everyone. "She's pregnant. Leave him alone for a second. He'll get himself back under control." She clapped excitedly, watching my reaction.

"Pregnant!" Tyrande gasped.

"Congratulations!" Jadelyn squealed and was echoed by the rest of my mates.

"Mine," I roared, pushing her against the wall and marking her shoulder over and over.

Yev put a soft hand on my cheek and cupped my chin to pull me up to her lips.

"Yours, my mate. I suppose I'm off to your hoard," she grumbled, but a light was lit in her eyes. While she didn't want to be out of the fight, she now had our child to protect.

I sniffed her again. Now it made sense. The subtle shift was a change in her hormones. It was a slight change, but enough for a dragon nose to pick up.

"Mine," I growled once more, but I let up and relaxed before stepping away.

Every time I smelled her, the beast inside of me went wild and wanted to wrap myself around her. "Get in my hoard, stay safe."

"I will. But you better come get me, us, soon." She grabbed my hand.

"Of course." I looked at her and all my other mates that were going to stay back. "I'd be a fool to lose this all."

"Damn right," Kelly replied as she strolled away from the rest of my mates.

I growled. "Where do you think you are going?"

"What use is it being the pack leader of over five hundred wolves if I don't get to use them when shit hits the fan? I'll meet you out there. It sounds like there's an entire city of vamps that need to be turned into chew toys." Kelly put her hands on her hips, just daring me to fight her.

For once, she was not being my submissive alpha mate. She was being the head bitch of my harem.

"What about me, Furball?" Morgana cocked a brow at her jab at vampires. It also broke the tension and gave me a way out.

"Not you. You are growing on me, Blueberry, kind of like mold." Kelly laughed and took her leave. While I wanted her safe, her plan made sense. We'd likely need the help while we took on the heavy hitters.

The group split up, Yev taking the lead and bringing part of my growing harem back into my hoard. It was hard to be apart from them, but I knew they would be safer there. I needed a clear head as I went on the hunt for Beelzebub.

"Zach. I appreciate you including me. But I need to get back to my family." Maeve caught my arm.

"I understand. Good luck." I realized that Maeve could handle herself, and she needed to get back and warn the fae.

She gave me a brilliant smile. "Don't worry about me." She flexed before turning and whipping her long silver hair behind her.

I gave her a smile before heading towards the garage.

As I moved, Polydora walked up next to me. "My king. I know you wish to get personally involved, but it might be best for us to handle the combat."

"Not a chance," I told her, my voice calm.

It was strange. A sudden calm had come over me now that we had a target. Rather than being angry, I was cold and calculating.

Poly didn't argue with me, and as we walked into the garage, we skipped right over the gun rack. The fight that was coming would render those useless. This was a fight for magic and claws.

We were all quiet as we filed into Morgana's car.

Trina had claimed the passenger seat while Sabrina was in the back with Amira. That left Polydora and me to take the middle two seats. I buckled my seatbelt in preparation.

"Hang on." Morgana smiled as she floored the gas. The car's tires squealed as she whipped out of the spot.

Amira flew across the back, having not buckled in, but the rest of us had prepared.

Polydora had a huge grin on her face. "That was pretty fun."

"Fun?" Amira climbed back into her seat with Sabrina's help and buckled in as Morgana's van flew out of the parking garage, bouncing onto the street.

"Fun," Polydora confirmed before changing the subject. "We should inform the detective."

I was already on that, hitting his contact and putting the phone on speaker.

"Zach? Any news?"

"Yeah, actually. A lot of news. Susan Garrison was running a human trafficking operation, which turned into a blood donation business for the vampires. Till is taking her back to the station. We'll use the human trafficking to cover everything else."

He grunted, but didn't seem to have anything else to say, so I continued.

"But we also now know that Beelzebub is in town and playing a part in all of this." I paused, assuming the detective knew about the demon prince, and when he let out a slew of curses, I assumed the name registered. "It seems like this is a Gregorian play for the fae."

"Idiots," Detective Fox spat. "Why would they do this? It's just sloppy."

I nodded, but something about it made sense to me. "They might have been influenced by Beelzebub, or another demon of gluttony. I don't know how deep their relationship goes, but it's a problem. At the very least, they are currently being influenced by Beelzebub, and it's likely skewing their decisions."

"True. Either way, it's a mess that we now have the pleasure of cleaning up."

While the detective was talking, the sounds of phones ringing off the hooks sounded behind him. I could hear him shuffling around before he paused.

"One moment." He put the phone down, and there was the scuffing of boots and background chatter that picked up several volumes as he opened the door to his office.

A minute later, he picked up the phone again. "So we have a situation. We are getting calls all over the city of violence, specifically an increase in bites."

"They know we are close and are letting their minions loose," I said, realizing the situation and staring up at the roof of the car. "Do what damage control you can. We are going to make a pit stop."

"On it. Bye," Fox breathed and hung up.

"Where are we going?" Morgana asked.

"We need more magic power, someone who can take on an army in the streets. I think it's time to visit an old friend at a nursing home." I thought of the perfect person to help in the event of an army in our city.

Morgana winked at me in the mirror. "You are crazier than I am."

"Why are we going to a home of old people? We need to take down a demon," Polydora asked.

"An old friend of Morgana's lives in the home. He keeps a low profile, but if we have a big problem, there's no one better to clear a battlefield." I thought of the stories that had popped up around T. I'd been shocked that the crotchety old man was such a feared being.

Morgana swerved off the highway onto an early exit and barreled down the exit ramp, not even stopping for the stop sign.

"Stop signs are for everyone's safety," I reminded her as she swerved to avoid someone running across the street, and a vamp came charging after them.

Morgana was quick, pulling a SMG out of the spatial pocket in her bra and turning the van hard. She skidded to a jarring stop as her window came down.

In the confined space of the van, the gunfire was deafening as she sprayed down the vampire to Swiss cheese.

Trina held her ears and cursed. "Warn a girl first. Envokus." She flicked her wrist, and the skin melted off the vampire even as it was trying to heal.

Polydora sat beside me with her arms crossed and a pensive look on her face. "We are far too exposed. This is a nightmare."

"Agreed. It's time to end this. Quickly." As I said it, I was slammed back into my seat as Morgana took off once more.

# CHAPTER 26

"I won't be able to magically solve this," Morgana reminded me. "But he would definitely be a heavy hitter against an army of newly turned vampires."

"T?" Polydora frowned at the name.

We rounded the last corner to the idyllic little nursing home as dark clouds rolled overhead, and the first lightning flash announced the coming of a storm.

"He's an old friend of Morgana's." As I replied, two hungry vampires attacked someone in the parking lot ahead of us, and each took a side of the nurse's neck. It was like the scene where two lovers share a pasta noodle, only far less cute and a lot more grotesque.

Morgana gunned the van and hopped the curb, going into the parking lot and expertly clipping just one vampire, ripping them off their victim.

I threw my door open and growled. "Contego."

A shield came to life, separating the other vampire from the nurse. Polydora was racing around my shield, pouncing on the remaining vampire.

I caught the nurse and picked the poor woman up. "Are you okay?"

"Uh don't know," she answered with a slur and a glazed expression. The venom worked almost too well on humans.

There was a splatter noise as Polydora got a hold of her vamp, and Morgana got out of the van, flicking her blades and killing the other.

"Not good!" Polydora dropped the dead vampire onto the pavement, ready to rush into the nursing home, but she stopped dead.

I turned to the entrance of the nursing home. A tall, gaunt, old man leaning on a younger elf came to the entrance.

"They are drawn to you," T replied.

I assumed he was looking at me, but it was hard to tell because of his damn bushy eyebrows.

"Hey, old man. There's a big problem in the city, and we could use your help," I replied. "On behalf of the council, I'd like to ask for your help in subduing the wave of vampires coming through the city."

Another thought occurred to me. "And if possible, we would appreciate you partnering with the fae to create a potion to stop any recently turned humans."

"Oh?" A spooky light flashed underneath T's eyebrows. "My help?" He stopped leaning on his daughter, Hestia, and stood up straight. "Too bad my knees ache during storms."

"Cut it out, you old windbag." Morgana stormed up to him. "Yes or no?"

"Morgy," Hestia scolded her friend and stayed close to her father.

Another vampire came streaking across the parking lot towards our group.

T lifted his hand, and the vampire screamed as its flesh was ripped completely off its body, leaving nothing but the bones that didn't fall to the ground. Instead, the bones hung there a moment before solidifying back in place as two spooky lights that looked just like the ones that had been in T's eyes a moment ago appeared.

"You say the council has allowed me to act?" T replied, curious.

"I'll take the full burden if there are problems. But you have my support, the fae's, and the sirens'." I was honest with him. "Do the best you can to minimize damage and exposure?"

T looked up at the storm, which seemed to be growing quickly in intensity. "I think people will be off the streets here shortly. It is about to get quite dark."

"All vampires on the street are free game," I told him. "Except our favorite one." I grabbed Morgana's hips.

We had said we'd give them time, but that was clearly over. The attacks had escalated beyond a point of return. It was time to clean up the streets.

T's eyes flashed again, and another vampire died across the street in a puff of black smoke. "Deal. But I get to keep any reagents I find, and I'm too old to do much more than these little guys."

I didn't believe a word he said. Age shouldn't really bother a lich. "Any help is appreciated. Wonderful to see you again, old man. Keep an eye out for my wedding invitation soon."

"Come back, I've been working on my hair styling just for you." The old man smiled as he pulled out a pair of scissors and clipped them in the air a few times.

I shook my head. He always wanted pieces of me, even nail clippings or hair clippings, to use in his potions.

"We'll see. I'll come by though. I certainly owe you a favor," I promised as I headed back for Morgana.

T had already shown that there was nothing to fear in leaving him alone. The ancient elf waved with a smile on his face like an elderly neighbor. He was so happy to have a favor; I wondered if he'd ask for skin scrapings or my toenails next. But he'd fought in quite a few battles back during the seventeenth century. As I understood it, liches were immortal.

We all hurried back into the car. Once the doors closed and the car got moving, Trina spoke up.

"He's a lich. A fucking lich, Zach?! I thought they were all wiped out. How can you give a lich carte blanche like that?"

"T's harmless." Morgana waved a hand as if to dismiss the concern.

Trina choked. "Harmless? A lich could fucking wipe out the eastern seaboard."

"He's not so bad. He's helped us out a few times now," I backed Morgana's assessment of T.

"I'm going to need to check any and every potion you get from a lich." Polydora's tone brooked no argument.

"His daughter is the one that makes the fertility potion for the pack," I reminded her, letting them put the pieces together.

Amira wrinkled her nose behind me. "You mean she has access to your seed? Do you understand the horrible curses she could place on you with that?"

"Morgana grew up with both of them before T became a lich. She trusts them, and I do too. He's done nothing but help me so far." My tone said that there was no room for further argument, and the girls settled down as the van's engine roared and we swung from one side of the van to the other as she took corners far too quickly.

"I'm going to be sick." Amira held her mouth as Sabrina rubbed her back.

"I thought dragons would be tougher than car sickness," Sabrina stated.

"We do fine when they aren't driven by crazy people!" Trina shouted back with a huff.

Little did she realize that such a statement was only more of a challenge to Morgana. Morgana sped up, forcing me to cling to the oh-shit handle. But we were crossing into the industrial area, and I could see the grain silos pop above other buildings.

"At least we haven't seen more vampire attacks since T's," I said, trying to find something positive to talk about.

But as I said it, the lights flickered all around us and then went out. Most of the city seemed to have lost power. It only made it spookier as dusk was rapidly approaching.

"That's not good," Sabrina observed.

"I'd bet money that the council just cut the entire city's power and cell towers," Morgana replied, far less concerned. "Things have gotten terrible. It's the only way to stop somebody from getting a video that goes viral. When the dust settles and everything comes back online, we'll work to scrub whatever goes up. But this is a last resort."

"Meaning elsewhere in the city, shit has hit the fan." I rubbed my chin. If their ultimate target was the fae, then we needed to go to Wissahickon park after this.

The brewery came into view, and the place was a hub of activity as people moved about in a hurry. Large pallet crates were stacked up everywhere amid the loading zone, with the bay doors wide open. The brewery was far too busy, even for a business.

One car pulled up, and two vampires sped out of the front two seats before opening the trunk and pulling out a couple. The couple was bound and covered in blood.

"What are they doing?" Trina frowned, watching the spectacle.

"Setting up a long-term feeding solution," Morgana answered as she pulled in, not even attempting to slow down.

Our van quickly caught the attention of several vampires moving about. Morgana sort of stuck out like a sore thumb, and they started shouting in alarm.

"If they swarm the city and the fae, they need many people to bleed daily to keep all the new vampires fed," Morgana commented before gunfire hit the van and bounced off.

While the vehicle was safe, the sound of the bullets hitting the metal was still loud as shit.

"My king, allow us." Polydora, Trina and Amira all shifted, tearing their clothes.

Poly was first out of the van, throwing open the door amid the gunfire and charging out. The gunfire focused on her, the easiest target, but it did nothing as the bronze warrior charged through them like a meat grinder.

Trina and Amira shot out behind her. The copper was like Polydora, with a form like my dragon knight, but Amira was different. She was hunched over, more like a werewolf. And her head had shifted more to match the dragon.

I had seen the varied hybrid forms amid the conclave, and now some of Amira's difficulties made sense. She identified more with being a dragon than a human, even in the modern world. But her form certainly had an advantage. She fell on all fours and moved far faster than Polydora and Trina.

"Like they get all the fun," Morgana scoffed, throwing open her door and stepping out as she whipped out her curved blades. She started expertly spinning them before she blurred away.

Some vampires were already screaming to retreat; they could see that, despite their numbers, they were outmatched.

"Sabrina." I closed Poly's door to protect the succubus from gunfire. "You're here for the magic. Can you support us from inside the car?"

The dragons weren't in any danger from the small fries, but Sabrina might be.

She nodded before shaking her head. "I'm fine. Just give me a little juice?" She held the edge of her glasses, not taking them off as a smile lingered on her lips. "Remember what you said about the next time I did this? I do."

Her statement caught my full attention as she lifted her glasses, letting her succubus nature flood the inside of the van like a pink cloud of lust.

I breathed in deep, remembering my promise that I'd mark her the next time she did it. The beast in me did too, and I lurched into the back seat of the van and pressed the hot and sexy succubus to the seat.

But despite the desire churning through my body, I was at least present enough to know that we didn't have much time. I needed to help the others, including my mate.

Leaning down to mark Sabrina, she claimed my lips first. I lost myself momentarily in the pillow softness and tender sweetness of those lips. I rubbed myself against her as I felt my body becoming red hot.

I could also feel her feeding from me as my lust continued to swell. But it didn't affect me at all beyond the sensation. It didn't last longer than a few seconds.

When she was done, Sabrina had to push me hard to get me off her, and my jaw crackled as I looked at her shoulder.

"Do it. We'll play later if you come out of this alive." She gave me a lusty look, her pink eyes sucking me in.

I found myself nodding as my jaw finished shifting and my teeth became sharp.

"Mark me then," she whispered.

My teeth clamped down on her, and magic flooded my mouth. I left my mark on her, branding her with magic that I could always follow to find her. She held the back of my head for a moment before I felt the lust pop like a water balloon, suddenly far more aware of the battle noises outside.

I pulled back to see a furiously blushing Sabrina that was having trouble looking me in the eye.

"That was lovely." I pushed her chin to force her to look into my eyes. "Mine."

"Yours." She blushed so completely red that I thought for a second she was returning to her succubus form. "I-I'll work on tracking down Helena."

"We need to get out there before they do all the work," I chuckled, dragging Sabrina back out the side of the van where Morgana had exited less than a minute before.

Small arms fire was going off sporadically, but the four ladies had torn through the welcoming party while I'd been powering up Sabrina. I felt a little guilty, but there was no time to dwell on the moment. And Sabrina had needed the strength to protect herself.

Sabrina stepped out next to me and her hands swirled in the air with red magic, creating a diagram in the shape of an arrow. "Give me a minute."

I caught Polydora walking back in our direction. "Any injuries?" I shouted at the leader of my honor guard.

"No, my king. They fought us here until they realized they were outgunned, and then the vampires retreated into the building." She stared over to where the bay doors had been closed. "We were cleaning up outside the building while you... occupied yourself."

I snorted to hide my embarrassment. "Sabrina is fully charged up and ready to help us," I tried to defend my distraction.

Poly's nose flared, and she stared at the stretched and torn collar of Sabrina's shirt. "And marked." There was a low growl from the bronze dragon as her eyes flashed with jealousy.

"Let's go." I slipped out of my clothes and shifted into a gold and red dragon knight form. I had yet to announce to the world that I was the son of Bahamut and Tiamat, but I figured I'd need all the power I could to fight a demon prince.

Sabrina finished her diagram, and the arrow fell parallel to the ground. Then it swiveled to point at a wall of the brewery. "It isn't a GPS with turns, but it should help find her. Let's go through one of the bay doors."

I scoffed. "I'd rather make our own door. They'll have less time to prepare that way. Trina, Amira, Morgana, to me."

I pulled Sabrina along with me, following the direction of the arrow up to the concrete industrial building's side and wound back my arm. Then I punched right through the slab, sending cracks in every direction before I got a grip on it and tore open a hole.

I went to move into the opening just as a big ice lance shot out of the hole. It caught me in the chest and pushed me a step back as it shattered like broken glass that covered me. Thankfully, my scales prevented anything besides the impact.

Polydora crashed through the hole a second later, and a vampire screamed as she tore it apart.

"Are you okay, my king?" Trina went to heal me.

I pushed her hand away. "Let's go. We are hunting vampires."

Inside the building, the vampires were older. They knew how to use their magic, even if it was simple.

"Contego," I shouted, creating a barrier against a barrage that peppered us on entering.

"Stay together. Amira, Poly, you two go first. Trina, Morgana, cover our backs." I pointed down a hall that roughly matched the direction of Sabrina's magical angel compass.

"Yes, my king." All three of them echoed their agreement, but Morgana just chuckled and bobbed an eyebrow at me, taking charge.

Poly and Amira wasted no time in their task, charging down the industrial hall, taking magic and small arms fire as they found pockets of vampires.

"There are a hell of a lot of vampires here," Trina commented, looking over her shoulder often and sweeping the nearby areas. "You said they were stocking up, Morgana?"

"Yeah, I know this place. They make bloodwine for the vampire community. Normally, they either source it from blood banks or from willing humans. But it looked like they were trying to significantly increase their operations." Morgana kept her hands on her blade handles as they smacked against her leather clad rear.

"Willing?" Sabrina said with doubt.

"You'd be surprised." Morgana rolled her eyes. "Humans love a good high."

We walked slowly behind Poly and Amira as they cleared the way for us.

Soon we came up to a hallway that opened into a large main processing area. There were storage tanks and pipes everywhere, winding around walkways. But my eyes went to the leader.

Ricardo stood in the middle, surrounded by a small group of vampires facing us.

"Congratulations, Dragon King, but you are too late. My master will take what he wants from this city. Not even you can stop him." He stood calmly, clearly sure of his advantage.

Further behind Ricardo and his group, Helena hung chained to a balcony.

A female vampire wearing an outfit that was more leather straps than actual coverage turned away from the angel, with eyes that glowed red like Sabrina's magic.

I recognized her. She was the woman that Deniz had fed on at the club and was present when they had captured Helena.

"Dragons are such greedy, gluttonous creatures, wouldn't you agree?" Beelzebub, I assumed, stood. I noticed that their stomach was shrunken in, almost as if she was in a permanent state of starving.

Gazing at Beelzebub hit me like Sabrina's lust, only I wanted to devour everyone in the nearby vicinity, starting with the three juicy dragons around me.

"Zach?" Sabrina asked with wide, worried eyes.

I wanted to tell her that she was safe. That I would never eat somebody marked as mine, but I was too focused on the tasty dragon morsels near me.

# CHAPTER 27

S abrina seemed to notice my attention and hunger as I gazed at the dragons in front of me. They had turned, eyeing me as well. I smiled, my stomach churning with hunger.

Sabrina acted quickly, taking off her glasses and blowing a pink mist into my face. Instantly, all thoughts of eating were cut off, and instead, I wanted to take my two mates in the back of the warehouse to enjoy them.

"Zach, focus. Kill the demon." Sabrina's eyes bore into my own, and I regained what little sense I had.

I might be a giant dragon packed with power, but it seemed my emotions still ruled me—a flaw that demons could use.

My three honor guards were staggering. Polydora kept shaking her head. Amira threw herself at me. I grabbed onto her and slammed her into pipes that sprayed steam into the air, blocking my vision of the rest.

Beelzebub's voice was wrong somehow, like a male voice layered over the female voice of the body as he laughed. "Too easy. Now it's time to feast, my little vampires. I never thought we'd see his kind."

Faintly in the back of my mind, I registered that he knew what I was, but that was soon overwhelmed by the desire not to let Amira take a bite out of me as she lunged again.

"Off," I roared, punching her in the snout. I knew the move worked on sharks, so I gave it a try with dragons.

Amira dipped her forehead at the last moment, taking the fist on her much harder brow before rolling with me and slamming me into the metal bracing on a tank.

I groaned, and the noise was echoed by the tank itself as the bracing buckled. Rolling out of the way, the tank came down on Amira with an enormous thud. Red, frothy liquid exploded into a wave over all of us. Vampires landed on top of me, and I crushed one against my shoulder before throwing the other off of me.

Polydora and Trina were sluggishly resisting several vampires as well as simultaneously fighting off Beelzebub's effects.

I glanced over to check on my mates. Morgana and Ricardo were fighting. The former vampire leader of Philly had a rapier that I could barely see beyond the sparks that appeared as he fought Morgana. The two were actually well matched.

Sabrina had several red diagrams surrounding her as she fought off her own vampire. But I couldn't see Beelzebub anywhere in the glances I could take between vampires trying to get at my throat.

The collapsed tank shifted, and Amira wobbled to her feet, a hint of clarity in them for a moment. "My king!" Her eyes flicked over my shoulder.

I had just enough time to jump out of the way before the emaciated vampire that Beelzebub inhabited splashed into the space where I'd been in.

"Contego." I threw up a shield between us to buy myself a moment.

But the demon-possessed vampire was fast. It blurred around my shield as his jaw unhinged and grew impossibly wide.

I tried to smack him aside, only for him to bite and latch onto my arm. To my surprise, his fangs actually sank through my scales and pierced my skin. He'd barely broken skin as he sucked like I was an almost empty juice box.

I froze. It was like someone had stuffed a vacuum to my arm as his entire mouth suctioned to me.

I reacted instinctively; my fist crashed into his face, breaking bones and sending him flying.

"My king." Amira rushed Beelzebub in my name, jumping on the demon prince before he could recover. Then she began tearing into him with her black claws.

I had to shake my head clear as potent vampire venom flooded my system, and my arm felt numb as it recovered.

"Amira, help the others," I shouted. Then I moved and hoisted up the wet, demon-possessed vampire. "Where's the bloodlord?"

The demon gave me a choking laughter, even as his vampire body healed. "Now, why would I tell you that? I'm just here to consume and revel until my body is crushed." He kept on laughing.

It was all a joke to him, and that pissed me off even more.

I slammed him against a concrete wall, breaking more of his bones before he could heal. "Who says you have to go?"

Another fist to his chest was a stark reminder of how much pain I could inflict on the demon prince before he had a chance to get away.

"You can't stop me. But I will be back. What fun would it be to live a week in the Dragon King's body?" The demon prince only smiled, and the eerie red glow faded from the vampire's eyes.

The vampire had a hint of their own clarity for a moment until their face became gaunt. Their skin shrunk down onto their bones, and everything in them seemed to waste away until the vampire's body was a husk, like the other victims.

I tossed it to the side, and the brittle husk collapsed on itself.

The three dragons had finished taking out the stronger vampires, and Sabrina had protected herself throughout the fighting. Morgana had done the hardest job. Ricardo was disarmed and pinned to the floor, his dark hair wet and sticking to his face.

"Where is it?" my partner demanded, pushing his face into the floor.

"I can't," Ricardo whined. "He made me. He's the one who made me."

The Spanish man looked like he was on the verge of tears. But I just couldn't bring myself to give a shit.

"Either you provide information, or I eat you. Those are the only options. Either way, you'll be useful. So choose." I stepped up to the downed vampire, still keeping my senses alert for any other threats.

The battle had seemed almost too easy.

"Poly, Trina, Amira, you all okay?" I asked the dragonettes while Ricardo considered his answer.

They all nodded.

"Good. Fan out and make sure we don't have any stragglers to surprise us." I put my foot on Ricardo's back to relieve Morgana. "Now, where were we?"

"I can't." Ricardo pressed his cheek to the wet floor.

Morgana stood and pushed some wet strands of hair out of her face. "If this bloodlord is the one who turned him, then there's little he can do if they recently put a compulsion on him." She sighed. "Ricardo, answer me this, how much of all of this was by force versus free will?"

Ricardo didn't even try to look at her, instead looking at the ground. "A lot of it was me. You don't understand. You stay well clear of vampire politics, and you can because of your connections. The rest of us are forced to be a part of it, mired up to our eyeballs in the conflicts of the three houses and our masters."

Morgana snorted. "I'll throw you a pity party at your funeral." Morgana didn't have any sympathy. "You killed hundreds, maybe even thousands, of people with your plans today."

Ricardo just laughed. "You haven't fed on humans for years. They aren't people. They are nothing but cattle led around by the nose of whatever talking heads are on TV. Even those we bleed for months here were given a TV and electronics without an internet connection. And they were happy as could be. You should see it when you give humans food, shelter and entertainment. They just stand around, happy, just like cattle."

"I'm sure vampire venom had no part in that." I rolled my eyes, increasing the pressure on his back. "Tell me something useful or I'm going to make you useful," I reminded him of my threat to eat him.

The ruined vampire only smiled, showing off his fangs. "You have much to learn, young dragon. Don't think this is nearly over." Moving quickly, he tried to grab my other leg.

In response, I crushed his back, paralyzing the vampire while Morgana's blade flicked and a tear in space severed Ricardo's head.

"This was too easy," I stated my thoughts out loud to Morgana and Sabrina as they approached.

Though, I looked down with a frown. He would have probably been rich with mana, but it bled out of him, and I wasn't about to lick the floor.

"Agreed. But they likely wouldn't want to split their forces. They have another battle planned." Morgana turned and gazed at the concrete walls like she could see through them. "We need to get to the park and help the fae."

Sabrina finished one of her enchantments and frowned at the diagram. "There are still a lot of humans here."

I nodded, knowing it was going to be messy. "Work with Morgana and the dragons. Clear the place and lock it up tight with them inside. We'll have to come back for them after. We just don't have time or manpower to rescue dozens of people."

As I said it, my eyes flicked to Helena hanging from the chains. I was glad that she hadn't been possessed yet, and we could use her in the fight against the fae, even if she was weakened.

Morgana nodded and hurried off with Sabrina, who was holding up her enchantment to help direct them to the humans.

"Now, let's see if I can't help you, Helena." I went over and broke the chains, pulling her down into my arms.

Her eyes fluttered open as they flashed with magic.

"Mmm," she moaned, and her eyes were hazy as she gazed up at me. "My hero," she mumbled, and a feeling like a heavy warm blanket settled over me.

I felt like I suddenly had fallen in love with Helena, and she with me. It was such improbable, yet inevitable, instant love. I was so relieved to have her in my arms, to have her safe from everything. The comforting warmth that squeezed in around us made me want to hold her forever.

Somehow, even after all the tension between us, it just exploded and became love here and now as I saved her.

There was a familiar smile on her lips.

"Too bad you are alone." The same distortion that had been in the vampire's voice who had been possessed by Beelzebub was present in Helena, and I felt myself bristle before more of that warm blanket settled around me and calmed me down.

The woman I was looking at meant something to me. I loved her, and I would fight for her. The beast raged in my chest for me to mark her and mate her.

And I didn't want to suppress that urge, but there was something buzzing in the back of my head like a nagging fly.

"My hero. Thank you for saving me. I'm just a damsel in distress, and I think I love you after saving me." Despite the distortion, her words were like sickly sweet honey to my ears. I couldn't help but savor them, desperately clinging to them.

I put her down gently, dismissing the buzzing in the back of my mind as she hung her arms around the back of my head.

"Oh, the Dragon King is a romantic," Beelzebub said with Helena's mouth. "Come, love me, feed me." She chuckled in what felt like the cutest giggle I'd ever heard.

I loved it when she laughed.

I loved everything about her.

The buzzing grew even louder, and I tried to swat the feeling away even as the beast in my chest became a love-struck puppy and begged to be with the woman before me.

But as I stared down at her, I processed what was wrong. She was mine, but at the moment, I was sharing her. And I did not share.

MINE! The thought raged in my mind like a burning inferno even as my jaw crackled, ready to mark the nephilim. The rage going through me gave me purpose. Whatever was trying to take her from me would pay. It would pay so dearly for touching my angel.

Anger and love pushed through me as I latched onto her shoulder, magic burning through my jaw and searing into her flesh.

"Ah!" her distorted voice screamed as she bucked in my arms and grabbed my head. "Stop that." Beelzebub raged and our eyes locked.

His magic welled up in Helena's body, and I could see purple light reflecting off her eyes as wild fae magic burned in my own.

The two magics clashed, forming between our eyes as the windows to our souls. Then it felt like I was falling into her eyes, tumbling and twirling through the soulful pools and into something else.

When I finally landed, I was surrounded by a dark blue world with silver wisps of people running back and forth.

"Helena!" a woman scolded the young girl with wings who was clambering and climbing up onto a table. It looked like the little girl had knocked over a ceramic bowl and shattered it on the floor, spilling berries everywhere.

I waved my hand in front of the woman, but she didn't react.

"I swear. You are nothing but trouble." The woman put her hands on her hips.

"Sorry, mom." The young Helena looked down at the ground like a properly chastised child. And then she took a step back, fear covering her face.

The woman's back suddenly had wings, and she grabbed Helena by the hair, forcing her to look up at her. "I love you so much, dear."

Young Helena burst into tears. "I love you too, mom."

But I could tell that her mother was using her magic on her daughter.

"That's why this is going to pain me so much. I really do love you, my little Hel, but look what you've made me do? All because you won't listen." Her mother continued to hold her by the hair, pushing her love onto her before she started to slap her.

I winced.

It was brutal, absolutely brutal, to force her child to love her and then weaponized it against her like that. The way Helena acted made so much more sense. And the way her mother called Helena her 'little Hel' didn't sit right with me. It didn't sound like a term of endearment.

Anger at how she was raised rushed through me.

I hadn't had much time to process being a father, but I knew that once Yev finished her pregnancy and the egg hatched, I would be a better parent than the example in front of me.

I moved on through the bleak landscape of Helena's soul.

Helena's memories sprang up, tinted with foul emotions. Her mother continued using her power on Helena like a thousand-pound chain, dragging her down and tying the young Helena to her.

She constantly made Helena love her, only to use her.

I watched as Helena was pushed into combat training that she didn't want. And then when she was pulled away from one of the Nashner's maids that had stepped in to fill the parental void.

And then... oh god. She was forced to remove the maid herself just to prove to her mother that she loved her. Helena's mother twisted her around the bond between them, cementing it with the full might of the archangel of love's power.

It was no wonder Helena didn't change sides until she thought her mother couldn't reach her anymore. Helena was clearly simultaneously terrified of the woman and eager for the barest scrap of attention and love.

I watched as she grew up, loathing the very idea of love.

At some point, Helena seemed to understand that the way she'd been treated wasn't right, but it was still hard for her to do much to change it. She'd been so conditioned by her mother that it was painful to watch.

A few paltry attempts at rebellion were squashed brutally by her mother until she became a grudging, but effective, soldier for the celestial plane and the church.

As I reached adulthood, I skimmed past the parts I knew, like our time in Switzerland. But what really caught my attention happened after she had fled from where the archangel of justice had died.

For a long time, she just flew. Flying from mountain to mountain, she sat atop the peaks and gazed at the world below.

I imagined that she was savoring her freedom, but Helena didn't talk or meet people. Instead, she remained on her own and eventually crossed the Atlantic Ocean on her own wings, arriving in America, where she started anew in New York City. She reinvented herself, starting her work as she became an agent for the FBI and started protecting paranormals.

She'd worked her way through the organization quickly. She'd learned how to manipulate people and circumstances to her benefit. Helena had learned from the best. But she did seem to be using it for the good of paranormals. Helena was actually trying to solve problems, at least in her own way.

As I moved into the present moment, I noticed that the surrounding space was quite large. And it was marred by red veins as a fat demon laughed. He sat in a chair with Helena restrained and leaning up against it.

"You've come. But you are a fool. This is not where dragons should be fighting." Beelzebub was tall, well over eight feet, with jowls that flopped against his neck as his belly bounced.

He was the perfect picture of excess.

"I'd say something heroic like 'let her go', but we both know that won't happen." I flexed my hands. I'd remained in my dragon knight form, and I hoped it would shield me as well as it did in the real world.

Helena tried to yell something at me from her position, but it didn't get through the cloth around her mouth.

"Yes, well. We can see just how strong the soul of the Dragon King is. After all, I see hints of Bahamut and Tiamat in you." Beelzebub's eyes flashed greedily. "Tell me, is that true?"

"Why don't you come and find out?" I widened my stance and prepared for battle.

# CHAPTER 28

Beelzebub cackled and pushed the bound Helena sharply to the side to make way for his girth as he stood. But surprising me, the demon moved from his seat to standing in front of me in a flash, completely defying his otherwise overweight appearance.

"Boo." He laughed.

His fist buried itself in my gut, and I folded over it before being thrown back into one of Helena's memories. She was screaming something at Jared.

Ignoring the memory playing out around me, I rolled over and got to my feet, my whole body aching.

"This is a battle between souls, Dragon King. You might be incredibly strong physically, but here? You are weak." Beelzebub was on me again, sending me flying through more of Helena's memories. "I'm going to beat your soul to a pulp, then I'm going to ride you back to your body."

Fuck.

I felt weak. The strength that normally flooded my limbs seemed absent. After two hits, my arms shook as I tried to lift myself off the ground.

"Don't feel bad. Age has a lot to do with the strength of the soul. You are just too young to fight a ten-thousand-year-old demon." Beelzebub put his foot on my back and pressed me back to the ground.

"I'm going to have so much fun working through your harem and hoard. Dragons really are gluttonous creatures." Beelzebub sloppily licked his lips.

Even from the ground, I could smell the foulness in his breath. It was like he had spent all ten thousand years letting fish rot in his mouth. My mind barely registered his words, but they slowly and surely etched their way into my mind.

"Mine," I growled as images of him touching my hoard, my women, flipped through my mind. "Mine," I said with more force as I pushed against his foot.

"Greed and Gluttony are so intertwined," Beelzebub chuckled, leaning harder down onto me. "Don't think you can overpower gluttony with a little greed."

I lifted my face off the floor, and the purple light of Ikta's magic shone off the floor in front of me. It was coming from my eyes.

The fae supposedly felt their emotions greater than other paranormals. Yet neither angels nor demons tried to influence them. Whether it was Helena's love or Beelzebub's gluttony, both were hitting me, pushing on my soul and draining it of mana. They were weakening me because I couldn't control myself.

But these were my emotions. Mine and no one else's.

I took hold of my emotions and reined them in. They would obey me, and me alone. As I crushed the connection between Helena and myself, I felt strength return to my limbs. I lifted Beelzebub off of me enough to roll out.

"It isn't that I'm weak, but that you are actively weakening me," I growled knowingly, pushing out the thoughts that he'd planted in my head.

The battle in Helena's soul wasn't just physical. It was a battle of wills and internal strength. When I rose to meet my opponent, his eyes were like staring into a fire pit.

"Don't think your succubus will be here to save you this time," he replied, smiling at me.

I felt my mouth water as hunger seeped into my every thought. That strength that had started to build became a sieve as he pushed on my gluttony and fed off of me.

My dragon nature wasn't strong enough at that moment to fight the desire that flooded me, but I wasn't just dragon magic anymore. I thought back to how some of the fae were insufferably confident in themselves and tried to channel my inner Ikta.

Nothing could stop me.

I repeated that thought like a mantra as the gluttony dimmed in my mind, and I stood up straighter. "You know, it's a little cowardly to hide in souls."

Beelzebub laughed. "I know my strengths. That's why I bounce from soul to soul, squeezing them for everything they are worth before moving on. A physical fight? Well, that just sounds like work."

Cracking my knuckles, I smiled. I was more than happy to make him do a bit of work.

Rather than running to him, I followed my instincts. I imagined myself in front of him, punching deep into his gut. I made it my full intention, and sure enough, the strange world we inhabited in Helena's soul responded.

I was suddenly in front of Beelzebub and slamming my fist right into the fat bastard's gut.

Beelzebub wheezed a laugh as his stomach sucked inwards like it was hollow. His skin split open, only for a vast suction to appear in the middle of his chest, trying to draw my fist into it.

"I will devour you one way or another." Beelzebub grabbed my shoulders and tried to push me further inwards.

I quickly realized that I needed to be bigger.

Rather than truly shifting, I once again focused on my intentions. One moment my hand was a fist, the next a claw as my view changed to look down on Beelzebub from up above.

I had become my dragon form, towering over the demon. A low growl pulled itself from my throat. But from up here, I saw something else.

Helena.

She was tied up, looking up at me feebly. Knowing her body had been tough in the real world, I hoped that would prove true in her soul world. Taking a breath, I washed the entire area with fire, hoping to break the binding on her.

"Hah. Fire doesn't bother a demon, son." Beelzebub grew larger to match me. "We bathe in hellfire."

"Who said I was aiming for you?" I commented as a pissed off nephilim rose behind the demon with silver ire in her eyes.

"You fucking pig," Helena screamed. A spear formed in her hands, and she stabbed it into the giant Beelzebub's back, tearing it out the side and leaving behind a large gash.

Beelzebub certainly screamed like a pig. But his scream did nothing to Helena. She was in a full rage as she kept stabbing the demon.

He tried to back away from her, but I was there, my claws tearing into that prodigious stomach again as my jaw clamped down on his shoulder. The taste of the demon was absolutely foul in my mouth, but I held on because the incensed Helena was quickly whittling away at Beelzebub.

"Die, pig! How dare you come in here and take my body? You only won because you surprised me," Helena screamed and grew several times in size to match the two of us.

"I'm going to cut you into a thousand pieces for touching me. I will never be able to shower enough!" Helena kept tearing into Beelzebub.

I lost my bite, and as I let go, Beelzebub was clearly afraid. He was backpedaling, barely keeping his head from being removed as her silver spear flashed out again and again.

Helena was incredible to behold. A blindingly bright silver ball of rage, she pummeled the weakened Beelzebub.

Any attempts he made at trying to control her with gluttony washed right off of her. Her anger was so bright that it couldn't be penetrated by the demon's power, and she now was prepared to defend herself.

"You will both pay for this. This fraction of my soul might perish. But I, Beelzebub, will be back." The demon roared before Helena overtook him and stabbed him with her spear, flooding his body with silver light and exploding it into tiny ribbons of demon soul.

Her anger only cooled marginally as she whipped her spear to the side and turned to look at me over her shoulder.

"Why are you still here?" she asked, her voice still filled with anger, but her eyes slightly softer.

"Uh, I don't know how to get out," I answered honestly.

Her eyes glowed again, and it felt like I got hit by a truck.

I found myself thrown out of her soul back into my body.

My jaws unclamped from Helena's shoulder as I blinked away the disorientation. As I came to, I realized I had Helena pressed to the ground with her arms around the back of my head.

There on her pale shoulder was the thin scar of my mark. The mark I placed on all of my mates.

She returned to her body as well, and her soft expression hardened to the hard shell I'd seen her put on after her mother's abuse.

I didn't wait to get yelled at. I pushed off of the nephilim in an instant, making space between the two of us. "Sorry. You really had a hold on me with your magic."

She frowned and brushed her shoulder, watching me. But as she touched her shoulder, I saw the moment she registered that something was different. It wasn't long before it twisted into anger.

"What the fuck have you done?" she screamed at the top of her lungs. "You marked me!"

In an instant, her wings were out, and she was before me.

The slap had the full force of her strength, and even in my dragon knight form, my bones were jarred. I wanted to be angry, to hit her back, but the beast locked up, fighting my movements.

Despite the situation, my instincts registered her as my mate.

"You shit! I will tear you to pieces" She came swinging again.

I went to cover my face, but the strike never came.

Helena stood before me, huffing and puffing with anger fixed on her face. "Fight me, dammit. I'm not one of your floozies. Do you understand me? This mark means nothing! I still hate you."

I was mostly baffled that she wasn't hitting me.

But as I looked at her, I saw the need for me to attack her back in her eyes. She was almost hungry for that kind of conflict. It was the only kind of love she'd really known.

"I didn't save you only to fight you." I stopped trying to protect my head. "All I wanted to do was get rid of Beelzebub. You've been out for a while, and shit has hit the fan."

She paused in her anger. "Tell me. Now."

"Till is aware of the paranormal, and as a result, she's also my servant now. She's helping me sort out the issues in the city, covering some of it up with a human trafficking operation that we discovered. But I have to go now, and you are done. Clearly, you don't have the strength to join the current fight," I tried to piss her off.

Helena got up in my face. That sharp cut of her white hair swayed as she was forced to look up at me. "Bullshit, you wouldn't have defeated Beelzebub without me." She stabbed me in the chest with a finger.

"We'll never know. Pretty sure I just let you vent a little anger there," I replied, keeping a charming smile on my face.

"Don't smile at me." She poked me with her finger again. Her face was so close, my instinct was to lean forward and kiss her.

I shook it off, not wanting to take the risk of getting stabbed by the angry nephilim, even if I thought there was a boatload of sexual tension sparking off between us.

Helena's eyes were stormy, but there was something more in them. And with her heart-shaped face, she was still a bit cute when she was pissed.

She blew out an angry huff. "My case isn't over until all accomplices are accounted for. What was happening here?" She looked around at the mess we'd made of the brewery, her eyes landing on several bodies of vampires.

"Vampires working with Beelzebub?" she commented to herself, looking back over her shoulder at me for answers.

"Look, like I said, I think you are done. We'll go handle the rest of the vampires and the bloodlord that is making a move on the fae. Till is at the police station. You can go help her fill out some paperwork." I brushed her off, trying not to smile and give away that I was riling her up.

She poked me in the chest again with her finger and whirled, storming off. As she moved, her wings unfolded, and she flew forward, slamming her spear into a wall to vent her anger before flying off.

"That was interesting. You know she's going in the direction of Wissahickon park, right?" Sabrina asked from behind me.

"Was there any lust coming off her, or was I imagining it?" I asked the succubus.

"Oh, I thought for sure there was about to be a hate fuck here on the floor. No way she'd do makeup sex, just take all that anger and vent it through rough sex," Sabrina clarified.

"Good. I wasn't imagining things. She's all twisted up. I doubt she even knows what love is outside the angelic power. Damn." I shook my head, remembering her past. "Either way, we need to get going."

"Morgana is wrapping up. I came back because I felt demonic mana again, and thought you might need help, but you seem to have done okay."

I shook my head. "No, that was pretty rough. How can I fortify myself against those types of pulls?"

"We'll work on it later. Maybe you'll need some summer school for your independent study." Sabrina smirked, and something told me that class with my new succubus mate might get very interesting indeed.

But at the moment, we needed to move. The main event was about to happen, and it would take all of our strength to keep the city intact.

I took a deep breath and bellowed with my dragon's voice. "Morgana, dragonettes, we are leaving."

Sabrina blinked and stuck a finger in her ear. "Please tell me before you do that next time."

"Whoops, sorry." I gave her a sheepish grin.

"What?" she yelled, looking closely at my mouth as she tried to read my lips.

"Sorry," I repeated more slowly.

"Yeah, me too." She completely misread my lips. "Help me back to the van." Sabrina leaned on me, and I felt the warmth of her body. Despite the situation, I felt my body suddenly grow excited.

The beast begged to take our succubus back to our hoard and cement our mating. But as much as I wanted to, I couldn't then.

Sabrina must have felt my lust as she patted my arm. "I'm going to ride my dragon later. Don't worry about that."

The beast acted as if she had talked to it, sitting down and patiently waiting like a dog when you picked up a bag of treats.

"You really know how to tame my dragon instincts," I said into her ear as we walked back out to the van.

"Of course. Though, if you wanted, we could always do a quick round in the van. Wissahickon is a good fifteen-minute drive." Sabrina's hearing was back, and she looked up at me through her eyelashes as she blushed.

I loved that she was feeling more confident and bold, embracing a bit more of her demon nature.

We reached the van, and I shifted back to my naked human form. Then I picked her up, carrying her with me to the back seat of the van and planting her in my lap.

Morgana was next, hopping in the front seat as Sabrina and I kissed in the back like a teenage couple trying not to be caught. "I see you two are having fun. How do you feel about being with a woman, Sabrina?"

The succubus pushed off my chest, and her eyes flashed a bright pink before she turned to Morgana. "I'm sexually fluid, but I don't think I'll enjoy anyone else, at least not without my mate present."

Morgana only chuckled as the three dragons joined us in the car. Each of them was naked. We hadn't brought a change of clothes with us, and we'd likely be shifting again soon, anyway.

"The succubus beat us all," Amira grumbled, finding her seat and buckling in.

"I'm even naked, and he barely spared a glance," Trina whined. "Stupid Dragon King. Your dragonettes are naked."

"Splendidly so," Polydora agreed, turning around in the seat in front of me and giving me a full view of her naked breasts.

Sabrina ground her skirt against my hardness, and a growl escaped me. I wanted to take her right there, but our first time after mating wasn't going to be a quick rut in the back seat of a van.

Sabrina piped up, ignoring my growl, "I can assure you all that there was a vast change in his lust as you three naked girls showed up. He's just trying to keep a lid on things because we have more important matters to handle."

Then she wiggled again on my lap. "I'm just working to feed myself. He has to keep his succubus full now, doesn't he?" She turned around and straddled me, rocking back and forth with her arms behind my neck.

I leaned back. It was both torture and pleasure. And I was so going to get her back once we got back to my hoard.

# CHAPTER 29

I barely registered the ride to Wissahickon park as Sabrina's body made mine nearly combust with heat. I found myself appreciating Morgana's driving in a new way as Sabrina bounced and shifted from side to side with Morgana's sharp turns.

"Guess the council has it all on lockdown," Morgana commented as the van came to a screeching halt.

Ahead of us, there were lines of military jeeps with mounted guns and sirens manning them.

"Shift as you get out," I told the dragonettes as I placed Sabrina to the side.

As we became physically separated, my mind was suddenly clear of lust, focusing on what I saw beyond the jeeps. A huge vortex of magic cascaded over the park.

I clambered over the dragons, shifting into my gold dragon knight form and stomping forward.

The closest siren saluted me. "Dragon King. We have orders to let you through."

The others filed out of the van behind me.

Morgana tossed her keys to another siren. "Park it for me. And don't even think about scratching it."

I rolled my eyes. That van took hundreds of bullets and didn't leave a scratch. But it was Morgana's prized car.

The dragons stood behind me in their hybrid forms as the line of jeeps parted for us. One jeep peeled away from the rest and came forward to pick us up. There was a siren waiting for us in the back.

I hopped in the back with the others; the jeep sank under the weight of four dragons. "What's the situation?"

"Vampires swarmed the city. They just completely overwhelmed everyone instantly. Thousands of them. They ran over any defenses that we had in place and were able to turn more humans. The concentration seems to be here at the park though," the siren laid down the basic details.

"Current strategy?" I asked.

"Uh..." He paused as if my question was far above his pay grade. "My group is keeping humans away as a fucking war starts. We have reports of several groups clearing the city ev-even a l-lich." The very mention of T had the siren stuttering.

"Ah, yeah. Don't worry about him. The lich is a friend of mine. He's killing vampires by ripping their flesh off of them and turning them into skeletons." I realized the added details may not bring full comfort to the nervous siren, but he nodded stiffly.

"So he's on our side?" The siren seemed skeptical.

Morgana interjected, "Absolutely. T wouldn't hurt a fly."

I begged to differ, considering he was killing vampires, but I left it alone. "What's the situation here?"

"We got here and laid down fire into the park, but the vampires just shrugged it off. Some escaped into Faerie, and their masses were hard to whittle down. But then the elves slammed down a huge shield around them, cutting them off from the city and keeping them contained."

"Yeah, but it's not currently cutting them off from the portal. They want into the fae lands more than anything. That's why they're here." I eyed the current shield.

The siren shrugged. "We didn't have the firepower to take them on. I think they'll drop the shield once we have some of the bigger hitters like you here."

The siren pulled up closer to the park, and the huge magical vortex seemed to end in a shimmering dome that flickered as vampires tried to get out of the park. The lower section of the park was completely teeming with vampires. And I could spot fighting and struggling among them.

Based on the party, I knew they were fighting each other to get to the portal that held the fae world.

"Bring us to wherever the elven command is set up." I felt my marks and sensed Kelly hurrying in this direction. And Helena had already arrived, circling high above. I tried to find her with my eyes, but the vortex of magic made it difficult to spot her amid them, even though I knew where to look.

The siren relayed my order to the one driving.

"Do you think you can take them all?" Sabrina asked, her eyes wide as she took in all the vampires below.

"I'm going to lay down some runs of dragon fire. That ought to take out a lot of them."

"Or push them all into the Faerie," Morgana commented, watching the situation closely. "There must be something on the other end of the portal, or they wouldn't still be here."

My eyes flickered to the area where I knew we'd find the portal. "Yeah. Hopefully, Maeve and the others are okay."

"What's the Faerie realm like?" I asked, realizing we may end up taking a trip through it.

"It isn't often that outsiders are able to enter," Polydora spoke. "But my understanding is that Faerie is split into two major parts."

"Summer and Winter." I grinned, happy to know something about the paranormal world.

"No." Polydora popped my bubble. "There is a large area that is tamed, about the size of Germany is how I've heard it sized. Then beyond that there is a boundless, wild, untamed Faerie. It is incredibly easy to get lost among it. Paths aren't straight, and turning around doesn't bring you back the way you came."

I paused. "That sounds impossible to inhabit."

She shrugged. "There are some who do. Winter and Summer are ever expanding their tamed territory, taking back the wild. It is important that, if we enter the Faerie, you never go into the fae wilds."

Morgana cleared her throat. "But you were partially correct. The part of the Faerie that the queens control is split between Summer and Winter. They push on each other's territories constantly with their war."

"So, where does the portal exit?" I asked. It seemed like a lot of power to give to one side versus the other.

But the surrounding paranormals just looked at each other, clearly not sure of the answer. Wonderful, I thought, hoping it didn't drop us in the middle of a battle line or something.

The jeep came to a stop where a tent had been erected, and a dozen old elves were working magic, constantly reinforcing the barrier.

Sebastian was standing back, watching with his arms crossed, and he turned to see me approach. "You," he scowled.

"I knew you missed me." I hopped out of the Jeep. "Good news. I've gotten rid of our Beelzebub issue for the moment."

At least, I was pretty sure I had. Helena seemed to think so, and she knew more about how demons worked than I did.

The elf's eyebrows shot up. "Beelzebub?!" he hissed.

"Yeah. Recent development. I may not have had time to report it more broadly," I continued on. "Helena, the nephilim, has also been freed."

I looked up at the sky, trying to spot her once more, but failing.

"What's the situation here?" I brought my eyes back to the barrier.

"I'm not sure this is a bigger problem than Beelzebub in our city. Are you certain that he's gone?" Sebastian put aside his issue with me, focusing back on the issues of the city.

"Helena dealt the finishing blow. Though he made it seem like only part of his soul had come."

Sebastian nodded. "Yes, that would give me confidence. Demon princes rarely enter our world completely. They are far too cautious for that." The old elf looked at the current situation again. "I assume you want the barrier down so that you can get in there?"

I paused, trying to decide the best course of action. "Maybe just open up the top for me? I'd like to see if I can't clear out many of them with my fire," I suggested.

Sebastian rubbed his chin. "We can collapse it starting from the top and see how slow it goes down. But at most, we are talking a minute before it's fully gone."

"Perfect." I grinned, feeling a little feral edge to my face.

I was ready to cook the vampires below.

"My king." Amira slammed her hand to her chest. "We would love to fly with you."

I had been ready to ask them. "Of course. Let's get ready. Sebastian, give us the signal when you will start."

The elf nodded. The normal hate he had for me was replaced by a sense of duty in solving this crisis.

Walking away from the tent, I stretched myself out. It had been a few months since I'd gone entirely dragon. I realized that I understood more of what Herm had been saying when we were at the fae party. The city did make it hard to stretch your wings.

"Zach." Sabrina caught my arm. "Stay safe." She kissed my cheek and pulled away with a blush blazing to life on her cheeks.

Morgana was next. "I'll be right behind you as you head into the fae realm."

I snorted; she knew me too well. I fully planned on charging into the fae realm as soon as the vampires outside of it were less of a problem.

My bones cracked as my mates stepped away to give me room, and I rapidly expanded. Gold scales grew along with me as my face elongated and an enormous tail sprouted from the bottom of my spine. Stretching out, my wings unfurled from my back.

I continued to grow, towering over my two mates. They were only the size of one of my claws when I was finished. My scales were gold, but with a little focus, the gold bled away. Aspects of red flickered along the scales, showing my full dragon heritage.

Polydora, Trina, and Amira shifted beside me.

None of them quite matched my size, but Polydora was certainly trying as she held her head aloft.

"You are showing off your nature," Polydora stated, squinting her draconic eyes at me. "It looks good."

I smirked but became distracted, as I could sense Kelly growing closer.

"Alpha!" a lumbering brown werewolf shouted at the front of the pack as hundreds of werewolves charged behind her and echoed her. "Alpha-alpha."

She shifted as she stopped before me, and so did the red wolf that had been keeping pace with her. Taylor gave me a wink and a little flirty wave of her fingers.

"The elves are going to drop the shield, and we are going to thin these vampires out. As soon as the shield is down, we push through them and into the Faerie realm." I gave Kelly the rough plan. I had no idea what was happening inside the Faerie realm, and I planned to find out.

She grinned and howled only for the rest of her pack to echo her. "I'll be right behind you, alpha."

"I will too, alpha-alpha." Taylor bowed, her naked form flowing downward.

Kelly only rolled her eyes, but it seemed she'd given up on correcting the 'alpha-alpha' thing. "Get in there, my mate." Kelly gave my foot a gentle push.

I chuckled and crouched low before launching myself as high as I could. Stretching out my wings, I beat them a few times, sending out a torrent of wind that ripped up the tents below. I cringed a little, hoping they wouldn't be mad that I'd destroyed their temporary structure.

But I had a job to do. I circled, climbing high into the sky. As I moved up, I noticed a black cloud that seemed to be crawling towards us from the north. I assumed that was T heading towards us.

The three dragonettes joined me in the air as we circled over the barrier erected by the elves.

A magical firework lit up the sky, and I knew that was my sign. They were about to bring the barrier down. We hovered just over the top as the smallest hole formed; the barrier peeling away as the spell collapsed.

Not wasting time, I dove, my dragonettes close behind me. I gathered my fire in my throat before swooping lower and releasing a gout of fire that exploded out of my mouth under high pressure. I nearly filled the inside of the magical barrier.

Through the flickering flames, I could see vampires throwing up red shields to protect themselves and those around them. My fire was powerful, but with such distance and spread, many of them could huddle around the shields and survive.

My dragonettes worked to fire on the vampires as well, but it had a similar effect.

My scales shifted from red and gold to silver and white as I banked my wings hard, coming around for a second pass nearly as soon as Amira laid down her blanket of death fog.

I spewed freezing fog into the collapsing dome, turning it into the largest snow globe ever. And as soon as my breath cut off, I was already coming back around for another, my scales shifting to blue and bronze.

Lighting crackled around my jaw as I built up another blast, but this time, I dove straight into the center of the mess as bolts of lightning raced from my mouth like the most epic thunderstorm ever seen. The bolts arced between vampires and lighting up the park.

I landed with an enormous thud as the barrier finally collapsed, taking in the scene around me. My wings beat hard, throwing vampires everywhere.

Charred and frozen vampires were scattered all over the field, but many were pushing and shoving each other, trying to cram themselves through the portal into the Faerie realm. Any that couldn't get away turned and gave it one last go, charging me.

I let loose a roar that shook the earth and filled the air with more arcs of lightning just as Kelly and her wolves came sprinting down the hill. Vampires tried to leap onto me like ticks and bite, and the deep howl that came from Kelly made me proud. My mate was a true Alpha.

The werewolves came from behind them and crushed the remaining vampires as I swatted them with my massive paws, trying not to take out werewolves in the process.

I found myself feeling cramped, trapped in the middle of the battle on the ground. A vampire clung to my snout, even as I tried to shake him.

"Hold still, alpha-alpha!" someone shouted, and I froze as Taylor's red werewolf form latched onto the vampire and tore him off my face, only to roll and land on top of him. She emptied his chest cavity of any organs with a single swipe.

She grinned up at me. "You are impressive, alpha-alpha."

I snorted at the compliment. "Now I just need not to crush any of you on my way to the portal." It would crush Kelly if I killed one of her wolves.

The field had become utter chaos as the wolves tore through the vampires, and I tried to figure out the best way to make it to the portal.

"Make way for the alpha-alpha!" Taylor shouted, ending her command with a piercing howl and running ahead of me.

Surprisingly, the wolves parted, throwing their combatants to the side or completely abandoning them in my wake. I had no qualm snapping my maw down at any vampires in my way as I made a path towards the portal.

Taylor happily led me like a truck escorting oversized loads, running in front of me and howling commands.

The vampires caught on that any in my way didn't fare well and joined in moving aside, making it all a little easier. One vampire tried to jump Taylor, but I managed to catch him with a claw, and in my attempt to tear him off of Taylor, I tore him in half.

"Thanks, alpha-alpha. Almost there," she cheered, far peppier than I'd ever seen her before.

Three other bodies landed near the portal as my honor guard dropped in their hybrid forms, making a much more graceful appearance.

Behind them, a pair of trees leaned slightly, their branches twisted together. All my senses were screaming at me; there was a massive amount of mana flowing around them.

I looked back, wanting to make sure my mates were okay. The battle still raged. Morgana had gotten caught up working with Kelly. The two actually fought together very well.

I wanted to let loose more blasts of dragon breath over the crowd, but I couldn't risk harming the wolves, and they seemed to have a simple time killing the vampires.

"My king. None of these possessed the power of a bloodlord. The stronger vampires are still alive." Polydora looked at the portal warily. "Allow us to head through first."

I nodded, and she darted in with her hybrid form.

"So, multiple colors?" Taylor asked, looking me up and down. "Now you are bronze and blue."

"Multiple colors," I agreed. "Long story."

"How about you tell me over a few drinks some time?" Taylor made her shot.

"Did you really just ask me out?" I chuckled as I shrank back down to my dragon knight form. I sure as shit wasn't fitting through the portal as my dragon.

Taylor shrugged. "A girl has to try if she wants to get into the Dragon King's harem. So, drink?"

Polydora ducked back through the portal amid Trina and Amira, scowling at Taylor.

"Rain check. And Scarlett has to give the okay," I told her and focused on Polydora, who was lightly dusted with snow.

"We are in Winter's realm. There's no sign of the vampires, but there is an enormous palace just outside the portal. I think we may be right outside the Winter court," she reported.

I shifted my scales back to silver and white, bracing for a freezing cold. "Let's go."

"Be safe, alpha-alpha. I'll hold the portal and wait for that rain check!" Taylor stood on her tiptoes as she waved to us.

# CHAPTER 30

I moved through the portal into the fae worlds, coming out the other end immediately buffeted with the frigid winds of a snowstorm. Snow swirled around our group, and the leafless trees creaked as the weighed down branches of ice were blown about by the strong wind.

"There. My King." Polydora pointed through the storm towards a vast castle coated in ice rose amid the storm.

Even with the fresh snow, enough vampires had been passing through the portal that there was an obvious trail heading up to the giant structure.

Yet there were none here at present.

"That's where our vampires went," I stated the obvious and pushed through the snow that was nearly knee deep, even in my dragon knight form.

The other three dragons fell into line behind me.

I had left many allies behind to deal with the vampires at the park. But I'd expected to find the fae battling them already and planned to join their forces.

"My king." Amira kept pace with me. "If there was nothing on this side blocking the vampires, why were they not entering the Faerie realm in greater force?"

I frowned as she restated my concerns. The elves had been wrong; the fae hadn't put up a fight. At least not by the portals.

Only one answer made sense. "Greed. The bloodlord and his direct followers must have wanted the fae for themselves. They likely ordered all the younger vampires to stay out. It also provided them a bit more protection."

But that meant he also left behind an army. So how did he plan to take on the fae? "Vampires don't simply grow stronger by feeding more, do they?" I asked.

Polydora shook her head. "No, not exactly, but feeding replenishes strength. And age matters. At the point that a vampire becomes a bloodlord, they are old enough that they cannot drink enough blood to reach their full strength."

So this bloodlord could increase his personal strength by feasting on fae.

I sped up my steps as I slogged through the snow up towards the castle. As soon as the castle entrance was in sight, the situation became clearer.

Fae lay slumped and dead along the entrance, their skin shrunken. There was barely a drop of blood on the ground.

"Drained. They are draining them all." My pace quickened as I could get out of the snow and onto the cleared paths of the castle. I wondered what unlucky fae had the job of clearing paths that were under eternal snow, but then I realized that it was probably magic.

Reaching the entrance, I jogged into the castle.

The bloodlord and his followers had at least a half an hour head start on us, and it showed. The halls of the castle were lined with dead fae.

I stopped at an intersection, trying to use the dead bodies to direct me in which direction to take, but it wasn't clear.

"This way. I hear a battle." Polydora dove down one hallway.

I was hot on her heels as she cut through several more paths. Sure enough, the sound of metal on metal and people yelling became clear to me as we grew closer, and I overtook Polydora with my longer strides.

We finally arrived, stepping into an enormous chamber. A throne rose above us in the back of the chamber.

Fae fought in a half circle around the entrance, while a several layer deep group of vampires attacked. The entire room shook from the impacts of the fight beyond them.

There were more vampires than fae, but the fae were using the hallway to limit how many of them could join the fight.

"Zach!" Maeve was amid the fae, fighting.

A vampire tried to take advantage of her distraction, but the Fall Lady parried his sword, swishing it out to the side and followed it up with a quick slash under his arm that caused him to stumble back. But his injury only lasted for a moment. He healed right up and attacked her once again.

I hoped that the Winter fae were at least partially resistant to ice as I took a deep breath and blew a thin bank of freezing fog at the back of the vampires.

But as the blue cloud rolled over them, different pieces of jewelry on them glowed for a moment, and the fog rolled onto the fae, who shrugged off the chill.

A nearby vampire rounded on me, scoffing. "We came to fight the Winter fae, and you think we're that unprepared?" He paused as he noted my half-silver, half-white appearance. "Kill them."

Given their numbers, the vampires easily carved off some of their forces from the fae attacks and moved them towards us.

"Enchantments," Trina scoffed. "They have something to counter frost magic." A little purple fog moved off with her breath.

I had wondered why the fae were all fighting with swords.

"Don't use your breath; we'd kill the fae too," I reminded her.

The vampires moved on us in a blur.

I took a swing at the first vampire to reach me, but he ducked around my attack, and his sword scraped against my side. My scales took most of the blow, but the blade worked its way under a few of them, leaving a shallow cut.

"Contego." I filled the hall behind the vampire that had scratched me, trapping it alone with four dragons.

He was fast, but Polydora was skilled and snapped a kick where she expected him to be and bend his knee in the wrong direction.

"Whoops." Polydora smiled before her claws flashed forward and tore chunks from the vampire, severely challenging his regeneration.

Trina pulled him back, even though he was already recovering at a remarkable rate, and blew a thin stream of death breath onto him, decaying his body even as it tried to heal itself. She kept it up for several heartbeats and his body fell apart.

Vampires cut at the shield several times before backing up and hurling red bolts at it.

Seeing how well Trina's death attribute had worked against the vampire, I let my scales shift as I held the shield. I became copper and black, much to the shock of the vampires.

"Envokus." I had practiced this spell to where I wanted to puke saying the word again.

Focusing, I tried to make the spell start in the center of one vampire.

He moved, and my aim was off. The spell instead started in his shoulder. The dark purple mist oozed out of him as his arm melted off, but his regeneration snapped into place and quickly reattached it.

Amira was following my lead. "Envokus," she growled, but hers was more precise. She'd clearly had much more practice as the power wasted away half the vampire's torso.

The vampires screamed and threw everything they had against my shield, trying to get around it to take us down. They might have prepared for Winter fae's magic, but they weren't prepared for dragons.

But before I could get too smug, I noticed that the vampire with half his torso gone was healing back up far faster than I would have expected. It felt like we were fighting something that was near immortal.

"They've feasted on the fae on the way in," Polydora acknowledged as the other two dragons continued flinging death magic.

My focus was on holding the shield, but I could only hold for so long before it sustained so much damage that it shattered.

"Contego," I roared again, putting my anger into the spell and throwing up a second shield to stall for more time.

As I went to throw another spell, the palace shook with extreme force, and I saw Maeve turn with startled eyes.

"Zach. Push through! My mother needs your help."

"Ready?" I checked with the girls quickly, prepared to answer Maeve's call.

"Allow me." Polydora ducked her shoulder, a spark of battle filling her eyes as she charged forward.

I waited until the last moment to dismiss my shield as she plowed through the vampires. And I stayed right behind her, and the others behind me formed a single file chain of charging dragons.

The vampires tried to cling to us and catch a ride on the dragon express, but we threw them off as we moved. As we neared the front of the vampire's forces, Maeve and another fae parted to let us through. The Fall Lady skewered a vampire that had been on Trina's back.

A few vampires tried to use the opportunity to get through the fae ranks, but only two were able to make it.

"We'll handle them." Amira grabbed one vampire off Polydora while Trina went for the one that was trying to attack the fae's back. "Help the Winter Queen."

Now that the vampires were out of the way, I could see the battle raging behind the front lines.

Winter was pinned, face against the wall as the blood-lord drank sloppily from her neck.

"Get off of her," I shouted as I charged the bloodlord.

But I only got several steps before he whirled around and hurled Winter at me, forcing me to catch the fae queen.

She whimpered in my arms, and I realized she had bite marks all along her body. Her clothes were shredded, and she was in awful shape and wasn't going to be much help.

Even at her weakest, the Winter Queen wasn't someone to be trifled with.

Her frost eyelids fluttered for a moment as she struggled to remain conscious.

"I was just finishing up with her. Has dessert come already?" Deniz grinned and licked the blood off his lips.

Something clicked now that I was seeing Deniz, yet I also knew he was the bloodlord behind all of this. We'd been played.

"You aren't Deniz," I said calmly. "He's probably dead, isn't he?"

We had gotten his name from Ricardo, and Morgana had checked with a contact that Deniz had indeed come to Philly. But now that we knew it was the vampire that had turned Ricardo, it fell apart.

Wallachia had sent Deniz, and he had died, the Gregorian bloodlord before me having taken his place.

"Yes, the Wallachia have such an old view on things. Peace. Can you believe they want peace?" The bloodlord chuckled. "You can still call me Deniz, though." He didn't tell me his real name.

"Is that what you want? War?" I stalled, hoping to have some additional reinforcements. He radiated strength after having fed on the Winter Queen.

"No. What I want is power. Once you become immortal, few other things matter than having the power to stay immortal. When you secure enough time, anything else is possible. And now you won't live long enough to know. Though..." His eyes wandered my form. "Your coloration intrigues me."

I put Winter down on the steps up to the throne. "I don't care what intrigues you."

I glanced in my peripheral vision at the battle, which was still roaring. It would not let up anytime soon.

Deniz saw my distraction and darted forward, his fist planting itself in my chest.

I prepared for a typical vampire attack, but what came was entirely different. It felt like I just got hit by a dragon as my body flew backwards, crashing into the wall and cracking some of the ice off of it.

"Pathetic," he snorted as I shot back to my feet and let out a dark cloud of death breath.

The cloud washed over him while he was gloating. As he moved, the speed caused enough wind in its wake that the cloud dissipated. He was almost entirely unharmed, except for an already fading rash on his face.

He didn't speak again as he charged me.

I threw my arms over my face to block the impending hit and was pounded back against the wall. I tried to re-member what Morgana had taught me. There had to be something that I could do to counter his speed. I knew he was softening me up before he'd bite and feed off me.

Taking a deep breath, I blew out a cloud of death around myself to buy a little time. Then I shifted in the dark purple cloud, changing just as he zipped through the cloud and missed me.

Hoping it would work, I slammed down an aura of fear over him, followed up with the spell, "Envokus." I roared out the spell, putting everything I had into it.

A dark purple mass exploded out of his arm as he moved. The arm ripped right off of him, and I felt a moment of satisfaction before it regrew right back.

Annoyed, I changed tactics yet again. I had to find his weakness. I let my scales shift to red and gold, feeling the wild strength that came with those colors and punched out.

But Deniz bobbed around my fist just in time to come in at my side with a hammer fist. My ribs felt like they were on the verge of breaking as I was thrown across the room.

The cold ice of the fortress pressed against me, and I had a new idea.

Before Deniz made another move, I let loose a fire breath, melting the ice that clung to the walls and ceiling of the chamber. The water pooled together further into the chamber, and I dove towards it, putting all of my strength into my legs and throwing myself across the room to the water.

I just barely avoided Deniz's next blow as I landed on my knees in the water. I splashed into the puddle as my scales shifted again, and I breathed lightning into the water.

Deniz had nearly reached me as I let the lightning go. His body shook from electrocution as he got a taste of my strength.

The shocks might not have fried him, but they certainly locked up his muscles long enough for me to throw myself on top of him. My jaws crackled and became larger as I turned the tables.

If he wanted to eat me, then I'd eat him.

My teeth clamped down on his leg, and I let myself continue to shift larger into my full dragon form. Then I swung him by his leg, my teeth and the motion tearing his leg off and throwing him against the far wall.

It was a gamble that wouldn't work too many times, but I'd hurt him again. I chewed his leg, feeling the richness of mana in him and salivating for more of it.

His leg was already growing back, but from my larger mouth, I blanketed the side of the room in huge cords of branching lightning that echoed off the chamber walls, deafening everyone.

Deniz looked a little charred after my attack. Not wanting to give him much time to regenerate, I dove to swallow him whole.

My jaw clamped down, but it didn't close as he held it apart with his hands, despite my teeth nearly splitting them. Using the full strength of my jaw, I tried to crush him.

Deniz screamed something in another language, and a detonation went off in my throat, burning me and making me wheeze. I tried to toss him, but he'd wedged himself inside.

He did the spell again, sending another explosive bolt of magic down my throat.

I roared as my colors shifted back to copper and black, biting down to make sure he couldn't escape as I breathed an immense wave of death breath on him.

The room filled with the purple fog, and I felt his strength holding my jaw open weakening. That moment was all I needed to crunch down on him.

I felt him fall out of my mouth, and I saw that I'd cut him from shoulder to hip. But despite being that wounded, he still was maneuvering to get away, using his one remaining arm as his body attempted to regenerate. Fae blood was apparently potent.

"Not on my watch." I pinned him with a claw and bent down, getting his head between my teeth and finishing him off. Morgana always said that removing the head was the best bet to ensure death.

And because he was so tasty, I finished the rest of his body, feeling bloated as I turned to see the rest of the room.

Fae were huddled around the throne with Polydora, while Amira and Trina had their wings out, trying to beat back the cloud of death breath that had blanketed the floor.

I realized that my attack had done more than I'd initially realized. I'd been so panicked as Deniz had sent blasts down my throat.

Taking a deep breath, I sucked the death breath back out of the air. "Sorry. I was focused on the battle with Deniz."

"Thank you." Maeve bowed. "I'm not sure we would have survived." Her gaze flickered down to her mother, whose chest was barely moving. "Please, can you give us a ride out to the battlefield between Winter and Summer? I need to see if our healers can do anything."

"Of course. Dragonettes, carry the queen. Maeve, you can show me the way." I shifted back into my dragon knight form, preparing to race us out of the castle.

# CHAPTER 31

Maeve and my honor guard rode me to the fae battle ahead of us. I was curious to see this eternal battle between the seasons for myself.

And it didn't disappoint. The battle from above it was awe-inspiring. The two forces seemed to stretch all the way to the horizon on either side.

But news of Winter's fall spread; every winter fae could feel her weakened state. They quit the battlefield and retreated as one.

But it seemed organized. The Summer fae allowed their retreat if only to push their battle line forward and regain another half mile of the field.

"Fighting will start at dawn again tomorrow," Maeve said as she stood over her mother. "We've done what we can."

When we landed, five prominent fae healers had rushed to come to Winter. One had been killed by Maeve for supposedly trying to kill her mother.

Fae were notoriously conniving.

"I thought fae were always trying to climb higher," I questioned. "Surprising that you'd expend so much effort to help your mother recover."

Maeve snorted. "I'm not ready to be queen. It's not just about the strength my mother possesses. I still want to live life without those burdens. For a fae, I'm not that old." She chuckled, grinning to herself.

I didn't know how old she was, and I doubted she was going to tell me. "Are you going to be okay if I leave you here?" We needed to get back and clean up the park, as well as the broader mess of the city.

Maeve was still for a moment as she stared at her mother.

Taking a chance, I stepped up behind her and wrapped her in a hug. "It'll be okay, and I need you to come to me if you need any help."

The proud fae lady leaned her entire weight on me. "Okay. I'll keep you to that."

"Besides, apparently, you already have a plushie," I joked, as if the little golden dragons were binding.

"Yes. I do, but I have a feeling I'm not going to make it in time for your grand wedding thrown by the Summer Queen." She pushed herself into my chest like she was trying to bury herself in my arms.

I didn't have an answer for her besides holding her in my arms for a moment longer.

Polydora cleared her throat after a minute. "My king, we need to get back and help return the city to normal."

"She's right." Maeve pushed herself out of my arms. "Go, deal with the problem, but maybe come back? I'll be out in a few days once things stabilize here. The healers said that she'd wake up soon."

Maeve turned towards the area where Summer had gained ground. "But get ready for a hot summer," she added.

I wanted to stay. Despite her strong appearance and her words, I could tell that Maeve needed support.

"If you need anything, please send for me." I kissed the top of her head, making her blush. Evelyn, who was never far from Maeve, was grinning from ear to ear. "That goes for you too, Evelyn. Come running if you or she need help. I'm counting on you in case Maeve is too stubborn."

The Fall Lady stuck her tongue out at me. "Shoo. Go clean up your mess, Dragon King. The Winter fae are hardy. We'll be fine. Tell Jadelyn that I sent you back without stalling you too long, and put in a good word with Scarlett for me."

"Will do." I nodded to her and walked out of the tent, parting the frosty blue material amid the war camp for the fae.

I kept on moving towards an empty field, ignoring stares of many of the fae. When I reached an open spot, I didn't hesitate. I stripped out of my clothes and put them and my honor guard's clothes in my bracer before we shifted and headed back to the portal.

"My king. I worry about you getting involved in the fae war," Trina commented, flying up beside me.

I nodded. It was a natural risk of being closer with Maeve. "We'll see. So far, I've been trying to split my attention between the two, as to not openly favor a side. But that might be changing. And I'm concerned about Winter. She was so weak."

"A fae queen is strong," Polydora tried to reassure me, but I still had this feeling that her weakening might have kicked off a cascade for the fae.

We flew further into the frozen land of the winter fae until the palace came into view, and I dipped back down into the familiar woods, shifting down to fit through the portal.

Coming out the other side, I let myself return to my dragon form, complete with my multicolored scales.

"Alpha-alpha!" Taylor cheered for me amid a scene of absolute carnage.

I shouldn't have worried. Wissahickon park was a mess of charred, bloody bodies. Wolves were already working to clear it. But at Taylor's shout, many of them turned to see me return and cheered along with her.

Even after everything that happened, they were uplifted by my return.

"Alpha-alpha. Can I call in that rain check yet?" Taylor bounced her eyebrows.

Kelly came up behind her and had to go on her tiptoes to smack the back of Taylor's head. "Quit being so forward with my alpha."

Taylor only gave her a wide grin in response. "He's my alpha-alpha, and he didn't say no to my date. I'm perfectly happy being a mistress as long as he fills me with pups."

Her words brought me back to Yev, and an overwhelming need to see her and know that she was okay filled me. The dragon in me grumbled that I had more to clean up first, but I could at least tell through the mark that she was okay.

"We'll talk about it later, Taylor," I grumbled as the other dragons came through the portal but remained in their dragon knight forms. "I assume the council is gathering?"

"They are up on the hill where the elven tents were set up." Kelly pointed. "Give a girl a lift?"

I dipped my head, and Kelly sprang up on my head before I climbed out of the small valley in the park.

My big red and gold head rose over the ridge, and I paused before going further. The council wasn't far away, and at my appearance, they had turned and were coming my way.

There were many familiar faces, and some I hadn't expected. Till and Helena were present along with Maddie, whom Morgana had a protective arm around.

"The bloodlord has been dealt with, but he used this opportunity to attack the Winter Queen and her court. She's gravely injured, and many of her fae were bled," I summarized the events for them.

But several of them seemed to have trouble not staring wide eyed at my dragon form.

I was most amused by Till's reaction. Something about the look on her face made me think she was playing through all the insults and jabs, maybe regretting them just a smidge. I snapped my teeth at her in jest, and she let out a nervous chuckle.

Maddie just had eyes that were nearly popping out of her head as I climbed a little higher, and more of my dragon form was visible.

"So, the threat of the vampires is over?" Detective Fox cast a nervous look over his shoulder towards T and the small army of skeletons with him.

"T, thank you for your help in clearing up the danger in the city. The threat is gone, and I'd ask that you dismiss your forces," my voice rumbled over the crowd.

The old elf did a slight bow. "You are very welcome. I'm excited to see that you are even more than I had expected, Dragon King."

As he rose from his bow, the skeletons lost the light in their eyes, and they fell to the ground in piles of bone ash.

"If you don't mind, I need to get back to my barber skills. Come by when you want another haircut." T waved at the crowd and turned back.

There was a murmuring among the council. Many were talking about my red and gold nature, wondering what it meant. Only those with longer histories were putting it together.

Sebastian glared daggers at me. "You brought a lich into this?"

"I did. And I'd say he was a tremendous help eliminating the problem here. I trust T. If you have a problem with his actions, you can lay them on my shoulders." I took responsibility, confident I had made the right decision.

The elf leader snorted. "You can be sure that I will. But for now, we have a much bigger problem to solve." He looked over towards the city.

From my vantage, I could see that the city was still dark and without power. "Do we have any control over the ISPs to control communication going out?"

The council shook their heads.

"A few of the gnomes are embedded in the local offices, but nothing at this scale." Tilly waved his little arms to get attention as he spoke.

I turned my attention to the rest of the group. "What options do we have?"

A few side conversations developed as everybody tried to come up with a plan.

Helena took the moment to step forward with Agent Till. "We've wrapped up a plausible reason for some of it that we can address within the FBI, but so much has happened. It complicates our story."

"We'll start the news spinning up stories as soon as the power comes back," Rupert offered. "That'll help control the narrative."

I was still frowning. There was no way there weren't hundreds of people who caught video of the vampire's rampage through town, or saw it and now would be more paranoid as they moved around town. We had to do something.

"We could try to read in someone higher at the FBI?" Till offered.

I shook my head.

"They would inform their superiors, and it would go all the way up to the white house and congress. We self-govern in the middle of the states; there's no way that doesn't end up in a power struggle," Rupert spoke up first. "We keep our involvement with agencies to lower levels."

"The best thing we can do is let the story ride out with nothing to follow it up," Grim, the leader of the dwarves, said with his arms crossed. "A single night of strangeness will bring some people to investigate, but it won't splash on national media."

I hoped his reasoning was right, but I wasn't sure.

"Fine. Do what we can. Let's clean up here and everyone goes home. What's the story?"

Rupert scratched his head. "There was a death cult in our city. They went wild and crazy, thinking it was the end of the world. Military rolled in to stop it, but it took some time to get a lid on it. Thankfully, the lich kept a cloud of darkness around himself while in the city, so any videos out there will just be vampires going crazy and our jeeps mobilizing."

My father-in-law looked exhausted. He had a lot of work ahead of him to keep it all under wraps.

"What about satellites?" Till pointed up in to the sky.

"The fae have provided protections for the park for ages," Sebastian said. "We don't have to worry about Clifford the big red dragon showing up."

I laughed, completely not expecting the joke from the curmudgeonly elf. "Okay, if we can get through putting this under wraps, then we can talk about what we do with vampires from now on. They must feel the anger of the other paranormal at the risk their kind brought to our doorstep."

Morgana raised her hand to get everyone's attention. "I will be reaching out to the Wallachia through Deniz."

That made me groan. "Deniz is dead. The man we met was someone else. I never got a name, but the man claiming to be Deniz was behind it all. Please reach out to the Wallachia, and make them aware. I will inform the dragons of what transpired in our city."

"Sentarshaden will know as well," Sebastian agreed.

"As will El Dorado," Grim agreed. "We need to tell everyone of this. Pressure must increase against the vampires, and they must take accountability. Even if we came out the other end okay, this was too close."

I nodded. "Then it sounds like we all need to get to work and then get some rest. It has been a long day."

Pulling myself up over the ridge, I let my body shrink back down so that I stepped on the grass as a naked human. Kelly hopped off mid transformation and let her eyes rove over my naked form for a second.

"The pack will finish cleaning up and then head back. I'll see you in your hoard later." She winked. "Oh, and don't encourage Taylor too much. At least, not until you give me my first pup."

I pulled out clothes from my bracer and got dressed. Then I took out my phone and texted my mates waiting in the hoard. "Yeah, she's persistent. But for now, you're my only wolf I want to put pups in."

Kelly cracked her knuckles. "Excuse me then. And here comes Blueberry anyway." She raised her voice so that Morgana heard her use the nickname.

"Shoo, Furball. You have a pack to take care of. I'll keep our mate company."

Maddie was looking back and forth between the two, bewildered by their play. "They really don't mind sharing you? Even when I know vampires exist, it's still hard to wrap my head around harems existing."

I went to respond, but she just continued on. "Also. Holy. Shit. You are like a legit dragon! Huge!" Maddie stretched her hands as far as she could, like she could stretch to the point and give me a reference. "Also, hoard? Can I see all this gold?"

"Where's Frank?" I asked, realizing he wasn't with her.

She looked away. "He needed a moment after everything. He's back at Bumps with an open tab. I think what is really getting him is that he can't be my sole blood source. Somehow, the idea of me feeding on anyone else bothers him."

I scratched my chin. "We'll figure something out. Maybe we can help teach him to use magic. The magi I've seen have a higher capacity for mana and could work."

"Really?" Maddie was all smiles. "He'd fucking love that."

"Do you guys have anything to wrap up before we leave?" I looked at Morgana and extended the question to Sabrina, Till, and Helena, who were nearby.

Helena snorted. "Who says I'm going anywhere with you?"

"Tyrande will be there. I thought you could finally give her that apology you promised." My expression was sharp.

And I also really needed her to apologize to Tyrande. I was going to be in such deep shit the second Tyrande saw that Helena was marked. But if Helena made amends, it might turn out okay.

"We can head back. But I'd rather not sleep under house arrest again." Till crossed her arms and tapped a finger against her arm.

"Of course not. You are welcome to rooms in the Scalewright manor. I'd like to wrap up tonight and discuss things in the morning. The two of you should consider relocating to Philly's field office." Before they objected, I added, "You could do a lot of good here where you are in the know of the real problems."

Helena surprised me with a quick nod. "That makes a lot of sense, actually."

Till only let out a small noise, acknowledging that she'd heard me. She was still upset about the status that the council had thrust on her.

Sabrina's arm slipped in mine. "I'd like to solidify this mark. I also used up a lot of energy today and need a little refill." She wiggled her eyebrows at me.

Till wrinkled her nose while the others laughed. "Let's go. We'll drive separately."

"Don't want another show, agent?" Polydora called after her with a laugh and turned back to us. "Here I thought she enjoyed the show in the limo. Oh well, more dragon king for us."

I chuckled. "Let's let the poor agent process all she's seen today. Come on, ladies, let's go home."

# CHAPTER 32

Morgana had closed Bumps for the Night because of the outage, and we were making the best of the situation.

We had pushed tables together in the dining area, and everyone was in attendance. All of my mates, Till, Helena, and the dragonettes. The only one missing was Maeve. Even Maddie and Frank had joined us, and it felt damn good to have my old life and new life finally less separated.

"I left Taylor with a pile of work once you said this was happening." Kelly walked in to get hugs from all my mates.

The lights were still off, but Morgana's staff had lit candles. Candles made spaces look romantic in online photos, but somehow it made our current space look like some sort of haunted mansion with all the dripping wax.

"Shh." I held a finger to my lips, my eyes trained on the entertainment that was going to begin.

Helena was standing before Tyrande with her head bowed as she muttered an apology.

"Oh, it's Birdbrains." Kelly paused, and then her eyes widened. "You marked Birdbrains?" Kelly asked, surprise filling her voice.

"Long story. It wasn't exactly on purpose. But yes, I've marked her now." I was still torn on how I felt about it.

Every instinct I had told me that she was mine, but she clearly wasn't ready to be mine yet.

Tyrande said something that I couldn't quite hear, and Helena's head snapped up ready to argue. The Highaen princess held up her hand like she would hear no argument.

Kelly snickered. "Shit. I want to see how that turns out."

Helena's shoulder slumped but she nodded.

"Birdbrain at least seems very dedicated to make up." Kelly kept a smile on her face at having a secret I didn't know.

"Spill?" I pushed my mate to let me in on it.

"Nope. But I think you'll see it tomorrow." Kelly snickered and moved on. She wasn't very good at keeping secrets, so it appeared that her strategy was just to give a little space.

Kelly was quickly replaced by Yev, who stood in front of me staring at me with an intensity that I'd never felt, before taking my hand and pressing it to her stomach.

"My mate," she started.

Smiling, I leaned in and kissed her stomach gently. "I promise I'll do everything I can for both of you."

She blushed. "I want to move in to your hoard."

My heart clenched, and I had to plaster on a stiff but giant smile. I coached myself to play it cool. I so wanted to stuff her in my hoard and keep her safe there.

"Sure. How... uh... I feel like I should know more about how this works." My gaze wandered back to her belly which didn't look any different, yet I knew there was a life in there.

"In about forty-five days, I will lay the egg. And then a year after that it should hatch. I want to lay and brood the egg in your hoard. I promise not to move things around too much."

"Is there any danger with the gold elemental?" I asked.

She only snorted and tossed her hair. "I dare the elemental to get close to my egg," she replied.

I chuckled, imagining just how ferocious she would be to protect our baby dragon. "After this, I'll take you to go see if we can't meet it."

Yev smiled. "Then we'll see where my gold can fit into your hoard. I'm going to add it all, and mix them in until you don't know which ones are yours and mine. Then I'm going to have my egg, and as soon as I have the first, I'm going to seduce you into getting me with another before it hatches." She pushed up against me and nuzzled into my neck.

"Mine," I growled.

"Yours," she happily sighed.

"Congratulations again, mistress." Trina came from the side. "If you and the King wouldn't mind, I'd love to name myself as your physician for the short term of your pregnancy, and also for the egg once it's out."

"Yes please," Yev squealed. "I don't really know anyone who would have any knowledge about this."

Trina stuck out her tongue. "I know a bit about dragons and medicine. But if I'm honest, this will be my first rodeo too. Hopefully not the last." She bounced her eyebrows.

"Better than nothing," I agreed. "Please, would you take care of my mate?" I formally asked Trina, wanting her to feel the position officially extended to her.

She nodded quickly in response. "You are just glowing, mistress," Trina continued to lay it on thick.

"I come with a feast!" Morgana came out of the kitchen with a bevy of her people behind her carrying out tray after tray of food.

Though the power was out, the gas had still worked, and Morgana had taken the excuse of clearing out the food they had in the fridge.

"Everyone, order your drinks too, except Yev." Morgana pointed at the dragon. "Do not serve alcohol to the pregnant dragon," she instructed her staff.

Yev puffed out her cheeks in a fake pout, but went along with it, finding her seat at the extended table.

Frank looked at me from across the room and mouthed 'pregnant' with a wild gesture.

I grinned and nodded.

He hurried across the room. "Congratulations, dude. Dragon babies?"

"Baby. Singular. At least, I hope so." I chuckled at the thought of more than one.

"Congrats." Maddie squeezed her eyes shut with her smile.

"Thank you."

"And for the new vampire." Morgana had set her tray down and come around with a full wine glass of sanguine red liquid.

"Blood?" Frank asked.

"Bloodwine," I clarified. "The vampires are generally pretty refined. They've managed to turn blood into a variety of alcohols."

Maddie took a sip and had a face of surprised delight. "It's good."

Frank eyed it and held out his hands, taking a sip as well. But his face recoiled in disgust. "Tastes like drinking rust."

"Vampires." I rolled my eyes. "Pretty sure her taste buds changed with the transformation. Come, sit, you two." I pulled the two of them over to sit on my left as I took the head of the table.

Scarlett took the head on the other side while Sabrina took the seat on my right, with Yev and Tyrande next to her.

Yev was ladening her plate with multiple steaks.

"Just because you are pregnant doesn't mean you get to be a piggy," Tyrande teased her sister.

Yev let out an offended chuckle. "Just remember that when you get pregnant. Besides, I don't eat like a pig; I eat like a dragon. Have you seen how much our mate packs away?"

Frank was paying attention to them. "Wait, so dragons eat more?"

Multiple voices spoke up. "Dragons eat a shit ton."

I laughed and without even asking, one of the servers just kept putting steaks on my plate until I held out a hand for them to stop. "Maddie saw my true form tonight."

"Huge." She threw her arms out wide. "Dude was like a walking school building, and everyone was really impressed that he had two colors."

"Okay. I need you to back up. Were you always a dragon?" Frank asked.

"No. Well, yes. I was born one, but my parents died, and I ended up being raised by humans. We think my dragon was magically sealed. So I had no idea until recently. Remember that time I got into it with Chad at the bar?"

Frank turned to look down the table at Jadelyn. "Yeah, you fought over Jadelyn. Wait, did you kill him and take his girl? Intense."

"No. Nothing quite that dramatic," I cut him off, but Scarlett piped in.

"He did kill Chad though. Pulled the guy's mouth open and breathed dragon fire down his throat." She stabbed into another piece of food and ate it with a casualness like she'd just stated the sky was blue.

Frank felt otherwise, holding up his hands and insisting we go back to the start, ever since I'd learned I was a dragon.

And every time one of my girls came up in the story, they pitched in and added their own details with excited gestures and their own thoughts as they became involved. And the dragonettes seemed to be eating it up. I had no doubt they were strategizing how to get closer to me through what they were learning.

The night got away from us, and even as the lights came on in the city, we sat, eating and drinking together.

I didn't know how much damage control was happening or where the next day would bring us, so I just enjoyed the time with my chosen family.

***

Everybody was stuffed full of food, and more than a few of us were feeling the drinks. Morgana's servers had been very diligent in resupplying our drinks whenever they got low.

Frank had it the roughest. He'd fallen asleep in his chair only partway into the night. Trying to keep pace with paranormals wasn't his smartest move.

"I think I should get Frank back." Maddie came over to him and hoisted him easily out of his chair.

"Anything we should worry about?" I asked her honestly, wondering if she had herself under control.

"No. I'm pretty satiated after that wine, and if I'm honest, his blood isn't that tempting." She looked guilty as she said it. "If you don't mind, I'll tell him about becoming a wizard or something."

"We are happy to help," Sabrina agreed, grabbing my hand on top of the table.

She had been very touchy feely through the dinner. I had a feeling that she was going to be in my bed that night, and I couldn't wait. I could feel her succubus nature ever so slightly tugging at me as she touched me.

Maddie nodded and headed off towards the Atrium to use it to get back to Frank's apartment.

As soon as she left, Scarlett clapped her hands to get everyone's attention. "We have two new marked mates among us. Though... one doesn't claim to be a mate. So, I suggest that we let Zach and Sabrina have a little time together tonight. The betting on who wears who out can commence after they've left."

The alcohol flowing through the room was evident as many of the girls started giggling and whispering with not-so-subtle gestures.

"We'll talk in the morning? I'm sure the council will have a session early tomorrow, and I'll want to understand what they've found as they've turned power back on," I suggested to the girls.

"Breakfast in the east parlor," Jadelyn confirmed, once again assuming the position of host. "Those of you that don't have a room are welcome to stay at my place tonight."

Feeling like they all had somewhere safe to sleep, I stood. Sabrina stood as well, pulling at my hand and tugging me away. Her move only increased the laughter and gestures behind us.

"Whoa." I tried to slow her down, but the succubus turned to me with a little flush on her face from drinking as she bit her lip.

"Having second thoughts?"

"Not at all." I stepped in and swept her off her feet, carrying her like a princess. "Just normally, it is me dragging the girl back to the room."

"Oh, it's unlikely I'll ever get enough." Sabrina's eyes were hungry.

It seemed that a little alcohol brought out the succubus in my nerdy wizard.

She started to kiss along my neck as my body heated up several degrees. Her succubus nature was leaking out around her glasses, and her breath was leaving behind little pink puffs.

"Take me," she whispered into my ear.

My pace quickened, and I let my hand cradling her torso reach around to squeeze her chest. As I squeezed, I could see desire flash in her eyes. They turned pink with little golden flecks. There were only a few flecks, but they sparkled in her eyes.

She had gotten them when she had last fed on me, and I really wanted to see if I couldn't make her eyes go completely gold. My dragon preened at the idea of somehow marking her as mine even more.

I pushed past the door to Morgana's and my rooms, closing it behind me and nearly diving into my room.

As soon as we were in, I pushed Sabrina up against the wall and kissed her as my growing erection nestled itself between her legs. Feeling like a horny teenager, I couldn't help but grind it against her.

"I'm going to take my glasses off," she warned me before she reached up and pulled them off, tossing them aside along with the ties holding her hair back.

Her skin flushed a subtle pink, and she became the epitome of temptation as she arched her back against the wall. Her top could hardly contain her curves. Somehow, everything she wore that was once baggy seemed like it dripped with sex appeal.

She pulled my head closer to kiss me.

Her lips tasted like berries ripe for the picking as her sweet breath washed over me, and I continued to press her to the wall until it felt like our bodies had melded into one. I groaned into her mouth as my body ached with the need to fill hers.

Sabrina started to suck the lust-tinted mana from me, and it kept coming in waves. I couldn't have wanted my succubus more in that moment.

I pushed her head aside and kissed down her neck to where I had marked her. Satisfied with the mark, I kissed along the thin scar that was even more apparent with her pink skin. "Mine."

"Prove it." Sabrina flushed and looked down at our still clothed bodies.

I went to rip her clothes off, happy to remedy the situation, but she held back my hand.

"That's no fun. Go sit." She was suddenly a little dominant as she pushed me off of her and made her way over to the bed.

It was about everything I could do not to get up and slam her against the wall once more.

Gold coins clinked on my bed as I settled down, and she smirked as she leaned over, putting her hands on my thighs and continuing to kiss me for a moment before she stood up and slowly undid the buttons on her sweater.

The smoldering look she gave me had me panting for her.

I was torn. I still wanted to rip her clothes off of her, but I also recognized that, if I was patient, I was going to get an incredible show.

Sabrina's chest seemed to bounce out after the third button, pushing against her frilly bra. Then Sabrina pushed her arms against their side, squeezing them even further up as she bent down for me. "Put your face right there."

I leaned forward, my nose filling with her feminine scent as I pressed my face softly into her mounds. Her hand came behind my head, pushing me even further into them before she shook them against me.

"Oh, grab them," she moaned.

I didn't need to be told twice, grabbing them roughly and kneading them in my hands as I started peppering them with kisses.

After a moment, she pulled back and turned around to sit in my lap. As she sat, a thin spaded tail came out of her skirt and curled around my thigh as she rocked her butt in my lap, rising and falling as she rubbed herself against me.

"Mine." I grabbed her chest in the new position and pressed her back against my chest as I bit at her clavicle again.

Sabrina kept grinding against me and moaning as she finished unbuttoning her sweater and tossing it off to the side. "Want to pull my skirt down for me?"

She lifted her hips off my lap, and I pushed her skirt down to her ankles as she returned to my lap in white and pink undies, grinding against me. "Now, we need to do something about your clothes."

I went to hurry to get my shirt off, but she stopped me and turned around to sit in my lap, still swaying her hips.

"Let me." Her eyes were smoldering with the gold flecks as she started to work the buttons, agonizingly slowly apart on my shirt.

She leaned forward with every button, moving the fabric back just the slightest bit as she kissed the newly exposed area of skin. The little succubus knew exactly what she was doing to me as my body started to shudder with need.

Unable to hold back anymore, I pulled her forward, claiming her lips and pulling her across my lap against me.

Sabrina smiled with glee but just tsked back at me. "Silly, we'll never get to that if you keep distracting me. Your buttons are so small." She grinned mischievously, but this time as she got back to work, she moved a little quicker, clearly also bursting with need.

I made it through the rest of her undoing my shirt, but at that point, I was so pent up that I wasn't able to wait any more. I grabbed her horns and pushed her down to work on my pants next.

Sabrina only chuckled as she quickly undid my pants and pulled them down, my cock springing free.

Her breath hitched and her pink misty breath wrapped around me. I could feel every inch of my erection stiffen, stretching further in an attempt to slip into her mouth with just a little more length.

Leaning forward, she parted her lips, and I pushed her down by her horns. A sigh of relief ripped itself from my chest as I finally felt her mouth surrounding me.

Her warm, wet mouth wrapped itself around the head, and she resisted me as I pushed her slowly down further. Her tongue began drawing shapes all up and down my length.

"Faster," I groaned.

But she continued to tease me slowly, driving me mad with lust. When she didn't speed up, I pulled out of her mouth and tossed her on the bed.

"My mate, can you not hold it any longer?" Sabrina stretched out on the bed, her eyes holding a little challenge as a flush crept along her cheeks. But her pink eyes swallowed my attention as I kicked off my pants, crawling over her.

I lifted her chin and kissed her lips. "Mine."

"Take it then." She grinned in response.

I lined myself up and pushed into her sex. Relief flooded me as she pulsed around me and breathed more pink mist in my face, drawing me closer and kissing me.

I wanted to go fast and hard, rutting her, but Sabrina controlled the motions in ways I never even realized a woman could do from the bottom.

Instead, I ended up in an agonizingly slow build up as I savored thrusting up into her. A little delirious from all of the sexual energy in the room, I came hard, my vision spotting as I released into Sabrina.

Sabrina arched her back and screamed as she got her first taste of my mana-filled seed. Her legs hooked behind my back, pulling me deeper into her as I continued to twitch and roll right into a second climax after the first.

I kissed her, and she pushed her lust demon powers to the max, driving me wild as I continued to unload into her. Part of me hoped it would never stop.

But eventually, I felt spent, and she eased up on me and rolled me over onto my back.

"Satisfied?" She grinned as she kept me in her, still rocking on my hard cock.

I looked up into her eyes, noting that her succubus nature was only growing stronger as more flecks of gold filled her eyes. At this point, it was just under a quarter of her iris.

"No way. The Dragon King can last much longer," I shot back.

It had felt like she had emptied me with that one go, but I knew my stamina. I'd likely recover quickly, especially with her fog's help.

Her tail wrapped itself around the base of my cock, squeezing it before she started to ride me. She leaned down over me, kissing me again before pulling back enough to look into my eyes and speak.

"Good. Because there's a bet among the girls."

"Which one of us has more stamina?" I asked as a fog of pink breath rolled out of her. She seemed to be filling the room with a pink haze.

"I aim to win the bet," she stated.

Then her sex did something strange. It felt like her mouth, slowly sucking on me. I let out a little gasp, surprised at the sensation before I groaned and embraced it.

"After all. I am a sex demon." Sabrina grinned and moaned as she started to ride me again, using all of her wiles to try to win the bet.

# CHAPTER 33

"So who won?" Jadelyn asked as soon as I came to sit down in the east parlor with Sabrina. Sabrina's succubus nature was still on display; she'd left her glasses back in the room.

After we'd finished, she had announced with glee that she was so full that she didn't even feel the need to suppress her nature.

"He did," Sabrina admitted as she slumped down into the chair next to Jadelyn and leaned against her. "I should feel shame at losing that challenge, given what I am, but all I feel is very satisfied."

The girls giggled.

Most of my mates were in the parlor. But only two of the dragonettes were present, and we were still missing Helena. As I noted her absence, she rounded the corner, and my jaw nearly dropped.

"If you ogle me, I will tear your eyes out," Helena scowled at me.

"That doesn't sound very maid-like," Tyrande scolded. "I thought you were going to be my maid for a month?"

"This is not a maid uniform. Did you get this from a sex shop?" Helena picked at the latex maid uniform.

"She borrowed it from me," Morgana clarified, and I nearly choked.

Once I recovered, I turned to Morgana. "Do you have other outfits like that?"

She smirked, shrugging. "I tried it, but I never really got into it."

Tyrande held up her cup of coffee, and Helena came over, snatching it out of her hand and walking off to refill it.

"Is this really okay?" I checked with Tyrande.

"If she can put up with this for a month, then I'm convinced that she really wants to repent. Otherwise, she's my enemy and I'll never forgive what she's done. That means Sentarshaden won't either." Tyrande crossed her arms as Helena came back and slammed the coffee down on the table.

Tyrande cleared her throat, and Helena begrudgingly added, "Your coffee. M-m-mistress." She struggled with the word.

"Thank you. That'll be all." Tyrande shooed her away with the wave of a hand.

"I need some as well." Till held up her hand to get Helena's attention, but Helena just tipped her chair over, smirking down at her partner. "Do it yourself. I'm only Tyrande's maid."

My elven mate happily sipped her coffee again.

"So, any news on the council's efforts to keep the paranormal secret suppressed?" I asked no one in particular.

But I wasn't surprised when Jadelyn jumped in with the answer. "It's going badly. There are a lot of videos floating around. We are doing what we can. Apparently, my father is getting a bot farm, whatever that is, and trying to suppress them. The news is running out an alternative story, but there's a lot of chatter online still."

Till cleared her throat as she came back with a fresh cup of coffee, righting her chair. "I have worse news. We turned in our case report on the congressman, and we got a lot of questions that weren't even about our case as follow ups. They were coming from on high too. We were asked if we would consider relocation to Philly before I even asked."

I leaned back in my chair. "Then we stay quiet and hope this blows over. Besides, we have a wedding here in a month and a half. The Winter Queen might need some support, so I'm turning my focus from Philly to the Faerie realm for the time being."

Till opened up her laptop and logged in only to nearly spill her coffee all over it.

"Which one of you did this?" She held up the laptop and angrily glared at the dragonettes.

"I don't know what you are talking about." Larisa bat her eyelashes innocently.

I got enough of a view to see that her background now had a golden plushie on it before she stormed over to Larisa shouting about how she broke into an FBI laptop.

"Is it wise to get involved with the fae?" Scarlett asked, pulling my attention back to the table as she still scratched at the base of her tails.

But before I could answer that, the door opened, and Maeve stepped in.

"Hope I'm not interrupting anything?" She eyed Helena's current outfit, but she didn't say anything.

"No, we were just talking about the fae. How's your mother?"

"Awake, but not well. She's insulated herself among some of her most loyal people, and our army has their spirit back for the fight. They took the field this morning without a problem." Maeve sat down, biting her lip not to directly laugh at Helena. "I see we have new staff."

The angel snorted. "Serve yourself."

"Fae princess." Maeve pointed to herself, and as she said it, Evelyn glided into the room and prepared Maeve's coffee.

"So, tell me more. What were you discussing?" Maeve focused on me.

"It seems that we nearly blew the lid off everything, and even the FBI are curious. So we need to be quiet, and I can't think of a better way than supporting the Winter Fae if you need me."

Sabrina cut off a piece of waffle and fed it to me. She needed me in top condition if I was to keep feeding her sex demon nature.

"I can't see the future. But for now, how about you focus on your first child, getting married, and getting some of your ladies pregnant?" Maeve countered, and the faces around the room perked up immediately.

"Yes please!" Kelly raised her hand. "If the Dragon King isn't tired of sex, I'd take another roll in the sheets. All the pregnant bitches around me really make me want to have a tummy." She made the shape of a pregnant belly with her hand.

I shook my head, my beast nearly purring in interest. "We'll work on it tonight."

"We do need to talk more about the wedding." Tyrande perked up. "Since we recruited the help of the Summer

Queen, I wanted to talk about flowers. I always thought one of those vine arches was absolutely perfect."

"Sure and we could make it from gold," I added, trying to subtly work in more gold, but the blank stares I got in return said I wasn't very subtle.

"It's got to be white," Jadelyn interjected.

"For once, I agree with her. It has to be white," Tyrande added.

And from there, the conversation shifted into wedding detail upon wedding detail. As they sank deeper and deeper into their discussion, I scooted back from my chair, tiptoeing away. I was ready to escape to my hoard.

I made it to the door before Yev grabbed my arm.

"Let's go look at your hoard." She whispered it so that she didn't catch the attention of the other women. But she also did a little skip of excitement. "My parents said that if you come with that bracer of yours, they'll let you take away my hoard."

I had a feeling the powerful family had another way to move her hoard, but they likely wanted to get me alone.

"I can go tomorrow if you set it up?" I replied.

She made a cute noise as she nodded. "Done. They'll be excited to see you again. My parents have been wanting to talk to you even before I told them about the pregnancy."

With the extended Atrium connecting all the way to Sentarshaden now, it was easy for us to get back and forth and make a day trip.

We walked through the Atrium and entered my room, but as soon as we entered, my attention was caught. The little gem that held Tia was active as she bounced up and down in the window.

"This is your mother, right?" Yev went closer to inspect it, and Tia beckoned to her.

As she got closer, Yev's knees buckled, and I dove to catch her.

"What the hell?" I picked her up and looked at the crystal, frowning.

Yev was in the middle of what had become a courtroom with Tia manning the judges bench and Bart looking grumpy as the stenographer.

"Tia, let me in there. What are you doing to Yev?" I shouted at the crystal.

My mother looked at me and frowned before crossing her arms.

I knew exactly what she wanted. She didn't like it when I called her Tia. "Mother, please let me in."

She smiled at my correction, and I only had a moment to sit down with Yev in my arms before my perspective warped and I landed in the middle of a courtroom.

"Today, we call to session the judgment for one Yevanara Highaen." Tia banged a gavel several times.

"Mother, what is this?"

"You spoke out of turn." She banged the gavel again. "Don't do that in my courtroom or I'll kick you out."

"This isn't—" I started, but she raised the gavel threateningly, and I wondered if she could actually eject me out of the crystal.

I cursed silently, wondering what the hell my mother was up to.

"My apologies." I crossed my arms.

"Good. Now, Yev, you are guilty of becoming my daughter-in-law and even bearing my grandson without even coming and asking for my son's hand." She banged the gavel several more times in anger. "Unacceptable."

Yev did a small curtsy keeping her head bowed. "I'm terribly sorry, mother. I hadn't intended to become pregnant already. May I have your permission to be with your son?"

Tia's gavel hung in the air. She'd clearly expected more of a fight. "You aren't supposed to just roll over." She flailed the gavel about. "You are chromatic. Fight me!"

But Yev just shook her head. "I'm sorry, but your son has already tamed my wild chromatic heart, and you are his mother. Given your strength, Tiamat, I can see how he could only be your son." She kept her head bowed.

Tia leaned back in the judge's bench and played with the gavel while she squinted at Yev. "I want to see my grandson every week."

"Mother, I don't know if this space is healthy for your grandson to enter often." I looked to Bart for support. Coming into the space had given me headaches before, and my body was far more resilient.

"No. No. No." Tia banged her gavel and shook it at me. "No speaking, son. You make too much sense. I want to hold my grandson."

Yev was still bowing to my mother. "If nothing else, I think the crystal that you can view the world from should be brought to some dinners with our child so that you can see him," Yev offered up the suggestion.

"Yes. Yes. Exactly that." Tia punctuated her words with gavel. "Bart, I want speakers on the crystal."

Bart just sighed. "We need someone's help to modify the exterior of the crystal, and a little more power wouldn't hurt," Bart commented from his station where he certainly wasn't typing up notes.

"Sabrina is pretty skilled. If you come up with it, I'm sure she can do it," I offered.

"The succubus? I'm sure she's quite skilled." Tia narrowed her eyes on me. "I need to vet the rest of your ladies. If they are going to possibly bear my grandchildren, I need to meet them." Tia swung the gavel around before smacking it into her hands like a thug about to crack some skulls.

I sighed. There was no sense in trying to argue with her.

"I'll happily help you vet them if you'd like, mother," Yev said, rising from her curtsy finally.

"Yes." She squinted at Yev. "I just got my baby boy, and now all of you are taking him from me."

Yev's expression shifted to sadness as she rubbed her stomach. "I might not have been able to understand you before, but I can't even imagine such a thing. And I've only known I was pregnant for a day."

Tia nodded rapidly as Yev spoke. "Exactly. Now you understand. I needed to meet you, and now you need to help me meet the other women. Bart, make up the enchantments. We'll use the succubus to get the changes done. I still wish we knew what happened to our latest reincarnations. If I ever find her, I'll throttle her for not raising my baby boy and bringing me the memories." She shook her gavel angrily in the air.

"I wish I knew more, but nothing has surfaced. It's hard to believe that they lived in this world." Even with the full resources of the dragons and sirens, months of searching had turned up nothing. It was like my biological parents were ghosts in the system.

"Mother." Yev added as much sweetness as possible as she spoke. "We were on our way to add my hoard to your sons and check in on an elemental he created. Perhaps we could come back another time?"

Tia hugged herself. "How romantic. The gold part, not the elemental. Bart has made a few that he used to cheat on me."

"I never cheated on you. We were never together when we were alive." Bart sighed. Clearly, it was a conversation that they had already had multiple times.

"But now we have, and since I'm the only one for you, then all the previous girls were cheating." Tia crossed her arms and stuck her nose out.

Bart sighed once more as he waved his hand, ejecting Yev and me from the crystal during her moment of distraction.

I blinked, finding myself back in my room with Yev in my arms. As quickly as I could, I picked her up and moved away from the crystal. But out of the corner of my eye, I could see the two of them arguing.

"She's... fun." Yev suppressed a giggle.

"Want to play in my hoard?" I asked her instead.

"Yes please!"

I lifted my mattress and let Yev enter first.

She climbed down and started surveying the gold. "I want to see the elemental. I need to make friends with it if I'm going to be sitting on an egg and not really able to move a ton."

"Well, Herm told me to try and feed it some mana. It should find my mana familiar." I pushed my magic into a ball in the palm of my hand and held it out over the massive pile of gold that was my hoard.

I really had gone a long way in learning magic, this would have been a foreign concept to me not that long ago.

There was an instant reaction as I could hear the tinker of gold shifting a little ways away. It was like something was swimming under my gold. The tinkling stopped about four feet from me before the elemental launched itself out of the gold, snatching the ball of mana from me, and landing back on the gold. It took a bite out of the captured mana.

"It's so cute!" Yev squealed.

"Yeah..." I stared at the gold elemental. It was now almost the size of a house cat, and it hadn't been bigger than a rat before. "It's gotten bigger."

"Aren't you cute?" Yev bent down.

The elemental moaned, but it didn't sound like it was in pain, it sounded like...

I smacked my face with my hand. I hadn't been doing much talking in my hoard, so if it were to start mimicking sounds...

Sure enough, it moaned, mimicking someone's sexual moans before saying a breathy 'yes' on repeat.

"I think I've failed to teach it to speak. Instead, it learned... from other activities." I shook my head.

Yev broke out in hysterical laughter, tears streaming down her face as she continued to crack up.

The elemental continued to mimic moans and cries of ecstasy to try and communicate with me, and I had no idea what to do. After finishing the mana, it relaxed into the gold it was on and took a vaguely humanoid form as it continued trying to communicate.

That only made Yev laugh harder. "All you've taught it is sex."

"Shut up." I knelt down by the elemental and gave it more mana. "You need to speak if you want to communicate," I told it. "Those noises are for a certain kind of happiness."

The head on the elemental tilted in confusion before it took the ball of mana and bit into it again and rubbed its belly.

Yev rolled over to face it. "This thing really is quite cute. And there are a lot of uses for an elemental."

The elemental perked up and walked over to Yev before going down to her belly.

Yev put a hand between it and the precious new life growing in her out of instinct. "What's it doing?"

"I think it feels some of my mana in the child." I knelt on the gold. "That's my child. Will you help me protect it?"

The little gold elemental turned its featureless face to me and nodded before turning back to stare at Yev's stomach.

I wasn't sure just how smart the creature was. Part of me thought the moaning proved it was still rather simple minded, but now I was wondering if it had been messing with me and was smarter than I thought.

"Come on. Why don't you come with us as Yev picks out how to arrange a nest amid my hoard. She's going to have a baby soon." I tried to talk more to the gold elemental, hoping it could pick up speech.

It nodded again, moving around with us as Yev took in the full hoard to choose where she wanted to nest.

I smiled as I watched her begin to arrange the coins. I'd get her settled in, and then I'd go figure out how to make sure we didn't end up with a very warm summer. I had a feeling I was about to get a crash course in the Faerie realm.

# Afterword

That was a lovely book five for the series, if I don't say so myself. We got to know Sabrina and Helena much more while setting up some fun back in Philly. Even though it was still a pretty colossal disaster, I was happy to wrangle the story back into Philly.

Book 6 is set up to start and end with a wedding in the faerie, with a journey through the fae wilds to rescue the Winter Queen as well as uncover where Zach came from and how he ended up the way he is. So get excited for that one coming down the pipe for December.

Until then, I have SSV3 coming out in October and Dao 4 in November. Both should be exciting in their own rights. Though SSV3 took on a path I didn't see coming, so get ready for Melody to get her bad self on.

Otherwise, things are great. The break was good, reset some of my writing/editing cycle to include another editor. I went and did some whirlwind family tours with the little guy. Then last but not least, moved across the country. Thanks for letting me pause for a month and get that all done. I'm back and hope to keep to my monthly schedule for a while before another break.

I also couldn't not keep busy and I tested dozens of artists and now am producing my own manga for Saving Supervillains.

So, now I'm not allowed to take any more breaks because, according to my wife, I just make up more projects for myself. She's not wrong, but it is a very fun and nerdy wish fulfillment of a project. I don't know when the manga will be done or how I'll distribute, but we are 3/4 through the first chapter and I expect chapters to take about a month per.

Please, if you enjoyed the book, leave a review.

Review Dragon's Justice 5

I have a few places you can stay up to date on my latest.

Monthly Newsletter

Facebook Page

Patreon

# ALSO BY

Legendary Rule:
Ajax Demos finds himself lost in society. Graduating shortly after artificial intelligence is allowed to enter the workforce; he can't get his career off the ground. But when one opportunity closes, another opens. Ajax gets a chance to play a brand new Immersive Reality game. Things aren't as they seem. Mega Corps hover over what appears to be a simple game. However, what he does in the game seems to effect his body outside.
But that isn't going to make Ajax pause when he finally might just get that shot at becoming a professional gamer. Join Ajax and Company as they enter the world of Legendary Rule.

Series Page

A Mage's Cultivation – Complete Series
In a world where mages and monster grow from cultivating mana. Isaac joins the class of humans known as mages who absorb mana to grow more powerful. To become a mage he must bind a mana beast to himself to access and control mana. But when his mana beast is far more human than he expected; Isaac struggles with the budding

relationship between the two of them as he prepares to enter his first dungeon.

Unfortunately for Isaac, he doesn't have time to ponder the questions of his relationship with Aurora. Because his sleepy town of Locksprings is in for a rude awakening, and he has to decide which side of the war he is going to stand on.

## Series Page

The First Immortal – Complete Series

Darius Yigg was a wanderer, someone who's never quite found his place in the world, but maybe he's not supposed to be here...Ripped from our world, Dar finds himself in his past life's world, where his destiny was cut short. Reignited, the wick of Dar's destiny burns again with the hope of him saving Grandterra.

To do that, he'll have to do something no other human of Grandterra has done before, walk the dao path. That path requires mastering and controlling attributes of the world and merging them to greater and greater entities. In theory, if he progressed far enough, he could control all of reality and rival a god.

He won't be in this alone. As a beacon of hope for the world, those from the ancient races will rally around Dar to stave off the growing Devil horde.

## Series Page

Saving Supervillains – Complete Series

A former villain is living a quiet life, hidden among the masses. Miles has one big secret: he might just be the most powerful super in existence.

Those days are behind him. But when a wounded young lady unable to control her superpower needs his help, she shatters his boring life, pulling him into the one place he least expected to be—the Bureau of Superheroes.

Now Miles has an opportunity to change the place he has always criticized as women flock to him, creating both opportunity and disaster.

He is about to do the strangest thing a Deputy Director of the Bureau has ever done: start saving Supervillains.

Series Page

Dragon's Justice

Have you ever felt like there was something inside of you pushing your actions? A dormant beast, so to speak. I know it sounds crazy.

But, that's the best way I could describe how I've felt for a long time. I thought it was normal, some animal part of the human brain that lingered from evolution. But this is the story of how I learned I wasn't exactly human, and there was a world underneath our own where all the things that go bump in the night live. And that my beast was very real indeed.

Of course, my first steps into this new unknown world are full of problems. I didn't know the rules, landing me on the wrong side of a werewolf pack and in a duel to the death with a smug elf.

But, at least, I have a few new friends in the form of a dark elf vampiress and a kitsune assassin as I try to figure out just what I am and, more importantly, learn to control it.

Series Page

Dungeon Diving

The Dungeon is a place of magic and mystery, a vast branching, underground labyrinth that has changed the world and the people who dare to enter its depths. Those who brave its challenges are rewarded with wealth, fame, and powerful classes that set them apart from the rest.

Ken was determined to follow the footsteps of his family and become one of the greatest adventurers the world has ever known. He knows that the only way to do that is to get into one of the esteemed Dungeon colleges, where the most promising young adventurers gather.

Despite doing fantastic on the entrance exam, when his class is revealed, everyone turns their backs on him, all except for one.

The most powerful adventurer, Crimson, invites him to the one college he never thought he'd enter. Haylon, an all girls college.

Ken sets out to put together a party and master the skills he'll need to brave the Dungeon's endless dangers. But he soon discovers that the path ahead is far more perilous than he could have ever imagined.

Series Page

There are of course a number of communities where you can find similar books.

https://www.facebook.com/groups/haremlit

https://www.facebook.com/groups/HaremGamelit

And other non-harem specific communities for Cultivation and LitRPG.

https://www.facebook.com/groups/WesternWuxia

https://www.facebook.com/groups/LitRPGsociety

https://www.facebook.com/groups/cultivationnovels

Made in the USA
Monee, IL
12 January 2024

51638258R00223